To F...
Thank
Much Love,

Gracie

Caitriona Coyle.
xx

ORLA
KELLY
PUBLISHING

Caitriona Coyle

Orla Kelly Publishing
27 Kilbrody,
Mount Oval,
Rochestown,
Cork,
Ireland.

Printed and bound in Ireland by www.printmybook.com

For Mum and Dad. Always.

Acknowledgements

I am so grateful to a number of people who helped me to write this story.

For listening closely to every chapter as I read it to her, I thank my lovely friend, Frances Roberts. For a second time she has been my sounding board and strongest supporter, urging me to write from the heart and never hold back. Thank you my friend.

For listening to my legal questions and answering them with precision and patience, I thank Brendan Kelly and Frank Dorrian. Thanks so much to Dave Lordan whose positive feedback bolstered my belief that I was on the right track.

To my family, Frank, Kate and Holly, thank you for your enduring love and support; special thanks to my girls who are constantly pestered to help me with the 'computer stuff'!

A very special thank you to Gregory O' Connor (R.I.P.) who worked in The National Archives of Ireland. Gregory went beyond the call of duty and searched for the court papers relating to the legal case at the heart of this story, despite me giving him dates that were years out! On the day that I collected the documents from the Archives in Bishop Street, Gregory met me quite by accident in the lift as I was leaving and accompanied me to the front door. He seemed fascinated by my story and when I voiced some doubt that it needed more drama, he winked and said, "I think you have enough drama there to be getting on with!" He will never know how much his words meant to me.

Finally I thank you Mum and Dad for instilling this story in my heart. I carried it for you until the weight grew too heavy, demanding to be heard.

Contents

Ann

Ann Cox ignored her husband's warning to come away from the window as she hunkered down on the landing, peeping through a hole in the netted curtain, bird-like. Spying on her new neighbour, who stood on the footpath below, buttoning her red winter coat.

Ann figured she was young. Younger than her anyway. Probably younger than most of the women in the village.

She felt the sting of jealousy, watching her tying a headscarf tightly under her chin. Wheeling her bicycle off the path, glancing quickly around, before perching straight-backed on the saddle. Peddling past the Post Office, slowly and gracefully. Up the lower road towards the school.

Kitty and Mona were at the shop door, watching her too. She cycled past them, looking straight ahead, her flat black shoes working the pedals.

The linoleum began to feel cold as Ann rose from her vantage point on the landing, grateful for her panoramic view of the village.

They called it a village, but really it was a smattering of two-storied houses on either side of a wide street, with Cox's pub standing sentinel at the mouth of the hill road. A tiny hamlet, nestling at the foot of the mountains. The tallest hill, Bunbin, towered over them, facing the school, guarding the village lough.

From the landing, Ann had a clear view of Mona's shop and Mickey's garage opposite, two busy spots, depending on the day of the week. She could get a decent look at Logues next door, with the right twist of her head and see all three roads that led people to her door. It was her favourite place to watch her customers coming and going.

Most of them arrived on foot, a few on bicycles, a very odd one by tractor or car, all sober. They left, staggering down the street, stopping to light cigarettes. Some talked to themselves or sang and she killed herself laughing if Johnny Neils fell on his arse because the soles of his wellingtons were threadbare. Or Andy Dore collapsed into the bushes with his fly still open, trying to take a leak.

They were pathetic old boys, most of them. But as long as they kept throwing their money across the counter at Ann, she'd keep giving them plenty to drink, along with her false smiles and cutting remarks, when required.

She moved towards the stairs, stopping to open the bedroom door where Nora had slept when she was their lodger. Nora, who paid 15 shillings a week for two years, a nice wee supplement to what they made in the pub. She was an easy tenant, who ate whatever was put in front of her and spent most evenings at the fire correcting copies and preparing work for the following day. She had her Leaving Certificate and was a very bright girl; a Junior Assistant Mistress who could teach in any school in the land. But thanks to this new one next door, Nora was gone. Back to live with her parents and her 15 shillings were badly missed. The jab of bitterness hit Ann as she slammed the bedroom door, gritting her teeth, running downstairs to boil the eggs before Nevin came down for breakfast.

The morning ritual was always the same.

Eating eggs and toast at the kitchen table, Nevin telling her how much the takings were from the previous night. Ann recounting a funny story about one or two of the customers, then the work of the day began.

The most unpleasant job was cleaning the toilet. Some of the men were such bad aims, frequently missing the bowl. More used to emptying their bowels in cowsheds or shitting in fields, wiping their arses with grass. The squares of newspaper Ann cut and hung on a cord for them went unused. Far too advanced for the savages.

The clawing smell of Jeyes Fluid rose, wafting through the pub. Nevin carried out crates of empty stout bottles. He washed dirty glasses and restocked shelves, looking up when the pub door dinged. Announcing Jimmy Owen, a bachelor farmer from down the road, whose brother John was hot on his heels. Both men were in their sixties and had probably never known the feel of a woman. After their parents died, they let their land go to swamp and rushes, surviving on the dole, throwing every penny of it across the counter at Ann or Nevin, even owing money.

Their debt grew bigger by the month.

The blue jotter under the counter kept a record of their tab.

Ann didn't mind that they owed them money, that it was unlikely they would ever square their bill. She had her plan, and knew well how the ultimate payment would be made. Which was why she kept smiling at them like a Cheshire Cat, encouraging them to have a whiskey with their stouts, not forgetting their packets of Players or Woodbines. Those neglected acres would be hers and Nevin's someday. Plenty of sites to sell, or maybe a site to build a house for themselves when they retired.

She smiled, watching the two brothers. Two pigs at the swill, slurping their bitter flat stouts, brown stains forming around their mouths.

Nevin's portfolio of land was increasing with every year that passed, thanks to Ann's intelligence and vision. She had a gift for sniffing out the old boys with no close relatives. Not a niece or a nephew or first cousin in sight. Not one shrewd relation who might know what they were entitled to. And once sniffed out, they were marked men, seduced by Ann's kindness. The odd plate of stew, plonked on the counter on bitter cold days. Mugs of hot sugary tea with a few penny biscuits, keeping them on the bar stools for another hour.

Nevin was part of the game too.

Giving them lifts home at night. Up lonely hilly lanes to dilapidated farmhouses, with starved dogs lurking at their doors.

On election days he took them to the polling station, provided of course they voted for deValera.

Ann checked the seats afterwards, retrieving notes and coins that had fallen out of drunken pockets. Money they thought they spent on drinks, too inebriated to remember. When the time was right, Nevin took them to MaCausland, the solicitor, where they made their wills. Leaving the lot to Ann and Nevin, those kind interlopers, whom the villagers had taken to their hearts.

John and Jimmy Owen weren't your average dullards though. Ann would have to work harder on them, especially John. He seemed impervious to her charms, detecting perhaps the poison therein. Sharp-tongued and well able for Ann's sneering ways, he could silence her with a quick retort. She hated that about him, that he had that power. Especially when she was trying to be nice, however implausible it was to hide the contempt in her voice. She glanced at him, noticing the sunken eyes, the hangdog look. He sat staring hard at his reflection in the mirror that ran the length of the bar, behind bottles of spirits.

"What are you looking at John?" she laughed lightly, only a hint of sneering detectable.

"I'm looking at the man who spent all my money!"

His deadpan tone reminded her that he was no fool.

She would have to tread carefully. With a bit of luck, he would die before Jimmy, making her plans come to fruition without all the pandering.

Ten years had passed since they bought this pub, yet Ann felt the village was more a home to her than Fermanagh ever was. They had honeymooned here and fell in love with the area, both agreeing to buy a shop or pub, if one ever came up for sale. Saving every penny they could scrounge, hoping their dream would be realised.

They rented a small cottage on the outskirts of Enniskillen after they married, unwilling to commit to a permanent home or bank loan, when they both knew where they wanted to live. Nevin worked in Comber's bar on Main Street, starting there as a youngster straight out of primary school, working his way up to assistant manager, trusted and respected by Mr. Comber, the owner. Ann didn't work. After all, she was now a respectable married woman, done with looking after other people's children. The war was over, times were hard. Married women were better off letting men earn their living outside the home. Babies came along anyway, giving women plenty to do.

Ann did love money though.

She was ambitious for herself and Nevin, which was why the idea of owning a pub appealed to her so much. You didn't have to leave your own property from one end of the day to the next in order to make good money. The comfort of it, the security of it, appealed to Ann. She was good with people, being nosey by nature and rather gabby, as Nevin would say. That's what he loved about her. The customers took to her funny flirtatious nature, able to talk easily with her.

Nevin was less loquacious, quieter in his ways and more reflective, which was why they worked well together.

They married late in life, but at 33 Ann felt there was still hope of a child, though Nevin hadn't broached the subject with her. She fondly thought of them as Jack Sprat and his wife. Nevin being tall and lanky, with thick dark hair framing his long sallow face. Her being small and plump, with a round face and short mousy hair. His hooded brown eyes were deep and sensitive, in stark contrast to her pale green orbs that were always busy and vigilant. His movements were slow, his walk old, although he was only 40. She was a whippersnapper, full of energy, fit to move quickly and get the job done.

The villagers in this Donegal backwater didn't know their arses from their elbows, until Nevin and herself came along to teach them the ways of the world. The big broad world that they knew about, being from the North you know, where people were more outward looking, more advanced.

Now the women looked to Ann for guidance about all manner of things, from rearing their children to buying new corsets.

Mona, who owned the Post Office and shop with her husband Josie, consulted her before buying in new stock. Should she introduce fancy jams in the grocery end, or new hanks of wool and long johns for the drapery side?

"Get rid of the wool Mona," Ann advised. "None of the women around here can knit. The long johns are a good idea, but God help the poor women who'll have to wash them!"

Mona nodded in agreement, smiling behind her rimless spectacles, cutting thick slices of bacon for Ann and Nevin's tea.

Kitty Eddy stood at the counter, arms folded in her usual pose, the butt of a Players Navy Cut stuck to her lower lip.

"Oh Christ!" She said, "You better not get rid of the wool Mona, I hear the new teacher is giving the youngsters knitting lessons."

"Who told you that Kitty?" Ann's tone was sharp, her narrowing eyes rounding on the older woman who meant no harm.

"I met Bridget Roarty at the well this morning, all her wanes had the news home with them yesterday. They're going to be learning to knit in the next few weeks." There wasn't a trace of malice in Kitty's voice.

"O now they won't be able to knit very much," Mona was colluding with Ann, hoping Kitty was confused, watching Ann's mouth set hard, waiting for Kitty's reply.

"Well, she's teaching the wee ones to knit scarves, and the big girls are knitting jumpers. Isn't it great?"

Kitty's drawly question floated on the air, lingering around the pots and pans that hung from the shop ceiling, drifting around the bacon slicer and back to Ann, who gave a high belittling grunt.

"I'm surprised Master McFadden is allowing that nonsense, letting her have the big girls when they should be doing their sums."

Mona was thinking she would hang on to the wool all the same, though she threw her eyes to heaven as she handed over the rashers that Nevin loved so much.

Ann crossed the street, temples throbbing, stumping annoyance, almost kicking the ground. She stared hard at the new sign above the door of her neighbour's premises. 'Logue's Bar', in raised silver lettering, shiney and hopeful.

She grunted again. It would take more than a fancy new sign to build up customers for that business. Sure the aule doll who had it before Logue, ran it into the ground. She came out of America before the Depression with her fortune intact and bought it as a hobby, not opening half the time, lucky to sell three bottles of stout a week. She didn't need the money and she wasn't a threat. Unlike this new pair, Ann thought, slamming the kitchen door behind her, sitting at the range for a minute to settle her nerves.

She could hear Nevin's quiet drone floating down from the pub, trying to keep a conversation going with Barney Cam, who could make a bottle of stout last longer than any man Ann knew.

He was born with a crooked leg, so they nicknamed him 'Cam'. His right name was Gallagher and when he was drunk Ann loved teasing him, reciting the rhyme about the crooked man who walked a crooked mile, just to see him thump the counter with his fist, slavering at the mouth, demented. Nevin and her would still be giggling long after he had hobbled home to his crooked house.

All the same, it was hard to believe ten years had passed since they settled here in the village, making a good living, getting on the best; though she knew at 43 there would be no children.

At the start the women watched her like hawks for signs of a swollen belly, wishing her pregnant. Misery loves company after all.

Some of the customers even asked her about it. The bad-mannered men, who hardly knew how many wanes they had at home themselves. It was hard to keep smiling, especially when their teasing crossed a certain line, but she brazenned it out, vowing secret revenge as they mocked.

"You're keeping nice and slim Ann, hehe."

"Aye, nothing stirring at all, heh?"

"You'll have to get Nevin to put a spurt on himself."

"Or we'll need to get this new buck to look at ya. The AI Man! hehe."

They didn't talk like that when Nevin was around. Ann wondered how he felt about having no children. He never showed any signs of sorrow or disappointment, so that was fine.

They were better off just the two of them, foraging away, building up their nest egg. Adding wee parcels of land to their expanding farm and keeping an eye on the villagers, leading them along gently by the noses. Children were overrated, though she didn't let anyone know she felt that way, not when most of their customers had a houseful of them. At 50, Nevin probably felt the same. He had more important things to do than run after a brood of wanes. Let the simple couples do it, it suited them better.

They weren't Jack Spratt and his wife any longer. No. They were the King and Queen of the land, with many loyal subjects, like the two in Sing a Song of Sixpence, reaping their bounteous rewards. Until now.

Ann's heart was beating faster than usual. What exactly was she feeling? Why did the thought of this new pair next door fill her with such rage?

Maybe she was afraid of change, when everything was lovely just as it was.

Something about the arrival of this young couple, with their new sign and new bicycle and new knitting classes, rattled her. But she would deal with it. No better woman.

Nothing and no one was going to swoop down and peck off her nose.

Gracie

———

Gracie Logue closed the top button of her red winter coat, shivering in the cold January wind. She wondered if Ann was on her perch spying. She fought the urge to look up, knowing that if she did, the netted curtain would twitch and she'd feel silly for having bothered. It was exactly one year since she came to the village, a year to the day since she wheeled her bicycle onto the street and peddled up the gentle incline to her new school. Ann was watching her then too, but it was the eyes of the other women that surprised her, standing rigid on their doorsteps, arms folded, staring and unapologetic.

She remembered thinking it was a mistake coming to this backward closed off place, where she was an outsider, a curiosity. By the looks on the women's faces, an intruder.

Jim and herself weren't even married a week, when they moved into the two storied neglected building they would call home.

It was a source of great pride to Gracie that home included a pub, or bar, as Jim called it, thrown in for good measure. Along with a kitchen, indoor toilet, 4 bedrooms and a miserable looking tin shack of a scullery, with an enormous Belfast sink. There was a turf bog too, that came with the premises, waiting to throw out hard black turf, plenty to keep fires blazing all winter.

When Jim told her about the bar he sounded secretive, like a little boy with a packet of sweets, afraid to show joy, in case someone took them from him, a punishment maybe for being bold. He wanted to buy it so badly, he said, pulling the 'poor wee me' face that made Gracie laugh, bribing her with a compliment. Saying she looked like Maureen O'Hara, when she starred in The Quiet Man. Maybe he thought she wouldn't help him to buy it, that she'd balk at doing two jobs: teaching during the day and serving drinks in the evening. Well he needn't have worried, she wanted it just as much as him.

She was anxious at first, afraid she was taking on too much, but it didn't matter now anyhow.

Their name was above the door and a part of Gracie liked that, the furtive part where she stored feelings no one knew about, hidden from Jim, even from herself.

She was aware that owning a bar carried weight in a community, commanded respect, like having a priest in the family or a doctor or a teacher. When she calmed down and thought about it, she realised Jim was right. He was a publican, she was a teacher, doubly blessed; destined to be well off and successful. A bit like John Wayne and her lookalike, without the fighting, please God.

Fr. Coyle offered Gracie the village school when he heard she was marrying Jim; her reputation preceded her he said. Married women were banned from teaching, but he told her not to worry about that. deValera's mantra, 'One Man, One

Job', would be overturned soon by a strong Teachers Union, the I.N.T.O. He was sure of it.

Since leaving Carysfort College, Gracie had taught in four different parishes, doing substitution for women on maternity leave. They were defying the ban too and they all loved Gracie, because she was gifted with the Gaelic. By the time she was leaving each school, she handed them back their classes, fluent in their native tongue, impressing the Parish Priest and the Inspector, but most of all the parents. They rejoiced when Gracie told them their boys and girls now qualified for a £5 reward the Government gave each year, to every child who could speak in Gaelic.

Two weeks before her wedding, on a bitter January morning, Fr. Coyle walked into her classroom in the townland over the hill, where Jim was from. He stood warming his hands at the fire, catching Gracie off guard. Mrs. Duffy was returning from maternity leave the following day, so she reached for the notes ledger, to show him what she had been teaching these quiet timid children on loan to her.

"You don't need to show me that Miss O' Brien," he waved the ledger gently away.

"I know you did a great job here; the parents are never done praising you."

Gracie blushed, a shy pride filling her up, watching the children dip their nibs in the inkwells to write carefully in their jotters. The white collar and black suit a warning to them, to be on their best behaviour.

"I'm delighted you're taking the position," he said, "we need someone like you down in the village, fully qualified and fluent in the Gaelic."

"What about the ban Father? In two weeks, I'll be a married woman, will that not go against me?"

"Don't worry about that," he urged. "Plenty of women are defying the ban. I guarantee that as long as I live, you won't be put out of that school."

Two weeks later, on a cold Friday morning, January 31st, Gracie married Jim.

It was at 9 o'clock, with only her younger sister Hannah as bridesmaid and Jim's brother Tom as best man.

They stood in the big draughty chapel and made their vows, promising to love and honour one another, the obeying part was Gracie's alone. Afterwards Tom drove them to the wedding breakfast in the local Hotel. Her mother Kit joined them at the breakfast, along with Marjorie, Jim's mother, who sat beside Fr. Coyle. It was a quiet affair, with awkward silences falling between the relatives, who seemed to have very little to say to one another. Gracie was relieved when Tom announced that it was time he drove them to the depot in Letterkenny.

They took the bus to Dublin, Jim in his wedding suit, Gracie in her navy going away suit that Mary, her older sister, had tailored for her.

Fr. Coyle recommended the North Star Hotel, so that's where they stayed. Alone finally, they dined in the big comfortable dining room, watching the other guests talking and laughing easily, both nervous about their first night in bed together. Gracie had no one to talk to about her anxiety, certainly not Hannah who was still waiting to be courted, or her mother, who squeezed her hand before she left, telling her quietly to do her husband's bidding. Mortified, Gracie pretended not to hear her, assuming this was the obeying part of the marriage deal. She sensed Jim's shyness too, which he masked with halves of whiskey, as they sat together in the lounge after dinner. She waited for him in their room, wearing her new nylon nightdress, hoping Jim wouldn't turn the light on when he came up. The starched white sheets felt cold as they climbed beneath them, Gracie praying silently that Jim would know what to do. He touched her awkwardly at first but she moved towards him, responding easily, naturally, allowing herself the freedom to enjoy what was happening between them. They were married in the sight of God after all and although there was pain, there was passion surging through her, spilling over when Jim moaned with pleasure, saying her name over and over and over.

"Gracie, Gracie, Gracie. I love you."

"I love you Jim. Will we say a wee decade of the rosary together, ask God to bring us good luck in our marriage."

Maybe he found it an odd request but he didn't refuse and she loved him even more, safe in the darkness listening to his voice close beside her, knowing she was different and would never be the same again.

In the morning, too embarrassed to look at each other, they blurted out words at the same time, trying to keep a conversation going over breakfast

Gracie

Jim didn't hold her hand as they walked along O'Connell Street, but she was happy. They sat near Nelson's Pillar and Gracie pointed to the trams that used to take her pals and herself back to Blackrock in her Carysfort days. They walked through the busy city streets, stopping occasionally to look in the fancy shop windows, laughing at their reflections staring back at them, innocent and stern. The biting breeze that blew down O'Connell Street, propelled them to the comfort of the open fire, blazing in the hotel lobby. They ate dinner in the big airy dining room and Gracie felt a new excitement fluttering through her, knowing she would enjoy the warmth of Jim again that night, taste the musky sweetness of whiskey and tobacco on his lips.

"Here's to our new life together," Jim raised his glass, "and thank you Gracie for helping me to buy the premises."

"You're welcome," Gracie smiled. "To our new life and new adventure together."

"We're a very lucky couple Gracie, long may it last."

"With God's help it'll last as long as we live Jim."

Their love making was better the second night, knowing what to expect, what to enjoy, trusting Jim's touch and her own explosive feelings that had frightened her the previous night. She slept fitfully, hearing Jim's gentle purring beside her. Tomorrow the real dance began between them when they returned to reality, and the village.

Sunday evening, Gracie put away her pale blue wedding gown, folding the matching lace veil and gloves into the tall boy of her new bedroom.

Jim entertained his first customers in the bar below.

The honeymoon was short and wonderful and over too soon. She felt different though, more complete, anxious too that she would be a good wife, strong and capable.

She thought about tomorrow, when she'd wheel her new bicycle, a wedding present from Jim, out onto the path that ran the length of the house, to cycle up the street and take on her new full time position in the village school. She was 26 years old, Jim was nearly 30, their whole lives were ahead of them.

She'd been lucky in her previous posts. The Masters were welcoming and kind, helping her to settle in, allowing her the space she needed to get on with the job. They minded their own business, trusting her judgement and her qualification. She had even been a lodger in Master McLaughlin's house in Buncrana. Travelling to school with him in his car, home with him in the afternoons, to the cute cottage where he lived with his wife and two teenage sons. It wasn't ideal, of course not. She felt childish going to the cinema with them once a week, pretending to enjoy the cowboy films they liked so much. She fell asleep at times in the dark smoke-filled cinema, waking with a start as the lights came on and everyone stood up around her.

The ceili once a month in the parochial hall was where Gracie felt less confined. She joined the local girls being asked to dance the Waves of Tory or the Siege of Ennis, feeling at home among young men who reminded her of her brothers and young women in similar flared skirts and Aran cardigans as herself.

There were boys who liked her, she knew that, but Gracie wasn't ready for romance. Her mother's advice was foremost in her mind, when she felt them watching her, not just on the dance floor but everywhere she went. Waving at her on the road when she passed them, sitting in the front seat of the Master's car, blushing. Staring at her in the chapel on Sunday mornings, walking down from holy communion, keeping her eyes fixed on the seat she came out of.

"Na bac leo", she could hear her mother's voice, "Pay no attention to them. Time enough for that. Get your diploma first. Save your money," and that's exactly what Gracie was going to do.

Only six weeks into her third post, things changed. The Master, a thin pious bachelor twice her age, got the strangest idea that Gracie was ripe for the picking.

It was a harsh winter that year, yet he walked to her digs, in driving sleet, convinced she would accept his proposal, for after all he was doing her a favour. The landlady made herself scarce, while they sat at the kitchen table, Gracie bewildered when he produced a hard backed notebook and pencil. Asking her question after question about herself, to see if she fulfilled the criteria he required in a wife.

Bemused, she watched him ticking boxes, jotting down words, until realisation dawned. This is not a scene from an amateur play, this buck is serious! She stood abruptly, assuring him she was not interested in marriage at that time, thank you very much. Walking him hurriedly to the door, while he fumbled with his notebook and pencil. Ignoring his shocked eyes and angry mouth, she dispatched him into the driving sleet from which he came.

"Did you send the poor man away?" The landlady pretended to scold. "You could at least have walked him up the road a bit."

Gracie didn't answer, she wasn't amused. What a silly man. What an arrogant man, thinking she would want to lie with him for the rest of her days on God's green earth! The very thought made her shudder.

Her last weeks in the school were strained and awkward. Filled with stony silence on the Master's part. Gracie's part filled with longing to do well when the Inspector called and get out of there before any more nonsense occurred.

Her last position before coming to the village was in Jim's town land, high up in the hills, overgrown with fearns and gorse and dotted with sheep. Gracie found lodgings in a house near the school, owned by a Protestant brother and sister in their fifties, both unmarried. Both eccentric in ways that intrigued and amused her. Agnes had a dark moustache and liked to wear hob-nail boots and trousers, never once appearing in a skirt or frock. A petite slim little woman with short grey hair, Agnes knew how to cook and keep a clean house, which made Gracie love her, even if she did talk to the hens and hang her faded bloomers out to dry on the gorse bushes, for the neighbours to see.

When he was around, Sam was warm and amiable, though he didn't seem to do much by way of work. He had a reputation as a ladies man, going out most evenings, sometimes staying away for days at a time. Returning to have a long rest, in his bed under the stairs where he slept. It dawned on Gracie that he had given up his bedroom, so they could take a lodger as a source of income.

The digs were reasonable. One pound three shillings a week. With her wages being four pounds five shillings a fortnight, her savings were building up nicely, yes indeed. If she could just get over her final two inspections and get her Diploma, life would be grand. She could buy that new watch she kept promising herself, maybe a bicycle too; she heard Raleighs were good.

Sam insisted that Gracie use an old bone-shaker belonging to him. A man's bike with a crossbar that took her to school and back. Her brave old warrior, she fell in love with, ferrying her all over the parish.

The locals wondered about the dark-haired young woman, working in the school. Word spread that she was a qualified teacher from over west, staying in Sam and Agnes'.

Gracie had some sense that she was pretty, 'doighuil', her father would have said, God rest him. She couldn't recognise the girl who was emerging from the folklore building around her though. The whispers on the wind, reaching her ears, testing her genuine modesty.

"She's a fine figure of a girl."

"You should see how blue her eyes are."

"Her dark hair is so shiny it would blind you."

"They're saying you're the best-looking woman they've seen around here in a long time," Sam winked. Himself and Agnes watching Gracie's face, both beaming with pride.

Gracie tried to dismiss the compliments, raising her eyes to heaven, indicating that she'd never heard such nonsense. A sneaky smile lingered on her lips, the flattery percolating inside her. The essence of what she was hearing rang true, making her walk taller, happy to smile and wave at everyone she met on the road.

Word of her teaching skills reverberated, reaching Fr. Coyle's ears, in the neighbouring village. It ignited a hope in him, that perhaps he could poach this capable young woman, supplanting the Junior Assistant Mistress in the village school, and breathe new life into a tolerable situation. He was biding his time, letting serendipity play its part, when his new housekeeper arrived from the same townland as Gracie, over west.

She enticed Gracie to visit the parochial house four or five evenings a week, cycling six round miles from her digs and back. Delighted, Gracie drank tea and ate slices of fruitcake with Brege, her old neighbour, who was fast becoming her friend and confidant.

The aging priest put his head into the parlour from time to time to say hello, building a gentle familiarity between Gracie and himself. Stepping into the room on occasion, to comment on the weather or wonder if Brege and herself were warm enough, telling them not to spare the turf on such cold winter nights.

There was no doubting Gracie was a good girl, reared in a decent home where the rosary was recited every evening and Mass attended religiously. Each borrowed conversation he had with her confirmed what he knew to be true. Gracie was of sound moral character, and if God spared him he would live to see her ensconced in the village school.

And God spared him.

Indeed, God seemed to collude with him, in the shape of Jim Logue, a handsome young man of twenty-seven who lived in the hills above Sam and Agnes. The youngest of four, his mind had lately turned to a notion that he needed to marry.

Gracie had seen Jim often, couldn't miss him on the hilly landscape, driving his brother's lorry that choked and farted on the corkscrew roads. She returned his wave when he passed, thinking there was something attractive about his freckled face and cheeky grin. It was only when she watched him at the Sunday Sports, warming up before a race, that she realised her heart had sped up and she lost her appetite for the bag of chips Brege had bought her.

She watched him at the starting line, his sandy hair falling in a rakish kind of way. He flicked it back with a quick jerk of his head, earnestly watching the steward's gun. There was something wild or untamed about him, she thought, startled by the firing gun, watching his lithe body taking off down the track. Jim won the race with ease, punching the air in triumph, glancing quickly towards the sideline where Gracie stood. Her heart was still racing, even Brege caught a hint of something, a frisson so remarkable, she had to comment.

"Are you alright Gracie?" she asked. "I hope you're not catching a cold or something worse, I'm looking forward to the dance tonight."

"I'm grand," Gracie smiled, "We'll meet outside the hall at 10 o'clock, the band will have started by then."

She took extra care getting ready that evening.

Changing into her good slingbacks. Making sure the seam in her nylons was straight, licking her fingers and running them up the back of her calves. She had good legs, even her mother allowed her that, when she wasn't telling her to be like Blessed Virgin Mary, pure as the driven snow.

The parish hall heaved. One waltz ended and another began. Gracie and Brege took mincing steps along the wall, avoiding the dancers, finding a seat on the ladies side, near the stage.

Jim was on the floor with a local girl, steering her around artfully, a kind of exhibition Gracie thought. She knew he saw her, though his conversation with his dance partner continued and became more animated. They whirled around, and for the first time in her life she felt the pain of jealousy in her sternum, forcing herself to sing along with the music; 'Little brown jug....da dee de dee.'

The set ended and Gracie was relieved when Jim returned to the men's side of the hall, standing with his friends, talking and smoking, moving his weight from foot to foot, rangy and agile in his smart suit. He was out of place among the others, with their baggy pinstripe trousers, shiny at the knees, their ill-fitting jackets with wide flapping lapels.

She wondered how he could afford such expensive cloth and was about to share her musings with Brege when the first strains of the 'Tennessee Waltz' struck up and Jim's hand was out, asking her to dance. The same hand firm on her back, gliding her across the floor, his head arched gracefully, a ballroom matador, staking his claim. They moved in harmony, Gracie's footwork matching his. They must have looked good together, all eyes were on them she noticed, their mouths set in conclusion.

Gracie wished them to be right, prayed that Jim would ask her to stand on when the set was over. She knew right then that these were the arms she wanted to be in, now and forever. That was a resolute certainty.

Few were disappointed then, when romance bloomed and within a year Jim had proposed to her. Except for Sam who said something; a silly comment Gracie thought, though her mother called it 'greanwhar!', strange.

"Watch yourself," Sam said. "He's a flighty boy, that young Logue fella."

She tied the flowery scarf under her chin, shivering in the cold January wind, remembering.

Remembering that two years had slipped by since Jim waltzed her around the dance floor, sweeping her off her feet.

She was a teacher and a publican's wife. And now, a mother. She wanted to surprise Jim with the news, tell him in a cute way, instead of just being blunt about it. He seemed impatient with her efforts at coyness though, when she told him their honeymoon was very productive, that one and one made three, that the stork was on his way. His frown relaxed when she finally made it plain and simple; she was expecting their first child. His beaming smile said it all. No, she hadn't done something wrong at all, she was the best wee wife any man could have.

Yes. A young mother, leaving her baby boy Malachy for the first time in five weeks. Leaving him with a hired maid, to return to her post in the village school.

The women were on their doorsteps. Mona stood at the shop front watching her cycle past slowly. Up the gentle slope that felt steep now to Gracie, her legs struggling to turn the pedals, her body heavy with worries.

"Stay strong," she prayed deeply, the school coming into view.

Surely things will improve.

The villagers would accept her eventually. Jim would settle into his responsibilities.

And next door, Ann and Nevin would really become the kind friendly neighbours they pretended to be.

Nevin

At 52 Nevin felt he was getting old, though he didn't dare let Ann know that, because she was still like a spring chicken. His gait had always been canny and considered, which helped him now to disguise the stiffness in his hips and the tightness he felt in his back when he bent to restock the lower shelves with bottles of stout. It was getting uncomfortable, leaning on the low wooden counter, chatting to the customers. He didn't want to give in to sitting down while he served, Ann wouldn't like it. Anyway, he had to be careful not to show any signs of weakness, or the locals might start seeing him in a different light; he couldn't have that.

For twelve years he had steered a steady course through calm waters, commanding the unquestioned respect of the people within a ten-mile radius and he wasn't going to display any vulnerability now. Not now the waters had become a bit choppy, with the manoeuvres of the two next door.

Nevin smiled, thinking of the Friday morning, over a dozen years ago, when Malcolm Black left his 'Derry Journal' behind him on the counter of Comber's bar. Nevin poured over it, taking a few seconds to realise what he was seeing on the property page. The picture came into focus before his eyes, with the words For Sale written underneath.

His mind and his heart were racing all morning, all afternoon, checking the wall clock every two minutes. Only half listening to the cattle dealers just back from the Fair Day in Belleek, their pockets bulging with bargained notes. He strained on his leash until 6 o'clock, when his shift was over. A sideways grin on his face walking into their rented cottage, handing over the paper to Ann, tapping the picture of the pub twice with his index finger, ordering her to peruse.

She shrieked in excitement, not in the least bit put off by the price tag, £800. She knew Nevin could make it happen, though she hadn't two pennies to rub together herself.

And make it happen he did, using his bit of inheritance from Uncle Neil who died in Boston, along with his own savings and a small loan the Bank gave him, on account of his consistent hoarding over the years.

There were no other bidders on the property, which included a three bedroomed house, the pub, a piece of turf bog and two acres of land ideal for grazing cattle.

Mr. Comber drove them to their new Donegal home in his black Ford Anglia. Their few belongings in the back seat beside Ann, who hadn't stopped smiling since they drove over the border into the Free State.

Their premises looked long and imposing, pebble-dashed with tiny shards of coloured glass, glistening in the midday sun. A square of black render over the pub door waited for the new proprietor's name. The door dinged as they stepped inside the dark hollow den, with low ceilings, a low wooden counter and ancient stone flags beneath their feet. The shelves were bare and the grimy latticed window blocked out the sun. Still nothing could deny the charm, oozing from every wooden board that panelled every inch of wall, in that cozy old room, whispering to Nevin of long profitable days ahead.

The spell was broken in the living quarters, with a cold dirty pantry that led into a pokey kitchen, housing a range that spilled its ashes over the faded linoleum floor. A rickety table with two weary chairs sat by the window, the grey netted curtain sagged, weighed down by years of dust. What was once a parlour was now a storeroom, strewn with wooden beer crates and empty crisp tins wrapped in red tartan paper.

The bedrooms upstairs held no delights either and Nevin knew that Ann would struggle to bring comfort or order to these sparse rooms longing for homely domesticity, the kind of nurturing Ann didn't possess. He noticed her wavering smile beam again as she stood on the landing, looking out over the village; she could almost see inside the Post Office door.

In the short few months after they married, Nevin learned that housekeeping was not Ann's talent, no; nor was she a middling good cook. Her cheeky wit made him laugh though, and in his long heavy bones he knew she would be a great landlady.

And wasn't he right.

They were barely opened a week, when word spread of the sparky wee woman who took over Power's pub. In dribs and drabs the men came juking down from the hills and in from the fields, to study her over their glasses of stout. They were suspicious at first of her loud Northern accent and constant smile, but the way she remembered their names won them quickly, and once won, they were hers forever.

The people of the village were rudderless, moving aimlessly through their lives it seemed to Nevin, hearing their dull limited conversations about wet fields and whin-bushes and bindweed taking over the land. He knew they needed a stalwart to guide them, steer them in the right direction.

Ann knew it too, flushing out their simplicities with clever questions each night in the pub. Nevin soothed their concerns by day, when they nipped in for quick stouts, dragging on their cigarette butts, listening. Listening to the best information, on politics, education, livestock prices. You name it, Nevin knew about it. His advice was being sought on a regular basis and followed verbatim.

Yes, he was originally from Fermanagh, so was his wife, but they were both rooted in the area now. They grew kindred to the locals, especially in their love of deValera, backing the Fianna Fáil candidates with passion. And always, always, deeply interested in the lives of the people. It was hard to remember that they weren't born and reared there.

Within five years Cox's pub was the seat of the village.

There were no chains adorning Nevin' s neck, but he was the Lord Mayor of this sheltered hamlet, nestled snugly in the shadow of the hills.

It wasn't until Ann turned forty that it dawned on Nevin, he wouldn't be a father, probably not.

He couldn't mention it to her though, she wouldn't like it. They both knew that line of conversation was out of bounds. He heard the men teasing her when the drink loosened their tongues and they thought he wasn't around. He remained calm, standing in the pantry, listening to their cruel taunts, which he was certain Ann instigated herself, with the usual barbs she aimed at their drunken heads, goading them.

They were both too old to start a family now, and anyway, there were enough snotty-nosed wanes running about without Ann and Nevin adding to them. That side of things was slowing down between them, which was grand; they had had their fun and now they had higher roles to play.

When numbers began to go up in the village school, Master McFadden called a meeting in the pub on a Friday evening in late October, a few days before Halloween. Fr. Coyle, the Parish Priest, was there too, quietly official, watching the parents gathering in. Mothers in their coats and head scarves, behind their husbands, shy and uncertain in that male domain. Nevin told Ann earlier to offer the women a wee sherry on the house, but she said a glass of diluted peppermint would do them fine, he was too much of a softie for his own good. She smiled at them all though, calling them by name, as Nevin brought up extra chairs from the parlour and the meeting came to order.

The Master did most of the talking, deferring to Fr. Coyle from time to time, who nodded his head in approval.

There were 27 children attending the school, now the Duffy family had emigrated back from Scotland. That meant they were entitled to a second teacher, a Junior Assistant Mistress, who would teach infants up to second class. Indeed, they were in the process of putting up a dividing partition, creating two separate classrooms, each with its own fireplace. Master McFadden was hoping the parents would donate more turf in future, if they could manage it.

These were exciting times, Fr. Coyle told them, when the Master sat down.

He turned to Nevin then, making a big display of thanking him for his advice, on procuring a Miss Nora Boyle from Killygordon, the new J.A.M. for the school. He praised him for his generous donation of a tractor load of turf, that would help to keep fires burning until well after Christmas. Nevin nodded humbly in acknowledgement. It was really Ann who deserved the credit for finding Norah, because Ann's people were originally from Norah's neck of the woods. So Ann was not only responsible for upgrading the education in the school, she also found a lodger willing to pay them fifteen shillings a week, for the long foreseeable future.

Nevin tittered with satisfaction, climbing into bed beside Ann that night, content that their sovereignty was going from strength to strength. They lay for a while rehashing the evening's events, when a mouthwatering notion seized Ann.

"Do you know what we should do, Nevin?" She licked her lips at the thought.

"What are you scheming now?" He was already laughing.

"Wouldn't it be gorgeous if we could fix Master McFadden and Norah up!"

"You're not using your head pet."

"What do you mean Nevin?" She was crestfallen.

"If you fix them up and they marry, Nora might have to give up the school and we'll lose our lodger."

"Christ! I forgot about that, are you sure she would have to stop working?"

"I'll find out. I'm fairly certain that that's the way it is."

"It's a silly idea anyway, you're right Nevin, sure she wouldn't live with us if she got married."

The conversation ended and Nevin fell asleep, knowing Ann would never do anything silly to jeopardize the extra money Norah added to their healthy bank account. So healthy, he had paid off their small mortgage, making them the owners, fair and square, of Cox's pub. The deeds were safe, in a tin box on top of the wardrobe.

It was a good idea getting Ellen O' Donnell from around the corner, to come in and help Ann tidy the house before Miss Nora Boyle's arrival. Ellen was such a capable woman. In no time at all she had the guest bedroom looking clean and presentable. The wooden floor was scrubbed white, with a nice wee raffia mat thrown down to cover a hole in one of the floorboards. She made the bed fresh and smooth looking, smoother than any bed Nevin had ever seen. The tall boy and drawers stood polished and shiny, leaving a fresh smell in the room, masking the odour of stale beer wafting up from the pub below.

The parlour was the hardest job, after all Norah would need a place to sit in the evenings, to mark her copies and prepare her lessons. Ellen set to work with gusto, clearing out the empty crates and boxes, down on her hands and knees scrubbing the wooden floor. Ann up and down from the bar overseeing progress.

Jackdaws had nested in the chimney. Andy Dore arrived with his brushes, amid curses and grunts and soot and fragments of old nests, to clear it. By the time Ellen was leaving, the fire in the parlour was drawing nicely. The room had reclaimed a little of its former elegance, now that you could see the mustard armchairs and the green patterned rug, pushed up against the brass fender.

Norah was shy at first. Nevin watched with satisfaction the way Ann coaxed her along, introducing her to the women of the village. She invited Fr. Coyle for evening tea, shortly after she arrived, knowing Mona and Kitty Eddy would be watching. News would spread that the J.A.M. was thought highly of by the school's manager. By Christmas she had settled in nicely and returned from her break in the New Year, happy to be back in her post. She filled Ann in on the gossip from Killygordon and she looked great, wearing a brown mohair coat, purchased in the sales in Derry.

They grew closer as the months passed. There was Nora and Ann, giggling on the landing, watching Cormac Brown across the street, piddling in broad daylight. Lolloping towards the Post Office, tripping, trying to regain his balance, the unbuttoned corduroy trousers falling down over his wellies.

Norah and Ann again, trying not to giggle the following afternoon, watching Cormac trampling back in his worn hobnail boots, nodding unwittingly at the friendly chat the women put on him.

"Afternoon Cormac, isn't it a beautiful spring day?" Ann nudged Norah.

"Oh, deed it is, a grand day altogether." He shifted uneasily, the thirst killing him.

"Go on in Cormac, Nevin will pull you a drink, and put a knot in that wee thing of yours, before you wither every rose bush in the village!" More giggles while Cormac smiled, then fumed, unsure whether he was insulted or not.

Norah and Ann, walking across to the Post Office to buy stamps, having a wee natter with Mona and Kitty; back over with a fresh batch loaf and slices of bacon for the tea.

Nevin watched them, delighted that Ann had a friend.

She was younger, a good bit younger than Ann, at twenty-three, but wasn't she lucky to have Ann showing her the ropes. She was a breath of fresh air, compared to the reeking buffoons Ann had for company, seven nights a week.

Things were going nicely, very nicely indeed.

Nevin changed the car. Traded in the old Anglia for a new Ford Zephyr Mark II, black with beige leatherette seats. Even Mr. Comber didn't have one of them. For years, Nevin had the only car in the village, until Mona's husband Josie bought the Consul, a fine model but showy, with her two toned colours in cream and maroon. He didn't mind that Josie bought a car. Himself and Mona had no children either and their hard work warranted a bit of luxury. It made life easier on Sunday mornings, now some of the villagers travelled to Mass with Josie, sparing Nevin the two trips he used to make to 11o' clock Mass. Ann grumbled about the loss in fares, though she soon saw it was a better arrangement.

When the buko next door arrived with his Hillman Minx, parking her in front of his new shiny sign announcing, 'Logue's Bar', it niggled Nevin something terrible. He was only in the village a wet week and he was driving a fine car, and just to be really annoying, he was teaching his wife to drive, if you don't mind.

He thought Ann would lose her reason the day she heard Norah was put out of the school. Fr. Coyle had found a new, fully qualified teacher, who came highly rated by all accounts, well, according to Andy Dore, and she happened to be marrying Jim Logue from over the hill, a townland barely in the parish.

Norah didn't seem half as disturbed as Ann, who sulked and ranted while Norah packed her things and sat at the kitchen table drinking tea, waiting for her brother to arrive.

"Don't you worry," Ann remonstrated, "Me and Nevin will get to the bottom of this. There's something fishy here, but we'll get to the bottom of it."

She was still making pledges, as Norah waved out the windscreen of her brother's car.

The women stood in their aprons, shaking hankies at her, until she was out of sight of the village.

Nevin fumed too at Nora's sudden departure. God knows they could have done without this upset and

Christmas nearly upon them. He had taken the toys down from the attic, to display in the parlour window as he did every December, but his stock of Snakes and Ladders was low, as was his supply of caps for the guns and holsters. It meant a trip to Raineys in Letterkenny, a journey he wished he didn't have to make. Not now, with Ann in bad form and the bar getting busy. She could be sharp on the men when she was irked. And she was irked. Now that Norah had gone and taken her fifteen shillings a week with her.

Two years ago, it didn't matter whether she sniped at the customers or not, when Cox's pub was the only show in town. Mrs. Dorian, the old American doll, was a rare duck, seldom open for business. Nevin wondered if she had a licence to sell liquor at all.

Well, the new buck next door put paid to that wishful thinking.

In the two years since his doors opened, he was doing a steady trade, even luring in women because he had a snug, which apparently was fashionable in the big towns and cities. Ann and Nevin's customers were loyal though, seldom defecting to Logue's Bar, except for Cormac Brown, who scurried like a goat into Logue as soon as he opened the door.

When his customers did sneak in next door, Nevin made it his business to wander in too, by the way, needing to borrow a bottle of Powers or a naggin of Johnny Walker until Thursday, when Mulrines lorry came around. Logue was always pleasant enough, handing over whatever Nevin needed, asking him to stay and have one himself, but Nevin declined gracefully, making sure he took stock of who was in the bar. He'd only be back behind his own counter five minutes, when the door dinged and the boys slighered in, all sheepish, hoping they weren't in the bad books. They were quickly forgiven, if they repeated every word, movement and gesture that took place, from the moment they went in, until the second they came out of Logue's Bar.

In a way it suited Nevin that his customers took a wrong turn, from time to time.

It gave him a chance to see the snug, how well his neighbour's shelves were stocked, and who Logue's regulars were. If the timing was right, he got a gawk at Logue's wife too, when she came in from school after 3 o' clock. She seemed to go straight to work behind the bar, so her husband could go back over the hill to help his brother Tom with the sheep. She wore her dark hair back in a bun, looking about shyly with her big blue eyes, not fooling Nevin one bit, acting like butter wouldn't melt in her mouth. The same lady was as shrewd as they came, and money mad. She came in the door from one job and straight into another, hardly feeding herself in case she would lose a penny.

He did feel a twist in his gut, the day he noticed her frock blowing against her swollen belly, walking in from school. He stood at the green gate between the two premises to steady himself, wondering if Ann knew.

It was a blow.

Here they were, only married a few months, with a child already on the way. Everything fell easily into their laps.

New business, new school, new car, new sign, and soon, a new baby.

How did they do it?

Thank God Johnny Neils had a big loud mouth and wasn't behind the door sharing how they did it.

"I hear the aule mother gave him money to buy the place."

Nevin kept polishing glasses. Ann couldn't contain herself.

"You don't say Johnny. Will ya have another stout?"

"Aye. He got the money, and the brother Tom got the farm," licking froth from his cracked lips.

"Now where would his poor mother get that kinda money?" Ann's smile was getting strained.

"Saved over the years, I suppose."

"And what about the wife?" There was anger creeping into her voice now.

"They say she's a brilliant teacher, but she'll soon be out for a while, there's a wane on the way."

The smile abandoned Ann.

Nevin ignored her sharp intake of breath, as she headed for the kitchen, her low-set arse defeated looking, the door slamming behind her.

She perked up the next morning though, when Nevin pointed out that Mrs. Logue would be needing a substitute soon, a chance to get Nora back.

Her arse looked livelier going out the door the following afternoon, to have a wee chat with Mrs. Logue. Point out that Nora would be the obvious choice to step into her shoes, while she was on maternity leave.

Wasn't she lucky to have a mature woman like Ann to guide her, Nevin thought, confident that Nora and her fifteen shillings would soon return.

When the time came, the brazen bitch put a cousin of her own into the school. A heavy set wan from over the west, fully qualified like herself, no less. Nevin felt mortified for Ann, having to phone Killygordon Post Office, to relay the message to Nora that the job wasn't hers after all.

It was dawning on Nevin that the two next door weren't playing a fair game.

Wasn't Ann right to dislike them from the very start.

Still, they were both as nice as pie when baby Malachy came along. Himself and Ann, the first into Logue's Bar to congratulate the new parents. Wetting the baby's head with the daddy, who was standing drinks all round him and barely able to stand himself.

She was upstairs recuperating and they had a good look at Jim Logue in action that day, draining the bottle of Black Bush. Bumming like a clown, about the fine son he produced and the lucky man he was to have a wife like Gracie, she was one in a million. If the ban on married teachers was lifted, the sky would be the limit for her.

Yes, himself and Ann kept smiling and nodding, clinking their glasses every time there was a toast to the first child born in the village for years. On the farewell clink their eyes met. Ann's resolve echoed his own.

This was a cat that needed skinning!

Jim

Jim sat up in bed and lit a Sweet Afton, waiting for the cup of tea Gracie brought him in the morning. The range would be lit and downstairs getting nice and warm, enticing him to rise around 10 o'clock. He would shave at the kitchen table and put on a clean shirt, left on the armchair for him by Gracie. Most days started the same. He soaped up his face, looking into the cracked mirror on the wall, glad that Malachy was asleep in his cot; the cot Gracie dismantled and carried down the stairs every morning, back up at night.

Peggy was out in the scullery, washing nappies in the big Belfast sink, sloshing away, while Jim tried not to nick himself with the blade he hadn't changed in ages.

Peggy came to them after Malachy was born. Gracie knew they would need a girl in the house when she went back to school. Madge, her first cousin, had been her substitute when she was on maternity leave, but she couldn't stay on as their housemaid. Gracie had to hire a girl to nurse Malachy and do the housework when her five week leave was up. Naturally they went looking for someone from Gracie's neck of the woods and found Peggy, willing and able, dying to set out on a new adventure. She was two years older than Gracie, heading into spinster territory, but Jim liked that she was sensible and capable, unlike some of the hired girls, constantly homesick, unable to cope.

Peggy was solid, the eldest of eight children, delighted to have her own bedroom and only have to deal with one small child. It helped that she had a lively sense of fun and baked the nicest bread Jim had ever eaten, even trumping his mothers. He didn't say that to Gracie mind you, for her treacle bread was passable and her apple tarts improving under Peggy's tutelage.

Mickey up in the garage had an eye on Peggy, but he was a bit backward in coming forward. It took him six weeks to pluck up the courage to say hello, though he was warming up lately, having wee chats with her as she passed by, wheeling Malachy in his pram. He was reared by his grandparents, who left him everything when they died, house, land and money; according to Andy Dore. The garage was starting to do well for him, now that people were buying cars, a change from working on tractors. He was getting a petrol pump installed any day. Peggy and Mickey would make a good match, not that he wanted Peggy to leave and neither did Gracie, not when she was in the family way again.

Gracie didn't want to hear about Mickey at all. She pulled faces and made crass jokes about his grimy fingers and oily overalls, whenever Peggy spoke about him at the dinner table. Jim's warning look didn't deter her one bit. She knew she had a good one in Peggy. They laughed easily together, gabbing away in Gaelic, using their own dialect. Giggling like silly schoolgirls, making Jim think they were talking about him.

Ann next door was a nosey bitch, scurrying towards Peggy five minutes after she arrived, trying to draw her out with sweet smiles and probing questions. Peggy knew a nosy parker when she met one, knew how to stonewall her, with the low set arse all business

Ann was mad that Gracie didn't hire Nora as her substitute, after she advised her to do so. The other women in the village understood that advice from Ann was really a set of instructions they should capitulate to. Gracie wasn't like the other women, whether that was a good thing or not; Jim couldn't decide.

He smiled thinking about her now, pulling on his ironed shirt, lighting up another Sweet Afton. Gracie had her own ideas and she could be damned stubborn when a notion got into her head, maddeningly so. Indeed there were times Jim felt driven to drink by her, questioning why he had married a woman from over west, without a long courtship that might have helped him to understand her ways. Tom was still courting Sally, five years on, with no sign of a wedding yet, although he was six years older than Jim.

Tom warned him to take his time, but Jim wouldn't listen. Too eager to gallop, once he had the bit between his teeth.

The local fellas were talking about Gracie for weeks before Jim met her or got a look at her, but he already had a clear picture of her in his mind. She was tall and willowy, with jet black hair and sapphire blue eyes and the fair skin of an Irish Cailín. She rode her bicycle from Sam and Aggie Dokes' every day, aloof and mysterious, ignoring the gawking town landers, on her way to teach their children. She was well in with Fr. Coyle apparently, and visited the Parochial House most evenings, where a friend of hers called Brege, was the housekeeper.

The local girls hated to see her and Brege appearing at the dances. Their prospective husbands spent too much time dancing Gracie, or watching her from the corner of their eyes, harbouring thoughts that required a valour they didn't possess.

Not like Jim, who knew in his heart he would win her, though he needed time to get a few bob together, to pay for the new suit Mickey-the-Tailor was making him. She would see that a certain man had style about him and didn't go flailing around the dance floor, with wide trousers flapping and big spags rotating, one going east and the other going west.

No, Jim wasn't your average local yokel.

He had brains and ambition, with no intention of staying on the hill for the rest of his life. Tom worked him like a dog, making him walk sodden fields in driving rain, looking for lost ewes. Making him stand at the dipping tank, on blazing summer days with the ears scalded off him, the fumes from the sheep dip catching in his lungs. He was stingy with payment too, but every penny Jim earned working the farm with Tom or driving the lorry for him, he spent on good suits and leather shoes, waiting for the right opportunity to present itself.

His older sisters Nelly and Teresa were gone for years, married in Scotland with big families.

Gracie

It was a given that Tom would inherit the home place and move Sally in with his mother, as soon as they got married. His mother approved of Sally, glad she was a local girl whose people she knew all her life; a strong hard worker, reared on a small farm similar to their own.

She fretted that Jim had notions; that he harboured a false pride that made him want things in life above his station, showing very little interest in courting the neighbouring girls who didn't seem to have what he was looking for.

She needn't have worried though, because Jim had a plan.

He would marry an educated woman. One with a career, who made good money and had a steady income, a backup to whatever line of business he would eventually pursue.

He was a bright man, but the love of learning was battered out of him, by that brute Master Sharkey, who despised the children from the hill, making them kneel in the school yard in cruel weather, for not knowing their sums. Hitting them so hard with rods, he left welts that stood out in swollen ridges on their arms and legs. He favoured the children from better off families, the merchants' and shop owners' wanes, who were invited to sit near the fire and told constantly how smart they were, when Jim could see they were a shower of dolts, the lot of them.

The resentments bubbling up in him boiled over the day he turned fourteen and Sharkey made fun of the hill children, calling them whelps and mongrels, standing them in a line, sneering at their tattered shoes and frayed knitted jumpers; making the dolts cry with laughter. The inkwell struck Sharkey just below the left eye, but Jim didn't wait to see if he drew blood. He was halfway across the hill before the Master knew what hit him.

It was a dull November day, when he stood pale and breathless in the kitchen where his mother was baking a white soda scone. He swore to her he would never go back to school. She didn't force him to return; nor did Sharkey send for him, and there ended his formal education. He regretted that; but the scar left on the Master's cheekbone was a branding Jim boasted about for years.

The first time he led Gracie around the dance floor, he knew all eyes were on them. His hand firmly on her back, his deft footwork keeping her in step, making her look as good a dancer as himself. He knew she was smiling, though he couldn't see her face, and he smiled too, as they waltzed to 'The Tennessee Waltz', the tilt of his head proud. Gracie's full skirt floated out behind her, pale blue shantung, that matched the lace gloves she wore, holding Jim's hand tightly in hers. The five guineas he paid for his grey tweed suit was money well spent, even if Tom did pour scorn on it, asking him who the hell he thought he was.

"You're Jim Logue, not Gentleman Jim," he sneered.

"You have no style Tom, that's your problem. If you want to get a woman that's a bit of class, you need to know how to dress."

"I know I could be doing better things with five guineas; Mickey the Tailor must be having a right laugh at ya."

Jim wanted to tell him he slaved bloody hard for it, thanks to being worked like a dog, but he didn't want to

Gracie

lose his temper or ignite Tom's. He finished knotting his tie, putting a red hanky in his breast pocket, before heading out to the dance.

He was still smiling when the set ended and they walked to the mineral bar, the eyes of the locals pretending not to follow them. Gracie glanced shyly at Jim as they sat together, drinking Orange Crush through paper straws as the band announced a ladies' choice and the floor remained empty. She seemed reluctant to speak much about herself, answering questions quickly, forcing Jim to do most of the talking. It was no problem talking about himself, about his dreams of being a great runner and missing his chance to go to the Olympics after the war. It was his favourite subject and not one he had an opportunity to engage people in for quite some time. His dreams were scuppered by Tom, he told her, who wouldn't give him the money for coaching or runners which he needed badly if he wanted to make it to London. He wasn't going to make a charity case of himself, begging the parish for money; he had a bit more pride than that.

He could see Gracie was upset on his behalf when she heard this, her mouth pursing slightly, telling him she was sorry to hear that.

Her big blue eyes encouraged Jim to keep talking, until the band announced the final set of the evening and Gracie went to tell Brege that Jim was walking her back to Agnes'. She would see her some time during the week.

"You could be doing with a new bicycle," Jim remarked, as they wandered along the dark lane that led to her digs.

Gracie was walking the bike between them like a shield, still letting Jim do most of the talking.

"It's not mine, it's Sam's," she said. "He was very good to lend it to me and it'll do till I can buy a new one."

She giggled shyly at the thought of Sam and Agnes. Jim smiled too, thinking he would like to kiss her, but not tonight. He would try and have patience, though he knew for certain Gracie was the woman for him.

He had a strong feeling she liked him too.

"Would you like to go to the pictures during the week? I'll get the lend of Tom's lorry."

"It depends which night," she said. "I usually visit Brege on a Tuesday."

"What about Wednesday then? There's a good western on with Yul Brenner, the bald fella. I'll pick you up around 7o'clock."

"That should be alright," she said, her eyes catching Jim's, making him want to kiss her again. Instead he leaned her bike against the gable wall and wished her good night.

He laughed out loud, walking back out over the hills towards home. No competition stood between him and Gracie's affection, the affection he'd already won.

One hand was as long as the other though and he needed prospects, a profession of some sort to make Gracie feel secure, feel she was marrying her equal.

A week later Tom and himself were driving through the village, below in the glen,when Jim let the engine stall and she cut out near Cox's pub. Tom fumed, shouting at him

"What the fuck are ya at!"

Jim wasn't listening. He was staring at the 'For Sale' sign, on Mrs. Dorrian's bar, the aule American doll; she finally got fed up and was moving on, maybe back to her people in the States.

"I wonder how much she'll be asking for it?" Jim was really talking to himself.

"Well whatever she's asking, you won't be able to give."

Tom's retort hung in the cab like a challenge.

"It's a grand wee bar, the house is in good shape too," Jim was still thinking out loud, a hint of excitement in his voice.

"Where the hell would you get the money? The bank wouldn't look at ya."

Jim knew where the money was, most of it anyway, and he pushed the choke in and tried to start the lorry again as Tom shouted.

"You're going to flood her! For fuck's sake, you'll flood her!"

His heart was beating fast; still surveying Dorrians, as the engine caught and he drove on through the village, ignoring Tom, who stared hard at him, making low exasperated gasps.

Jim's mother had been saving all her life; forty years of spiriting away egg money. She drew it all out of the bank the morning of the auction. £400; which she hoped would secure the pub for her youngest child, her pet.

The final bid was Jim's, at one thousand eight hundred pounds and he didn't worry one bit, as the gavel came down for the final blow. The Bank was happy to lend him and Gracie the residue, with Gracie's payslips as a guarantee of solvency.

It was a small mortgage in the scale of things.

MaCausland drew up the paperwork. A three page document that Jim signed with a flourish, before shaking the big warm hand of his solicitor, who wished him the best of luck in his new venture.

Everyone went to MaCausland.

He was a local man and you couldn't pass him, so Tom reckoned anyway.

It was the second of January and Jim drove Gracie down into the village in Tom's lorry. They sat beaming with pride, peering out the windscreen at Dorrians imposing facade, Jim vowing that a new sign would soon announce 'Logue's Bar'.

Himself and Gracie would be running a successful business.

They didn't get the keys until the week before their wedding, when Jim took possession of the premises, stocking the bar and tidying up as best he could, by himself. Gracie had gone west to her family, before the big day. Her sister Mary was making her wedding dress and she needed to have a final fitting and get things ready for the honeymoon.

His mother wanted to help in the bar, but Tom was in a sulk about the money she shelled out, so she stayed on the hill and made no fuss. She knew Tom would feel different after the wedding, when the bar opened and she could visit in peace, maybe even stay a few days.

McMahon's showroom had a fresh looking Hillman for sale, she looked almost new. If Jim had a good start in the bar, he would buy it in a month or so. Gracie would need a bicycle for going up and down to school, even though it was only a five minute walk, he liked the thought of her starting her new post with a bit of style.

They married in Jim's parish church, which was unusual. Gracie insisted, saying she wanted Fr. Coyle to marry them, after all it was the parish she would call home, for the rest of her life.

The chapel was cold and draughty, as they stood saying their vows, Gracie promising to take him for richer or poorer. Her blue lace gown with matching veil and gloves, highlighted her sapphire eyes, blinking slowly as Jim placed the slim gold band on her finger. Fr. Coyle joined them for the wedding breakfast in the local hotel, toasting their future that he said looked rosy.

They honeymooned in Dublin, staying two nights in The North Star Hotel, because Fr. Coyle recommended it. Jim drank a few whiskeys the first night, giving him the courage he needed to consummate their union, a job he seemed to do well, judging by the twinkle in Gracie's eyes the next morning. He noticed a spring in her step, as they wandered along Talbot Street, heading to Clerys. She wanted to browse, while Jim stood outside smoking, watching the trams and listening to the noises of the city. He drank a few more whiskeys the second night, while Gracie waited for him upstairs and all too soon it was time to go home.

On Sunday evening they were back in the village.

Jim stood behind the counter of his own bar, pulling bottles of stout and pouring whiskeys for the men who crowded in, thirsty and inquisitive. Some of the customers were from Jim's townland over the hill, there to show their support on opening night. Even Tom was there to show that blood was thicker than water.

The local men were all regulars in Cox's pub and Jim wondered as he greeted them warmly, shaking their hands in welcome, were they there for the novelty of the occasion or would they now divide their loyalty between the two bars; maybe even defect to Logue's Bar for good.

Gracie joined them for a little while, smiling shyly at the men, as Jim introduced her. They drank her all in, so they could describe her accurately to their wives, when they got home.

Jim was having a whiskey himself, sure why not?

It was nice to be convivial on his first night in the business, but Gracie reminded him again that she did not drink, when he offered to pour her a sweet sherry. She left them shortly afterwards, saying she needed to get ready for the morning, nervous at the prospect of starting in her new school.

Opening night turned into a loud garrulous affair, lasting well after closing time, with the last few men stumbling onto the footpath at one o'clock in the morning, pulling their overcoats closed against the icy night winds.

Jim's head was thumping, feeling Gracie's heat leaving the bed early, listening to her morning noises, dressing in the dark, not wanting to wake him by switching on the light. She went downstairs to light the range. The smell of turf wafted up through the floorboards. He imagined the heat spreading, hearing cups and plates being placed on the kitchen table. He rapped the bedroom floor with the heel of his foot, until Gracie came up the stairs to see what he wanted.

"Bring me up a mug of tea Gracie, three spoons of sugar and a good drop of milk."

She was rushing, she said, couldn't he rise and get it himself. Still, she brought him what he asked for, then he heard the front door closing, heading off to her new post.

He sat up in bed, lighting a Sweet Afton, thinking about the crack the night before, knowing the takings were good, though he still had to count them. The headache was worth it. If it persisted though he would have to get Mrs. Cullen's headache powders in Mona's, to tide him over till later. Till a wee hair of the dog later, when darkness fell and the customers gathered in again and the crack would be good all over. He imagined the money drawer filling up, with half-crowns and shillings, maybe the odd pound note.

It was another Monday morning, three years on.

Malachy was shaking the cot, crying for his dum-dum. Jim shouted to Peggy to come in from the scullery and see to the wane. He fumbled with the wrapper of a Mrs. Cullen's powder, dusting it into a cup of water, annoyed that his hands were shaking, making him spill some of it.

He knew Gracie was in bad humour with him, for constantly drinking behind the counter and she seemed jealous of the fact that he often went back over the hill to help Tom with the sheep.

He was beginning to notice that her moods changed, fluctuating at a rate he wasn't aware of before they married.

Her form was low after Malachy was born, but she picked up again when she went back to school, though there had been highs and lows since then. She rose some mornings at six o'clock, to clean out the range or scrub the wooden floor behind the counter, before heading up to school. There were Saturdays when she washed all the windows in the house, polishing them with old newspaper, ignoring Peggy, who urged her to sit down and relax on her days off.

These bursts of energy were often followed by Sundays where she fell asleep at the range after Mass, sitting in the leatherette car seat they used as an armchair, bone weary, staring into space or at the floor.

Jim hated her like that.

He'd throw disgusted looks in her direction when he came up from the bar to tell her Malachy was crying and she needed to lift him from his cot. She'd have to rouse herself and make the tea, for it was Peggy's day off and Tom was joining them for the Sunday fry, as usual.

The main task for Jim was keeping the customers happy, and he certainly knew how to do that.

He tuned in to each man who came through the door, getting to know his peculiarities or his ways, as Gracie called them. He tried making each man feel that he had something interesting to say, something Jim wanted to hear.

Johnny O' Donnell was a veteran of World War One, clearly too painful a memory for him to relive. He talked mainly about poaching salmon in the village lough, or snaring rabbits on his own land, with a view to selling them to his neighbours. He'd been posted to Siberia in 1915 and lost a few toes to frostbite, so his gait was lurching and awkward, and he spoke through his nose in a grunting unattractive fashion. Jim liked him though, and when it was just the two of them in the bar he would recall some of the horrors of the war, shuddering as he spoke, almost in a whisper.

Neil Fada came in the mornings, when it was quiet. He was a TB survivor, who knew there was muttered fear among the villagers, that he was still spreading disease wherever he went. He was middle aged and well spoken, having travelled a bit in his time, seeing some of the world. Like Johnny he never married and like Johnny he lived with his spinster sister. He loved to read and left novels in the bar for Jim, some of them a little bit salacious, which Gracie hated, though she knew they remained on a high up shelf, unread. Jim liked to hand them out to men like Johnny Neils and Barney Cam, because it tickled his funny bone, in a wry, pitying kind of way.

Neither man could read, but were too embarrassed to admit it, so they lurched off up their hilly lanes to light Tilly lamps and slabber over the sexy books, thinking they had pictures. They hid their disappointment always, telling Jim they enjoyed the stories and man wasn't Jim the wild man to have such dirty books about him. Jim winked conspiratorially at them, unable to confess who the books really belonged to, they would gossip that he was spreading TB about the place; a rumour that could close his bar and finish him completely.

Tomorrow was pension day and more aule codgers would be in, first to Mona and then to Jim, for their weekly blow out.

Cormac Brown would be first through the door, loud and boorish, kicking the counter with his tackety boots, hoping to rise a row before the evening was done.

John and Jimmy Owen would make an appearance too, but not for long, because they knew where they were expected to be and just when the crack was getting up. At a certain time of the night, when the yarns were flying up and down the counter, they both slid off their stools while Jim was in full flight, telling his favourite one about the Simie brothers' greyhound. No, they couldn't stay, because they had to go next door, before Nevin put his head in, to inquire if Jim had a bottle of Johnny Walker he could spare, until Mulrines lorry came round. Everyone knew why he was really there, as men shuffled next door in fear of some unspoken, nasty retribution.

Jim had his own regulars now; a small band of locals and a collection of men who came from outside the village, because they liked Jim's style. Liked his intelligent line of conversation. That he could drink with the best of them and man, he was great crack, the life and soul of the party.

Yes, some of his customers were ordinary simple men, but in the main they were smart, articulate fellas.

Not like the local yokels who frequented Cox's, running up Ann's arse, listening to Nevin with their gobs hanging open, like they never heard anything in their lives, till it came out of Nevin's mouth; the big aule string of misery that he was. A blow in from the North, who had conveniently adopted the politics of deValera, because he knew the villagers revered him, more than the Pope or God himself.

He set himself up as deValera's disciple, his St. Peter, the rock who kept Dev's flock loyal and true.

Jim was a Collins' man.

Now there was a man worth admiring. A handsome lion of a man, who would have done great things for Ireland. And when Jim was full of Black Bush, in the bar late at night, he cried bitter tears over The Big Fellow, taken down in his prime, by that miserable, specky, four-eyed de Valera, the stupid jealous bastard, who was never fit to lick Collins' boots.

Gracie would tell him to be quiet, still ranting as he climbed into bed beside her, when it was late and she needed to be fresh for the morning. Sometimes he woke Malachy, who would stand in his cot crying, fearful of the terrible angry sounds coming from Daddy's mouth, that he couldn't block his ears from hearing, not even in the loving comfort of his Mammy's arms.

Ann

~~~

The summer was almost over. The last of the Scottish visitors left that morning, heading for the boat to Stranraer. The Glasgow Fair brought them home in their hundreds and the parish heaved with cousins and uncles and aunts. The usual brigade, who landed every July, flooding the place with scotty accents and pockets ripe with holiday money.

Ann loved to see them arriving for a month or more, back to the farms they were reared on, eager to help out, saving hay and turf. In the evenings when they got scrubbed up, they came into the pub, thirsty and ready to spend their saved notes.

Charles Bayers played the fiddle and Nevin didn't call last drinks until the wee small hours of the morning. Ann couldn't carry the drink to them fast enough, laughing and smiling, watching their sunburnt faces, singing along with, 'I Belong to Glasgow', though she hadn't a note in her head.

It was quiet now, lonely even. She was glad things were back to normal and herself and Nevin could take it easy, heading into the longer darker evenings.

The school opened in another week. Ann wondered if Gracie Logue would be going back, or would she take extra time off, after the baby. She hadn't called yet to see the child, a girl. Cathy, she was calling her, after the aule mother over west, apparently.

She was born before the Glasgow crowd arrived, and Jim didn't sober for a week, putting up drinks on the house every night, like a right clown; according to Andy Dore. He made some kind of comment too, about Gracie being very delicate, when she didn't appear downstairs for weeks after the birth. Andy drank in Logues a fair bit, but Ann didn't mind, he always spilled his guts when he came into Nevin and herself, filling them in on the carry on next door.

The Peggy one had married Mickey up in the garage and Gracie had a new housemaid, the one from over her own country, the cousin who did sub for her again and couldn't speak a word of English. Ann met her coming across from Mona's shortly after she arrived and despite her warmest attempts at being welcoming, the creature didn't seem to understand one question Ann asked her. She had the same closed off ways as Gracie Logue, it wasn't hard to tell they were related.

Anyway, she would call down tomorrow she decided and go in through the bar to see for herself how the place looked. Jim would show her up to the kitchen and plamas her with the usual offer; a snowball or sweet sherry, which she always declined. She would cross the baby's palm with silver, a shilling would do fine, after all, they had a good season too and Gracie had her wages coming in all summer, without doing a day's work since early June. No wonder deValera didn't want married women teaching.

They were off having wanes at every hand's turn, putting in subs and neglecting the children's education, a fact Ann reminded the locals of, every chance she got.

It wouldn't be so bad if Gracie gave the substitution work to poor Nora, or a girl from the parish even, but oh no, she always had to go west to her own country for a sub or a maid and rub people up the wrong way.

It didn't go amiss on the locals, especially the McBride twins, Peter and Hughie, two farmers whose children attended the school and bright children they were.

"Does Master Mac Fadden not have a say in who does sub when yer wan next door goes out on maternity leave?" Peter asked one evening, sitting beside his brother, pouring stout sideways into a half pint glass.

"Aye, or wouldn't you think the Parish Priest would have the final say, isn't he the school manager after all?" Hughie wondered.

"She's a law unto herself." Ann was bristling. "Fr. Coyle had great time for her. He put her into that school, a married woman, and the ban on at the time."

"But he died not long after hiring her; she must have the ear of Monsignor McLaughlin too," Peter sounded baffled.

"You'll find they're paying a big stipend in the chapel." Hughie offered.

"I doubt that Hughie," Ann was bristling again. "Business is not that good in Logues and she watches every penny. Doesn't she make the children pay for material and thread for sewing class, they have to pay for wool too."

"That's true enough," Peter agreed, watching Ann's disgusted face. "Our wanes love the knitting all the same".

Hughie was nodding in agreement, but he knew the conversation had taken the wrong turn for Ann. He tapped a cigarette on the counter before lighting up, glad when the door opened and the Owens came in. Ann moved stridently down the counter to serve them.

"Our wanes love the knitting all the same!" Ann mimicked, when the last customer stumbled out and Nevin locked the pub door.

" Jesus! Do they think of anything besides knitting? That'll get them far in life; bloody knitting!"

She left the last of the glasses on the draining board and followed Nevin up the stairs to bed, aware that she would have to work harder at bringing the locals to their senses. Their eyes were not fully opened yet, to the threat this pair next door posed to the village.

Jim Logue was an opinionated show off, but at least he would stand and talk to you and be pleasant, even charming; but Gracie was impossible to read. Ann felt she was making no inroads with this aloof impenetrable woman.

Shortly before Malachy was born she had Gracie up for afternoon tea.

They sat down in the parlour with a nice wee fire on, drinking out of the good China cups Ann got as a wedding present. They ate slices of jam Swiss roll from Mona's shop and the conversation dragged along, with Gracie's blue eyes watching Ann suspiciously, as Ann tried valiantly to hit on a topic that might make the conversation flow.

"So how long were you and Jim courting before you got married?" Ann stirred her tea, giving Gracie her most generous smile.

"A year or so, I suppose." Gracie's face remained closed.

"And Fr. Coyle married you?"

"He did."

"He's not from your part of the county Gracie?"

"He's not."

"No, it's just that you seem to know him very well."

"He's a good man," Gracie sounded defensive.

"How do you find Master McFadden?" Ann persevered.

"He's grand," Gracie's languid eyes were fixed on Ann's.

"I hear he can be a bit odd at times," she was hoping to open up a hole Gracie might fall into.

"He has his own ways, but he's a great teacher," she was giving nothing away.

Ann's smiling face was beginning to pain her, holding some semblance of a grin in place, until Gracie put down her cup and saucer, announcing her departure. Jim was going up to help Tom dose sheep and she had to do the bar till he got back.

She stood at the kitchen door, watching Gracie's laborious walk down the footpath. Her smile vanished. She closed the door, disgusted that she got nowhere with the brilliant knitter, brilliant teacher, brilliant pain in the arse, who refused to succumb to Ann's magnetic charms.

Back in the pub with a weary step, she hoped someone would lift her spirits. Nevin recognised the frustration in the gimp of her shoulders and the low set of her arse. Barney Cam was at the counter looking sober, as was Andy Dore, both ready to listen to every word she'd say to Nevin. She moved further down the counter, until she was standing opposite the McBride twins, in for a quick stout before their dinner.

"Do you know that one next door is as odd as two left feet," she felt safe venting in Peter and Hughie's company.

"Mrs. Logue is it?" A hint of a smirk on Peter's mouth.

"That's right, she likes to be called Mrs. Logue," Ann was about to enjoy herself.

"Well she is the schoolteacher after all," Hughie quipped, "fully qualified it must be said, isn't that right Andy?"

"That's what Jim says anyway, nearly every time I talk to him, he says it." Andy could read the mood.

"What else does he tell you about her, Andy?" Ann was smiling again and winking at Nevin.

"Well, do you know what he told me there this morning? He said Mrs. Logue was going to get the local women knitting Aran jumpers, a kind of knitting circle he called it."

"The women around here could knit before she came to the place," Peter said, taking a quick look at Ann.

"Aye, but they'll get paid for it now; £1. 5 s. a jumper. She's sending them up to Dublin to some big shop up there," Andy sounded impressed, almost boastful.

"You'll find she's making a huge profit on them herself," Hughie snorted. "For by God, the pair of them are fond of money."

"Do Sadie and Frances knit?" Ann asked the brothers. She had a feeling neither of the wives were gifted with needles and wool, no more than herself.

"Indeed they do not," Peter was indignant. "They have more to do than sit on their arses all day, clacking needles and getting heat rashes on their shins, like some of the dirty women around here, who can't keep a house or keep their wanes clean."

Ann was happy to hear that.

She knew the Mc. Bride children were no good at speaking the gaelic either, so they didn't stand to profit from any of the schemes cooked up by yer wan next door.

She was delighted too that the card playing evenings were proving to be a success. It was lovely to see the wives coming in the door with their husbands for a change, enjoying a wee sherry or glass of Babysham, while they played 25's or whist. She didn't really agree with women frequenting pubs, but these wives were welcome on the odd occasion, joining their husbands in an evening's fun. It was Nevin's idea to liven up the place on a Friday night and it gave Ann a chance to strengthen her bonds with the local women. It was Nevin's idea too to get Charles Bayers to play the fiddle on Sunday mornings after mass, when the men gathered in. Most of them were tone deaf, which was good, for Charles' fiddle sounded like drowning cats squealing in the corner. It was a jolly few hours, until the bar closed and everyone went home for dinner, some returning in the evening when the cows were milked and wanes tucked up in bed.

They gave Jim Logue a run for his money, for he thought he was clever. Creating a snug next door, where the women could sit in private, away from the men. Even providing a bell for them to ring for drinks, so they didn't have to hear the garrulous dirty chat of the men. That's how Andy Dore explained it anyhow, repeating Jim Logue's words as if he was some big shot from America. Charles Bayer's wife Mary had been in the snug and declared loudly, in her daft eccentric voice, that it was a beautiful thing for the ladies of the area.

"O Ann dear, it's a darling little spot!" she yelped. Always decked out in the clashing motleys she loved to wear. She was born in Boston and still retained a hint of the Yankee twang, with a vague look of King George's wife Elizabeth, about her face. Charles was a gentleman, who carried himself like an old army Colonel, straight backed and elegant in dress and mannerisms. How he ended up with Mary, no one knew; not even Andy Dore. They had no children either, but Ann made sure never to identify too closely with Mary on that or any other subject. She was a silly woman, more to be laughed at than anything else. Most of the local women thought the same, except Gracie Logue of course, who had her employed in the knitting circle, a fact that left Ann weak with laughter when Andy told her, one evening in the bar. She laughed that hard, because she knew the cream bainín wool Gracie gave her would be black with dirt, by the time it was transformed into an Aran sweater.

Ann found herself wondering how much profit Gracie would make on the knitting circle, like she wondered about a lot of things in that woman's life, without getting satisfactory answers.

When Fr. Coyle died, a year to the day he put Mrs. Logue into the school, Ann and Nevin were sure that the new P.P, Monsignor McLaughlin would fire her, because of the ban; but he did no such thing. Instead he let her teach away, until the ban was lifted and she was home safe and dry, permanent forever, unless she did something wicked altogether. Ann wondered about that too. What would be so bad that you could lose your job over it!

When Nevin's brother, Fr. Manus, came home from the Missions last year and spent a month with them, she thought he might be able to shed some light on the situation, know the inside track on teachers and how they were hired and fired. Instead, he was asking Ann how this married woman had eluded the Ban, and how her husband had funded his purchase of the premises next door.

He seemed intrigued by the new pair, a little besotted with Jim, who worked his charm on him, standing free whiskeys, free cigars, making Manus think he was a grand fella, probably.

She heard Manus talking to Nevin at the breakfast table and Nevin was engrossed; hanging on his brother's every word. He asked Ann to open the pub, annoying her, because she was banished from the conversation. She heard enough to know that his musings would infiltrate Nevin's mind and give him the wee spurt her husband sometimes needed. Heading to open the pub, she stood juking around the corner, listening to their chat.

"It's in very good repair, the premises next door," Fr. Manus said, buttering his second piece of toast. "And young Logue has tidied it up nicely."

"It wasn't hard to improve on Mrs. Dorrian's setup," Nevin said. "It was gone to the dogs when she had it."

"Maybe that's why you failed to notice its possibilities," Fr. Manus cautioned. "The house is in good repair, as is the bar. Sturdy looking out buildings with the premises too."

Nevin was endeavouring to laugh in an amazed kind of way.

"What would Ann and I have wanted next door for, in the name of God? We're making a grand living here, we didn't need two pubs Manus."

"No I'm not suggesting you did, but licences are hard to come by. You would have cut out all competition, if you had purchased it and let it sit there for a rainy day."

That was as much as Ann heard. Johnny Neils rapped the pub door and she ran to open it.

She didn't resent Nevin having time with his older brother, he'd been abroad for so long. But he was home for good now, retired really, though he liked to say Mass in Enniskillen and here locally, when he was invited to do so.

Monsignor McLaughlin was an austere kind of man, prancing around in full regalia at all times, wearing the full length black surplus, a small five cornered hat on his head, with a purple Pom Pom. He kept to himself, declining offers of tea, or invitations to dinner with certain families after Mass on Sundays.

Ann tried to ingratiate herself with him after he arrived in the parish. Going up to the sacristy after Mass the first Sunday, welcoming him, extending a warm invitation to dinner or evening tea any time he wished. She informed him that she was the landlady of Cox's Pub in the village, but he remained polite and distant, not a bit impressed it seemed, by Ann's winning ways.

Herself and Nevin had their own designated pew in the chapel; five rows back from the altar, left vacant for them at all times, no matter how late they were in arriving.

Nevin had to drive a load of villagers to church first, before going back for Ann. They both walked up the centre aisle, smiling benignly at the faces who peered back at them, making their way to their pew, bolstered by the pleasant winks and nods of their loyal subjects.

Gracie Logue usually went to early Mass, at eight o'clock on a Sunday morning. Lately though, she was taking Malachy to eleven o'clock service, sitting a few rows behind Ann and Nevin, the child tucked safely in beside her. She showed him the Latin words the priest was saying, pointing to them in her brown leather-bound missal. Jim Logue wasn't much of a Mass goer, Ann noticed, but now and again he did accompany Gracie and Malachy, sitting behind herself and Nevin, never returning Ann's nod of approval as she entered her seat, or echoing her brilliant smile.

Malachy was three now and looked like his father, with the same freckled complexion and light brown hair. He had his mother's big blue eyes though and boy didn't he know how to use them, in a begging appealing manner that always worked on Nevin.

Ann wasn't fond of the child.

He had taken to Nevin in a big way and seemed to be always hanging around their front door, especially since the summer had come. He loved sitting in the Zephyr, pretending to drive and Nevin gave him bars of chocolate from the confection they kept in the bar, which he scoffed like a savage who never saw a bite in his life. It was obvious to Ann that the pair next door weren't half as generous to the child as Nevin was. Too consumed with making money to look near him, or pay him any attention. The Peggy one was rearing him, until she married the garage man Mickey and was pregnant five minutes after the wedding.

Gracie had the new maid now, who seemed to be twice as backward as Peggy. A fully qualified teacher too, by the way, hired to do sub for her when Malachy was born and asked back again before Cathy arrived. Madge, as they called her, stayed on as housemaid then, which seemed odd Ann thought. Maybe her qualifications were no better than Nora's!

She had the same hidden ways as Gracie, God help us, which made her the chosen one. She'd come up looking for Malachy, with the broad accent and the fat ankles on her, like something let loose.

Ann had a good laugh with Nevin about her.

"We must take a drive over the west some time Nevin, I'm dying to see how they live over there."

"You mean, the Wild West Ann," Nevin laughed.

"*Me name is Mauge!* Ann mimicked, *"An a ave big stout legs!"*

"She'll be looking for a husband too, that's what brings them over here." Nevin climbed into bed beside her.

69

"O! Do you know who would suit her nicely? Barney Cam, with his big flat feet and his lisp when he speaks, hah! Can you imagine the pair of them?"

"They would make a lovely match," Nevin said.

And Ann roared, giddy with delight. She felt good falling asleep, certain that Nevin wasn't that fond of Malachy.

Didn't he smirk when she teased the boy, pretending to give him sweets. Watching the disappointment on his face, when the bag was only filled with stale pieces of bread, the tears appeared in his big gullible eyes.

Everything was fine. Her and Nevin were as right as ever.

Unlike the pair next door, who weren't suited at all. He spent more time over the hill, helping Tom on the home place, than he did with his wife; bolting the minute she came in from school. Probably trying to get away from her, as much as possible. He taught her to drive, but they rarely went anywhere in the black Hillman, parked up at the door most of the time. The Tom fella seemed to drive it more than they did and Ann wondered what that was all about.

She was drifting towards sleep, when she thought of the new baby next door, Cathy, and the pang she felt earlier in the day, when she looked into the crib at those sweet cherub lips. The huge blue eyes, the smile on Jim's face as he stood looking in at her too, a smile she would never see on Nevin's face.

She pushed the image away and concentrated instead on a plan to introduce Miss Wild West to Barney Cam, certain they would produce right ugly offspring.

Gracie

Gracie couldn't believe how quickly time was passing. Cathy was a year old and the memory of her difficult birth had faded.

Life was back to normal.

Malachy had turned four and Gracie brought him to school for the last two weeks in June, getting him used to the environment and the routine. All the new infants came out for those last two weeks, and for Gracie, who was already exhausted, it was a trying time.

Like every June for the last five years, these four year olds had to be handled with kid gloves. They were little frightened rabbits, hardly able to tell Gracie their names; constantly wetting themselves. Sitting with puddles forming on the floorboards beneath their benches, afraid to tell the teacher they were wet. Gracie allowed their big brothers or sisters to sit with them for the first few days, until they calmed down, becoming accustomed to their new surroundings. Some clung to their older siblings for longer than Gracie deemed necessary, but the effort to part them wasn't worth the hysterics.

"Spoiled scuts!" Jim called them, when he heard who they were, the children whose daddys drank in Cox's and never darkened his bar.

There were more Mc. Brides and Mc.Claffertys and Roartys, with one or two new surnames appearing for the first time. She could tell to look at them who they were. She could tell who the smart ones would be. Who would be left sitting silent and dour at the back of the room, because they could learn nothing and Gracie hadn't time to give them individual attention.

Malachy was well behaved, although he called her Mammy, instead of Teacher like the other children. Gracie corrected him gently every time, knowing he would eventually make the switch in his little head.

It was comforting to have him beside her every morning on the short walk to school, answering his questions, telling him about Bunbin hill that towered above them and how St. Colmcille slept in a cave there, a long time ago. As the weeks went on, he ran ahead of her, eager to play with the other boys in the yard, before the ringing bell announced school.

Peggy had moved on; now a new mother herself, which was fine, because Madge was proving to be a tower of strength. Better than Peggy ever was, and a cousin of her own into the bargain. She had been in Carysfort with Gracie, a year behind her, but hadn't found a permanent job yet. In the meantime, she was delighted to do sub again and stay on as housemaid after Cathy arrived.

Gracie really needed her then, because she was run down after the birth, just like after Malachy. Three weeks passed, before she got out of bed, even nurse Kelly, the midwife, was losing patience with her. Jim was angry, telling her to pull herself together, every time she cried. Sometimes he was gentle, putting soothing arms around her, though he kept asking her what was wrong.

Gracie didn't know what was wrong.

Maybe it was trying to juggle teaching and the bar and motherhood all at once. Maybe it was the hateful Master Mc.Fadden, hateful Ann next door, the hard set hateful faces of the local women, who rarely smiled at her on the road. Maybe she just needed a good bottle of tonic, like her mother suggested.

Anyway; she did finally pull herself together, thanks to kind Dr.Melly. He prescribed tablets for her, that made her a bit shaky at first and drowsy, but over the weeks she felt stronger, calmer, able to cope with the idea of returning to school at the end of August.

Master McFadden didn't offer congratulations, nor did he welcome her back; nodding curtly behind his desk, as she walked through to her classroom. The new Infants sat with first and second class, all with arms folded, waiting for her. The Roarty boys had the fire lit although it wasn't cold, just a slight nip in the air made it a welcome sight. She looked at the new scared little faces, some tear stained, hoping Mrs. Logue would be kind, beside the older familiar faces, who knew she would be.

By October the days had turned dark, the weather bitter, and the Master was back at his old tricks.

"That fire is far too big," he admonished one morning, marching into Gracie's room without the courtesy of knocking.

"Turf's precious you know!" He eyed the red sods heaped high in the grate.

"I have plenty of turf at home," Gracie didn't lose a second in replying, "I'll get Jim to drop a load in the yard, for my own use."

He turned, disgusted, striding back to his classroom.

He resumed his other favourite trick though; watching her through the partition windows. Eyes followed her, as she walked between the desks, checking the children's copies, admiring the little houses the infants had drawn, the sculptured figurines they had fashioned out of marla.

He was getting handier with the rod too, taking out his pent up frustrations on the older pupils, when they didn't know the Proclamation off by heart, or the names of the heroes of the 1916 Rising. Gracie winced as the rod swished through the air, slashing into outstretched palms.

She'd assemble the children quickly before the fire, a choir, to sing Baidin Fheilimi; panicking to find the right note with the tuning fork. They could still hear him ranting, while the big boys gulped down tears, repeating after him the names of Connoly, Pearse, Joseph Mary Plunket.

On Friday afternoons, he charged the same boys with discarding putrid buckets from the outside toilets and cutting fresh sally rods from the wood, near the school. He stored the rods in his locked press, beside rolled up maps of the world.

The older girls loved going into Gracie, on Tuesday and Thursday afternoons. They sat quiet and industrious, in the warmth of her classroom, while the small boys went into the Master's cold miserable room to do extra sums. They dragged their feet as they left, trailing school bags towards the partition door, with no hope of reprieve.

Gracie rarely used corporal punishment, but now and again she did use the ruler, lightly she hoped, on small palms, when they didn't know their tables or spellings. She fought hard against the spite she felt for some of the children; especially those whose fathers were deValera supporters, who 'ran up Ann and Nevin's arses', as Jim said. She fought against loathing the Master too, with his mean pedantic ways, despite Jim goading her on, telling her to take no guff from him, mimicking his walk in the bar some evenings, making Gracie laugh hard; he had him off to a tee.

She did enjoy his miserable face, the afternoon Andy Dore drove his tractor up to the school with a trailer full of turf, shouting over the noise of the engine that Jim Logue sent him and where should he unload his 'precious cargo.' There wasn't a hint of sarcasm in Andy's tone, repeating what he was instructed to say by Jim. He had no notion that Jim was in the bar howling, knowing he had antagonised McFadden. Knowing too, that Andy would relay the entire scenario in Cox's bar that evening.

Gracie lit big roasters for weeks, aware she was being watched, feeling his spiteful eyes trying to weaken her power. She read Putsy Ryan, from the Far East magazine, making the children chuckle with glee, forgetting their shyness, pleading loudly with her to read it, again and again.

Her confidence was growing, surging through her, making her almost belligerent.

She remembered her first year, when the ban was on. Fr. Coyle promised that as long as he lived she would not lose her post. A year later he died suddenly and Brege and herself wept at his funeral, certain that neither of them would retain their jobs, under the new PP, Monsignor McLaughlin.

Brege was right. He arrived regal and haughty, with his own housemaid in tow, dispatching her back to the west, to live with her mother and knit for a living.

Gracie waited to hear her fate, petrified. Until he stood one evening at the kitchen door, in his full length cassock, trimmed with red, a stiff looking five cornered hat on his head. Her heart thumped, watching him stand in her kitchen, oblivious to Malachy, who stood rattling his cot, wanting to be lifted.

"Who gave you the teaching position in the village school Mrs.Logue?" Inquisitional tone, accusing; peering at Gracie, through square black rimmed spectacles.

"Fr. Coyle offered me the post, Monsignor. He told me the job would always be mine," Gracie sounded calm.

"Indeed," he mused. "Well Mrs.Logue, new Kings make new rules."

Gracie didn't respond; unsure of his meaning. She showed him out, his enigmatic pronouncement unexplained, the swish of his cassock like a warning as the door closed behind him.

Jim came up from the bar, eager to hear what the Monsignor had to say, interpreting what Gracie relayed as a certainty that she had lost her job in the school.

"What odds," he said, "We'll manage. Let him keep his job and stick it up his arse."

Gracie wasn't going to give in so easily.

Jim pleaded with her on Monday morning not to go up to school. She would be the laughing stock of the village, being told to go home by Mc.Fadden. Boy would he enjoy that; the bollocks that he was.

But nobody told Gracie to go home.

The fire was lit in her room as usual and the children sat with eager little faces waiting for the teacher, waiting for Mrs. Logue. They stood to say their morning offering, loud and robotic, their hands joined in gentle supplication.

Jim felt sure that every day would be Gracie's last. Until Easter arrived and they relaxed, both aware that a small miracle was taking place, keeping Gracie in her school.

She was praising the Infants, for picking such beautiful buttercups and wild irises for the May altar, when Monsignor Mc. Laughlin strode towards her in full regalia, right hand extended, his smiling face mystifying Gracie.

"Congratulations Mrs.Logue!" he gushed, reaching for her hand. "The ban has been lifted. The school is yours for the rest of your life."

She wanted to say the right thing, show gratitude, but no words came. Aware that her eyes were welling up, she smiled, a weight she had grown used to, lifting off her shoulders.

Jim was jubilant in the bar that evening, sharing the good news with all his customers, holding Malachy in his arms, telling him his mammy was the best wee woman in Ireland. Gracie laughed, though she felt embarrassed that he praised her like that in front of Andy Dore and Cormac Brown.

Andy's son Steven was in second class, and like his father he was too nosy for his own good. It galled Gracie that he carried the title tattle of the village into school every day, sharing it with the other children, having heard it from Andy the night before, on his return from the pub. He was a clever lad, rarely giving Gracie an opportunity to use the ruler on him. She knew from his gaze, the way his ferret eyes followed her, that he was privy to glimpses of her life she resented him having.

Jim was silly at times, opening his mouth in the bar, when he should have kept it closed. Bumming about the great salary Gracie had, how profitable the knitting circle was for all of the women, but especially for Gracie. He was proud of her, which was lovely, but she wished he would show more decorum and keep his own council, like Nevin next door, who was as deep as the village lough.

Jim wasn't cute enough either in his dealings with the customers, giving them free drinks, extending their credit for too long, afraid to ask them to square up their overdue tabs.

Gracie kept an eye on him, making sure to check the red hard backed leger she kept behind the counter, reminding Jim frequently that certain people weren't paying their bills; Jim always said he would see to it, but he never did.

She blurted it out sometimes in the bar and the men would go quiet. Jim's red face was enough to let her know she would have to listen to him later, calling her all the names under the sun, wailing about how embarrassing she was. Once they paid up Gracie didn't care. She just turned her back to Jim in the bed and faced the wall, praying to Our Lady or to St. Jude, that he would run out of steam and fall into a deep snoring slumber.

Before Cathy was born, Gracie was finding it hard to cope. All energy left her. Replaced by a heaviness that stole her longing to scrub sheets on the washing board and hang them on the clothes line, admiring their brilliance. Malachy was in his own bedroom, trying to be a big boy, getting ready for his new brother or sister who would share the room with him. He was wetting the bed, but Gracie still hadn't put the rubber sheet on his mattress.

The high Formica counter in the bar needed scrubbing, the smell of stale urine wafted up to the kitchen, every time the back door opened. Buckets of disinfected water stood unpoured, too heavy for Gracie to manoeuvre. She constantly nagged Jim about keeping the place clean, while he was trying to drink down a Mrs. Cullen's powder, making pained faces to indicate his agony and annoyance.

He was disappearing over the hill to Tom, using her bicycle because the Hillman wasn't going right, the car he paid too much for, Gracie thought. She nagged him about that too, accusing him of cowardice, afraid to go up to Mc Mahon's in Milford and demand his money back. Tom and himself did eventually go up, but according to Tom, they got nowhere with McMahon. He refused to change the car that leaked like a boat and sat like a dud outside the front door. Gracie ranted, vowing they would never do business in that garage again, adamant to stick to her guns, no matter what Jim said.

When Peggy left to get married, Gracie found it hard to cope.

With a month to go before maternity leave and Madge not arriving till the last minute, her only resort was to send for her mother. Jim nodded agreeingly at the suggestion, which he had no intention of allowing.

Ellen O' Donnel, who lived around the corner, arrived the following morning, after Nurse Kelly left, with her sleeves rolled up, as if she knew Gracie was floundering and needed help. She was a widow, who's grown up children were all married and gone, except for Bernadette, who worked part time in Joe and Mona's shop; a terrific grafter like her mother. Ellen washed the sheets from Malachy's bed and his little stained vests and drawers; along with Jim's white shirts and anything else she deemed ready for the washing board. The comforting smell of Lux flakes reached Gracie's nose. She lay in bed, imagining the clothes line hanging proud; the counter gleaming in the bar. Stale urine sloshing down the gully at the back door and Ellen working to lift the burden off Gracie's worried mind.

She was a decent woman and a decent neighbour. So was Bridget Roarty, who sent over scones of homemade bread, even though she had eight of a family to rear. Kitty Eddy wasn't a bad sort either, though she did like to stand in Mona's all day, smoking and gossiping. The fact was, she had a good heart and was always friendly to Gracie. Just like Mary Bayers, who was sneered at by many of the locals, because she wore a yellow coat and patent orange shoes and laughed after every word she spoke, as if she was always telling a joke. In the knitting circle, Mary's jumpers were always finished on time. Gracie pretended she didn't notice they were grubby, accepting them, smiling her thanks, until she got home and sponged them down. Eventually her blackberries and twists emerged in high relief, as elegant as the other knitters, stitch perfect.

The warmth of these women wasn't powerful enough though, to offset the cold that emanated from the bulk of the wives and mothers who met Gracie on the road, or watched her going up the aisle on Sunday mornings. The deValera women. The ones whose husbands drank in Cox's and made Gracie feel guilty of some vague crime she stood accused of without hope of reprieve.

She had driven up so many country lanes in search of knitters, the back seat piled high with hanks of bainin wool, dispatched to the willing and able.

At the Mc. Bride houses Sadie and Frances held their doors ajar, talking to Gracie in the half light; a rabid dog that might savage them. They declined to be her knitters, indignant at her cheek, driving patronisingly to their homes, suggesting they needed her measly few pounds in order to survive. They dismissed the idea of their children being examined for the £5 reward too, refusing to have their fluency inspected.

Gracie reassured them their children were well prepared, but she wasn't convincing these closed faced women, grunting their disdain, closing doors against her.

Andy Dore's wife Sadie was the same, and the Gallagher women and the Mc. Clafferty wives.

The virus was spreading.

Only a handful of ladies were immune. Time passed. Gracie began to realise what the antidote was, one she would never willingly swallow.

Gracie was here to stay.

Her position in the school was permanent and safe. Nothing and no one would drive her out.

Even Master McFadden was thawing a little, acknowledging the pupils who advanced to his room were well grounded in their sums and spellings, almost fluent in the Gaelic. She was pleasantly surprised by his admission, but not surprised by Jim's reaction to it.

"He should be down on his knees thanking you, the bollocks! Aren't you making life easy for him?"

"I suppose you're right," Gracie agreed. "I wonder what's putting him into good humour these days?"

"Maybe he got himself a woman," Jim sneered.

"I think he had an eye on Norah when she was there and that's why he was unfriendly to me when I arrived." Gracie was only sharing her theory with Jim now.

"I doubt that. I was only codding about him getting a woman. The same boy is as bent as a five penny bit."

Gracie's eyes bulged in mock horror because there was a ring of truth in what he said. There was often a ring of truth in what Jim said, but she didn't let him know that.

"Well whatever is making him more pleasant these days, long may it last," Gracie said.

"Indeed," Jim agreed, "Pity the parents wouldn't get a bit nicer too, show some thanks instead of looking at you as if they were chewing on a sour sweety."

"There's a jealousy in them I think, like they're wishing the worst for me."

"Don't you know," Jim said, "And don't forget it either or give them any excuse to get at you!"

There were no question marks over Gracie's ability to teach the children, she was sure of that, despite the fact that some days her mind felt foggy, her legs reluctant to move. She pushed through the miasma, a dogged determination willing her on.

When Inspector O' Mara visited, checking her notes ledger and the children's jotters, he always used the same word; 'impeccable'. He commended each small initiative she undertook, especially the sewing and knitting classes. He praised her little choir, singing sweetly for him, his favourite song, Trasna na Dunta; the crows miming, as Gracie had instructed them to do on such occasions.

Mona was happy to show the big girls to the back counter every October, to choose wool for their jumpers, which she ordered specially in a surprising array of colours, creating excitement, even competition among the girls. Gracie cast the stitches and set the patterns and by Christmas their crimson and purple and mint green jumpers were finished, ready to wear. Mona was ordering spools of coloured thread and needles and swatches of calico fabric too, without the courtesy of thanking Gracie for putting the new business her way.

The virus had spread to Mona, causing her to be cold in her dealings with Gracie, constantly trying to pawn her off with stale loaves or bacon that was on the turn. She hated that

Mrs. Logue returned every unworthy item Peggy or Madge arrived home with, returning the goods herself, making sure the replacements were up to scratch. She constantly haggled over her bill, when she paid up on the last Friday of every month, disputing the final figure Mona came up with. The constant denial that she purchased raspberry jam or tinned stewed steak was infuriating. Exasperated, Mona stopped giving Malachy a juicy red apple or small bag of sweets from the American Can Mixture; a tradition adapted for her customers' children on the day they squared their bills. She certainly wasn't going to give the Logue brat free sweets, when his mother was such an annoying awkward woman.

Cathy was barely two months old when a General Election was called.

The parish went into a frenzy of electioneering Gracie had not witnessed before in her life. Every gable, every wall, was plastered with posters, all of them campaigning for Fianna Fáil. Neil Blaney's smiling face followed Gracie, peering out from every angle, as she walked to school and back.

Cox's pub became the epicentre of political activity, packed every evening with deValera worshipers, certain their party would be victorious again. Nevin was driving his Zephyr to remote doors, canvassing for Blaney, ferrying old bucks down to the pub who hadn't seen a drink in years.

To Gracie it felt like war was imminent, with Jim in the wrong trench, about to be savagely dispatched. He was on the Fine Geal side, being just as vocal as the others in his admiration of their candidate, Paddy Harte. He seemed reluctant though, almost afraid, to put up the posters of Harte that lay on the kitchen table, feeling outnumbered by the Blaney camp.

Gracie wasn't political, but something dogged made her mix the wallpaper glue, one Saturday afternoon. Madge and Jim watched her plastering the wall opposite the house with Harte posters, three of them in a row, walking back to the kitchen, her head high in vanquished satisfaction. An hour later Madge was shouting at the window and Gracie ran in from the scullery to see what the hubbub was about.

"Jesus, wou'd you look at that bloody clown!" Madge's face was blotched in anger.

"Jim! Jim!" Gracie was shouting now too. "Come here till you see what Barney Cam is at!"

Barney was pulling Gracie's posters off the wall, tearing them to smithereens, while some of the locals looked on laughing.

"Isn't he the dirty bastard," Jim came up from the bar, his breath smelled of whiskey. "I'll go out and kick the living shit out of him."

He moved towards the door but Gracie held him back, pleading. Madge moved to help her, telling Jim to have a bit of sense and not be disgracing himself.

"I'll put manners on him," Madge muttered, reaching for three more posters from the kitchen table, marching across to the wall, sticking them over the Blaney posters. The McBride twins stood outside Cox's, with the McClafferty's and Owens, watching her, nonplussed. Ann was at the pub door, Barney beside her like a snivelling lap dog, ready to do her bidding.

"You're a disgrace Barney Cam!" Madge roared, brandishing the glue brush like a weapon.

"Ah now Madge", Ann smiled, "Sure it's only a bit of fun."

Jim returned to the bar, swallowing a Black Bush, with only a few mavericks like himself for company; Cormac Brown, already drunk; John O Donnell, lost in the fog of World War One. Andy Dore braved it in, dispatched from Cox's to see how the land lay down in Logues, for he had a knack of being likeable, even if he did talk out both sides of his mouth. John and Jimmy Owen came slinking in too, standing beside Andy at the counter, trying to make Jim see the error of his ways. Fianna Fáil was the party of the people and deValera was the greatest leader the country ever had.

"He's nothing but a big aule string of misery!" Jim's temper flared. "Didn't he have Michael Collins shot, the stupid arsehole! Now there was a man who would have made something of this wee land of ours."

"deValera is an aule hooore! A hooooore!" Cormac Brown was kicking the counter, as Jim's voice lost control.

Cathy began to cry for her bottle and somewhere in the background Malachy was asking Gracie for something. The hurdy gurdy was in Gracie's head again and Madge told her to go to bed, she would see to the wanes.

Rain spilled down outside. Someone had discarded the Fine Gael posters again. Scraps of Paddy Harte's face ran in rivulets along the village street. Neil Blaney's confident eyes stared out at Madge from his pole position on the wall.

Gracie was relying heavily on the tablets Dr.Melly gave her. Upping her dosage some days so she could leave the house. Walking to school, holding Malachy's hand, trying to answer his worried little questions. Why were their posters torn down? Why was Daddy in bad humour and the bar so quiet?

On Election Day, the school became the polling station.

Gracie locked her press against nosey parkers, resenting that the whole townland could traipse through her classroom, taking in every picture, every chart, every stick of chalk.

Nevin was on overdrive, carting voters to the school, whose walls were destroyed with Blaney posters, Hart nowhere to be seen. Malachy begged Jim to let him stick one poster on the school wall and Jim relented, walking up with his son to oversee proceedings; warning Barney Cam who stood at the gate, he would break his fucking neck if he touched the boy's offering.

It was a landslide victory for Fianna Fáil.

The triumphant sounds travelled down from Cox's pub, the odd shriek from Ann, whose arse would be fairly bristling, as she uncorked bottles of stout for John and Jimmy Owen, winking at Hughie McBride, deep in conversation with Nevin, lilting along with Charles Bayers' croaking fiddle.

Jim was having a quieter celebration in the bar, putting up a drink for the boys. Paddy Harte got elected; a small victory for Fine Geal. God knows, maybe they would live to see a Taoiseach from their camp some day.

He was in good form since Cathy arrived, although he hated that Gracie's energy levels plummeted after her birth. Hated when she took to the bed, leaving Madge to do everything. He was making more of an effort with Malachy, bringing him to the village lough to fish, buying him his own little rod and showing him how to dig for worms in the backyard.

Business began to pick up in the bar.

New customers were appearing. Men who had returned after years of emigration in Scotland or America. Men who were able to build new houses, who had a few bob to spend in Logue's at the weekend. Andy Dore and the Owen brothers were coming in more often, managing to strike a balance between the two pubs, though they still scuttled next door if Nevin put his head in, asking for a spare tin of crisps or bottle of black rum, until delivery day.

The Aran jumpers were piling up on the kitchen table. Madge helped Gracie press and parcel them, ready for the railway lorry that called to Mona's once a week. Gracie was making a clear profit of two pounds ten shillings on every sweater, which she skived away in the Bank, along with the children's allowance and most of her wages. Any money she could take from the drawer in the bar when Jim was over the hill with Tom, went the same way. The mortgage on the premises was easily managed, their account looked healthy.

Gracie got news she secured a summer job, teaching Gaelic in a school over west and the dial on her energy levels turned, soaring to new heights.

She'd been to the Bank late that afternoon and a thought stuck her as she walked into the weak evening sun. Across the street in McMahon's a new Hillman Minx sat inside the showroom window. At five hundred and sixty pounds it didn't come cheap, but if Nevin could buy a new Zephyr and Joe and Mona a new Consul, surely Jim and herself could drive a new car too, and she liked the colour of this one.

"Coffee Cream", the young salesman called it. Gracie wasn't going to deal with him though. She asked to see Mc Mahon himself; wanted to give him a piece of her mind. She'd remind him about the heap of rubbish he sold Jim and use her favourite form of torture to shame him into compliance.

It would cost eleven pounds a month over five years, MacMahon said, using his sincere tone, disguising his impatience at dealing with a woman. Undaunted, Gracie described every leak, every draught in the car she was driving. The mortal sin he committed by selling such scrap to loyal customers. She couldn't drive through a puddle without getting soaked up to her two knees and Jim wanted to tear the eyes out of his head over it. She ranted loudly, attracting glances from a couple who appeared to be closing a deal on a second hand Anglia at the back of the showroom. Mc Mahon was at the end of his tether, rubbing his big red head with a checked hanky, agreeing with Gracie's figure of nine pounds a month for five years and a full tank of petrol for good luck.

They collected the car the following Saturday and drove her to Letterkenny. They ate dinner in Gallagher's Hotel and Jim enjoyed a few celebratory whiskeys. He was jubilant, urging Gracie to drive their new car home to the village. He praised her prowess behind the wheel, though she revved the engine a few times on the windy road near the village lough. He was laughing, telling her she should get herself a new winter coat because he was ordering a new suit from Micky the Tailor. Gracie felt his hand on her back as they pulled up at the bar, clapping her gently, for she was the best wee woman in the county.

Madge stood on the footpath with Cathy in her arms, admiring their new purchase. Malachy sat behind the steering wheel pretending to drive, Jim pointing to the dials, explaining what each one was for. Andy Dore passed up heading to Cox's and it wasn't long before Nevin had to carry out a crate of empties and do an impression of looking surprised when he saw the new Hillman on the street. He sidled down to admire her, quietly complimenting. Ann put her head out the kitchen door to tell him tea was ready and she shrieked in amazement, oohing and aahing, shouting 'your health to drive it!' disappearing in the door again.

Tom took possession of the old model, driving it over the hill, muttering something about giving Jim a few bob for it, but no money ever materialised. Gracie reminded Jim about it every chance she got, until he told her to shut her trap and not be always nagging him about money. She dropped it verbally, but it soldered in her mind, joining all the other hurts and slights that were piling up there, which Gracie intended to rectify at some point down the line.

She had no intention of inviting Ann down for tea, she just invageled her way in after Cathy was born, startling Madge who was taking bread out of the oven; rousing Gracie from her slumber on the leatherette car seat near the opened range door. They had to make tea and listen to that loud forced voice of hers, trying to think of things to say back. She nattered on, taking in every move Madge made, the smile never leaving her mouth. She wouldn't have much to gossip about, Gracie thought, for the kitchen was spotless and the baked bread delicious, not like the miserable stale cake she produced when she had Gracie up for tea to that draughty fusty parlour of hers. And it was twenty questions, only Gracie always heard her mother's voice; "Na habair a dhath", say nothing. Her mother's opinion of Ann matched her own; "Nil an bhean sin deas, ar chor ar bith." That woman is not nice at all.

She had her twitching nose stuck everywhere. Pretending to say extra prayers after Mass on the Sunday Gracie had to kneel at the altar to be churched. Too mortified to wait in the chapel, Jim dragged Malachy out to the car, his concerned little voice echoing. "What's wrong with Mammy?" seeing Gracie make her way up to where Monsignor was standing waiting for her. Only Ann's hateful smile greeted her, turning from the altar humiliated, her face burning, hurrying down the aisle, screaming in her head, "Striopa! Striopa! Striopa!" It was the worst curse she could allow herself to use, because the Gaelic softened it and she could never utter 'Whore', not with the same conviction. Malachy's kisses, like butterfly wings against her wet cheeks, soothed the drive home. Both aware of Jim's temper, pulling the handbrake so hard he almost broke it, parking outside the bar door.

It was silly she knew, but Gracie couldn't quell the blink of fear that troubled her, whenever Jim lifted Cathy into his arms, carrying her down to the bar, showing her off to

Hughie Fada and Johnny O' Donnell. The thought that he might drop her made Gracie follow Jim, taking Malachy with her by the hand, trying hard to disguise her terror. Jim could be thoughtless like that, never considering her feelings or the possibility that Malachy was lonely since Cathy arrived. He blundered ahead and bought a pink cot, with reindeers painted on the base, without consulting Gracie. She said nothing about the splurge because it meant she no longer had to carry Malachy's turquoise one up and down the stairs twice a day. The boy was happy in his single bed now, but he longed for the attention Jim rained upon his baby sister. Gracie compensated, telling him Cathy would be his little pal, big enough to play with before long. It was trying though, constantly repeating the promise and Jim's mantra began to grate on Gracie's nerves.

"You're spoiling that fella so you are," his accusing tone igniting Gracie's ire.

"Well there's not much chance of you spoiling him, that's for sure," knowing what he'd say.

"Oh the aule thickness coming out again."

Something she said must have rang true, she thought, when he called Malachy down to the bar to help him with little jobs, making him feel he was daddy's boy. Gracie could see how he responded to Jim's attention, delighted by his approval.

"Thanks Jim," she said to him one evening in the bar when it was just the two of themselves. "For what?" he asked, slightly amused.

"For making more of an effort with Malachy, he loves being around you, you know."

"Don't be silly woman, the young fella is grand. You molly him far too much!"

Jim was impossible to talk to at times. Always ready to be embarrassed by her or blame her for something. And they rarely liked the same people, both defending their positions against each other. Gracie declared that Master McFadden and Monsignor McLaughlin were good men, while Jim snorted and sneered. She mocked him, when he admired his cousin Teddy, who landed the job of court clerk because brains ran in the family and he was as smart as any high court judge.

The maddening thing was, that when Jim disliked people it made Gracie wary of them too and more inclined to like the people he admired. He was always saying he could read people like a book so she never admitted she felt like that.

She dismissed on the face of it his unflattering opinions of people, his spiteful comments about the men who rarely darkened their bar, preferring to pass on up to Cox's. Privately Gracie felt bitterness towards them too, itching to use the ruler on their children, especially after the election.

They lit bonfires for Blaney's victorious homecoming, prancing around the village smug and triumphant. Most of the time she was controlled, and if she felt herself becoming reckless, she gathered them into their choir positions and sang and sang until she felt exhausted and had to sit down.

Master McFadden didn't look through the partition window so frequently anymore, accustomed to her ways now she supposed; too busy trying to get scholarships for the big lads who wanted to go to college. She, on the other hand, spent more time looking through her classroom window, down to the village lough, when the children were busy writing or drawing, feeling the stillness that rose from it, drifting towards her in a grey misty cloak.

The customers talked sometimes about The Lady of the Lough, a mysterious figure who came to the rescue of drowning souls, dressed in white, always carrying a lamp. It was strangely comforting, she thought. At Halloween she encouraged the children to tell the stories they'd heard about the Lady, laughing when Steven Dore said he saw her lamp one night moving over the lough, standing at his bedroom window. The next day his daddy told him Cormac Brown had nearly died after falling in drunk the night before. The whole classroom gasped in colluded awe when they heard that Cormac couldn't swim. He felt himself being tugged gently to the safety of the bank, where he lay until dawn broke and he could see to walk home. Gracie shivered at the miracle, the drama of being rescued from the edge of death. How many other desperate souls had The Lady saved she wondered, or was the village lough silted with bodies of the unworthy, unbaptised, unwilling to be rescued souls, like so many lonely loughs that buried their tragic shameful secrets.

Master McFadden didn't bother watching her surreptitiously anymore. She was just getting comfortable with him when he announced his departure from the school. Gracie's mind worked hard trying to process what he was telling her, that Friday before Christmas; he was leaving to join the Christian Brothers because he always felt he had a vocation.

Jim behaved as if he had won some small victory when she told him the news.

"I'm not one bit surprised," he said, "didn't I tell you there was something odd about him. He'll be able to batter all around him now!"

It wasn't fair. He was the devil Gracie knew. She wasn't looking forward to meeting the one she didn't. He would arrive in the New Year with a whole new set of habits and ideas she would have to endure, all over again.

At least there was something to look forward to.

She was going to teach over west that summer; convinced she would love it. Returning to her home place would be nice. Hannah and her mother would pamper her and look after Cathy and Malachy during the day. She would only teach the July term to begin with, maybe do two terms next year, if she liked it and the money was worthwhile.

She needed a break from Jim.

Lately he always seemed to be scolding her about something, especially when the Johnny Walkers were on board, or the Black Bushes.

She was fed up listening to him and to the old codgers in the bar. Their constant grumbling and slurring was boring, sitting for hours sucking on the same bottle of stout, while Gracie's dinner plate cracked in the oven.

Jim enjoyed the company of his customers, protective when Gracie mocked. Insisting they were harmless crathurs whose lives were lonely or very bright men who craved interesting conversation. She knew he was right. In the main, decent people patronized their bar, except for the new unexpected fella.

She could not warm to him, at all.

Ann never mentioned that Nevin had a brother, a priest. Jim gave Gracie one of his dirty looks when he glided through the bar door, pompously announcing that he was Fr. Manus Cox.

Gracie thought it was a joke, although he was dressed in the black suit and white collar of a priest. She was still sneering when Jim called him Father, his hand out welcoming him to their bar.

He stayed a month in the village, coming in for drinks every afternoon, telling Jim about his travels and ministry in Biafra, impressively wise and knowledgeable.

He was Nevin's brother though, Ann's brother in law and he went back up to them every evening carrying tales no doubt.

Gracie never lost sight of that. Her mother's voice came to her, "Never speak ill of a priest," but she couldn't obey this time. He was too warm, too sweet by far. Something 'glick' about him, sly, and she warned Jim not to talk too much around him or be too generous with free drinks and cigars.

"He's not like a priest at all," she told him in bed one morning, knowing it was the best time to get him to listen.

"What do you mean?" he asked, slightly impatient.

"He just doesn't have the ways of a priest about him." Her attempt at elaborating was clumsy. "You hardly think he's making up all those stories about working on the Missions do you?"

"No, I just mean he doesn't have the nice holy ways about him you'd expect in a priest Jim."

"Like the Monsignor you mean?" Jim's tone was scathing. "Maybe he's a better priest than that pompous fucker!"

"I don't care what you say Jim, there is something about the Manus fella I just don't trust; but of course you won't listen to me!"

"You're full of notions. Go down and light the range and bring me up a cup of tea like a good woman."

I am a good woman, Gracie thought, hearing Malachy's little feet on the landing. Madge would be up soon to mind Cathy. She stood at the kitchen table, stirring a third spoon of sugar into Jim's tea. Are you a good man Jim Logue? Are you a good man?

Nevin

Now every house in the village had an indoor flush toilet, with a cold water tap at every sink. No more going to the pump with buckets, on bitter frosty mornings, to find the well frozen stiff, or dried out on drought-ridden summer afternoons. The secondary roads were being tarmacadamed, leaving no trace of the opened drains that housed fat orange pipes, bringing water into houses.

Nevin smiled thinking about it; the progress that enveloped them since Blaney was elected, a reflection of his own ability to back the right horse and recognise a winner. And how grateful were the locals, who hadn't stopped smiling since last summer, relieved that Nevin steered them in the right direction. Not that there was any danger of them wandering off course, the children of deValera, who raised their glasses to their new President and to Nevin, behind the counter solemn and tall like the Long Fellow himself.

Paddy Harte made no impression on the county that he could see, even if Logue was claiming him as a great intellectual and visionary. It was the same tripe he spouted about Michael Collins, when the talk next door turned to politics or history, as inevitably it seemed to do at every hand's turn; according to Andy Dore. He wasn't exactly lying low and licking his wounds as he should be, or conceding defeat, though Nevin detected an anger in Logue he hadn't noticed before, breaking through the suave exterior he hadn't quite perfected.

They still exchanged pleasantries when they met on the street, or Nevin returned a bottle of Rum he borrowed the previous week, consciously mapping the bar. Aware now that Logue was abrupt with him, clipped with his, "You're welcome." Deep down he must know he's on the losing side, wondering how he can defect with dignity.

Well let him figure it out himself, Nevin certainly wasn't going to hold his hand, initiating him into the winning gang. He would have to work hard, do a bit of snivelling before that happened.

John Owen came into the pub every day, since burying his brother Jimmy in February. His footfall grew heavier with the weariness that gathered around his shoulders. Ann was magnificent, beyond the call of duty, soothing him with big mugs of sweet tea and raisin biscuits, murmuring her reassuring words.

"Don't you be worrying about your tab John pet, we know you're a man of your word, don't we Nevin?"

"You are very good to me," John bleated, "It's hard to manage now, with only the one brue coming in."

"You're not on your own John, remember that. Our door is always open and Nevin will drive you anywhere you need to go."

"Ah, suppose the only car I'll need soon is the long black wan," his voice was almost a whisper.

"That's silly talk and you know it," laughter in Ann's voice. "Nevin is heading to Milford one of these days to see MaCausland, you can be with him for the run."

It was the jolt Nevin needed, reminding him of Fr. Manus' wise words.

"Don't let things slip through your hands, Nevin. Strike while the iron is hot!"

A wise man indeed; his older brother, back home in Enniskillen after years of dedication to the African Missions and Nevin looked forward to his visits more and more

Ann was fond of Manus too, her head always leaning in, anxious in case she missed a word of his musings or advice. He brought clarity to every idea, introducing frontiers Nevin and herself hadn't dreamed of.

He had a knack of gleaning the pertinent details when conversing with customers in the pub. A fact that was fool's gold to most, became a nugget of gold to his ears.

He discovered that Barney Cam had a sister in America who wrote to him on occasion, which was no surprise to Nevin; sure Mona knew this as postmistress and no more needed to be said. Did Nevin know the sister's address in America? No? Well Manus did. Barney let him read one of the letters he kept in his dirty corduroy trousers. What Nevin would do next, was, write to said sister, informing her that Barney was living hand to mouth and as his only living relative she should send a few dollars over, to help him keep body and soul together. Furthermore, she should address them to Cox's pub, allowing Ann and Nevin to see to it that the money was handled in a fit and proper manner.

Within three weeks of doing what Manus suggested, Nevin received the first air mailed letter containing ten dollars, with a well penned note, thanking him for his kindness towards Barney, it would be a monthly arrangement.

How they laughed at the kitchen table, holding the dollars up to the light; Ann and Manus certain that Barney wouldn't recognise a dollar if it bit him on the arse. Fr. Cox was right of course, too much money in the hands of a simpleton was a mortal sin. Better to bank it for him in Nevin's account, releasing it when he needed new wellingtons or basic supplies, like tea and sugar.

Such good sense. Such benevolence.

Indeed Barney was another candidate for MaCausland's office, since his sister was fifty years in the States. When she didn't make a claim on the home place before now, it was unlikely ever to happen. Barney was illiterate, but Manus was confident that Ann could teach him how to engineer his way around the letter X.

The local men had all returned to the fold.

No longer darkening Logue's door, since he kicked with the wrong political foot.

They were angry at his lack of respect for Dev. His belligerent insulting behaviour deserved a wide berth. He was doing himself no favours. Men like the McBride twins voted with their feet, more fiercely loyal to Nevin than ever.

Logue entertained the clowns; oddballs like John O'Donnell, who was still hearing shells exploding. And Cormac Brown, whose trousers were more often around his ankles than on his waist. He was welcome to them.

Logue was attracting some new customers at the weekends though, men from outside the townland who drove good cars and wore suits like Logue himself. They brought their wives with them too, lured by the snug maybe. It was handy that Andy Dore and John Neils still patronised next door and still spilled their guts when they staggered into Nevin before closing time. Ann smiled through her resentment, serving the two of them, waiting to hear the latest news from Logue's, adamant it wouldn't affect her one little bit.

"The buck from over past Creeslough is a potato inspector, the wife's a nurse," Andy was trying to extract coins from his trouser pocket.

"You don't say Andy. What about the couple with the blue Anglia?" Ann's eagerness was obvious.

"Blue Anglia?"

"Yes Andy, a blue Anglia, I noticed it there this past few Saturdays."

John Neils was more lucid.

"That's his cousin Teddy from Letterkenny, you know him, Teddy Donnigan, the new County Clerk."

"County Clerk indeed," Ann's voice was hitting a new octave. "How did he land that job I wonder?"

"He'll be highly intelligent," Hughie McBride's sarcasm rankled.

Peter's voice was quick to support. "Only wild, intelligent people go into Logue's bar, isn't that right Andy? Highly qualified like?"

"Ah now I wouldn't say that," Andy was back in the running, "They're nice enough people, plenty of crack in them when they get going."

"What about the wives?" Ann winked at Nevin.

"You don't see much of them. They seem to spend most of their time up in the kitchen with Mrs. Logue, having wee sherrys at the fire."

Nevin called time, telling the men to drink up when he saw the smile freezing on Ann's mouth. She was picturing the convivial scene in the kitchen next door. The heads of the women washed and set, handbags on arms, perfumed wrists, all talking at once, lifting elegant little glasses to frosted pink lips. And Gracie Logue, smiling that sly smile of hers, talking with the guttural accent, trying to fit in with women who would get on far better with Ann, if they had the wit to drink in Cox's.

It was good that Nevin had news about Gracie Logue, to muddy the vivid picture in Ann's head and bring a genuine smile back to her face.

The brilliant teacher next door had taken two days off school the previous week. Went missing on Thursday and Friday and the new Master, Master Ferry, had to send Hughie McBride's oldest girl Sarah into her room, to mind her pupils on both days. They assumed she was sick, until Andy Dore heard she was at Madge's wedding over west, taking a long weekend to herself no less, without a by your leave to anyone.

There was more.

Monsignor McLaughlin called to the school on Friday, appearing perplexed when he discovered Mrs. Logue's absence, so Steven Dore said. He pulled his five cornered hat off in a bad temper and marched into the Master's room, making a loud rattle with his fancy shoes on the ancient wooden floor. Steven said the whole room stayed quiet as frightened mice, trying to hear what was being said, but the two men walked out into the yard to talk. Steven couldn't hear them or see them properly through the cracked grimy window.

Ann stood in the bedroom, still as a statue, afraid to move in case the story would take a turn for the best.

"The McBrides are not happy," Nevin made it sound ominous, "neither are the Gallaghers or the McClafferty's. She's getting big money to teach their wanes, not to swan about at a wedding as brazen as brass."

Ann hadn't blinked. Her heart was probably racing, imagining the possible outcomes of this crime. At last she knew what to ask.

"What's going to be done about her? She can't get away with this carry on."

"I advised Hughie and Peter to round up as many parents as possible, we're calling a meeting in the pub tomorrow evening. We'll open up the lounge so we can have a bit of privacy."

"Oh! Good man Nevin," she was bristling again. "Should we invite Monsignor McLaughlin?"

"We'll meet first ourselves, judge the mood before we include him."

He knew by her twists and turns that Ann slept very little after that, indeed his own mind was racing with the gravitas of the situation. He wondered if he should ring Manus for advice. He was being called on to be statesmanlike, leading his troops in the right direction.

It was the sneakiness of it, typical Logue behaviour, not telling anyone that the Madge wan was getting married. No one knew she had a boyfriend, never mind getting married.

They laughed about it the following morning, anticipation rearing up in them, bursting to get out.

"Poor aule Mr. Cam! He won't get his hands on MAUGE now, no day out for us Ann."

"There'll be another cousin from over that country to take her place; a BREEGE or a SHUANNE".

"Aye or a THRAASA."

The meeting was a quiet affair, short and intense. Six men attended, led by the McBride twins, Andy Dore arrived late. No wives appeared. Ann didn't mind doing the bar while Nevin held court in the lounge. The fire was lit and they had their bottles of stout and halfs in front of them, even Nevin was having a bottle of Phoenix.

Ann was evasive when Barney Cam asked what was going on. Johnny Neils and a few more bachelors sat waiting for her answer. It was nothing they needed to bother their heads about. She kept smiling when John Owen said they were meeting to see who would put the bell on the cat. The others didn't react, but Ann knew there was something in his comment that made her uneasy.

At ten o'clock the lounge door opened and all except Andy Dore walked straight through the bar, heading home.

Andy had just about time to swallow his whiskey when Nevin called time, it was a Monday night and John Owen still had to be driven home.

Ann stood on the landing, listening to Cormac Brown roaring as he left next door, Logue's voice shouting after him, then the slamming of the bar door. She was anxious till she saw Nevin's headlights turning the corner.

"Well, what was the outcome?" she asked.

Nevin was at the bottom of the stairs taking off his coat.

"Hughie and Peter are going to visit Monsignor tomorrow morning to lodge a formal complaint against herself," he mounted the stairs, "I wrote it all down for them what to say."

Tuesday afternoon, Nevin was checking the car seats for lost change, when Monsignor's car pulled in at Logue's door. The purple Pom Pom fluttered as he alighted, nodding sternly at Nevin, who was unsure whether to nod or wave back. He had time to do neither. The billowing cassock disappeared in Logue's kitchen door without the civility of knocking. Herself would be caught off guard, the sly smile and big blue eyes would hardly be enough to get her out of this mess.

Ann kept the light off on the landing, her eyes peeled on Monsignor's car, still on the street at five o'clock. It was too dark to see his face when he emerged, slammed the driver's door at half five, revving the engine, headlights turned on, to drive out of the village.

Nevin stood on the landing with Ann the following morning, convinced Gracie would not be walking up the street holding Malachy's hand, heading to school.

He was wrong.

There she was, standing on the footpath, handing the boy his tan leather satchel, wearing a brown astrakhan coat Ann hadn't seen before. They were both wrapped up in Aran scarves with matching mittens, and despite the harshness of the last day of February Gracie laughed when Malachy jumped on the frozen puddles. Up through the village they sauntered, leaving fractured craters, silver and opaque behind them.

Nevin could see Ann's breath exhaling frustration, rising from her kneeling position with a grunt. She stared at him, willing him to explain. Was Gracie Logue defying the Monsignor? Was she a thick bitch or just off her bloody head? Nevin thought she was all three, but in that moment he couldn't invent an answer that would calm his wife's goiter eyes, bugging out in her head, pounding down the stairs before him.

It was a long day, waiting for Andy Dore to appear and shed some light on the situation.

They knew young Steven would carry the news home from school, propelling Andy over the Tome road, from his home near the village lough. The squeak of his wellingtons came into the pub at four o'clock. He climbed onto the high stool with the gravity of a man who discovered there was a fourth secret of Fatima that he was unwilling to divulge.

Nevin kept washing glasses, ignoring Andy, hoping Ann would follow suit, scuppering the notion that he was presently in possession of some power.

"That's a bitter one," John Owen's voice was unexpected.

"It's a cold one alright John," Ann responded quickly, her eyes focused on Andy.

"I'll never forget the big freeze of '47. Man dear, that was the harshest winter this country ever witnessed." John was warming up. They had heard it all before. The blizzards, the ten foot drifts, cattle frozen where they stood. If Andy didn't speak up now he would lose momentum. He cleared his throat after lighting a Woodbine, throwing the dying match into a tin ashtray on the counter.

"Mrs. Logue had an interesting wee chat with the youngsters today," he inhaled deeply, watching Ann's face.

It was the beginning of a story, no one spoke, only waited for Andy to continue, amid slurping and coughing, wet boots changing position at the counter.

"Aye. She explained to them where she was last Thursday and Friday. Told them to make sure and tell their parents when they got home."

Ann was out of patience. "What did she say?"

Andy turned the packet of Woodbine over and over on the wide pinewood counter.

"She was at her cousin's wedding and took two days off. 'Personal Days', she called them. Said she was entitled to them because she taught Gaelic in the school over west this summer."

"Does she think people are stupid Andy?" Ann's head was making rapid jerking movements. Nevin knew she was getting upset.

"She wrote the name for it on the blackboard and told them to copy it into their jotters. Here, I tore the page out of Steven's."

Nevin lifted the page, reading out loud. 'E.P.V.=Extra Personal Vacation. Rule 58 for National Schools."

He asked Andy if he could keep the page, he intended to check the facts. Hughie and Peter and the other men who were at the meeting would have to see it too.

"Ah! Suppose there'll be no bell put on the cat after all!" John Owen got off his stool, staggering. The pub door dinged, closing hard behind him.

Andy was still on his stool when the McBride twins arrived along with Francie McClafferty, confirming for Nevin what he feared was true.

Monsignor McLaughlin understood their concerns, however, Mrs.Logue was perfectly within her rights to take two days off. In fact, she had more personal days left to take at her own discretion. This was a rule he had only recently become acquainted with himself. Before Hughie got a chance to complain about Sarah having to leave her own learning to mind yer wan's class, the Monsignor added that Mrs.Logue was most considerate not putting in a qualified sub for those days, sparing parish money he as school manager would have to pay.

Nevin could sense defeat; they poured their stouts, shaking heads disgusted at the injustice of it. They were waiting to hear some wisdom from him, something to alleviate the bitter sensation that a new system was in place, one they didn't understand, alien and impenetrable.

"She got away with it this time," Nevin tried to sound like Manus, "but she's a loose cannon, she'll make a mess sooner or later."

They left; encouraged by his prediction and Ann's directive: watch Gracie Logue like hawks. Question their youngsters every evening about her. Be on red alert for the day she did something that would give them a chance to put manners on her. For once and for all.

They didn't have long to wait.

March arrived, ferociously cold, bringing men in earlier in the evenings so they could go home before treacherous freezes made country lanes difficult to engineer. Nevin had a hefty fire lit behind the counter, the heat bringing rosy hues to peasant faces and thawing out the silence.

Steven Dore had been carrying new tales about Mrs. Logue's propensity for checking the children's necks and ears for dirt. O aye, she was doing it every day. Andy seemed amused and said she told one of the Gallagher lads he would soon be able to grow spuds in his ears, they were that dirty. She was giving wee tips on hygiene, telling them to use face cloths and bars of carbolic soap to scrub their necks good and hard with. They should have hot baths every Saturday night, change their vests and drawers and get into clean nighties and pajamas.

"Is that right now?" There was a glowering edge to Peter McBride's voice that banished Andy's smile.

"Does Danny Gallagher know about this?" Nevin asked.

"You can be sure he does not," Hughie McBride answered, ignoring Andy's gormless face.

"I'll put him in the picture tomorrow, he'll be in when he collects his brew in Monas." Nevin nodded his conviction.

Ann came up from the kitchen, confirming there was a telepathy between them, making her appear when he needed his second in command. She raised her eyebrows, inviting him to fill her in, which he did, despite John Owen's phlegmy cough forcing him to pause now and again.

"The cheek of her. Who does she think she is?" Ann's shoulders were jerking, as well as her head.

"I'm sure the women around here know how to wash their wanes and keep them clean, they don't need her from the arsehole of nowhere telling them their duties."

"Suppose, that's another way of looking at it," Andy seemed cowed.

"She's getting handy with the ruler too," Peter was still glowering "but the Malachy fella never gets a slap."

"According to our Steven, she hit wee Brian McClafferty with such force yesterday, she made his nose bleed," Andy was back in the fold.

"By God! I wouldn't stand for that," Hughie was outraged, staring at Andy longer than was necessary.

Nevin could see Ann's eyes bugging out, fuelling him to keep passions going in the right direction.

"We'll have another meeting about the wonderful teacher next door. I doubt if there's a rule for National Schools she can hide behind this time."

Ann was radiant.

She would light a massive fire in the lounge the following evening. Nevin should drive around to as many homes as possible in the morning, informing them about the meeting. Impressing upon them the urgency of the matter.

Again there were no wives, no convivial head scarves and sweet sherry. Just a dozen or so tired men, summoned after a hard day's work, willing to listen to what Nevin and the angry McBride twins had to say.

Monsignor McLaughlin would not be contacted this time. No. They would take matters into their own hands and use a tool their Fenian brothers had taught them.

They would boycott her.

Nevin was heartened by their response.

There were a few potential welshers, reluctant to take a stand because their wives were in the knitting circle, or their wanes got money for having the Gaelic. In the main, these fathers were ready to vote with their children's feet.

It was a starry Friday night, the hungry mist bit at the men's faces, as they walked out solemn and empowered, vowing there would be an empty classroom to greet yer wan on Monday morning.

Jim

~~~

Jim noted in defeat, that January came in the way December went out, with a harsh cold that was cruel and relentless. He took some comfort in the box of bog fir he managed to save along with his turf the previous August. He had cut extra binks, which allowed Gracie to take more peats for the fire in her classroom. The bar was empty during the day, except for Neil Fada, who still braved it out, wading through snow drifts four miles from his Blackstone town land, wearing rubber galoshes he procured in America.

They were running out of conversation in the dreariness of the mornings and the silence that pervaded the village; not a bicycle or a lorry or car stirring.

Even Mandy the Post abandoned his faithful Dandy scooter, trudging instead up steep hills and down narrow lanes obliterated by heavy falls of snow, perishing fingers barely able to extract the letters from his big canvas mailbag.

Andy Dore and Johnny O'Donnell didn't have to walk as far. Jim had a decent fire lit by the time they appeared, bringing the darkness in with them.

Gracie allowed the youngsters down to the bar on quiet nights like that.

Malachy sat on an upturned crate near the fire and Cathy on Jim's knee, both drinking banana flavored minerals and sharing a packet of Tayto, Gracie's big blue eyes shining in their little faces. When Cormac Brown was there, he made the children laugh, telling them they could catch foxes by putting salt on their tails. He had stories about wee brown trout that lived in the village lough and Malachy didn't like when Jim teased, asking the men if they wanted to buy a wee boy or girl, he had two going at a good price. He would run back up to his mother in the kitchen, unsure whether Jim was willing to sell him or not.

Cathy seemed to relish the idea of this sudden adventure, begging Jim to let her have her pink coat and matching bonnet, eager for change. She would go with Andy or John, even Cormac, despite his gravelly voice and clownish appearance. The men would laugh and give her big brown pennies, always saying the same thing.

"Here's a nice fat hen for you Cathy," Andy's voice, always kind.

"There's a wee harp on the back if you want to play a tune." John's voice, less appealing.

When the men went home, Jim closed up early to sit in the kitchen with Gracie, watching her knitting. The hypnotic click clacking of the needles soothing them, the open range door revealing the turquoise flames, heralding in another stormy night. The Arthur Mee encyclopedias Gracie bought were a good investment, Jim thought, opening one to read to the children: Jack the Giant Killer or Rumpelstilskin, and their favorite, Hansel and Gretel.

Cathy was still sleeping in her cot and Malachy was no longer wetting his bed, the single bed Jim threw his

Crombie on to keep the child warm, along with his blankets and hot water-bottle. It wasn't unusual for one or both of the youngsters to crawl in between himself and Gracie these nights, when bogeymen visited or Jack Frost hunted them into the warmth of mammy and daddy's double bed.

Jim was trying to have more patience with the children and with Gracie, particularly Gracie, now she was in the family way again and the past few months had been hard on both of them.

The new Principal, Master Ferry, was cold and harsh like the weather, indeed he made McFadden look like a gentleman. According to Gracie, he spent half the day looking through the partition window, spying on her. Obsessed with timekeeping, he stared at his watch when Gracie arrived each morning, implying that she was late. He asked to see her notes frequently, like he was the bloody inspector. He wasn't as fond of the sally rod, though he annoyed Gracie even more with the fawning manner he adopted around Monsignor McLaughlin, practically drooling at the mouth whenever the padre visited.

It was hard to know whether Gracie had notions, or was she accurate in what she felt to be true. When she told Jim one evening at the end of September that she knew some of the parents had a spite at her, he was dubious. Mind you, when she named the suspects, all deValera worshippers, the list of names did make sense. It bothered him, but he tried to quell the resentment rising in his chest. The caged anger burst out of him though, the day she came in from school tense and shaken, standing in the empty bar holding Malachy's hand.

"Monsignor McLaughlin came into the school today to see me," her voice was thick with emotion.

"He said there were serious complaints about me from a number of parents because I went missing for two days without explanation. They accused me of neglecting the children, of putting a daughter of Hughie McBride's in to do the job I'm getting paid for."

"Man, they're the shower of bastards!" Jim's rage was instant. "They never opened their mouths about McFadden and him away at meetings half the time and the rest of the time battering round him like a fucking animal! I warned you Gracie not to take them days off, but I might as well be talking to the bloody wall!"

"What the hell are you saying Jim?" Gracie exploded. "I explained to you at the time that I was entitled to those days and I explained it to Monsignor McLaughlin today. I told him it was all written down for anyone to see in the I.N.T.O. booklet."

"And what did he say to that?" Jim was calming down.

"He said he would like to look at the booklet himself. I told him I had it here in the house, so he's calling tomorrow after school."

"Jesus! The whole place will be watching this performance, can you not take the bloody booklet up to the school and show it to him there?"

"I didn't think of that Jim. He took me by surprise."

"You shouldn't have been one bit surprised when you know they have it in for you."

"But I did nothing wrong Jim; that's what I'm trying to tell you, I'm within my rights to take those days off and I explained that to the Monsignor. He's calling tomorrow and I'll show him the booklet. That should be the end of it".

"Well I hope he'll see that you're right Gracie, but you'll have to watch what you're at. They're only waiting to get you on something. No more personal days, for weddings, or anything, because you don't know what that shower could do."

Gracie was not so easily cowed.

"They can do what they like," the thickness was back in her voice. "I know my own rules and regulations. I'm a paid up member of the Union. Let them try their best, they won't get far."

Gracie's pronouncement only added to Jim's lingering anxiety about the security of her position in the school. There was an ominous veil that seemed to hang over them. Like a mist hanging around every decision Gracie and himself made.

Since Blaney got elected the triumphant sneer on the local faces felt hard to take.

It galled Jim that they always needed a hero, an emperor they could bow down to and blindly follow like complicit sheep. He heard them talking in the bar in awesome admiring whispers, about how Blaney brought the water pipes to the village and the indoor taps and flush toilets and proper sewage. Christ! if they managed to wipe their arses properly, they gave Blaney the credit for it.

Jim had to watch he didn't make his resentments obvious during conversations with the customers. He needed the business, knew he shouldn't alienate anyone, despite what his visceral bile was telling him to do. He'd remind them that Paddy Harte was a good man too, would prove to be a great politician yet, but the low grumblings that filled the bar then did little to bolster Jim's audacious musings. He was caught between his hostility for them and his instinct to survive, which covered the bar and Gracie's job.

He was conflicted about so many of Gracie's choices, most of them centering around money.

He didn't want her to teach in the Gaeltacht the previous summer and take the children over west for the guts of a month. She took the car of course, leaving him to cycle over the hill to Tom, which he did less and less as July wore on. The Glasgow Fair brought a crowd home and the bar was heaving day and night for two solid weeks. He enjoyed her absence then, reveling with Johnny Walker and Paddy Power; the Wild Colonial Boy ringing in his ears and Cormac Brown trying to sing along with "I belong to Glasgow…" , watching the lovely crisp Clydesdale notes hitting the counter.

The sore heads were worth it.

He sat up in bed smoking a Sweet Afton, thinking about the night before, suddenly convulsed with laughter. The sight of Cormac Brown, bare arsed at the counter, too drunk to feel shame that he shat his corduroy trousers and left them lying at the back door for the flies. Streaks of excreatment reeking on his Aran socks and hob nailed boots. In a gesture of chivalry Jim cleaned him up and poached a pleated skirt from Cox's clothesline, pulling it up on Cormac's waist, telling him to stand still. Cormac danced around the bar, before staggering home to his bog locked farmhouse, the night's summer breezes caressing his loins. John Owen watched the performance with glee, but he wouldn't inform Ann, neither would Andy Dore. They helped Jim to pull the skirt up on Cormac's waist, all of them apoplectic with divilment, worrying Jim that John's heart wouldn't stand it. Teddy added to the fun, waltzing Cormac around the bar floor at arm's length, telling him he was a fine figure of a woman.

The crack was mighty.

Gracie wouldn't complain when she'd count the takings in the cigar box under the bed, before depositing them in the Bank in Milford, along with her own wages from the Gaeltacht.

He smiled at the talent Gracie had for skiing money away. If he got her into good humor she might change the car again and they might get a few days away at the Galway races.

He knew he got too cross with her at times.

He hated how guilty it made him feel when he lost his temper. Malachy put his little hands over his ears and Cathy sobbed, "No Daddy, bold Daddy!"

He would turn from them and drive over the hill to Tom, or on into Milford for a drink in the Hotel to settle himself.

He never apologized, neither did Gracie. They thawed out slowly over days, making up in their own particular fashion.

Gracie always looked embarrassed when she told him she was pregnant again.

Last October when she stood over him at the kitchen table pouring his tea, he tried to hide his annoyance that she was going to have another wane.

There were big families in every townland around the village. The McClafferty women and the McBride and Roarty women seemed to thrive on having eight or nine wanes, but Gracie wasn't like them.

It took her weeks to recover after Malachy, months to get back to herself after Cathy. God knows what would happen this time. He knew she was worried too, poor thing, he could see it in her eyes and in the slump of her gait. But Lord how his heart froze only days later when she stood in the empty bar, again at lunchtime, pale and distraught, unable to gain composure.

Jim called Ellen to take Malachy up to the warm kitchen and make him something to eat. Ellen was struck by the sight of Gracie, but she kept her eyes downcast and shepherded Malachy up, closing the door gently behind her. Jim had never seen Gracie crying, but she cried now in fitful exasperated gasps, sitting heavily at the big table inside the bar door. She pulled off her knitted hat and mittens, leaving the buttons closed on her brown herringbone coat.

"When I went into the classroom this morning most of the youngsters weren't there," she trailed off, sobbing.

There was a trickle of cold sweat running down Jim's back.

"Is there a bad dose going?"

"Aye, there's a bad dose going alright, but only certain families have it," her sobs were giving way to anger.

"Christ! Will you spit it out Gracie, what the hell is happening?" Jim moved from behind the counter, drying cloth on his shoulder.

"Hardly any of the youngsters were there. My room was nearly empty. Only the Roartys and Duffy's were there and the wee cratheurs didn't know what was happening, no more than myself. Master Ferry was watching through the partition and came marching in to know why most of my pupils were absent."

"Oh he would, the bastard! What did you tell him?" Jim's patience was gone.

"I hadn't time to open my mouth. Steven Dore, the wee know it all, shouted in from Ferry's room that he knew what was going on." 'Daddy said, they're boycotting the teacher sir!' says he, and Ferry went dark red with temper, his finger up close to my face calling me a disgrace."

"Jesus Christ! What the fucking hell did you do now?"

"Why do you always accuse me of being in the wrong Jim! I could do with a bit of support now. Steven Dore said I insulted the youngsters, calling them dirty and that I was getting far too handy with the ruler," Gracie's blue eyes watched Jim, hoping for understanding.

"Surely to Christ you didn't call anyone's child dirty."

"What do you think I am Jim! I was giving them hygiene lessons, part of the curriculum. I did hit Danny McClafferty's young fella a few taps of the ruler last Tuesday, for not learning his tables and a while later his nose started to bleed. I got the big cold key of the school door to put down his back, that always works, but he wouldn't stop crying. I suppose he went home like a big babaí and told lies about me." Her piercing blue eyes were still trained on Jim's grey suspecting ones.

"Sure if they don't send their children out to school the numbers will drop and you'll be out of a job. Jesus! They're a shower of bastards."

Jim was almost out of control, shouting violently until Ellen put her head around the door, asking him to stop, Malachy and Cathy were crying in the kitchen.

"Jim! They're just raging they didn't get the better of me over going to Madge's wedding, that's what's wrong with them," she tried to sound reasonable.

"It's all over. Don't you bother going up to the school anymore, for the job's gone." He went back behind the counter to pour himself a whiskey.

Gracie ignored his pessimism.

She returned to school after lunch, Malachy running in front of her, praying it was a one day event designed to teach her a lesson. The following morning her classroom remained almost empty. Ferry wasted no time informing The Monsignor.

At 10 o'clock sharp he strode in, surprised to see her stoking the fire while the infants played with marla, the few that were present. Those left in first and second class rhymed aloud their seven times tables. Gracie showed him the curriculum and explained things from her point of view. He seemed satisfied, buoyed up even by her calm stoicism.

"Continue with the good work Mrs. Logue", he said. "These things have a way of blowing over. No doubt the children will be sent back to school within a week."

Jim wasn't convinced. Gracie remained resolute.

The week dragged on. He could feel her angst, walking through the bar every afternoon shaking her head and sighing disappointment.. She persevered, despite Jim's negativity, which he hated himself for. She prayed all weekend to St.Jude, patron of hopeless cases, "Please, please, send the children back to me on Monday."

When Monday dawned and her classroom remained almost empty, Gracie began to despair.

She didn't show it though. Not to Jim, below in the bar, predicting the end of her career. Not to Ferry, still glaring at her through the partition window, fogging the glass with his contempt. Her heart was racing, so was her mind, but she'd brave it out another day or two, maybe St. Jude would still come through for her.

The following Tuesday and Wednesday the McBride and McClafferty children trickled in, followed by the Gallaghers, sitting at their desks unsure of the reception that awaited them. Gracie smiled confidently and filled their ink wells from the white delft urn. She read Putsy Ryan, making them laugh despite themselves, easing back into the routine they had all missed, praying under her breath. "Thank you, O thank you St. Jude."

She walked through Ferry's room on Friday afternoon, nose high in the air, like Jim instructed and for the first time she was able to think about the new life growing inside her. She was hoping Jim would be in good humour, when she got home.

Jim was relieved.

He was careful not to bring the hateful word boycott into conversations in the bar. He still wasn't fully convinced that Gracie didn't bring trouble on herself and wouldn't incite another disaster, somewhere down the line.

Ellen from around the corner was a good housekeeper, though Gracie didn't trust her the way she trusted Peggy and Madge. She was kind and affectionate with Malachy and Cathy, encouraging their excitement, as Christmas loomed. She walked with them up to Cox's parlor window, where the toys were displayed every December. It was a sideline Nevin started when he bought the pub, making the business of Santa easy for the locals. Ellen coaxed gently their desire for toy soldiers and Ludo and rag dolls, saving Gracie the bother of travelling to Letterkenny in her condition.

She was exhausted most of the time and the boycotting business siphoned every drop of energy away from her.

In the New Year, it wasn't just the spiteful weather that caused Gracie's mouth to set in hardened bitterness, kneading bread at the kitchen table, sitting at the range, writing her school notes in the blue ledger, unaware that Jim was watching her. He felt her notching up all the slights, all the hurts and attacks, and it frightened him. He could disguise his anger, but he wasn't sure Gracie could.

He had terrible premonitions of her lashing out some day with the ruler, breaking one after the other, over the upturned palms of the offending offspring. Or running at Ferry with the ink urn, smashing it over his bald skull, as he stood pointing out Australia on a map of the world.

There was no doubt in Jim's mind where the boycott idea originated and who led the pose.

Cox, the hateful string of misery, was still smiling at him on the street, greeting him good morning, talking about the wicked weather. Jim felt compelled to respond with as much civility as he could muster. Tom tried to coax him up to Cox's pub on occasion, but Jim's civility couldn't stretch that far.

Nevin was nothing but a slither. Jim knew he was constantly juking about looking for news, hoping for the worst where him and Gracie were concerned. Didn't he open the back door to the bar unexpectedly one day, to find Nevin standing there, his ear cocked, listening. Muttering awkwardly about needing a bottle of Jamaican Rum, he followed Jim into the bar like a limping sheep; not fooling anyone. Only convincing Jim more than ever, that Cox was a treacherous sneaky hoor.

You couldn't credit that Fr. Manus was his brother.

Such a classy well educated man, able to converse on any topic Jim brought up. He was staying with Ann and Nevin a lot lately and he spent a few hours in the bar with Jim every morning when it was quiet. They could talk about something other than snaring rabbits, which was Johnny O'Donnell's favourite topic, or spraying bentweeds, which was Cormac Brown's area of expertise.

He loved to ruminate about his time in Africa working with the missions and Jim made sure that he knew about the box Gracie kept on her school desk for the black babies, filling it every year. About her donations to the Colombian Missions, who sent her the Far East magazine, which she sold to some of the parents. And read Putsy Ryan from, delighting the children with his antics. Jim asked him about prejudice in America and his thoughts on the Klu Klux Klan. That led them on to Martin Luther King and Jim said he was a brilliant orator, like Michael Collins. They agreed that Kennedy was the greatest President the U.S.A. had ever seen.

"Not like the miserable specky four eyed latchico we have," Jim got in. Mad that Manus ignored his comment about Collins.

He gave no reaction to the dig, as if he didn't hear it, only boomeranged to the same topic always, making Jim's shoulders go back and his head feel elevated, a pleased smile spreading across his face.

He loved Jim's bar.

The high Formica counter was perfect for a man his height, far more than the low wooden one in Nevin's pub. The snug was a marvelous creation, where the fairer sex could congregate, to enjoy their own feminine company in safety. Wasn't Jim wonderful to have thought of it.

He delighted Jim with his turn of phrase, when he said that Jim had been intuitive and progressive as a publican. When he was given a tour of the storerooms and the turf shed full to the roof with fodder, he made low whistling sounds, as if he was impressed. He was in danger of breaking the 10th commandment, he said; he envied Jim's bar so much and would love to own Logue's himself.

Imagine that.

Wait till Gracie heard that; that a man of the cloth would like to own Logue's bar! He was a card, that's for sure, and he had good taste too. Jim knew he wouldn't rell Gracie about his chat with Fr. Manus. She would only sneer and make snorting noises and drive Jim round the bend. She embarrassed him, the way she looked at the priest whenever he called into the bar, giving him dirty looks, always saying the some stupid thing when he left.

"He's a wolf in priest's clothing!"

Then it was Jim's turn to snort, telling her to keep her silly backward sayings to herself. She wouldn't recognise class, if it sat on her head!

He did his best not to fight with her though, for she was getting bigger every day.

By May her walk was awkward and labored. Before she went out on maternity leave, she took Cathy to school for a week, to get her used to the classroom. The week was cut short though, because Cathy was wild and headstrong, refusing to sit at her desk and do as she was told. Gracie hadn't the energy to cope with her and Jim was secretly delighted to have her back home.

The Monsignor suggested that Gracie give the sub position to his niece on this occasion. She was joining the nuns soon and could do with the teaching practice. Jim knew she didn't warm to the veiled order, particularly as her payment came from Gracie's own pocket, but Madge wasn't available anymore. Jim reminded her that she owed McLaughlin, after him being so supportive during the debacles the previous autumn.

So the soon to be young nun would bring out the new infants in June, a task Gracie said she was happy to miss.

For the first time, she was having her baby in hospital, in the new maternity ward in Letterkenny. Jim felt relieved that she wouldn't have to apply to the County Council offices in Lifford for medical care or midwifery services this time. He didn't want them bloody Councilors knowing their business, most of them Fianna Fáil. Probably all patrons next door, telling their business to Nevin, no doubt.

She was entitled to six weeks maternity leave.

She finished up in mid May and shocked Jim by announcing that she was going to teach in the Gaeltacht again that summer. Not just for one term either, but two, July and August. Her mother would mind the baby and Hannah would manage Malachy and Cathy. She intended to keep Ellen on for a few days a week while she was gone, to help Jim in the bar and house and do a bit of cooking. He didn't react when she outlined her plan, certain it would never happen. Certain that she'd be in the doldrums again after the birth and laid up for weeks, maybe months.

Jesus! He dreaded the thought, but at least business was picking up again, after the foul weather that had dogged them for nearly a year. No one was sad to see the back of it, especially the farmers who had lost livestock, cattle and sheep foundered in fields and on hills. Jim couldn't feel sympathy for most of them, though he tutted and shook his head whenever John Owen or any of the men talked about it in the bar. His heart had hardened against them, sure they were getting what they deserved. Punishment for their hateful backstabbing ways.

The mild weather was bringing customers back.

The men cutting turf stopped their tractors as they passed through the village after a hard day's work on the bog. They spent their shillings on cold bottles of Phoenix, pouring them with black scourged hands, licking their cracked lips in anticipation.

The men in suits were back at the weekends with the wives in tow, adding color and glamour to the bar, bringing a prosperous air with them. Gracie told Jim not to encourage any of the women up to the kitchen like he used to, she was too exhausted to doll up or listen to their silly gossiping chatter.

She shook Jim awake on Sunday morning the 2nd of June, saying her waters had broken and the baby was coming early. Jim didn't want to hear the details. He just about managed to swallow down a Cullen's Powder, before he found himself driving past the village lough, heading to Letterkenny, telling Gracie to stop moaning for God's sake, she was going to put him off the road. He gave the matron on duty Mona's phone number and drove home to open the bar for the hour after Mass, when the men called in for a few drinks before the Sunday roast.

Mona sent Joe across the street at 8 o'clock that evening. He stuck his big shiny head in the bar door to announce that Gracie had a wee cutty, eight and a half pounds. Jim was half embarrassed, but he forgot his shame quickly when the boys shouted for drinks all round, to wet the baby's head and man dear wasn't Jim the great fella altogether.

The crack got up.

Teddy was singing Boolavogue and Cormac was kicking the counter, worrying Andy Dore that he would mortify them in front of the ladies, if he shat his trousers again.

Jim didn't visit Gracie for three days.

The birth had been difficult and she needed to rest. The matron was a sharp bitch, who took him aside and told him not to show up again with the smell of alcohol on his breath. He had to bite his tongue, but he cursed her all the way home, until he ran out of steam, near the lough.

The following day he was straightened out and got in to see Gracie and his new daughter. He wanted to call her Jacqueline, after Kennedy's wife, but Gracie heard the Matron saying the next Pope was certain to be called Paul, so she was calling her Paula. She refused to budge on it, even if she did look wan and listless, showing no interest when a young nurse brought the baby in from the nursery, for Jim to see. Though he half expected it, it still stung when the matron took him aside, hissing that it would be a while before she went home. Her batteries were flat and they'd have to get her medication right this time.

He had a good cry to himself in the carpark, then drove home and told Ellen the truth of the situation, urging her to keep it to herself. He trusted Ellen, because she was a warrior. She came in early every morning, getting Malachy out to school for his last days before the summer holidays. She knew how to keep Cathy amused, cutting out pictures of film stars from magazines she owned herself, playing make-believe with her while she cleaned and cooked. There for Malachy when he came home from school and never left until the children were tucked up and securely asleep in their beds.

They asked Jim constantly where mammy and their new sister was and he kept them going with bottles of mineral and packets of crisps, sometimes pennies from the drawer, to go across to Mona's for pokes of sweets and ice cream wafers. Always reassuring them that Mammy and baby Paula would be home soon.

He was resigned to the notion that the Gaeltacht wouldn't happen, because Gracie would be sitting staring at the floor all summer. Then Mona's screech reached him, he was wanted on the phone.

He ran across to the booth inside the back counter, hearing the matron's bossy voice on the end of the line. Gracie had responded marvelously to the treatment and was ready to come home. She and the baby were waiting to be collected as they spoke.

Gracie did seem good, back at home, laughing with the children, hanging out nappies on the line. Too good, Jim thought.

He noticed she let Ellen take charge of Paula, rarely looking into the pram when she cried and she did cry a lot. Her energy levels were annoyingly high. Barely in the door from the hospital, when she wanted to inspect the red book, giving out that certain customers were running up big tabs and Jim wasn't getting the money off them. She would ask them out straight herself, she said, if he hadn't the gumption to do it.

New orders for Aran sweaters arrived from J. Hill Ltd. Londonderry, offering £4.5s a jumper. She was away in the car, up lanes resplendent with whins and ferns, whipping her knitters into shape. To put the tin hat on it, she declared she was heading west with the children, on July the 7th, to teach two terms in the Gaeltacht. She'd come home on the weekends, to make sure Jim was managing alright. His protests were faint hearted and he knew it, for the baby was cranky and cried so much. He would be glad of the peace when they went, though he was enjoying Malachy's company of late and would miss Cathy's sweet wee face. They came down from the kitchen often now, to sit with him behind the counter, listening to the yarns passing between the men. Laughing when Jim mimicked Barney Cam, lisping the same phrase, dragging his left leg behind him up the bar floor. "I'm a Sparney Scam and I lob Ann!"

Jim warned them not to repeat this, when Barney was in the bar, but Malachy couldn't resist at times, muttering it softly to Cathy under his breath, until she squirmed on the stool and Jim had to give him the look.

Their favourite customer was the new man in the village. Mickey Flood, back from America after forty five years in the States, back in the house he was reared in. He had plenty of dollars to refurbish his old home, which he did, creating a warm attractive cottage.

It was the talk of the village, for a while.

He ordered a twin-tub washing machine, to be shipped across the Atlantic, along with a fancy cooker with a grill and oven. It was the square box in his carpeted sitting room, perched low in a mahogany shell, its glass screen glinting, that drew Malachy and Cathy like magnets. They begged Jim incessantly to go across to Mickey's, 'Please', because he said they could. Jim would relent, feigning annoyance, on quiet evenings when Ellen did the bar and he would sit in Mickey's comfortable room watching a good Western, starring John Wayne or Garry Cooper, glad to be away from Gracie. She had no interest in television, only constantly grating on his nerves. Knitting or baking or washing or ironing, moving, moving with such intense vigour, he felt like tying her into the chair.

Mickey's sitting room became a cinema, on June the 26th, when Jim gathered with all and sundry, to watch John F. Kennedy coming down the steps of his big Boeing jet, shaking hands with Eamon deValera and Sean Lemass, hearing him speak so eloquently about his joy at finally being home. For days the atmosphere in the bar was jubilant and Jim always steered the conversation around to admiring Kennedy at Dev's expense, never missing a chance to put the boot in.

Timing was important.

He'd wait until the packed bar took a collective breath, all spent from agreeing profusely with each other, John F. was a man among men.

"Jesus it was embarrassing though, watching that performance with President Kennedy boys." The first shot across the bows.

John Owen looked up, "Why's that Jim?"

"To see a man the caliber of John F. Kennedy, standing on the tarmac listening to stuttering de Valera !" Jim sounded incredulous.

"Did you see the gimp on him? And the faltering aule speech he gave. 'We welcome you in the first place …… and in the second place…..' He was mimicking again.

"He did a grand job, I thought," Andy Dore took a chance.

"Ach me arse Andy! Why didn't he welcome the man with a bit of class?"

Teddy Donnigan was amused. "Christ Jim, you're very sore on Dev, I thought he represented the country well."

"Did you Teddy? Well, I thought Kennedy was bored out of his wits. Sure at one point he started to scratch his face, wishing to God he was someplace else. Jesus! Can you imagine how Collins would have looked, standing beside Kennedy? Now that would have been a sight to behold, one as handsome as the other."

Mickey Flood agreed with Jim. "He was a fine handsome guy, there's no denying it. He would have given Kennedy a run for his money."

The American twang added weight to his opinion. Jim shook his head, despondent.

"God, it's a shame. Look what we're stuck with: stuttering Dev; blind stuttering Dev."

They had heard it all before. Teddy changed the subject, to break the awkward silence that ensued.

"Won't be long till the Glasgow fair and the parish will be hopping again."

The thought cheered Jim somewhat, enough to set up a drink on the house, and the crack got up again. Teddy sang, Kevin Barry and Mickey Flood put up another drink. Cormac was kicking the counter in gratitude, shouting, "deValera's an aule hoor!"

Malachy didn't want to go west with Gracie, begging to stay at home with his daddy. Jim coaxed him to go, saying there were no other wanes his age in the village and he'd be lonely on his own. His Uncle Hughie would be home from Glasgow, with a rake of cousins to play with in Granny O'Briens. He waved them off on Sunday morning, delighted, smiling loudly, because Gracie promised they could change the car in late August, before she went back to school. It took the sting out of using her Raleigh bicycle to cycle over to Tom, who needed help with dipping and shearing sheep.

Some evenings Tom got cleaned up and came down to the bar to join in the crack with the men, which pleased Jim. He often thought that Tom was a bit sour over the way their mother had given most of her life's savings to him, when he wanted to buy the premises. Tom often went next door to Cox's for one, which Jim encouraged, because he'd fill him in on who was up above and how business was going for Ann and Nevin. He could be cranky though, scolding Jim often, for being too trigger happy with free drinks and encouraging fools like Cormac Brown and Johnny Neils to behave badly in the bar.

"You'll lose custom over the head of these clowns," he glowered.

"They're not doing much harm," Jim would placate, "Jesus the crack in here with them sometimes is wild."

Tom wasn't easily convinced.

He only brought Sally over to the snug, on evenings when the bawdiness was absent and her ears weren't assaulted by dirty chat, or the cursing hacking sounds they made, before spitting on the bar floor. Sometimes Sally went up to Gracie in the kitchen. Mostly though, she sat in the snug with the other wives, all backcombed in their summer frocks and sling backs.

By the end of July the cigar box under the bed was bulging with Clydesdale notes.

Tom had to drive him up to the Bank in Milford, the old Hillman spluttering and creeping over the hills. Jim treated them to a feed in the Hotel, to keep Tom from grumbling. He had a quick look into McMahons showroom, where a blue Anglia 100E caught his eye. He couldn't get a decent look at her though, with Tom harrumphing behind him, saying he was silly buying another car, he should wait till Gracie burned the clutch out on the car they had.

He could insult Gracie all he liked.

Jim recognized the whiff of jealousy wafting near him, so he didn't react. Her driving skills might be suspect, but her skills with money more than compensated for the odd bit of revving and crunching of gears. Bar trade was fair, but without Gracie's salary and the other accumulations she managed, their deposit account wouldn't look as healthy as it did. No wonder Mr. Walsh, the bank manager, had his hand out to shake Jim's, every time he saw him. They were fast becoming his best customers, with Gracie prospecting for gold in a number of mines. The Gaeltacht money was good, the knitting money was better, and she took out insurance policies of every kind. She even took out life assurance on Jim's mother and Tom had no idea.

If she had to spend money on bills or necessities she would find a way to claw some back, making Jim anxious that she didn't want to pay the hospital bill after having Paula. Or pay her subs in the school after each birth, waiting stubbornly for pay-outs from insurance contributions she said she was entitled to. Jim didn't know half the time what she was entitled to, or what schemes she was involved in. It made him nervous too, when letters arrived addressed to Gracie. Brown envelopes with windows; invoices from Rows of Dublin, or Cargill & McCandless of Malin, or whatever suppliers she was using for school supplies.

Eventually she would pay up, when Jim lost his head. She'd huff and puff as she wrote the cheques, marching over and posting them in Mona's, as thick as a donkey.

Jim paid £12. 0. 0. to the hospital after Paula was born, resentful that Gracie's stay had been so long. She ignored his dirty looks, saying she was due most of the money back anyway.

He reminded himself that he was grateful Gracie was well again, thanks to the doctors or St. Gerard Majella or Blessed Martin de Porres or the Dominican Nuns of Perpetual Rosary, or Jim's favourite , the Association of the Perpetual Lamp of St. Anthony.

Christ she was obsessed with Petitions.

A new envelope arrived every other day, from some religious order, thanking her for her donation, reassuring her that prayers were being offered for her intentions, at some altar or other. Money for religion was the only kind she didn't mind parting with and she loved sending to Brown and Nolan's in Dublin for books about Saints.

Lately she was leaving stupid bloody pamphlets called Temperance Catechisms, lying under Jim's nose. In the bar and in the kitchen, whatever her game was. He threw them in the fire in front of her, or flung them across the floor disdainfully, showing her what he thought of them.

She was coming back from the Gaeltacht every weekend, to keep an eye on things, she said. Driving around to check on her knitters, giving them wool, taking charge of their finished garments. It occurred to Jim that she was keeping an eye on him too, always examining the bar ledger, her dissatisfied blue eyes scanning the pages, seeing who still owed money. Pointing at names whose tabs were running into £4 and £5, threatening to call at their houses if Jim didn't get them to pay up.

She worked the bar on Saturday afternoons, while Ellen from around the corner nursed Paula and Jim took Malachy and Cathy to the matinee at La Scala in Milford. They sat up the back in the dear seats, watching Flipper or Lassie, eating tubs of ice cream and bars of chocolate that always melted on Malachy's good shorts and Cathy's pink summer dress.

There were constant niggles and nags from Gracie, but in the main she seemed happy when the Gaeltacht closed in mid August. She deposited her double wage in the bank, content enough to cross the street into MacMahon's, to look at the Anglia Jim had been gushing about.

She was a mid-blue, with silver trim and chrome bumpers and a big silver grill on the front. She was four years old, but a delux model in mint condition. Gracie breathed in the smell of the red leatherette seats, repeating the registration number over and over : ZP 4609. That was a good sign, Jim recognized. She liked it, and she sat in the driver's seat twisting the oversized steering wheel, trying to switch on the radio, attracting MacMahon's attention.

He wanted £350. 0. 0. for her, he said, because she was as good as new. Jim had to walk away, saying he needed a packet of cigarettes, because Gracie was already haggling and his face was boiling with shame. She chipped away regardless, until MacMahon relented and the deal was struck. He took back the Hillman Minx and accepted a cheque for £50. 0. 0. from Gracie's hand. Jim returned, to find himself stepping into ZP 4609, driving her carefully out the showroom door, over the hills, down into the village. Gracie beside him in the long front seat, still fiddling with the dials on the radio.

"Isn't she a beauty?" Jim asked Ellen.

She stood beside Gracie, admiring their new purchase. Malachy and Cathy begged to sit in the front and pretend to drive.

"You'll be a right swank behind that wheel," Ellen laughed.

Jim laughed back, feeling proud of Gracie, but most of all himself.

The days were shorter now Halloween was around the corner. Malachy was nearly seven and Jim bought him a false face in the shape of a fox's head. He taught him mummer rhymes, so he could entertain the men in the bar and be rewarded with fat brown hens or silver hares, maybe even a wolfhound or two, though knowing Cormac Brown, it would be a wee brown pig.

Cathy was four and wanted in on the act. Gracie dressed her in one of her old blouses and a wide brimmed picture hat belonging to Ellen. She joined Malachy reciting: "Here comes I, Johnny Funny, I'm the man, collects the money….", letting her brother take centre stage, shouting out the last line on him, "and if you haven't got a halfpenny God bless you!"

Everyone laughed and Malachy proffered his little tin box, delighted to hear the rattle of the coins hitting the bottom. They sat on the high stools drinking Colas, a treat for being so talented, answering questions about school and what height they were and when they were getting married.

Gracie made apple tarts with a fake gold wedding ring and thrupenny bits in them. Ellen bought a barm-brack in Mona's, which they all agreed was like Mona herself, hard as a goat's knee.

Things were trundling along nicely.

Master Ferry was keeping a civil tongue in his head and Gracie was busy helping the big girls knit their Aran jumpers, anxious to have them finished by Christmas. The Roarty boys had big roasters lit in Gracie's room every morning. She said a decade of the rosary with the children all through October and in November they were saying special prayers of intercession for their grannies and grandads in heaven.

Then one Friday the world changed. Forever.

Gracie seemed tired that afternoon and was late returning to school after lunch. Cathy and Malachy had stayed in the playground to play a game of football; boys against girls, with Master Ferry on the girl's team. Neil Fada was the only customer in the bar, himself and Jim, lingering over two bottles of stout, musing about the abolition of the death penalty and whether it was a good idea on the Government's part or not.

The day hadn't brightened.

A sudden shower of hailstones convinced Neil he should head home. When Gracie returned after three o clock, it was almost dark and John Owen and Johnny O'Donnell were on the high stools, listening to Jim, still wondering about the merits of abolishing the death penalty. He ate his evening tea in the bar, because Teddy was in and the fire was blazing up the chimney. A few of the Sunday night boys had come in for one, to mark the end of the working week.

When the commotion got up, Jim looked at his watch, thinking he lost track of time again and that Sergent Halligan was thundering through the door, but it was only twenty past seven.

Mickey Flood's voice was outside, loud and alarming, competing with the hailstones hitting off the porch roof. He fell through the door, forcing Andy Dore to catch him, holding him as he slumped at the table, the bar transfixed. He was sobbing uncontrollably, choking out the terrible news.

"Kennedy is dead! The great John F. Kennedy is dead."

Gracie and Ellen came down from the kitchen with Cathy and Malachy in their pajamas, their faces etched in shock and confusion. To witness a bar full of grown men sobbing. Their heads against the counter, leaning in shocked weakness, muttering despair. The children whimpered gently into their sleeves. Gracie and Ellen clutched at their bosoms, listening to the pained broken gulps of the men. Grieving for the loss of hope; for the lost promise that tomorrow the world would be a better place.

The world went into mourning.

On Sunday Jim wore a black tie to mass. He instructed Gracie to wear her darkest headscarf and brown herringbone coat. They walked solemnly up the aisle with Malachy and Cathy, sitting two rows behind Ann and Nevin. The Monsignor offered the mass for Kennedy and Jim noticed in disgust as the men moved up the left aisle to communion, that none of them, including Nevin, wore black ties, or carried themselves in a manner that represented the grief and heartbreak the entire world was feeling. The ignorant aule shits! They would fairly whail if stuttering Dev died. The cheek of the bastard, going over to Washington to attend Kennedy's funeral, when he was as bad as Harvey Oswald himself, putting a bullet in the back of Collins' head.

Gracie was off work on Tuesday and they attended mass again. Cathy in her pink coat, delighting Jim, she resembled Caroline Kennedy at her daddy's funeral. Malachy, though older than John John, asked to wear his blue overcoat, after watching the funeral on Mickey Flood's television. The coat Gracie had given up begging him to wear, having paid good money for it in McGinty's of Letterkenny. They stood, an elegant proud family, as Monsignor recited in Latin and

He stared at Ann, shocked at being addressed so cordially, swinging around awkwardly to gaze at Mary sitting at the corner table beside her husband.

"They're the latest trend," Mary tittered. "My sister sent them from New York, aren't they adorable?" Giggle, giggle.

"There's a new word for you Barney, adorable, her boots are adorable; go on say it," Ann ordered.

"Adobable," Barney barked, a trickle of stout running down his chin.

"They're a bit like your wellingtons, Barney," Ann couldn't resist. "If you put a lick of grease on yours, they would look as shiny as Mary's."

Mary laughed and continued to smile long after Ann had withdrawn; now serving the McBride twins at the other end of the counter. Barney gawked periodically at the beatle-boots, wondering if Ann was serious about the grease.

Johnny Neils was very ill, at a low ebb, Dr. Melly said.

Herself and Nevin were driving up to his decrepit cottage everyday, with soup and hot rum, trying to get him to recover. It wasn't his time to go yet; not until Nevin brought him to MaCausland to put his mark on the dotted line. His only living relative, as far as they knew, was a younger brother living in Australia. He hadn't been home since the day he left, nor had Johnny heard from him in years. A huge tract of land was gifted to him for free, in the Australian outback, according to Andy Dore, where he was a big sheep farmer, a wealthy man, if you could believe Andy.

Johnny's house was worthless and the land around it wet and swampy, but he had a few good acres across the hills and turf binks with the best of turf on them. Please God he would battle this dose and be back on his feet soon.

O that he was as healthy as Barney Cam. Hardy, like a whin bush.

Barney's house was nothing more than a wallstead with a tin roof, but the land around it was ideal for grazing sheep. It bordered Tom Logue's land and Tom's sheep often trespassed, which didn't bother Barney, but Nevin had every intention of fencing it off when it was his.

Barney's sister in America was still sending dollars and Nevin said they converted nicely, when there were plenty of them.

Barney didn't need much.

As long as he had bread and butter, with the odd pound of sausages, he was grand. A new pair of wellingtons often, for whatever way he dragged his left leg he was sore on wellingtons.

Yer wan next door, Mrs. Logue, don't you know, because she was a teacher, had another wane the previous summer. Ann hadn't been down to see her yet. She was christened Paula, after the new Pope apparently, but Ann couldn't be bothered visiting. Sure if you'd seen one wane you'd seen them all. And Gracie Logue was such an unpleasant woman, it was penance having to visit her. She wasn't let out of hospital for ages after the birth; Jim was telling everybody she lost a lot of blood and was run down.

Who did he think he was fooling?

She was only home five minutes when she headed west to her mother's, so she wouldn't have to face anyone, including Ann, who was all set to visit her then. Andy Dore said she was teaching Irish in the summer school, but Fr. Manus said it was more likely that her mother was caring for her and bringing her back to health.

How could a woman, who was nothing short of a headcase, be teaching big teenagers from Belfast and Derry, did she think they wouldn't recognise a headcase when they saw one?

She needed a third wane badly, when she could barely manage the two she had. Nevin was right when he said she probably wanted more children's allowance.

Hughie and Peter McBride weren't impressed when she took off before the baby infants went out in June, putting in a pasty-faced sub who didn't know her arse from her elbow. She left the wee pets sitting all day, crying and wetting themselves. Thank god they didn't complain, because she was Monsignor Mc. Laughlin's niece and not yer wan's relation, as they naturally assumed. She took her own Cathy home before the new infants came out, sparing her the misery of sitting shivering with the other wee crathurs; hadn't she it well thought out.

Monsignor was nothing but a snob, still ignoring Ann's invitation to Sunday dinner. He was only interested in dining with the big wigs of the parish. People like the Sweeneys, who owned two shops and had old money out of America; according to Andy Dore.

It was still a mystery to them why McLaughlin had such time for Gracie Logue, keeping her in the school after the carry-on of her last year. John Owen was only trying to annoy Ann's head, when he suggested it was because she was a brilliant teacher. Ann reminded him sharply, that Nora was a brilliant teacher too, brilliant teachers were two a penny. Even the boycott had no obvious effect on the bitch and the protest seemed useless when McLaughlin took her side.

Nevin consoled her with the promise that all good things come to those who wait.

Business had been slow since Christmas, but the stretch in the evenings was bringing the regulars out again on Friday evenings, when the cards were on. The dart's tournament was drawing a crowd too on Saturday nights, but Ann's favourite time was after Mass on Sundays, when Charles played his fiddle and the pub was packed and jolly.

There were no regular women customers in Cox's. The McBride and McClafferty wives had more pride in themselves than sitting guzzling Snowballs and Babyshams, laughing like silly hyenas. Mary Bayers was the exception and she was more to be pitied than envied. There were the uppity females who drank next door in Logue's snug and thought they were special. It was funny, considering the apes who drank along with them, men like Cormac Brown and Johnny O'Donnell.

Sergeant Halligan's wife Annette came into the pub occasionally, and if Ann knew in advance, she would light the fire in the parlor and the two of them would sip their Sherry's, having a good wee natter. A Northern woman too, with a great head on her shoulders and a wicked sense of fun. She could take off Gracie Logue brilliantly, speaking with a broad accent, guttural and backward, fit to make the cat laugh.

It was a comfort to have decent customers, regulars you could depend on. Men like Peter and Hughie McBride, who never missed a night, steady, canny, drinkers. Not men who got messy or made disgraces of themselves, like Cormac Brown and his ilk.

Logue was welcome to his clowns.

The likes of Neil Fada, with the odd looking face, infesting next door with TB, and Johnny O'Donnell, who made Barney Cam look swift on his feet. A voice on him like a rusty fog horn.

The carry on of them some nights was disgraceful.

Last summer when yer wan was over west, leaving Jim Logue to his own devices, they went out of control completely. The shouting and roaring was terrible, with Jim often the loudest. His own brother Tom looked disgusted that night last August, when he was in their pub. Cormac Brown squealing like a stuck pig and Jim and the Teddy fella on the street, shouting after him like two fools.

"Cormac Brown comes into town, with his trousers hanging down!"

Tom's face went purple. He got off the stool after gulping down his whiskey and left in a steer. Ann rang Sergeant Halligan the following morning to report Logue and he said he was keeping a tight eye on the same boy.

She knew her missing skirt was Logue's doing, but she couldn't prove it.

She shook with rage the day Nevin and herself were driving back from Letterkenny and there was her skirt, peeping out from a tuft of nettles at the bottom of Cormac

Brown's lane. Nevin wanted to stop and retrieve it, but she screamed at him to drive on and pretend they hadn't seen it. Mandy the Post quizzed her a few days later, saying he spotted it on the road near the village lough, a tartan one that he often saw Ann wearing. She denied ever having such a skirt and tried her best to laugh hard, when John Owen said it was the kilt Cormac wore when he was doing the highland fling.

In August the tinkers came around, not the usual tribe, whose faces and names they knew. No; these were a strange troop, who camped down the Tome road, near the bridge. A few of the men appeared in the village on a sultry evening around 5 o' clock and Nevin hunted them because they looked like trouble. They were dark haired wiry fellows, who just tipped their caps and headed next door to Logue's.

Nevin and herself watched to see what would happen.

Logue was on his front step, examining a bottle of wine, holding it up to the sun to see whether it was red or white. According to Andy Dore, the tinkers asked Logue to sell them the bottle and Logue said he had a full crate of it. If they were interested, he'd give them a good deal, because his customers weren't wine drinkers. It was superior stuff, he told them, but Andy knew it was hooch, left over from the time the American doll owned the place; the kinda stuff that would kill weeds, he said. The deal was struck and off down the Tome road the boys went; back to their camp to drink all night into the morning, howling like red Indians who might attack the village at any minute.

The sun was barely up when they landed back at Logue's door, rip-roaring drunk, accusing him of selling them poison and demanding their money back. Logue stayed silent and they railed for a solid hour, calling him every name under the sun, using the foulest language Ann had ever heard. The heart was crossways in her, standing on the landing with Nevin, listening to the rabble battering Logue's door, before moving up to theirs, banging and kicking and demanding entry, until they finally grew exhausted and staggered back to the bridge.

Ann rang Mona to warn her, thank God, because they were back again mid-day. This time at Josie and Mona's door, but the Post Office was closed tight and every door in the village locked against them. Nevin rang the barracks, but the Sergeant was out helping to stem a hill fire. By the time he got to the village, it was teatime and the tinkers were gone.

He walked down to the bridge with Nevin and some of the men. The sight that greeted them was what John Owen termed, biblical.

They had decamped, leaving a sordid battlefield behind them, turning on each other when they could find no other men to fight. Two yards either side of the bridge and the bridge itself was drenched red and Nevin assumed it was wine, spilt by the tinker women maybe. The Sergeant inspected, lifting wet hands to his face, repulsed that it was blood. There were blood spattered shirts, torn and discarded on the road, along with shards of broken bottles, glinting in the evening sun like crushed emeralds. Urine stained blankets sullied the ditch and a child's sand shoes lay in the shallow water under the bridge, laces missing.

It was a sight no one wanted to witness again. Poor Nevin wasn't the better of it for a week. Wasn't the entire village left shaken and anxious!

Ann's jaw was tightening at the memory of it.

The gall of Jim Logue! Who refused outrageously to admit liability. Telling the Sergeant he had a license to sell liquor, which is what he did. How customers behaved when they left his premises was their own business. No one was amused when John Owen sat tittering into his stout, repeating what Logue said in the bar, shortly after the affair.

"Jesus boys, it must have been like a scene from the Wild West, only without the guns. And Halligan ordered me to go down to the bridge and clean up the mess, because I was the cause of it. I will in my bollocks, said I, to the needle-nosed fucker."

John repeated Logue's words for the entire evening, his laughter filled with stupid admiration.

Nevin did go down, along with Andy Dore and Barney Cam, to clean up the scene, when a clap of thunder rumbled down the valley and sheets of lightning brought a deluge of rain in its wake. The men and the buckets were redundant. Ann spat that even the weather favored Jim Logue, but Nevin winked, saying Logue's luck was like the wine he sold the tinkers; it had a way of running out.

Fr. Manus comforted her too, with wise words and soothing noises at the breakfast table, cutting soldiers of toast and dipping them into his soft-boiled egg.

"Jim Logue is flying very close to the flames Ann, he's bound to get his wings singed, if not badly burned, one of these fine days."

"Well, he would deserve that Manus, for he really is trying my patience. He's full of notions too you know. You weren't here when John F. Kennedy died last winter, but Lord you should have seen the cut of him and her. Out at the memorial mass, as if they were the chief mourners. I think he thought he was Kennedy, walking up the middle aisle holding on to Malachy's hand. Her behind him, trying to look like Jacky, with Cathy, the brat, in a coat similar to wee Caroline Kennedy's. They were a laughing stock, that's what they were."

"There's no doubt he has big ideas," Manus smiled, more to himself than to Ann.

Easter Sunday was on the horizon and Monsignor McLaughlin invited Fr. Manus to concelebrate Mass, finally acknowledging his collar. Ann felt a thrill of hope that he would deign to eat lunch with them afterwards, in fact she was already planning the menu. Nevin had been fattening a pig in one of the outhouses behind the pub, waiting for the right time to kill it. Wouldn't a succulent joint of boiled ham be impressive or a couple of pork chops with apple sauce. Ellen from around the corner would give her a hand with the cooking, if she could prise her away from yer wan next door.

Mrs. Logue's big eyes would bulge, when Monsignor's car pulled up at Ann's door, walking in to enjoy a cosy meal, not leaving for hours. She thought she had a hold over him because he was the school manager. Convinced she had a privileged place in his affections because she prepared the youngsters each year for First Holy Communion. She spent all of Spring at that caper, the McBride twins said, neglecting the infants who were left sitting like dunces, except for Cathy, who was allowed to sit beside Malachy, one of the special communicants.

Nevin had the pig slaughtered and Bill the butcher cut it into joints, even cutting slices of thin bacon or rashers, as Manus called them, to give to the neighbours in a neighbourly gesture of generosity.

McLaughlin didn't come to dinner. He had a prior engagement, Manus said. Ann cooked the ham anyway, thinking it was his loss.

On Monday she went down to Logue's with some rashers, all smiles and lightness, in case yer wan got wind of the snub and was gleaning satisfaction from it. She didn't ask Ann to sit and have tea, she was changing the baby's nappy. A fine strapping wane, Ann noticed, ready to walk any day. She did thank her for the rashers, smiling pleasantly enough and she looked well, Ann thought, her blue floral blouse matching her eyes; her figure back in tact. Ellen was doing the bar, because Jim had taken Malachy and Cathy to La Scala to a matinee and it was all happy families as far as Ann could detect. A rag-doll she had often spotted Cathy carrying, stared up at her from the pavement as she walked back to her own kitchen. Fr. Manus stood attaching a clean starched collar to his white shirt, inquiring where she'd been. She banished the unease she always felt, after encountering Gracie Logue and answered Manus as calmly as she could.

"Would you ever consider doing up the lounge Ann?" he asked.

She lifted the kettle off the boil.

"It's hardly worth spending money on it," she replied, "It's only used for a few weeks in the summer when the Scots are home."

"Yes, that's a pity. If you carpeted the floor, put in soft chairs and lit the fire more often, you would attract female customers. On the weekends I mean, even in winter time." He worked on the collar as he spoke. Ann laughed and he looked up.

"I'm hardly going to do up a lounge for the likes of Mary Bayers, the silly creature. She's here every Sunday after mass, dressed like a clown, warbling like a head case. Self respecting women don't go into pubs," she added.

"Times are changing Ann. I've been telling Nevin this and I think he's getting the picture."

She watched him, sensing his wisdom, realizing her husband had absorbed every syllable Manus uttered the other morning, when she stood bare-footed on the landing, straining to hear their voices getting lower and lower.

They were prospering, Nevin said, making her smile. But the smile was wiped when the talk turned to next door, sparking her unease.

"He had a lucrative year, Nevin, especially the summer season."

What was Manus at?

"He doesn't have good regulars like me though, bringing in a nice steady trade. He's relying on the Sunday night boys and the Glasgow crowd for business."

Nevin didn't sound concerned.

"All the same, can you imagine if he wasn't there, not open for business, what the overspill would do for you Nevin?"

The question made Ann flush suddenly. She leaned nearer the bannister to hear what her husband would say.

"He's drinking the profits himself, the bit he makes. Isn't he steady putting up drinks for the bar? I hear customer debts are mounting too."

Ann nodded, good man Nevin.

"You're missing the point," Manus was emphatic, "If Jim Logue was gone, all the summer trade would be yours, plus his customers, including the Sunday night boys."

"Halligan will close him down, one of these days."

Nevin was sounding a bit desperate.

"He might burn the place to the ground some night too,"

Was Manus being sarcastic?

"I think you need to take control here, Nevin, not waiting for a miracle."

Their voices dropped to murmurs then.

Ann dressed quickly, to join them in the kitchen. They rose from the table though, denying her the satisfaction of knowing why Manus winked formally at Nevin and Nevin nodded ceremoniously in return. They walked up to open the pub then, like the sheriff and his deputy.

On a mission to clean up Dodge between them.

Gracie

The wireless was on full blast in the kitchen when Gracie and the children came in from school. Ellen's voice was loud in the scullery, singing along with Cliff Richard, slurring over the words of Bachelor Boy, pretending she knew them. Malachy and Cathy were excited, running upstairs to change into their old clothes, wanting to play outside in the snow, though Jim was calling them to sit at the fire in the bar with him. Neil Fada was in. She could hear him laughing at something Jim said. She smiled, despite her exhaustion, nearly too tired to take off her coat, which she did do, draping it gently over the end of the cot, hoping Paula would stay asleep for another while.

"There's a letter for you," Ellen was drying her hands on her apron. "I'll make you a wee pot of tea."

"That would be lovely Ellen. Whose it from?" Gracie examined the envelope as she always did, unable to recognize the handwriting.

"Open it and you'll find out," Ellen laughed lightly, pouring a cup of tea for Gracie from the small delph teapot.

The headed notepaper said, Premier Handknits Ltd., Tipperary. A new crowd, looking for Aran jumpers; the order was extensive. They wanted Gents cardigans and jumpers, sizes 44, crewnecks and polo necks, offering £3. 0. 0. a garment. Knitters would be supplied with enough wool for two garments each, with postage remunerated. Bags would be supplied for postage, once Gracie confirmed the number of garments she could send. Payment would be made by personal cheque to herself. The last line stressed that this work would be constant.

Another light in the dark tunnel Gracie thought, drinking her tea, leaning back in the leatherette car seat wishing she could sleep at the open range door. She wouldn't though, Jim hated when she did that. She kept her eyes open, thinking about this new bit of business and how she needed to hire a few more knitters. Ellen was already on board, with Bernadette, her youngest. The regular bunch were hard at it on the Dublin order, which was due in a week's time, including her own offering, laid out on the sofa ready for the raglan sleeves to be sewn in.

Last year was a trial she was still recovering from.

Paula's birth had been the hardest yet, followed by a wave of despair that swept towards her from every wall in the hospital and every voice that echoed through the maternity ward. It ambushed her, carrying her off to some distant place she longed to stay in. Only for the doctors and nurses she might never have returned.

She had been weakened at the onset of the pregnancy, trying to defend her position against the vicious slings and arrows aimed at her, but thanks to St. Jude and St. Martin de Porres, a miracle happened. Jim laughed when she said that, saying it was the wee blue tablets that did the trick.

At least he was kind when she got home, not scolding too much, more attentive really than he'd ever been.

Going to the Gaeltacht was the best healer of all. Her energy levels soared when she got there. She laughed with the cheeky young men from the North who pronounced her name so comically and insisted on dancing with her at all the ceilis.

Jim managed fine without them.

It was good to be out of his way when the Glasgow crowd arrived and he could do what he did best, be a publican.

Her mother had a knack with Paula, managing to settle her with earthy nurturing, putting Gracie's mind at ease for the six weeks she spent at home, over west.

Cathy and Malachy were bored at times, missing their daddy and the village, until her brother Hughie arrived from Scotland with three of his brood in tow and their moaning stopped. Hannah complained they were bold but Gracie let it in one ear and out the other, she had enough to be doing. She went home to Jim on the weekends, to keep an eye on things and bring him a supply of groceries.

The wireless was her first purchase in late August, when she received her Gaeltacht cheque, which Jim balked at, thinking she wouldn't look at the Anglia in McMahons. But he needn't have fretted. She had every intention of looking at it, hoping that it was as beautiful as Jim had said it was, more than once! She was determined to love it and drive it over the hill, informing the village and every townland in its environs of her strength and resilience.

She struck a great deal, putting McMahon in his place, ignoring Jim's embarrassment because he lacked the backbone to stand his ground where money was concerned.

He did delight her all the same with his takings in the bar all summer. Profits were remarkable, his stock taking was accurate. Unlike Nevin next door, who seemed to be forever running out of one bottle or another.

The only blot on Jim's jotter was the list of men in the red ledger who still hadn't paid their tabs, most of them men who could pay up rightly, Gracie knew.

When the school reopened in late August she drove the sleek Anglia up to the gate, parking it behind Master Ferry's rusting Morris Minor. Malachy and Cathy were jumping up and down in the back seat, the radio blaring out the driver's window.

He disarmed her though, coming out to admire, smiling and amiable. Gracie stood bemused, barely able to answer his questions about miles to the gallon and how many gears were on her. He got engaged over the summer he blurted, walking in together, Gracie managing to stutter out Congratulations, before moving into her classroom to face the row of new little faces sitting in the infants' desks, all scrubbed and anxious; a few whimpering quietly, needing their siblings to sit with them for a while.

Autumn came in cold and hardy. Ferry lit decent fires in his room, matching Gracie's and he looked just as surprised when O'Hara, the Cigara, made an unannounced visit in early November and another in mid-December. The Inspector was serious and official, asking to see Gracie's notes, satisfied that everything met his brief. He wanted to inspect the sewing boxes Gracie kept for the girls, in her big press at the back of the room. This prompted her to impress him further, displaying the knitting needles heavy with jumpers, ready to be sewn up, intricate with twists and cables.

"Don't you be silly," Jim warned her later that day. "That's Ferry's doing; getting O'Hara to call for badness on you."

"You're wrong Jim," she was adamant. "He's in great form since he got engaged; as shocked as myself when O'Hara walked through the door."

"Well if it wasn't him, it was the hangdog next door and his cronies. They'll be reporting you to the Department, still trying to get rid of you. That's the way those bastards operate, mark my words." His voice rose in a flourish of certainty.

He rattled Gracie, but her worries were calmed at the local branch meeting of the I.N.T.O., a week before Christmas. Teachers from other schools in the parish reported increased visits from O'Hara too, banishing Jim's neurosis from her mind.

Despite the snow flurries, there were two men up on Joe and Mona's roof, moving an aerial around trying to get a picture on their new Bush television, Joe in and out the kitchen door shouting up at them. They were the same men who sat on Cox's roof before Christmas and Gracie was thinking that Jim was right, it was time they bought a television.

Malachy and Cathy kept begging for one, since Mickey Flood arrived with his fancy American machine set into shiny wood. Even Andy Dore had one installed, along with the McBrides and their cohorts. It was time to capitulate. Anyway, she didn't want her children always running to someone else's house to watch films and cartoons. It was time they sat in their own home, before their own fire, watching together like a proper family.

Mickey was a good customer. She shared Jim's affection for him, warming to his constant kindness and generosity to the children, handing them the little brown hens to buy candy, as he called it. He had an American pension and always paid for his drinks, leaving the money on the counter all evening like cowboys in Westerns, his name never appearing in the red ledger. He was an easy man to like, warm and rotund in his checked fleece shirts, his smile open and pleasant.

Not like the Manus buck, who was tall and angular and far too slick to be wholesome.

He looked like Nevin; the same dark hair and deep set eyes that couldn't be trusted. Thin too like Nevin, wearing the white clerical collar like it was some kind of crown. Him and Mickey were polar opposites. It mystified Gracie how Jim could like two men who were so disparate. The contradiction seemed ridiculous, though she had given up pointing it out to Jim; it wasn't worth the aggravation.

The new business from Tipperary would pay for a television and Gracie realized when Spring arrived that joining the I.C.A.was a good move. It was fertile ground for recruiting knitters, increasing her circle twofold and opening up a social outlet she was badly missing.

They organized bizares and sales of work, where they sold home baked confections, with teas and coffees in the parish hall. Gracie was grateful that Peggy had improved her baking skills, when she presented her treacle scones and tarts dense with syrupy apples. The Protestant women produced homemade jams and pickles and crafted sandwiches cut delicately into triangles, served on paper doilies atop long silver trays bursting with fillings. These women were homey and easygoing, with an allied camaraderie that drew Gracie to them; and they accepted her quietly without fuss or judgement. They were stay at home wives, proud of their maternal roles. Gracie admired them, as she did the Catholic farmers' wives, who proffered their soda bread and rhubarb jams with as much skill and elegance as they could manage. There were teachers and nurses and shopkeepers wives in the mix, pioneering like frontier women, discovering a way to break out of their mundane hum-drum lives. Bridget Roarty was the only other woman from the village who joined the movement, gladdening Gracie's heart. She was spared the cliquish eyes of the deValera women. Free from their suspicious contemptuous looks.

The air was fresh in this new environment, where Gracie could breathe and bloom.

Even Jim and the children could feel it. Joining her at the gala occasions on Saturday afternoons, soaking in the joy, splurging on scrumptious treats, playing bingo and buying raffle tickets for boxes of chocolates and Crolly dolls.

Cathy squealed with delight the morning she discovered Gracie's new lurex dress, draped across a chair in the kitchen, silver and shimmering in the soft April sunlight. Mammy and Daddy were going to an I.C.A. dinner dance and the children didn't mope or whine, as Jim shaved at the cracked mirror, his frilled shirt and dinner jacket hanging on the door. Gracie with her makeup bag at the kitchen table, backcombing her hair into a swirling bouffant, her new black court shoes under the chair waiting to be slipped into. Bernadette from around the corner was babysitting and the children didn't mind at all, just excited to see Gracie and Jim looking distinguished and happy.

Gracie shone all night, swirling around like old times, aware of Jim's beaming smile and the ease with which they glided on the polished ballroom floor. These were the moments when she knew they were made for each other. Knew too that they were happy, despite the set-backs raining down on them from their next door neighbours.

Marjorie, Jim's mother, was visiting more often, at times staying for three or four days. She slept in the back bedroom that Ellen and Gracie swept and polished for her, making up the single bed that would soon be Malachy's.

Paula's cot was in the front bedroom where Cathy and Malachy slept, but that would soon change and the boy would have a bedroom of his own.

Marjorie was practical and uncomplicated, making no demands on Gracie, only baking soda bread in her floral crossover apron, quietly content. She walked Paula in her stroller and was generally ensconced on the two seater sofa opposite Gracie's leatherette seat, reading stories for the children from Mee's heavy red encyclopedias.

It was nice for Tom and Sally to have the house to themselves now and again, although they relied heavily on Marjorie when their own two girls came along and Tom needed Sally outside on the farm. Cows needed milking and hens feeding and his mother stepped neatly into the breach.

She liked to hear the bar filling up with customers in the evenings, sometimes peeping out the netted curtain when she heard a car pulling in at the pavement, calling out the registration numbers to Gracie, to discover their identities. Gracie could name them all, even finishing the numbers for her, asking if it was a grey Hillman or a brown Volkswagen. Marjorie would squint, pulling the curtain further back, till Gracie told her to stop, she'd be seen.

At times the garrulous tones in the bar would swell, morphing into loud and aggressive arguments. Marjorie would open the door to the bar then, amazed and abashed at the ferocity of the language reaching her ears. Occasionally, a punching match erupted between Cormac and Barney, amid goads and taunts from the counter. Mickey Flood and Jim tried to keep them apart, restraining them one each, until they diffused and order resumed. Jim would laugh and tease them, making his mother's head shake with concern. She scolded him in the morning when Gracie was gone to school and Ellen toasted bread on the toasting fork at the open range door. He rebuked her with his eyes, warning her not to talk to him like a child in front of Ellen.

When she asked to go back over the hill, Jim drove her, with Cathy and Malachy in the back seat, excited and eager to play with Mags and Maise, crouching in the hilly ferns playing hide and seek, or paddling in the fast flowing stream below the house, looking for wild ducks with baby ducklings in tow.

As the days grew longer they spent most Saturdays over the hill, willing apprentices to Tom, who taught them to milk cows and feed calves and gather eggs from the henhouse, to hand to Sally, knowing she'd fry them with sausages and sliced potatoes, browned in dripping on the heavy black pan.

Paula was in her playpen, scattering wooden blocks, rearranging them in shakey heaps while Gracie sat knitting, always aware of deadlines, humming softly, trying to enjoy the moments she had alone with the child. Even in these stolen moments of peace Gracie's mind was already turning to First Holy Communion in the spring and the worry that Monsignor McLaughlin would find her little postulants lacking in their knowledge of the catechism.

She steeled herself for conflict, before informing Master Ferry that her sets of penny catechisms were tattered beyond repair and she needed a new set. He nodded his head in pleasant agreement, a new set was badly needed and he would order them immediately. He was ebullient, saying he had ordered all kinds of books. Stories and folklore and nature and science, because the Department had given him grant money to set up a little library in each classroom. When the books arrived Gracie could pick the ones she thought would suit her pupils best. He was transformed, and she was finally convinced that this cheerful supportive man was here to stay. Gracie relaxed, enjoying their chats at morning tea break, a new tradition they established of late.

Jim didn't see what the big fuss was about.

Why wouldn't Ferry order books, didn't he get the money to do it, money that wasn't his after all. The memory of being beaten around the head for not knowing his catechism, still rankled. He balked at the notion of venial or mortal sins and told Gracie to stop filling the children's heads with nonsense, when he overheard Cathy asking Ellen in the scullery where her soul was and could she scrub it clean, the way Ellen was cleaning Paula's nappies.

"Your soul has to be immaculate, that's what mammy says," she sounded anxious, "I think I have stains on mine Ellen."

"If you have pet, they'll only be wee specks," Ellen soothed. "Sure what big sins would you commit?"

"I told lies about wetting the bed." She went on. "And I took thruppence out of mammy's purse for sweets when she wasn't looking."

Ellen laughed, but Jim didn't find it funny.

His ire was further spiked by the children's fear of the picture of the Sacred Heart hanging on the kitchen wall. They cowered behind the sofa, wondering if God could still see them, because God was always watching. He was able to see everything they did, especially the bad things, so he could punish them suitably, according to Monsignor, who had visited the school that afternoon.

"What kind of hateful tripe is he putting into their heads?" Jim asked Gracie. "I wonder how many mortal sins he committed himself, the same boy?"

"Now Jim, stop that." Gracie was firm. "You said it yourself that we should be nice to the man after he showed me such support last year."

"True enough," Jim conceded. "That boycotting business could have ended very badly for us, only for him."

"Exactly Jim. That's why you have to be careful what you say about him in the bar, there's always someone dying to report back every word you utter; you told me that yourself!"

His irreverence frightened her at times, but she knew where it stemmed from.

Before Maise was born, the Stations were due to be held in Jim's home up the hill, an honor that was long overdue for Marjorie and she urged Tom and Jim to help her get the place ready.

They went to Milford for whitewash and paint, to transform the house outside and in.

Marjorie and Sally scrubbed, till every cup and plate on the dresser gleamed and a new mat was placed on the step outside the front door. The bed from the lower room was removed to the barn. A makeshift altar was put in its place, with the fire set waiting for Mass to be read.

The house stood proud and ready.

The neighbors looked forward to Tuesday morning, receiving confessions and communion in Marjorie's home, before enjoying her tea and hospitality.

When young curate Boyce read out the notices at Mass on Sunday, Tom's face burned with humiliation. The Stations would not be held in his home. Instead, Mass would be read in a house in Cranford, synonymous with wealth and high standing. Confessions would go ahead in Logues beforehand, he said, but Tom was having none of it. He stormed the sacristy after Mass, unable to control his temper. His mother sat crying in her pew, ashamed of herself for being unworthy. Ashamed of her son who cursed in God's house and told the young priest he could stick his confessions up his arse. If his home wasn't good enough to host the entire stations, including the Mass, they could take themselves to fuck over the Cranford road and to hell with them. Tom stayed away from church after that, despite Marjorie's pleadings. Jim followed his lead, after the monthly stipend was announced off the altar and Tom's name was listed as having contributed not a penny. The names were stuck inside the church door for the parish to study and Gracie thought she would die of shame.

"They're nothing but a shower of bastards." Jim raged in the bar. "Religion is right! There's only one thing those boys are interested in."

"It's always been that way Jim." Mickey Flood was gently fanning the flames. "You know the Vatican is the wealthiest state on earth my boy? No wonder they're so powerful."

"O they have power alright, why wouldn't they, when stuttering deValera, spends his time running up McQuaid's arse, night, noon and morning."

"Very few priests died during the famine, did you know that boys?" Neil Fada joined the dissent.

"Of course they didn't die! Christ! If the starving crathurs had a bite to eat they gave it to the priest, before putting it in their wanes' mouths. Man but they were the stupid people too when you think about it." Jim was exacerbated.

Gracie had to work hard to take the edge off his bitterness, reminding him over and over that that kind of talk would reach Monsignor's ears and it would bode ill for her. She didn't want to be embarrassed, now that Holy Communion season was here and McLaughlin was visiting her every turnabout. She wanted to hold her head up and present her pupils for communion with a bit of class, a phrase she hoped would make Jim see sense.

It upset his poor mother too, that her sons had taken against the Church. It was a good day for everyone when Tom and Sally sent Maise down to be baptized, with Jim and Gracie as godparents. Slowly the Logue men returned to the fold. Tom paid his weekly stipend and Jim accompanied Gracie and the children to late mass. He sulked every Sunday though, grumbling about fasting and having to listen to McLaughlin's boring sermons.

This year was going well, thanks be to God and all his angels and saints.

The bad dreams were receding.

The Sunday night ones she endured all last winter, sending her out to school tense and exhausted. The sequence was always the same. Monseigneur McLaughlin flying slowly across the ceiling of her empty classroom, his black cassock cascading. Enormous black rimmed spectacles zoomed towards her, magnifying fierce red eyes. Swollen lips, stretched like grey rubber tubes whispering, "They're boycotting you.....They're boycotting you!" Ferry's shrill laughter echoing from the cold ceiling, pressing down on her head as she struggled to open the classroom door and escape. She'd cry out, waking fitfully, gasping for breath; Jim beside her telling her to shush, she was safe and well. The distress gradually faded, walking to school with Cathy and Malachy running ahead, giving her their laughter to focus on. Sometimes she listened to the blackbird talking to himself in the barren hedgerow, passing near him heavy with doubt.

She found herself studying the little faces in her classroom, watching for signs of discord. Afraid to use the ruler or scold harshly, yet avoiding obsequiousness, that might imply weakness or encourage mutiny.

Dr. Melly increased the dosage of her blue and white capsules, calming her thumping breast and banishing her headaches. She said nothing to Jim about that, for he would only whine as if she were upsetting him, making her feel weak and lonely. She prayed so hard and had so many novenas said, that one of them was bound to work.

There was no doubt that God answered something, by sending that lovely nurse from Monaghan to work in Letterkenny hospital and place her in the same digs as Master Ferry. She was the reason Gracie's life in school was truly comfortable for the first time in her teaching life.

Holy Communion went off without a hitch; gladdening Gracie's heart. She watched her little brood in their hand-me-down dresses and new Aran jumpers, walking to the altar with their tiny hands joined around plastic rosary beads, feeling special because Mrs. Logue told them that on this day they were all wee angels.

In early May the new library books arrived.

The classroom windows were stacked high, glossy and garish, in no particular order. Friday afternoons became library time, when her pupils moved freely around the room, choosing books to read or look at without scrutiny or examination. Just wallowing in the joy of turning the pages they pressed to their noses, inhaling the smell of new.

Summer approached, and Master Ferry booked a photographer to come to the school. He encouraged the pupils to bring the few shillings it would cost them and wear their best clothes for the occasion. The swish of the sally rod rarely bothered Gracie's ears now, nor had she heard the stifled gulps of the big boys for so long, her panicked reflex to reach for the tuning fork had all but abandoned her.

The May altar was fragrant and bright and Gracie was looking forward.

Nevin

As soon as Johnny Neils made a full recovery Nevin drove him up to MaCausland's office in Milford, to sign over the two acre field. He was glad to give it to Nevin, he said, for Ann had nursed him back to life when he was certain he was dying. He wanted to sign over the home place too and the land around it, but Nevin used his most saintly tone when he told him to leave it to his brother, after all it was the house he was born in. It was a glorified shed, festering away there on wet fields overrun with rushes, a liability Nevin didn't need.

Fr. Manus went with them for the run and he rambled up and down the street while they were in the solicitors, spending a long time staring in Fields' window, the Estate Agent, whose office was next door to MaCausland, facilitating a working arrangement between the two. The adverts were dull and sparse, he remarked on the drive home, sitting in the back so Johnny would realize he was the guest of honor on this occasion.

They dropped him at the head of his lane, telling him Ann would have a nice dinner ready for him at one o' clock the following day and they drove down into the village.

John Owen was the only man in the pub, so Ann was up and down to the kitchen eager to hear the details of their new inheritance. She was too impatient to sit at the table with the two men who were enjoying celebratory whiskeys, Manus already urging Nevin to get Barney Cam up next to Milford, before he kicked the bucket.

Ann agreed that Barney was looking frail of late, sighing annoyance when John's fist pounded the counter looking for more stout. When she returned to the pub Manus was suddenly urgent, describing the advertisements in Fields' window. The miserable looking houses and hungry looking farms he had for sale made him aware that business in the country was poor. Nevin agreed that times were hard, although he didn't feel it, with all the land and sites being gifted to him, even if Barney did die intestate it wouldn't matter. He'd hold back though letting his sister in America know he wasn't that well, her ten dollars every month was like a gold plated pension he did little for. He raised his glass to Manus again, intending to enjoy another chew on the glorious malt, almost choking when he heard his pressing question.

"Nevin, are you ready to take over Logue's?"

The coughing made his throat burn and his eyes water, so he couldn't reply.

"It's time we started planning our strategy, if you're serious about getting Logue out." Manus stared hard at Nevin.

"Jim Logue has no intention of selling Manus, why would he, he's doing well overall."

When Manus remained silent Nevin went on.

"Maybe if yer wan had lost her job at the time of the boycott, he would have sold, but with her earning good money he has backup. Anyhow, I would be the last man on God's green earth Logue would sell to; he would sooner give it away to the tinkers."

"There's truth in that for sure. Logue doesn't trust you Nevin, and she is totally hostile; but remember Ann's favourite adage; there's more than one way to skin a cat."

"He likes you Manus, but still, whatever chance you have of bringing him around, you have no chance of turning yer wan."

"She is one intractable woman, but we have two trump cards in our deck that we can use to our advantage," Manus smiled.

"You lost me there, Manus," Nevin smiled too.

"Think about it, it's staring you in the face. He likes to drink in his own bar, often, and to excess. And where does she go for two months of the summer?"

"She goes over west to teach Irish, but I'm not sure I get your drift." Nevin was still smiling.

Manus was about to clarify when Ann made another foray into the kitchen, wondering what the men wanted for their tea. He sat silent while Nevin told her scrambled eggs and toast would be lovely. She'd need Nevin to relieve her in the bar soon, she said, before skittering back up to the pub, her arse high and jaunty.

Manus used the time to assure Nevin that he needed to launch a new offensive against Jim Logue. A subtle charm offensive to warm up the icy air between the two houses and create the trust that was missing from the start.

Mrs. Logue was awkward and obdurate, there was no point in wasting energy on her. But Jim had a needy streak that was easily manipulated, with careful crafty tending.

Fr. Manus had been buttering him up for a while, but Nevin needed to row in now, opening up conversations with Jim on the street or outside Mass on Sundays. He should call into the bar when Manus was there and stay for the odd drink. Stand Jim one, and make neighborly gestures. Like handing over a bottle of ten year old malt, a gift, by the way, that he would never drink.

Make an effort with the children too.

Allow Malachy to sit in the Zephyr parked in front of his daddy's Anglia, maroon and majestic, drawing the boy like a magnet. Bring them back little trinkets from the Cash n Carry. Silly trifles that delight youngsters, like new pencils and erasers or books of pink and blue blotting paper.

Nevin wondered if Ann should be part of the performance, but Manus said no, Ann couldn't do subtlety. Her brand of kindness would frighten the youngsters and create alarm where Gracie Logue was concerned.

"I suppose it would do no harm if Daniel MaCausland and John Fields called into Logues now and again. They're the men we'll all have to do business with."

"Good Nevin," Manus was delighted. "Now you're thinking brother, now you're thinking."

"They'll want to know why I'm telling them to patronize Logue," Nevin was suddenly anxious.

"Suffice to say that Logue mentioned something in passing about putting his premises up for sale, but not to ask him about it. Just give him a bit of custom, to keep their profile high in Logue's mind."

Nevin would bring Barney Cam up to Milford on Thursday, after he got his pension and kill two birds with one stone. He needed Fields to take pictures of Barney's shack and the bits of scrub around it, for the advertisement he would put in the papers after Barney died.

Meanwhile he replayed the conversation he'd had with Manus, willing himself to be strong. Lord let him be cunning, lest Logue sniff out danger on the festooned path that would lead to his downfall.

The Gracie one was a stubborn mule; once you earned her scorn it lasted forever, but Jim was made of different stuff. Manus had found his ear, because they had no history together. Nevin would have to row back time. Smooth the choppy waters that would allow him back into the boat with Mr. Logue.

On Wednesday afternoon, instead of waiting for Manus to return from next door, Nevin stepped gingerly down the footpath, smiling pensively, attempting munificence, opening the bar door and peeping in like a child sent to retrieve an errant daddy.

Manus was on the high stool talking to Jim, whose head was bent in, listening to the respected older man. He shot an unfriendly look at Nevin, like a cross dog marking his spot. Nevin kept smiling, remembering Manus' salutary lesson, relieved when his brother beckoned him to join them for a drink, he needed to hear the hilarious yarns Jim was entertaining him with. He pulled a stool over next to

Manus, conceding that he might as well join them, seeing as his own place was empty and Ann was hot and bothered, scrubbing the wide pine counter.

"That'll keep her out of mischief for a while," Manus winked at Logue who looked uncertain for an instant, then sniggered lightly, asking Nevin what he would like to drink.

"I'll have a whiskey Jim, I see you have Johnny Walker Black. I'll try a drop of that." Matter of fact, not too friendly.

"Good choice Nevin, have one yourself Jim, it's hard to beat a drop of malt."

Manus used a gushing tone and Logue's shoulders began to relax. He poured three good whiskeys from the pewter spirit measure, spilling them into the glasses.

"They're decent measures Nevin," Logue sounded edgy, "Not like them wee thimblefuls you pour next door."

"You have a point there Jim," Manus interjected. "That new optics you installed Nevin discharges a very hungry measure."

"Do you know you're probably right," Nevin sipped his drink. "When I see you in action there Jim I'm convinced I'll go back to my pewter measure. I'll have to find out where Ann hid it." Hee, hee.

They talked about malt whiskeys, Logue displaying his knowledge, denigrating Johnny Walker as a blended brew. The king of the malts was Glenfiddich, only there was no point stocking it. It was too expensive, and anyway it would be wasted on most of the locals. Nevin nodded slowly in agreement, finishing his drink and dismounting the stool. It was time he went home, he said, telling Manus to take his time, tea wouldn't be ready for a while.

It was the first tentative step in the new courtship.

It went well, he mused, walking back up to his own kitchen door, aware of the warm April sun on his back.

Manus was approving when he appeared later, proud of Nevin's nobility, confident that the impasse had been punctured.

It was vital to keep going now, until the air between them resembled the warmer temperatures that were returning, as April dandered towards summer.

Barny Cam was the first in after dinner and Nevin told him to clean himself up on Thursday morning. He was taking him to Milford for a run out and they might pay MaCausland a wee visit when they were there. This cheered Barney, who got off the stool after his second stout, telling them he had to buy blades and a bar of red soap over in Mona's. John Owen came in as he made his announcement and seemed amused that some class of ablutions were imminent.

"Wash up and down as far as possible Barney," John urged, "and then wash possible." Hee, hee. Barney sloughed off, deaf to the quipp. John stared in the mirror, aware that Ann was glaring at him, vigorously drying a half pint glass in danger of shattering in her hands.

MaCausland had a warm welcome for them, shaking Barney's hand, telling him to sit down, as Nevin sat too, watching the portly solicitor take his seat behind his desk, the drill well practiced between them.

"So Barney, you're going to tie up the loose ends, that's a wise move."

Barney's doltish face smiled, his head jerking up and down until MaCausland spoke again.

"Did you bring a copy of your deeds Barney?"

Nevin was stung. He assumed that like Johnny Neils, MaCausland would have the deeds sitting pretty in his safe. He assured Nevin this was not the case. Searches would have to be made. If Barney's holding wasn't registered with the Land Registry, it would be impossible for him to make a will. Nevin kept the existence of the sister in America to himself for the time being, hoping the deeds would show up. Otherwise he would have to write to her explaining the situation, which he didn't want to do; there had to be some way around it. Barney was happy to comply when Nevin told him to go out and sit in the car, he had some more business to discuss with Mr. MaCausland.

"What's on your mind Nevin?"

"I believe Jim Logue is thinking of putting his place on the market," Nevin tried to sound casual.

MaCausland looked surprised, then doubtful.

"Really. It's not long since he bought it. I acted on his behalf. It can't be more than four years and he's doing well by all accounts."

"He's been there eight years and he's not doing that well. He has three youngsters now and his wife doesn't keep the best. He bit off more than he can chew."

"Is he selling the entire holding or just the bar?"

"As far as I know he's selling the bar and the house. Himself and Manus get on well and he confides in him."

"I find this baffling," MaCausland shook his head, "because I never saw a man who wanted anything as much as Jim Logue wanted that bar and everything that went with it."

"You know what they say Daniel, be careful what you wish for. To be honest with you, the pair of them have been nothing but trouble since they came to the village. He stays open all hours, especially at the weekends, serving some rowdy boys. He never bars anyone."

"What about the law?" The solicitor was indignant.

"Sergeant Halligan tried to put manners on him a few times, but he's a law unto himself and she always backs him up."

"She's a teacher isn't she?"

Nevin nodded.

"She was with him when they were signing for the place; a deep filly I thought, didn't give much away. She was the one with the money though, Logue had very little. Herself and his mother put up a fair bit of the collateral to purchase the business. She must want to get rid of it too."

"She surely does," Nevin lied. "She has to serve in the bar after a day's teaching and him drinking behind his own counter. She's money mad too, probably thinks she'll get interest on her investment."

"He was a bit of a peacock, the same boy, when I was dealing with him. Here in his fancy suit telling me how the law worked. He fell on his feet; but if you're telling me he's selling then I believe you Nevin."

"Thinking about it", I said, Nevin had to tread carefully. "I would prefer it didn't go on the open market Daniel, if you catch my drift? If he's selling, I'm buying, it's as simple as that."

"It will have to be done legally and above board," MaCausland was smiling.

"It certainly will," Nevin was smiling too.

"Leave it to me. I'll pop into John next door and see if he heard any whimpers about it."

"It might be an idea for yourself and John to call into Logue for the odd drink when you're passing that way; not together of course, he might smell a rat."

"That's not a bad idea, Nevin. I have an aged Aunt whom I visit occasionally over your way, I'll stop with Logue when I'm passing. I do that from time to time."

Nevin had a quick look at the pictures in Fields' window before driving Barney back to the village, weighing up the success and failure of his trip to Milford. He was confident that overall Manus would say it was a productive morning. If there were deeds to Barney's land, Daniel would find them.

He got the ball rolling, Manus said. If they played the game right, Jim Logue's tenure as a publican would be over by Autumn. They'd worry about Barney's place later.

In early May Malachy made his First Holy Communion and visited every house in the village, sporting a new blazer and long pants. Cathy ran beside him, hoping to share in the bounties. Ann guffawed as they trooped across from Mona's, warning Nevin that sixpence would do him fine. Nevin agreed, hiding a half crown in the palm of his hand, dropping it into the boy's blazer pocket. It was a surprise he wasn't to look at until he got home, and he winked at Ann who chortled loudly. He had a bar of chocolate for Cathy, her face beaming when she reached for it. Sure that her gift was worth more than Malachy's. He chased her down the footpath shouting that she had to share.

The maroon Zephyr lured them on Sunday afternoons, when adults read the newspapers and the Logue wanes mopped about the street, lonely and bored.

Nevin told them to sit in the front, removing keys from the ignition, warning Malachy not to touch the handbrake. He rolled down the driver's window, so they wouldn't melt on the hot sticky upholstery.

The following Saturday they ran and begged Gracie to let them go to Letterkenny in the Zephyr, because Nevin said he would take them, reappearing in their Sunday clothes, jumping from foot to foot, trying to open the car door themselves.

Ann's face was a picture as they drove off.

Cathy and Malachy ensconced in the front seat beside Nevin, waving frantically at Kitty Eddy who stood at Mona's shop door. The ubiquitous butt hanging from her lower lip, her arms folded at her waist. She was still on the street when they drove back three hours later.

Ann stuck her head out the kitchen door when she heard the car pulling up, bemused eyes absorbing the picture of chocolate stained mouths alighting, holding new pencil cases, smiling their bashful gratitude, before scuttling down the footpath home. The crumpled Oatfield sweet bag lay on the front seat, the weapon Ann needed to chastise Nevin with, chiding his foolish generosity where the Logue wanes were concerned. Why didn't he take some of the McBride children for a run to Letterkenny or wee Steven Dore.

Wouldn't it fit him better than carting those two brats who had plenty, around the country.

"They'll destroy the seats so they will." She was bristling again, helping to carry in cartons of cigarettes and boxes of crisps.

Nevin knew he'd have to invite her into the loop soon, but not yet.

She would love the plan and be too eager to execute it. Too sweet by far, which would excite Gracie Logue's innate suspicion of them and everyone they associated with.

"When they get their summer holidays I'll take Hughie and Peter's wanes for a big day out and get them ice cream cones. Steven Dore can come too," he placated. "All in good time Ann. All in good time."

Mandy the Post had been around the previous day and he didn't hide his awe when he handed the square parcel to Fr. Manus, pointing at the foreign stamps, that had come from far far away. He was hoping to be told what it was, but he had to slink off in ignorance, while Manus shaved at the kitchen sink and the package sat on the kitchen table unopened. The colorful stamps with a stranger's face stared up at Ann and Nevin. They clucked about, waiting for him to put them out of their misery.

Manus was jubilant but fastidious, removing the outer wrapping from the box of Cuban cigars Fr. Jose had sent him, all the way from Havana. He served his time in Africa too and was repaying a favor, Manus said. He handed a cigar each to Ann and Nevin, telling them to smell their richness, laughing that Jim Logue was in for a surprise.

"They're not for us Ann, we don't smoke dear," he explained, still gleeful despite the disgust etched on her face.

"These will appeal to Jim's ego," he winked, holding the box in his hands like the sacramental chalice, heading next door to Logue's.

Nevin checked the empty pub, then sat Ann down at the kitchen table.

It was time to give her a version of the plan, one that wouldn't induce her rancor or provoke a dam burst of venom. She knew where the enemy was, she just needed to know her role in launching their offensive.

Jim Logue had been bumming to Manus.

He'd been offered big money for his premises, from a couple of parties and he was seriously considering selling it. Yer wan was making great money, he said, so he could do a bit of farming with Tom and sell turf. He had plenty of bog and it would be a more relaxed healthy way of living. Business was slow enough and most of the week he was bored stiff, looking at the same old codgers lingering over flat glasses of stout.

Ann's snorts indicated that she was off on the wrong wavelength. Nevin had to slow her down, elucidate patiently.

"We don't want anyone else taking over that business and maybe extending it. There's plenty of outhouses and stores that could be converted to lounges and ballrooms or God knows what!"

She stopped snorting. The penny was starting to drop.

"So, we need to be the buyers Ann, and the only way to get Logue to sell to us is to use a bit of charm, that's what

Manus thinks. I know we don't need another premises, but we can let it lie there for a few years until we decide what to do with it."

Her protests were predictable.

She was absolutely correct that Logue would never sell to them, but Manus and himself had that all worked out. What she needed to do was be cute and casual, carry on as normal and everything would fall nicely into place.

Inevitably there was glee.

She wanted to rope in Andy Dore as a spy, which Nevin assured her wasn't a good idea. Nor was she to utter a word to the McBride twins or any perceived allies, no matter how tempting. This was strictly their own affair.

She didn't demur, especially when Nevin evoked images of Gracie Logue living up the hill with her farmer husband, no longer the glamorous publican's wife, surrounded by sheep and heather. She skipped from the kitchen, lilting up to the pub, making Nevin smile as he listened to her greeting John Owen who had dinged the door ten minutes previously and was now hitting the counter with his fist.

"Yes John, isn't it a lovely morning, what can I get you?"

She was on board. Good woman Ann. Softly softly catchee monkey.

Jim

Jim's head was stuck to the pillow, saliva crudding at his mouth. His own snores woke him. That, and the July sun glaring in the window. He'd forgotten to pull the curtains again.

Jesus, last night!

The memory of it swooped down on him, alighting on his chest like a boulder. He could hear his heart thumping in his ears, like someone marching over his grave.

There was another sound.

A dirty big bluebottle buzzing around the ceiling. How the hell did it get in?

He roused himself to a sitting position and opened his eyes. His suit trousers were thrown on the bedroom floor, the jacket on the end of the bed like a creased up rag; he was still wearing his white shirt.

Jesus, last night!

There were flashes of it zooming past his eyes.

He's in the bar drinking with Manus and Nevin. Laughter. Crack.

He's in the bar with John Fields. Taunting. Boasting.

Nevin was there. No. He wasn't. Or was he. He couldn't be sure.

Why did he feel such foreboding? Too much drink I suppose.

What the hell were they talking about all day? Was there a lot of talk about buying property and building property and selling fucking property?

Christ!

His chest felt tight, he must have done the dog on it altogether.

Sure what the hell, if the crack was good? It was only the pain of fun. Except, something wasn't right. Probably imagining things, sure what could be wrong? He needed to cop onto himself.

Ellen from around the corner was downstairs. He could hear her singing in the kitchen, trying to sound like Bridey Gallagher, warbling the Homes of Donegal. She was there yesterday morning. She might be able to fill in a few blanks. He would have to play it cute, whittle the details out of her subtly, as if he knew them already.

He pulled on his blue slacks and headed downstairs in his bare feet, every step hurting his head. The kettle was boiling on the range and he reached for it, filling the shaving bowl, aware that his hand was shaking badly. Ellen stopped singing when she saw him, a surprised expression spreading across her face.

"Well, you're up! I didn't expect to see you till evening time! You had a big day yesterday!"

It was a statement. Not a question. Jim laughed as self assuredly as he could, now resentful that she had been privy to what went on. He would talk as if he could remember everything, and it might come back to him bit by bit. That usually worked when Gracie put him on the spot.

"It was a great day's crack Ellen. I had no intention of closing up early, but the boys were pretty persuasive."

He expected signs of disapproval and waited to be admonished almost, though he doubted she would be so brazen. He couldn't see her face when she replied, only heard the intonation of her voice.

"Ah, it was hard to refuse an invitation like that."

He couldn't read her.

"What invitation was that Ellen?" He had to ask.

"Fr. Manus asking you to a fancy dinner in the Milford Hotel, I would have gone to that myself." She laughed. "If I was asked."

"You should've come anyway." Jim laughed too; he was beginning to remember.

Thursday was Mulrines day for deliveries and the lorry was only pulling off the street when Fr. Manus appeared in the bar, around 11 o' clock. He started helping Jim to carry heavy crates of stout and beer down the storeroom steps, appalling Jim who begged him to stop because a priest shouldn't be doing such heavy lifting. Manus only laughed panting, saying he had plenty of experience with manual labour in the villages in Africa. He insisted on helping to stock shelves behind the counter too, until Nevin put his long face through the door, followed by his long body, plonking a bottle of Glenfidich on the counter, tittering as he did.

"Mulrines left this with me by mistake. It wasn't on my docket, did you order it Jim?"

When Jim shook his head Nevin tittered again, saying it was a gift horse then, they shouldn't look in the mouth.

That's right.

Jim's memory was vivid now. Manus got three tumblers from the lower shelf and the bottle was opened, with no one but themselves in the bar.

It was twelve o'clock exactly.

Ellen was up and down the stairs, cleaning and making beds, but she made the odd foray to the bar too, looking for wet tea towels and sweeping the floor around the men as they became more garrulous, the further down the bottle they went.

Why did Manus decide to go to Milford?

Was it because Jim told them the yarn about the day himself and Fonsie O'Donnell went to a Fair Day in Milford years ago, before he was married and they drank the live-long day until the wee hours of the morning. Fonsie was carrying a tin of sheep marking, as they staggered out over the hills, a clearing visible on the horizon. They marked every animal that stood still long enough on the road home, with a bright blue cross, including Packy Wilhare's two dogs and Nelly Brian's donkey. There was a pose of local men trying to spring the culprits for weeks, but Jim and Fonsie lay low and got away with it. Jim could only admit to it years later, when tempers had died down. Manus enjoyed the story that much he suggested heading to Milford for a meal and a night's crack. The meal was on him, he said.

"Ann won't mind," he reassured, when he saw the doubt on Nevin's face. "Carpe diem men! Seize the day. Aren't the Glasgow crowd gone back and the pubs will be quiet tonight."

Ellen said she couldn't do the bar for Jim because her oldest son was home from London.

That was when Manus told him to close up early and take the day off, didn't he deserve it.

"Do you know what I'm going to tell you Manus, you never said a truer word," Jim conceded. "Gracie will be back tomorrow and a man won't have a minute's peace all weekend."

He needed to change into his good clothes and the boys said they would do the same.

He told Nevin the Zephyr was a fine car, as they drove out of the village, him riding shotgun, smoking a cigar. Manus in the back, apoplectic with laughter, slapping Jim's seat as he entertained them with more yarns. And then Nevin had to slow down because some of Tom's sheep were out on the hill road, looking naked and embarrassed with their sheared rumps marked orange and blue. Nevin asked were they Tom's sheep and then Manus was inquiring too.

"Is that your brother's home there on the hilltop?"

When Jim nodded, he said it was a magnificent setting, an extraordinary place to call home. Jim said it was a bit off the beaten track, but Manus wouldn't hear of it and neither would Nevin.

"It's God's own country," Manus patted him on the shoulder and Nevin admired the lush rolling fields, pointing out the deep dark stream that crossed the land, like a fertile prairie you'd see in a Western, he said.

"Aye, Tom and me are two right cowboys," Jim quipped, and Manus laughed heartily, slapping the upholstery again.

Jim had to relight the cigar, spitting the slivers of tobacco from his lips, surveying his home place as if seeing it for the first time.

He felt good there in the car with the two men; especially Nevin, who was turning into a decent fellow of late. He had mentioned this change to Gracie, but she fixed him with a sneering glare, incredulous that he would be so naive.

"Don't be an amadan Jim. Nevin and herself would love to see us in the gutter, don't forget that."

"Jesus Gracie, you must give the man some credit. I think he's making an effort to atone for his badness in the past."

She remained resolute and he didn't want to spend the weekend fighting with her and making the children miserable, so he let it go, secretly believing that Nevin was penitent. Down the line both houses would settle into a neighborly harmony, please God.

It was after 3 o'clock when they arrived in Milford.

Aware of his parched mouth, Jim was first through the hotel doors and into the bar, already packed with visitors. There were a few local faces, but no one of any consequence. Jim ordered a whiskey, asking the other two what their poison was. He felt a surge of euphoria for the morning's fun and the anticipation of the evening ahead. Nevin put a slight damper on things saying he would just have a bottle of Phoenix, but Manus upped the frequency again saying he would have the same as Jim.

They leaned against the counter, drinking and watching the lunch time diners flooding back from the dining room. They agreed to postpone eating for a while; none of them were hungry.

That part of the day was clear in Jim's mind.

He knew he did most of the talking. Didn't he have to keep the momentum going, telling yarns as only he could? The barman was reluctant to leave their end of the counter to serve other customers; he was enjoying the stories that much.

There was no crack in Nevin, but Manus was in rip-roaring form, grabbing Jim's shoulder, telling him he was a born entertainer who missed his calling. Nevin disagreed, saying he did not miss his calling. Wasn't he a brilliant barman? A bar on its own was too small for the likes of Jim. He should run a hotel, or better still Manus said, build his own hotel, over on the hill near Tom.

They all seized upon this idea and by the fourth round they had the hotel designed and built. The golf course manicured and coaches filled with American tourists driving up the avenue. On their way to Logue's Mountain Lodge, wallets bursted with dollars.

The crack was good.

And you know it wasn't that crazy an idea, Jim thought at the time.

In the sober light of day he could have laughed like a drain, only his head hurt too much and waves of cold sweats washed over him. Jesus, can you imagine running that idea past Gracie? She would dismiss it with a grunt, before throwing back her head and having a good guffaw at his expense.

Back to last night. What happened next?

At some point around six maybe, they headed into the dining room. This part of the evening was faded. He knew he ordered a T-bone steak that came out covering the entire plate. Manus ordered a bottle of red wine, which tasted light and fruity after the whiskey, but Jim drank it anyway, finishing the bottle with Manus. Nevin stuck with the lager, he wasn't fond of wine he said, not like his big brother who got used to the finer things in life when he joined the priesthood, hee, hee. They finished off with semolina pudding and ice cream and by the time they returned to the bar they were rightly sobered up.

Jim looked at the tea Ellen made for him, going cold on the kitchen table. He knew his hands were shaking so badly he'd spill it enroute to his mouth. He reached out, suddenly stung by a flash of memory; John Fields sitting in the hotel bar when they came out after dinner, waving at them to join him, pulling out comfortable chairs saying, "Look what the cat dragged in."

They barely had their arses on the seats when Daniel MaCausland, the solicitor appeared, looking serious in his dark suit, a chocolate brown fedora on his bald head. He joined them too, throwing his hat ceremoniously on the table, announcing that he'd had a busy day in court.

Jim's heart rate surged at the memory of MaCausland and he chewed on his lower lip, wondering why he was so bothered by it. Was he vexed at the manner in which the solicitor kept referring to him as, "Young Logue," as if he was an eejit.

"How are things in the bar trade, Young Logue?"

Manus answered for him, declaring that Jim was embarking on a new venture. He was building a hotel of his own, over the hill near Tom.

MaCausland raised his eyebrows, unsmiling. He stared at Jim, devoid of a sense of humor. Maybe he thought Jim would have two chances of building his own hotel; none, and fuck all.

Jim saluted Manus, then assured baldy head MaCausland that he'd been to the Bank earlier that day and was approved for the loan; that's what they were celebrating.

One word begged another.

John Fields was asking him if he was selling his premises and Jim said he would consider the right offer, just to annoy MaCausland and indeed the whole lot of them, for they were starting to get on his wick.

He rifted, and his chest burned. Jesus, he might be having a heart attack. Maybe he should try to throw up, only Ellen was in the scullery and she'd hear him retching in the lavatory. His head was pounding again and beads of sweat were breaking out on his forehead.

Man he couldn't remember things properly and this was the mother of a'l hangovers.

MaCausland didn't stay long in the hotel, he was sure of that.

After he left, things got blurry.

He rose from the kitchen table to peep out the window, every step reverberating in his head. The Zephyr was on the street. It was there. Parked above the gate.

So Nevin had driven them home.

Why was John Fields in the bar with Jim after that?

Had he stayed the night? Christ maybe he was upstairs, it wouldn't be the first time he had surprise overnight guests. He moved faster than he should towards the stairs, dizzy as he reached the landing, looking quickly into the other bedrooms all freshly cleaned and made up by Ellen.

No sign of Fields.

He sat on his tossed bed talking to himself. Come on Jim. Try to remember what happened between you and Fields.

They were drinking again. More whiskeys. But who else was there?

Did Manus go home? I think he did. I can't remember him being there. Nevin was.

I'm nearly sure. No. I'm imagining that.

Wait, that's right.

Fields had a brochure. Or a leaflet of some kind, that he kept waving in front of Jim's nose. Pushing it at him like a challenge of some sort. Like a dare. It was one of those adverts from his office window, maybe it's still down on the counter, if Ellen hasn't tidied it away.

He put on his navy and white striped tie, thankful that the knot was already done and pulled on his socks and shoes, walking down the stairs with measured careful steps.

"I'm going to open up Ellen," he said evenly, passing the scullery on his way to the bar. It was bathed in shadows and he moved to let up the blind, unbolting the door, allowing daylight to flood in.

Three empty tumblers stood on the counter.

He was certain Nevin had been there.

The silver tin ashtray was overflowing with butts and a crumpled Sweet Afton packet lay on the cement floor under a stool. It could stay there, if he bent to retrieve it he would collapse.

The angst was receding slightly.

Everything looked in order.

There were no overturned stools, no blood on the floor. So, they hadn't fought, thank God.

He should have known that, when his knuckles were perfect and there wasn't a mark on him. He lifted the three tumblers and put them in the sink, then reached for the dirty ashtray.

What was the stain underneath it? Blood. No. Ink.

Holy fuck!

Why was there an ink stain on the counter? He opened the drawer quickly where his fountain pen was kept and there it was, all clean and perfect in its box.

Right now. Settle down Jim.

You need a wee hair of the dog, maybe two and you'll be as right as rain before Gracie and the children get here, all chirpy and excited to be home.

Paula was too young to care, but Malachy and Cathy loved getting back home, where they could play freely around the village without Gracie's aule mother spying on them, constantly hampering their fun. They could watch television in peace, without the loud intruding conversations in Gaelic they had to endure, when Gracie's family gathered around the fire in the evenings.

He was looking forward to seeing them all, especially Gracie. He would say nothing about his day out in Milford. It is over now and best forgotten. Ellen would keep her mouth shut; he was sure of that.

He poured himself a quick half, swallowing the Black Bush with his eyes shut tight; the first one was the hardest. The second one would do the trick and let him get on with his day.

Johnny O'Donnell would be in Mona's, collecting his pension. So would Cormac Brown and John Owen. They'd be through the door any minute.

Ann

Ann thought she would die laughing at the sight of Manus, sitting near the kitchen table with his head in his hands, the opened bottle of Aspirin strewn before him. He was wearing his black shirt and pants. The clerical collar was probably still in his bedroom. The weather was too hot for it and lately he'd been wearing it less and less.

Despite the warm July morning, Nevin was on his knees trying to light the range, so the kettle would boil. He was looking fresh enough, although Ann knew he didn't get in until all hours. Manus was home before him, easily an hour before him, but she wouldn't ask too many questions yet, let them get some breakfast, then she'd hear all about their day out.

"Get me a glass of water Ann like a good woman." Manus issued the instruction knowing he would be obeyed.

"That's the first time I ever saw you with a hangover ," she handed him the glass, laughter in her voice." It's not like you, Manus."

"I only had a few bottles of beer," Nevin said. "And I'm not the best. Just bone weary."

"You'll soon have a new lease of life Nevin," Manus winked. "It was a rough night, my skull is still pulsating. All in the line of duty."

Ann changed her mind about waiting until they had breakfast. She had to know what they got up to with Jim Logue. She had to know now.

"I closed up last night around eleven. Things were quiet. By the time I got glasses washed and empties cleared away it was half twelve and there was still no sign of you two."

"I calculate that we arrived back in the village at one o'clock, Ann." Manus was precise.

"My alarm clock said ten past one when you came in, Manus. Nevin didn't get into bed until three o clock. I couldn't sleep waiting to hear the front door being locked."

She stared at her husband who was straining to rise off his knees, having lit the fire. Her eyes narrowed suspiciously, though the smile never left her face. When he made no attempt to explain his whereabouts she began to bristle, reaching for the sweeping brush to tidy around the range, where ashes and turf mould were spilled.

"Did you meet a few fancy women? Maybe you were up at Lough Salt with one of them, Nevin." She sounded a little desperate.

Nevin had to employ his calm, reasonable tone to explain that he had been below in Logue's bar keeping John Fields company, because Logue was as drunk as a sailor and talking a whole lot of rubbish.

"Why was John Fields in Logue's Bar at that ungodly hour ?"

"Because Ann, he had insisted on driving Logue home after the hotel closed, knowing where he would get plenty more drinks."

"What was Logue talking about?"

"He was spewing the usual claptrap about what a great fellow he was and the great things he was going to do and the great things he had already done and bemoaning the epic things he could have done in the past."

Ann was warming up now, her shoulders starting to flinch. "What else was Logue on about? Hee, hee."

"He was insistent that he could have represented Ireland in the 1948 Olympics and Fields believed him."

"Is there any truth to his claim ?" Manus asked, wanting to be reasonable.

"Not at all," Nevin dismissed. "He's been flogging that old chestnut for years, according to Andy Dore. He could run a bit in his day, I believe, but he wasn't in the same class as John Joe Barry. Andy says he didn't own a pair of running shoes. That he ran in the bare feet. Can you imagine him in the Olympics!"

"He did refer to Barry earlier in the day and something about the Irish flag. No such place as Eire, he maintained. Not sure what he was trying to say." Manus sounded tired.

John Owen was the man who could enlighten them on Logue's favourite boast, Nevin said.

Ann finished sweeping up and hoped that she would have the opportunity to grill John on the subject, later in the day.

John patronized Logue's bar occasionally and after a few whiskeys it was easy to whittle information from him about Jim Logue's history and how he conducted business next door, that's if he wasn't in a prickly mood. His lips weren't as loose as Andy's, unfortunately. His observation of human behavior was sharp, a fact that didn't always sit easy with Ann, especially when he trained his bloodshot eyes on her.

The kitchen door was thrown open to the sun, when Mandy the Post's bulk appeared with the letters, mostly invoices in long brown envelopes with windows. Ann handed them to Nevin, but the one marked AirMail she clung onto, recognizing the hand. She held it up to the light, using her mischievous voice, "In God we trust!" She sliced open the silky envelope with a sharp knife, but no greenery greeted her, just a letter written on flimsy paper in the usual elegant style.

Dear Mr. and Mrs. Cox,

I hope this letter finds you both well. I have decided to go home to Ireland and have booked my flight from Boston to Dublin for Saturday, August the 15th. I will reside in the Milford Hotel, as my home place is probably not in a fit state to receive guests. I will stay for a fortnight and hope the weather will be kind at that time. The heat here is oppressive at present.

I'm looking forward to my trip home. It's been such a long time since I was there, I hope I'll still recognize the place. Would you be so kind as to let my brother know my plans and reassure him that I will call to see him as soon as I get settled in the Hotel.

I hope to meet you both in person and get the opportunity to show my gratitude for your continued kindness to Barney.

My flight will arrive in Dublin shortly after lunchtime and I will take the train to Sligo,where I have secured a hackney to drive me to Donegal.

I will visit your public house in the course of my stay and perhaps we could dine together one evening in the Hotel.

Yours Sincerely,

Sarah Gallagher.

Ann's mirth was uncontainable.

The silly aule doll! Where was she running to? Did she have any idea what state Barney Cam's house was in? Fit to receive guests, that was funny. The only guests Barney received were four legged ones with long pointy tails, hee,hee. The gratitude word sounded promising though. Was the aule doll going to lavish them with fifty dollars, a hundred maybe. She was treating them to dinner in the Milford Hotel. Ann had only been in that dining room once; the morning of Josie and Mona's wedding, twelve years ago. They married late in life, later than herself and Nevin. The wedding breakfast had been a drab affair, with not as much as a sherry or sip of port in sight. This time she promised they would have wine and order the dearest thing on the menu, seeing as the aule doll was paying.

Nevin regretted having to temper her resolve by pointing out that Sarah Gallagher was younger than her brother, somewhere in her 60's, he'd say. She would be disinclined to show any gratitude towards them if they didn't spend some of her previously gifted dollars on home improvements for Barney and a few decent duds for him, that didn't involve holding up his threadbare trousers with rope, or wellingtons that made his feet look like canoes. They would have to employ Andy Dore and Steven to get Jimmy's rathole into shape before August the 15th. Nevin would go to the Co-Op in Creeslough and buy new boots for him and a couple of warm shirts; maybe a pair of Nevin's old trousers would fit him. Otherwise, Ann could forget about dollars, or any pearls she imagined were coming her way in a trunk from Boston.

"As for Milford," he watched Ann's face falling, along with her arse. "I've seen enough of it to do me for a life-time." "Oh I don't know Nevin." Manus said. "You'll be seeing plenty of that one horse town over the coming months." He winked again and Ann's dander was up, needing to understand the inference.

"It's like this Ann," Nevin spoke quietly. "Jim Logue seems to be serious about selling next door. It's more or less a done deal, he said as much yesterday. So it's vital that we say nothing about it for the time being. Fields and MaCausland have to work out the finer details with Logue. So behave as if you know nothing, we don't want him changing his mind."

"My God, it's nearly ours," her voice squeaked. "How much will it cost us?"

"We don't have a final figure yet, that's Fields' job. He'll get the best deal he can for us," Manus was explaining. "Be sure you heed what you were told Ann and the deal should work out favorably, in the heel of the hunt.'

Gracie's car pulled into the village late that afternoon. Ann stood watching from her vantage point on the landing, wondering if it was her idea to sell the place. Maybe it was finally getting the better of her, not cut out to be a publican's wife after all. She would set the price too, fix it good and high so she could build a big house up the hill, with change left over to deposit in the bank. She hoped Nevin wouldn't be silly and pay too high a price for it, she wouldn't cheek yer wan that she could gloat about fleecing them. No doubt Nevin knew what he was doing.

The old mother was in the car, holding Paula on her knee in the front seat, Malachy and Cathy jumping out the back doors before the car had fully stopped. She watched the old dear carrying the sleeping child inside, a crone dressed in black. In stark contrast to Gracie, who opened the boot with her dark hair swept off her face by a pink headband that matched her knee-length crimplene shift. She retrieved two grocery bags, all business Ann thought; ready to put Logue through his paces, God love him!

As much as she despised him, she loathed her even more.

If all went to plan and they moved up the hill to live, Ann could breathe easy again. Enjoy the peace of the village, without the flaunting and swaggering on the street every night and the annoying laughter of children every day.

She left the landing, remembering the Scotties were gone for another year and things would return to normal. She loved their arrival every July and their generous patronage, and she enjoyed their departure equally, when she could turn her attention fully to the locals with all their little aches and foibles.

The warm weather was holding.

July meandered towards August and the stammering of tractors through the village bringing home the winter's fodder, became a constant familiar percussion. Most of them stopped in the evenings at Cox's or Logue's, to dampen their thirst as the sun began to lose its power. The odd one stopped in the morning, needing a drink to kickstart the day. Logue mainly tended to their needs. He probably joined them. Drinking their Black Bushes and Grouses with eager greedy mouths. He did always manage to work the bog himself, saving his turf for the winter, making sure yer wan didn't founder in school.

She worked alongside him at times, turning heavy black sods and rickling hard peats with her determined hands, a job Ann wouldn't be caught dead doing. No self respecting woman went to work on the bog, it was more of the backward behavior inherited by the ones from over west.

July was a lucrative month for them in the pub. Logue had been busy too. And like all summers since he opened for business, the carryon in his bar was disgraceful. Ann had a good mind to put a flea in yer wan's ear because she didn't know the half of it; too busy swanning off to make more money. She remembered Nevin's talk earlier though and decided to say nothing, no point in rocking the boat now.

The Teddy buck was hanging around a lot of late, County Clerk, how are you! Driving his fancy pale grey car, an Austin A40, according to Andy Dore, who seemed very impressed by Logue's cousin. He wore sharp suits too, as if it were a family trait and brought a crowd with him from Letterkenny, mainly on the weekends, all driving snazzy cars and wearing mod outfits. He brought the wife sometimes, well Ann presumed it was his wife, though she was probably some floozy, for all Ann knew. They'd drive into the village on the weekends, with their back combed hair and short dresses in powder blues and lemon, like sherbet sweets. Following their men into the bar with handbags swinging, gabbing and giggling in their pointy toed sling backs. They were a silly looking bunch, ridiculously fashionable, trying to look English or American.

Ann was sticking to her pleated shirts and slip-on comfortable shoes, similar to the local women. They weren't running about making shows of themselves, like these dunder-heads.

Gracie Logue was nearly as silly as them, with her bright pink outfit and her supposed to be so intelligent; the best most qualified woman in the parish. She really didn't have the figure for those swingy type dresses she was wearing and she was getting long in the tooth too. There wouldn't be much call for style when she was up the hill running after sheep, hee hee.

One thing you could say about the female customers in Logue's bar, Ann realised; they brought a degree of civility with them, which was absent on the men-only nights. The goings on then were akin to the Wild West. Sergeant Halligan in his wisdom acknowledged that eleven o'clock closing was too early during the summer season. Twelve or half past made more sense, he said and Nevin and herself complied with his brand of reasonableness.

But not Logue.

His rabble spilled onto the street at half one, two o'clock sometimes and herself and Nevin had to lie in bed wide awake, enduring the rowdy bawdy onslaught night after night, with Jim Logue's supercilious voice always the loudest. Nevin's suggestion that they decamp to the back bedroom away from the street was resisted, because Ann was accustomed to her nocturnal spying, surreptitiously watching the antics behind her bedroom curtains. She enjoyed being outraged at Logue's cronies drifting towards their cars, dropping keys, fumbling and struggling to open doors as they wished good nights all round. Jim's voice carried on the air, calling them hoors and latchico's, endearingly, while they swerved up the street honking horns. It was insufferable.

His bar was smaller than theirs. He had the snug, but they had the lounge. And all through the summer Nevin pushed back tables against the walls and used the floor space, dancing Shoe the Donkey to Mandy the Post's melodeon and Charlie Bayers' fiddle. The local men brought their wives on Sundays or on special evenings, when they got their turf home and their hay saved. Now and again the younger generation arrived, wanting Mandy to play Elvis songs, so they could jive and do the twist. Andy Dore's wife Sadie was a great dancer and so were the McBride women.

Ann loved being a spectator, clapping and egging them on.

Mary Bayers was like a thorn in her side, spoiling her fun, always asking her to dance because she knew Ann had two left feet. She admired from a safe distance, knowing the flat feet God gave her would never look neat on the dance floor.

John Owen's beady eyes perceived as much, making him disagreeable and trying.

"You should hitch up your skirt Ann and hoof it out there with the rest of them."

"And who would get you your wee stout and whiskey then John?" she smiled.

"Ah go on," he was loud now and offensive. "Have ya auld bandy legs or thick ankles or what?"

She summoned control, knowing that soon he would be in the Zephyr, on his way to MacCausland to sign the dotted line and her smile remained radiant.

"Christ the Logues are like Ginger Rogers and Fred Astaire," he roared. "You and Nevin are more like Laurel and Hardy!" He laughed, shaking his head in mock despair.

Ann shot a warning glance around the counter. Andy Dore wiped the smirk off his face and stopped tapping his feet to the music drifting in from the lounge.

The pair next door might be great dancers, for all the good it would do them. Ann snorted ruefully, vowing to ignore John for as long as was humanly possible, no matter how loud he bellowed for his double whiskey, which he loved at the end of the night.

Gracie

Gracie was looking forward to her week off. The July term in the Gaeltacht had been wearing, mainly because the children hadn't settled in her mothers over west, despite the good weather and the attention lavished on them by Hannah and her brother John.

Malachy's attempts at snaring rabbits amused him for a few days, until he tired of the fruitless pursuit. Cathy loved the swing Uncle John engineered for her in the pine grove behind the house, swinging on the ancient tree, inhaling the spicy sap and feeling the coolness of the shade on her skin. Loneliness set in though, as she missed Jim and the village. Gradually the sunny days grew interminable for them. They sulked around the farm, immune to the charms of fluffy kittens and newly hatched day old chicks. Paula settled in beautifully, less fractious in her granny's arms. She thrived on unpasteurized milk and homegrown spuds, mashed with homemade unsalted butter; the same butter Malachy stuck his tongue out at and Cathy flatly refused to eat.

Their unbounded joy in the back seat as they drove home on Friday afternoon, convinced Gracie not to force them to return with her when the week ended and the August term was beginning.

She knew her mother thought the two oldest were spoiled, because Gracie didn't slap them or allow hunger to break their spirits, coercing them to eat food that made them retch. Frowning her disapproval when Gracie bought them sliced loaves and salted butter in the townland grocers. She'd leave them with Jim this term, who would balk at the idea straight off, until Cathy got to work on him, twisting him around her little finger and he'd say it was his idea all along.

The week apart for Gracie and Jim was a buffer, keeping them from squabbles and hurts, strengthening their resolve to be gentler, kinder to each other at the weekends. When Friday came around they were tense again in each other's company, like dancers who had temporarily fallen out of step. Since Paula came along their lovemaking had waned, not because their desire had, but mainly because neither of them wanted another child. They were both adamant about that and still they did take risks which Gracie always regretted, fretting for days until her period arrived and she could smile again. Jim had a way of making her feel invisible at first, when she greeted him on Friday evenings, apparently not seeing how lovely she looked or the effort she had made with her hair and clothes. She accepted it now, knew it would balance out as the space between them narrowed and thawed.

By Saturday evening, when she stood behind the counter with him, laughing and embracing her role as landlady, they were back in harmony again, tripping rhythmically along together. She expected that now, knew the pattern, which kept her heart from sinking when his greeting was distant and his replies cold. She carried in the grocery bags, confident that the chicken whose neck was wrung that morning, would gladden his heart later, served up plump and roasted and full of his favourite stuffing.

Malachy and Cathy would exaggerate how awful staying in granny's house was.

They'd forget to tell Jim about the fun at the ceili's, when they sat with Gracie and the musicians on the stage, watching the students weaving to the Waves of Tory or the Siege of Ennis. They'd leave out details about the stony beach and trips to the toy shop in Dungloe, arriving back with water pistols and bags of marbles that Aunty Hannah had bought them.

Jim liked to believe the worst about her home over west. His face, when he saw his mother in law standing in the kitchen with Paula in her arms, was almost funny. Wait till he heard she was staying for a week! It didn't matter, just more of the dance falling out of step. He'd have no choice but to endure it.

Kit, her mother, hadn't darkened the door of a public house until her daughter bought one with her son in law, making her quietly proud, broduil, as she called it. She was ill at ease in the largely male demesne and avoided the bar when customers came in, preferring the safety of the kitchen in the same way Jim's mother did.

She struggled to understand Jim, with his urbane suits and blustering ways. He was so different to her own sons, who worked the land; earthy physical men, who in her eyes were purposeful and productive.

Gracie explained that Jim enjoyed standing behind the counter serving drinks and conversing with customers, even on warm sunny days when potatoes were being dug and hay stacks built. He went to the bog when it suited him and now and again the outdoors called him when he helped Tom with the sheep. She encouraged Jim to welcome her mother and put her at ease, because she liked having her there. Paula loved her and it made life a bit easier for Ellen and herself. He did try to converse with Kit, but his Gaelic was rusty and their attempts at connecting were sparse and awkward.

Like Marjorie, Kit never grew accustomed to the cursing and vulgarity that reached her ears occasionally in the scullery or kitchen, when the door to the bar was left open. She would bless herself repeatedly, whispering prayers to the Sacred Heart as if the world was about to end.

She tolerated Jim.

Gracie knew there was no love lost between them. Her sighs of relief were loud and pointed when they drove west at the end of the week.

Lately Gracie had taken to joining Jim in the bar after Sunday mass, happy to chat with John Owen, who was coming in more often and staying for longer, before going next door to catch a tune from Charley's fiddle. Mickey Flood came in with two female cousins from Philadelphia and Gracie mused that Jim should hire a few musicians to play in their bar on Sundays too, after all there were still visitors in the parish and the music was drawing people next door. They could sing, she said, and dance, and Jim winked at her with pride in his eyes, saying he loved her and their dance was perfectly in sync.

On Monday afternoon Ellen from around the corner did the bar, while Kit minded Paula in her kitchen sanctuary and Cathy and Malachy went to Milford with their parents.

August had sneaked in warmer than July, clutching the lush fields and hills in her grasp, rallying the heather prematurely to pinks and purples.

They drove past Tom's and Jim muttered, "God's own country." Gracie smiled, wondering where he heard that phrase.

They were going to the Bank first to deposit the contents of the burgeoning cigar box, along with her Gaeltacht cheques. Gracie had no interest in the cinema, but she needed to keep her promise to the children that they would go to La Scala to see The Three Stooges and eat tubs of ice cream and chocolate bars.

Despite the hilarity on screen, Gracie fell asleep listening to the children's giggles. Only waking when Jim elbowed her shoulder, hissing that the show was nearly over and the lights would soon go on. He was silent on the drive home and she spoke quietly telling him not to be angry with her. She was just in the habit of sleeping in the cinema, that's all, and the children were so happy he shouldn't spoil their fun. She reminded him how healthy their bank account looked, maybe they should pay off the mortgage or maybe not. Maybe they should delay paying it and think about changing the car instead, a brand new one this time.

Perhaps it was the mention of a new car that cheered him, or Malachy singing Old MacDonald in the back seat, with Cathy squealing EIEIO, she wasn't sure. Gracie was just grateful that good humor filled the car again and she breathed a prayer of thanks to God for bringing her such good luck.

Paula was bouncing on Kit's knees, diddle diddle dumsey my son John. Ellen came up from the bar offering to make evening tea, but Gracie told her to take the rest of the day off, she would prepare it herself. There was cold chicken left over for salads and she wanted to show Jim that she still had some energy about her. The usual crew was below in the bar, Ellen said, adding that Nevin Cox had called earlier looking for Jim.

"What did he want? Gracie's tone was sharper than she intended, making Ellen react.

"How do I know what he wanted? I was hardly going to ask him."

"Nosing about as usual, letting on he wanted something I suppose. It's a wonder the priest wasn't sniffing about too, looking for a free drink."

"No, he's away back up north, John Owen was saying."

"Well good riddance to bad rubbish." Gracie softened her tone. "He'll be no loss around the place."

Ellen defended him, saying he read a nice mass and Gracie agreed because her mother was listening and she knew the golden rule; never ever speak ill of a priest. Gracie hoped Kit wouldn't overhear Jim's rants about the clergy while she was there.

She still found it peculiar that he liked Fr. Manus, he was generally a good judge of character. It made Gracie anxious, the niggle that tingled her gut whenever he was in the bar with Jim, but he was gone for now, so she could relax. If he never appeared again, she would put extra money in the black babies' box next year.

Jim seemed inordinately tense when she told him about Cox's visit, undressing for bed later that night. His tone harsher than hers could ever be, when he asked the same question, "What did he want?" adding , "the long string of misery." He tossed and turned in bed, kicking the eiderdown off them, grumbling in his sleep.

Maybe the sultry night was getting to him.

The week at home was productive. Every sheet and pillow case was washed and ready for ironing. The creases vanished under the new electric iron, bringing joy to Gracie's heart ; another good investment, she thought. If Jim had his way she'd still be shoveling hot coals into the contraption that was sitting at the back door, heavy with rust. A washing machine was next on the list, a twin tub like Mickey Floods. The days of sloshing about in the scullery sink, skinning knuckles on the washer board, were ending. It took two of them to wring out sheets, which was simple compared to wringing out blankets, when even Jim had to roll up his sleeves.

She was plugging in the iron again after lunch, about to do the last of the childrens' clothes, leaving everything in order for Ellen, before she went back over west with Paula and her mother. Her week had been so pleasant, she thought, when Nevin Cox's lanky frame passed the window. Jim was up and down to the storeroom, a sign that the bar was empty. She wondered if she should go down to the bar, in case Jim had left the money drawer open; she wouldn't put anything past your man. She relaxed when she heard Jim's voice, wishing he would refuse Cox the bottle of spirits or whatever he pretended to want. Cathy's little candy striped dress was ironing like a dream. She could hear her skipping rope beating the pavement outside the kitchen window. Malachy's football hit the gable repeatedly and not a peep emanated from the bar; maybe Cox was gone again, out the side door and up the back lane.

She heard the faint sound of conversation, he was still there.

Voices were beginning to rise, Jim's rising dangerously. Gracie stopped ironing. Jim was shouting now, his voice threatening. Cathy's skipping stopped. Malachy and herself were suddenly inside the kitchen door, her mother in from the scullery, suds up to her elbows.

"Get out Cox you dirty rotten bastard! Get out!"

Paula stood in her cot crying. Kit's mouth moved to speak but Gracie shushed her with an abrupt wave, so she could figure out what was happening. Jim was letting them down being so transparent in front of Cox, giving himself away. Nevin was calmer, she could hear him placating. Jim was incensed.

"If you don't get the fuck out I'll kill you with my bare hands." Hysterical.

The door slammed so violently, Gracie was sure it came off the hinges. Cox's shadow passed back up, swiftly this time.

Cathy was tugging on her apron, "Mammy what's wrong with Daddy?"

Malachy was standing near her, his sunburnt face etched in concern.

"Malachy pet, switch on the television and see if there's a nice wee programme on." Gracie sounded calm.

Kit lifted Paula out of her cot, soothing and rocking. Gracie walked down to the bar, steeling herself for what she was about to hear.

He was talking to himself, interceding , "Jesus Christ help me!" The offended door survived, with Jim leaning against it, his left hand running through his hair in agitation, his eyes fixed on the floor. He looked up, startled when Gracie spoke.

"What's wrong Jim, what was that all about?"

He might burst out crying, she thought, seeing his jaw move in a tight angry lock.

"You always said he was a bad one Gracie, but you had no idea just how bad he was." He continued staring at the floor.

Gracie sat down at the big rectangular table, her legs shaking beneath her.

"What did you do Jim?" It was a whisper.

"It's not what I did. It's what that bastard is saying I did," defiance was taking over.

"Well what did he say you did?"

He emitted a quick flabbergasted grunt. "He says I agreed to sell the place to him; the man is a headcase."

"Why in the name of God would he say that?" Gracie's heartbeat was increasing, she tried to ignore it.

"The Manus fella has been telling me for weeks about the great place I have here and the big money I would get for a premises like it. So for the crack I said I just might put it on the market, test the waters if you like. But I had no intention of doing any such thing. Now the string of misery is insisting we have a gentleman's agreement and I have to set a date to close the deal."

Gracie tried hard to process what she was hearing. Images of Manus' insincere face kept flitting across her mind.

"What's a gentleman's agreement?" she asked.

"It's where you shake hands on a deal, the way you see men doing on a Fair day, when they're buying or selling livestock," he sounded calmer.

"But there's nothing legal about that, it's not on paper even if you did shake on it, am I right?"

"Of course you are, but that silly fucker thinks he can convince me that I have to sell to him now, over the head of a handshake!"

"When did all this happen? Was it a while back? And why is he coming out with it now?"

"For Christ's sake, how do I know? He's saying it happened on this day last week when we went to Milford for a meal, but he's a born liar."

He was angry again. Gracie pushed on, needing to hear the details about this meal and the evening he spent with Nevin and his cleric brother, all eating and drinking together. Why hadn't he mentioned this before. Did Ellen know about it? The drinking was really worrying.

Did Jim drink whiskey that day?

She knew he could be reckless when he drank too much whiskey. He became mawkish and prodigal, handing out free drinks and waving the men's money away, spouting platitudes; "You only live once!" "What's life all about?"

Once he promised Mickey Flood the Anglia for free, because Mickey admired the car, saying she was a beauty. Jim said she was his when he bought the new one in September. He told Neil Fada he could take bags of turf from the turf shed anytime he liked, because he was too delicate to work the bog himself. Gracie put both men straight. Not that Mickey needed telling, but Neil might have taken up the generous offer. When Jim wasn't in the bar Gracie reminded Neil that Andy Dore had the best turf for sale and he would deliver as many tractor loads as Neil wanted.

Those transgressions had sailed into the ether without consequence, but this moment felt menacing in a way Gracie couldn't fathom.

"Start at the beginning," she persisted. "Tell me the whole story about this day last week from start to finish, leave nothing out."

His account of the morning didn't sound so bad; the bottle of Glenfiddich being shared at the counter with the two brothers; although Nevin's willingness to join in the drinking was suspicious. If only Jim had left it at that, but whiskey dismantled his resolve, always. She felt cheated that he closed the bar early, while Cox's bar stayed open all day. Logue's bar had lost money and Ellen from around the corner would have clocked it. She wished she could ask Ellen about that day, but she wouldn't, she'd keep her own council.

So, they had a meal in the hotel and a few more drinks and then they came home. Was that it, or was Jim being purposely obtuse? Was it the three of themselves all day or did anyone else join them she wondered, watching Jim pour himself a whiskey that he needed badly, after the shock of the fucker next door.

"That's right," he sipped. "John Fields came on the scene after dinner and Daniel MaCausland put his head in for one."

No alarm bells were ringing.

MaCausland was their solicitor, hadn't he acted for them when they bought the premises. John Fields had the details of the sale in his office, from when the old American doll was selling it. Both men patronized the bar occasionally, although they frequented next door more often. Still, they weren't strangers, like some people she could mention.

"Were Nevin and the priest drinking as much as you Jim?"

"Were they what! They were throwing it into them as hard as they could," Jim lied. "I don't know how we didn't go off the road at that bad bend near Tom's."

"And you went straight to bed when you got home?"

"O for fuck's sake Gracie," he was contriving now.

She watched him pour more liquor into his glass, a master at avoidance.

"John Fields came back here for a wee while, the man needed another drink; he stayed for an hour and that was that."

Gracie believed him.

She was going back west the following day with Paula and her mother. She needed to believe him, but it was time to lay down some ground rules. Under the circumstances she would get away with it, she'd meet little resistance, this was a part of the dance that needed practice too.

"No more whiskey Jim, it doesn't agree with you. And, no drinking in your own bar."

"For all the whiskey I drink, you wouldn't fill an egg cup with it." He screwed the top tight on Johnny Walker, replacing the bottle on the shelf.

"If it's quiet in the mornings, take the youngsters to the hill and get the turf saved for the winter. Book Andy Dore's tractor in good time, for he'll be busy."

Jim nodded quickly. Half compliance, half annoyance.

Gracie felt comfortable leaving the two oldest in the village for the August term. They liked Ellen, because she was jaunty and easygoing and kind. They behaved themselves around her, preferring her kindness to her sharp tongue, which sliced to the bone when incurred. It's a pity she didn't employ it with Jim last week. Gracie pondered, as she folded Paula's nappies into a straw bag, along with nappy liners and a tin of Johnston's baby powder.

Whatever the pair next door thought they were at, it wasn't going to work.

She had seen Ann earlier at her clothesline in the backyard. Was anticipating her usual fawning greeting followed by twenty questions. Strangely she seemed busy and preoccupied, unaware of Gracie on the other side of the hedge. She wanted to march up there and confront Nevin Cox and his hateful wife and ask them what sort of nonsense they were peddling. Jim beseeched her not to, and

Malachy said, "Don't Mammy," in a desperate little voice that stopped her in her tracks.

The very idea that Jim would sell their home was ridiculous.

The thought that they would ever sell it to the Cox's was laughable.

They would burn it to the ground first.

The fright of the idea was good for Jim though, it would keep him straight and away from the bottle. Maybe it was a godsend. He had the added responsibility of Malachy and Cathy now, who employed their own little wiles to keep daddy out of trouble and make him behave.

Gracie would be back in ten days.

All going well they would visit McMahon and find out what kind of deal they'd get on a new car. A Morris 11,00 this time.

She liked the look of them.

Nevin

It was mid August and Jim Logue was behaving as if nothing had happened, hoping it would all go away like a bad dream; only it wouldn't. The morning after the Milford scenario, Manus wanted to go down to Logue and outline exactly what had transpired, but Nevin forbade him and he was glad he did. He had the brainwave to send Manus back to Enniskillen, because he was a man of the cloth and couldn't be part of any scandal that might ensue. That's if Logue didn't play the game according to the rules. Manus was better off out of the way. His puppeteering skills were no longer needed and Nevin detested the possibility that he would be called as a witness if this thing went to court.

He let a week go by before he called next door, to sound out the vendor and sniff out the lay of the land. It wouldn't go smoothly, he knew that, so he set his teeth firmly, while he outlined for Logue the consequences of his actions. He spelt out the transaction he had entered into, then watched him gradually lose his head.

Nevin remained calm.

Although he was in danger of being physically attacked, he managed to get out the bar door with his jaw in one piece, having dispatched the first shot over Logue's bow. It was lucky that yer wan was there with the aule mother. They could all process the bombshell together and be planning their future.

MaCausland set the price for the premises and drew up the Bill of Sale, saying that inflation was non-existent, especially since Logue had acquired it. Wasn't a £100 profit welcome in any man's pocket? Jim Logue could buy himself a few new suits and a new coat for the wife, hee, hee.

"You could certainly build a hotel up the hill with the guts of £2,000," MaCausland sneered, as he watched Nevin signing the document. "Logue's Mountain Lodge indeed, I hope he embraces that plan wholeheartedly Nevin, hee, hee."

"Jim Logue has a big mouth," Nevin said. "It was always going to land him in trouble."

A few days later they brought Logue to the hotel and John Fields showed up with the document tucked safely in his inside pocket.

Daniel only put in a brief appearance, to ascertain whether the bold Jim was serious about selling and Nevin couldn't have written a better script if he tried.

It would soon be three weeks since he approached Logue with the news.

He was wondering if he should brave it down again. Surely Logue was seeing things more clearly now. He had to drive Sarah Gallagher to Sligo first though. Her holiday was over and she was returning to Boston for the last time; so she said.

Ann and himself were relieved.

They worried about her reasons for going back to the States, thinking that perhaps she had some relatives there who would inherit Barney's humble spread. Or maybe she was putting her affairs in order, to come back to the house she was born in and be buried with her own people. Anyway, nothing could have been further from the truth. She knew her grandfather hadn't made a will, neither had her father, and she fretted that Barney was left in a vulnerable position, the vultures could be circling, she said.

Nevin reassured her that Barney was being well minded by Ann and himself. The only one he could think of who might be harboring bad intentions was Tom Logue, whose land bordered Barney's. She wondered if she could have the few acres of hilly scrub fenced off, but Nevin advised against it. One Logue was enough to antagonize for the moment. When Barney was gone he would fence it himself over time and put a few sheep on it. Eventually he'd claim squatters' rights; possession was nine tenths of the law, according to MaCausland.

She was delighted with Barney's appearance, admitting that he had been a slow child who could learn nothing at school. He was lucky to have Ann and Nevin with their generous kind ways; it gave her peace of mind. She was a spinster who was in America for over forty years and at sixty eight she knew she would never return; her life was in Boston and that's where she would remain.

They dined in the Hotel on her second last night, bringing Barney with them at her request. They smiled benignly, Sarah too, when he slurped his soup, splashing it down the front of his white shirt. He gnawed frantically on the lamb chops, using his hands for cutlery, his gummy mouth chewing obscenely. It was orange squash all round, casting aside Ann's fantasy of fine wines and ports.

"When Logue's bar is ours," Nevin compensated, "we'll go back up with Manus and have the night of our lives. Frank Halligan and Annette will join us too."

He wouldn't go down to Logue on his own this time. No. He would bring Frank Halligan with him; the uniform might add weight to his case. The Sergeant had already been dragged into the debacle, because Jim Logue couldn't behave, only courting negative attention and shooting himself in the foot; again.

The Teddy buck was there day and night, giving legal advice no doubt; being a court clerk and all. It was ill advised of him though, to drive his cousin to Milford with half a bottle of whiskey in him, arriving at John Field's office, roaring like an ape, calling John an evil bastard and kicking the door that was locked against him. He went next door to Daniel's office and raised more hullabaloo, shaking his fist in the window, calling Daniel a double dealing hoor. Teddy got him back into the car, before the Milford Guards came on the scene. MaCausland rang Sergeant Halligan , telling him to call on Logue, warning that a restraining order would be issued against him if he didn't keep a respectful distance from himself and John Fields.

Sergeant Halligan had no compunction about marching into the bar the following morning official and stern, putting Logue on notice to behave civilly, if he knew what was good for him. He caught Logue off guard, for there wasn't a whimper out of him, only a big sad face, like a baby who lost his dummy.

Nevin spent every night after the Milford scenario going over the details with Ann. Lying in bed together, imagining what must be going through Jim Logue's head, surmising the predicament yer wan and himself felt trapped by.

They always reached the same conclusion; Logue wouldn't remember a damned thing about that night in July. Who was or wasn't present in the bar when the deal was sealed.

Nevin swore to him that Daniel MaCausland was there, as well as himself and Fields and he could see by Logue's face that he was uncertain.

"Why did you tell him Daniel MaCausland was there if he wasn't?" Ann was intrigued.

"Because, it copper fastens the legality of the situation. Logue talks big, but he's afraid of the law like the rest of us."

"What'll happen if he denies everything and refuses to go ahead with things? Yer wan will be advising him and you know how stubborn she is." Ann needed reassurance.

"He can deny all he likes." Nevin reached to put out the light. "But the proof is against him I'm afraid."

"We'll see how the big talker will talk his way out of this one." Ann sighed, looking forward to a sweet night's sleep.

John Fields was on the phone to Nevin, the day after Logue rattled his cage and Nevin struggled to put him at ease.

"I hope this doesn't come back to bite me in the arse," he whined. "Business is slow enough without rumours circulating that could do me damage."

"There'll be no rumours John. Who's going to spread rumours?"

"Jim Logue will tell any man that listens a whole load of shit and some of it will stick."

"Don't fret man. The same boy will keep his mouth tight as Fort Knox. He won't embarrass himself in front of his cronies, no fear of that."

"It was your suggestion that I put the brochure in front of him, the one I had from the time the American doll was selling the place." John was accusing.

"And whose idea was it to take new pictures of Logue's premises? I don't think it was mine," Nevin replied.

"I had to come up with something for God's sake, to warrant me having the original brochure with me in the first place. He thought I was photographing the place, to show him how good the bar was looking since he bought it and made all the improvements."

"What improvements did he make?" Nevin challenged.

"You know. The new sign outside and the snug inside for the women."

"I would hardly call them improvements," Nevin laughed. "But I suppose anything was better than the state it was in when the Yank had it."

"Well Logue thought I was going to produce a new brochure for him. That's why he signed the paper I put in front of him. He thought he was ordering the brochure. I know it's what Daniel and yourself told me to do, but it's not sitting right with me." He sighed.

"Do you know what will make it sit very well indeed John," Nevin suggested, "the thought of the remuneration you'll get when all is said and done, the reason you got onboard in the first place."

"Daniel should have been there, Nevin, do you not think?" He was wavering.

"Listen John, whether Daniel was there or not makes no difference. He signed a legal document, so hold your nerve and keep your mouth shut. You didn't do anything wrong."

When Nevin recounted the conversation later that night with Ann, she was unsettled.

"Maybe he's right. Maybe MaCausland should have been there, he is our solicitor after all."

"Logue might have his moments of weakness Ann, but he's not a complete fool. Daniel's presence that night would have signaled officialdom, scaring Logue off and we wouldn't have the outcome we got. It appeared to Logue that he was showing good faith in John and signing off on an impressive new brochure. Something he could show to his customers and boast that half the country wanted to buy his great premises. John had no intention of putting a new brochure together, there was no need to."

"Because yer wan would see the beautiful new brochure and knock the idea hard on the head. Am I right, Nevin?"

"Exactly my dear Watson," Nevin chortled. "Precisely."

Ann was behaving beautifully these days, moving up and down the counter, glowing and serene. There was a new energy about her, that not even John Owen could dim with his rancid humor, generally aimed at getting under her skin.

He was edgy of late and a bit sour, which was to be expected, since Nevin had taken him to MaCausland shortly before the Logue business, where he signed over the house and surrounding fields; at last. The house was waiting to be demolished, but it was the spot Ann dreamt of owning since the English crowd, the McCatridges, built a log cabin on a similar site, although theirs had a view of the village lough.

John had no one to will it to only Nevin.

Still, a dull resentment seethed inside him, which Ann ignored, plonking bowls of soup and buttered bread in front of him when he looked hungry. Mugs of sugary tea and penny biscuits when he needed sweetening up. He was drinking next door more often, with Andy Dore and Eddy McClafferty, but Nevin was confident the rats would desert the sinking ship, when they realized there were no lifeboats.

Yer wan didn't seem to be affected by what was going on, but then she was harder to figure out than a jigsaw puzzle with pieces missing. She returned at the weekends, often with her mother in tow and Ann said she showed no signs of worry or upset. She had a clear view of her from the landing window. And they knew what Gracie Logue looked like when she was in bad form, it wasn't a pretty sight. After the third child arrived, they barely recognized her, all bloated and glum, her eyes in the back of her head like a zombie. There wasn't a hint of anything resembling that now and Nevin almost admired her brazenness. Ann said she had no shame in her because she was too backward, like all of the wans from over west. Maybe she was delighted with Jim's decision, or maybe she didn't know half of it.

Logue left blanks perhaps and was living on a prayer.

How well he behaved himself when she was there at the weekends and the Letterkenny crew rolled into town, with Teddy Donnigan leading the pack. He still kept late hours which she wouldn't mind, with money flowing into the drawer; but there were no yelps or ye hahs or red Indian undulations as they drove out of the village, that nonsense had stopped.

Logue waited until Monday night when she was gone, to let rip at the top of his lungs.

Standing behind the Zephyr, screeching that Nevin was a treacherous dog! Manus was a mongrel pig! The Cox's had no more breeding than a sack of shit! He ranted until he was hoarse and Malachy's voice could be heard pleading with him to come into the house. Cathy in her nightdress leading him by the hand like a big lost wane. After the third night of railing, Ann agreed they should move to the back bedroom; she couldn't bear to hear his voice one more time. Sergeant Halligan paid him a visit to outline the consequences of his behavior, which was a waste of time.

When Nevin chanced down with Frank Halligan by his side, they went in the back door, hoping to meet Logue at the storerooms and avoid customers in the bar. He was carrying a crate of empties and stopped dead in his tracks, asking them what the fuck they wanted. Nevin tried to be fair and outline things in a plausible manner, although Logue's face was flushed and fierce. He displayed no violence because the Sergeant was there, but the outcome was the same.

He denied there was a gentleman's agreement, because on the night in question there were no gentlemen present, except himself. There was no agreement of any kind, verbal or written. Nevin could go to hell and take his guard dog with him. It was a futile mission. Frank advised Nevin to pay Daniel a visit, it was time for a solicitor's letter.

He drove to Milford the following day.

Although he had no appointment, the secretary ushered him into the waiting room, saying Mr. MaCausland would be with him shortly. He was due in court after lunch, so Nevin had to talk fast, outlining Logue's intransigence, which left him doubting that the deal would go ahead. It warmed his heart when Daniel reassured him that there was law left in the country, despite what Jim Logue thought and he would be ruled by it.

"This isn't the Wild West Nevin, or Dodge City, where we settle our affairs by brute force."

"I'd say that's where Logue thinks he lives," Nevin risked a snigger.

"Well he's about to get a rude awakening." The solicitor stood, indicating that the meeting was over. "I'll draft the letter on Monday, outlining his position. He'll receive it mid week."

He walked with Nevin to the door, resting his hand on his shoulder.

"It's a serious legal matter now, Nevin, so leave it with me. Go home and enjoy your weekend."

Jim

Summer was on the wane. August heather still bloomed on the hills around the village. Tom drove down for Jim on mornings when he needed help with lambs he was late dipping. Ellen kept an eye on the bar, serving Neil Fada and Johnny O'Donnell, lingering over bottles of stout, while she resumed her drudgery upstairs or in the kitchen.

It was a release for Jim working at the dipping tank with Tom, lowering nervous lambs, struggling and bleating, into the odorous bath. He liked being on the hill these days, walking beside his brother through the wide expansive fields. Enjoying his gruff muttering, his expert whistles, directing Roy the young collie to drive the sheep at a safe pace and worry them into pens and barns.

It was easier to breathe in the high clean air, where the heavy hand of worry pressing on Jim's chest could be forgotten or ignored, like an unwelcome guest beating at the door.

Cathy and Malachy loved it too. Hours spent hiding and seeking in the tall ferns behind the farmhouse with their cousins. They deferred to Malachy, the oldest and professed leader, who must always be obeyed. Only hunger drew them back to Sally's table, oblivious to Granny's scolding and screeching, grabbing at slices of warm bread straight from the oven slathered in butter and homemade rhubarb jam.

There was comfort in Sally's cooking, Jim thought. Her scrambled eggs golden on his plate, waiting for thick slices of hairy bacon still curling and crisping in the heavy black pan.

The weather stayed fine.

Afternoons were spent mending barbed wire fences that sagged or snapped under rotting pailing stabs, stopping now and again to talk or stand silently looking over God's own country, spotting pheasants and hawks on the distant slopes and hills.

They struggled to know what exactly they were seeing on one such afternoon, when a strange exotic creature came into view.

"What in the name of fuck is that?" Tom asked, shielding his eyes from the sun with his right hand.

Jim followed suit until the apparition came into focus. "It's Barney Cam. Christ, would you look at the cut of him!"

The splayed feet approached, awkward and stout, a spanking new pair of hob-nail boots; the gummy mouth pulled back tight with the effort of walking in them. Tom controlled his desire to guffaw, behind a stern look at Barney that was too cruel Jim thought.

"My dear Mr. Cam, aren't you looking swell," Jim encouraged. "Were you at a wedding?"

He recognized the faded sports jacket as one of Nevin's, the trousers looked familiar too, no longer held aloft with roped twine. Instead, a shiny buckled belt dazzled in the sun.

"Did I see that jacket before Barney?" Jim looked askance.

"Naw, it a new wan," Barney lisped.

Tom made a loud hacking noise, before lobbying a spittle through the air that landed on one of Barney's new boots.

"That'll help to clean them up," Tom sneered.

Barney loped to the grassy ditch to wipe his offended wader, shaking his fist at Tom, who pretended to run at him, sending Barney up the lane like a frightened goose.

"You were a bit hard on him," Jim said.

"He's a silly eejit ," Tom watched his flight. "Did you see he got the house done up a bit?"

Jim was surprised and wondered where he got the means to renovate.

"Cox had Andy Dore and Steven doing bits. They fixed the door and put new glass in his window. Sarah was home from America, I suppose she paid for it."

"I know she's been sending dollars to Cox for years and not many of them are being spent on Barney. He'll be trying to get her to sign over the place to him you'll find, probably drove her to MaCausland one of the days."

Tom doubted what Jim was deducing and his refusal to be convinced angered Jim.

"You should be trying to get Barney's place anyway, after all it borders your land. It would fit you better than spitting on his boots."

He was suddenly furious.

Tom didn't know half of it, he said. Hadn't John Owen confided in him, so had Johnny Neil, that they signed on the dotted line and God knows who was next. No he wouldn't fucking calm down because Tom never backed him, or supported anything he did.

Jim had calmed by the time they headed in for evening tea.

Afterwards Tom got cleaned up and drove them down to the village, staying in the bar until late. Jim was relaxed behind the counter, laughing with the Big Flood and Mandy the Post, winking at Tom when he complimented Andy Dore on his magnificent renovations on Barney Cam's palace. Tom returned his wink, though his gaze followed Jim's movements behind the counter, still puzzled by his fit of temper earlier in the day.

Gracie would be home on Friday, all finished up in the Gaeltacht for another year, thank God. By Wednesday the week was dragging, making Jim despair almost as much as the children that Friday would never arrive. Two more days he reminded himself, seeing Mandy the Post saunter across from Mona's, knocking lightly on the bar door, handing Jim a registered letter.

"There's something good in that one young Logue," he winked, watching Jim signing.

The only other such letter Jim received came to the house a month after his honeymoon, when MaCausland sent them their bill of sale for the premises, all signed, sealed and delivered. Gracie took the criss-crossed envelope and put it reverently in the tall boy upstairs where she kept all the treasures, hiding the tiny silver key away from curious fingers. This envelope looked similar, except for the color and the extra words typed in the top left hand corner; MaCausland and Fields, M.I.A.V.I.,Auctioneers; Valuers; and Estate Agents, Milford, Co. Donegal, Ireland.

He folded it roughly, stuffing it into his trouser's pocket, heading upstairs to the bedroom.

He sat on the unmade bed examining the envelope, aware of the weight pressing on his chest. Field's name seemed to spell hope.

It was the new glossy brochure he pretended to order. If that's what it was, he would throw it into the fire when Ellen wasn't looking and that would be the end of that.

MaCausland's name made his damp fingers darken the pale blue paper and the weight on his chest increased.

He wouldn't open it.

He'd go down and throw it into the fire and banish it from his mind. What you don't know won't harm you, his mother always said that. For once he was going to live by her edict.

Ellen was at the kitchen table with her back to him. He opened the range door and threw the letter in, pushing it down into the flames with the poker, in case one inch of it survived.

He closed the range and caught Cathy up in his arms as she rose from the table, swinging her high towards the ceiling, making her squeal with delight. Malachy, alert to his daddy's mood, asked if they could go fishing in the village lough. Of course they could, provided Malachy filled a tin can full of worms from the back yard and Cathy changed into her dungarees and wellies. Jim would get the big fishing rod with the heavy reel from under the stairs, along with the two smaller rods he rigged up for them last summer. He'd pull on his old trousers and wellingtons and away they'd go.

Ellen laughed at the sight of them setting off through the village, shouting at Jim to watch himself on the Bailiff; Jim shouting back that the Bailiff would be found feet up in a bog hole if he came anywhere near him. No English foreigners in a log cabin were going to stop him fishing his own native lough, whether they had the rights to it or not. He unsettled the children somewhat with his talk of stuffing the Bailiff in a bog hole, but a visit to Mona's for thrupenny pokes of sweets put all thoughts of violence clean out of their adventuring little heads.

Thank God Gracie wasn't there when the letter arrived.

And thank God for Teddy, the only one he could talk straight to, under the circumstances. He phoned him after Cox's first visit, when Gracie went back west, asking him to call, he needed to run something by him. He kept his voice at a low whisper in the phone box, knowing Mona's ears would be up like a sprung hare. Teddy shouldn't call on a Saturday, because Gracie would be there. He needed him on a weekday, early in the evening when the bar was quiet, empty even.

He drove down the following afternoon, bemused at the sight of Jim's serious features, his furrowed brow and tight mouth that normally twisted and twitched with divilment and yarning. John Owen was on the high stool, but he bade them 'so long' when Teddy arrived, recognizing when a man should make himself scarce.

Paddy Power stayed captive in his bottle, because they needed clear heads, Jim said and Teddy wondered if there was a blue moon in the sky. Unsmiling, Jim laid out the facts as accurately as possible, recounting his ill fated night with the Coxs' in Milford Hotel.

He sketched in the blanks with likelihoods.

Teddy listened with his legal ears, interrupting only when necessary, seeking clarification without being annoying. All roads led back to the same question; the most pressing burning question; did Jim sign anything? He needed to think hard, and start from the beginning again. Through all the permutations and possibilities, Jim remained certain of two things; Daniel MaCausland was not in the bar that night along with John Fields and himself. And no, he did not sign anything. Nevin Cox was there for a short while but he went home at some stage, leaving Jim and Fields in the bar.

Teddy was relieved.

So Jim had nothing to worry about.

A gentleman's agreement, no matter how many witnessed it, was not legally binding. It would hold no sway with a judge or jury, the very mention of which put the heart sideways in Jim, draining the blood from his face.

"Solicitors have a way of bamboozling people with their tricky legal jargon," Teddy warned, "MaCausland will be advising Cox and telling him what to say."

"I'm well aware of that, Teddy. Thank God you have a good grasp of the law, for I haven't been well with worry these last couple of weeks."

"If you're sure of what you told me, you can relax and get on with your business. Hold your head up man and run the bar with a bit of class. It might be no harm to lay off the whisky for a while," he smiled apologetically.

Jim's face flinched involuntarily and he attempted a joke.

"Christ Teddy, you're starting to sound like Gracie," and despite Teddy's sorry smile, he knew he had to be steady and on guard.

This was a volatile knowledge though.

When Teddy visited three days later, Jim had bolstered himself with nips of Jameson, insisting they drive to Milford because he wanted to clarify something with John Fields, nice and civilized like.

Teddy believed him.

Maybe Jim believed himself.

Until they reached Milford and the young secretary in Fields' office fumbled nervously when she saw Jim approaching, unsteady on his feet. She locked the door as if she expected trouble. His anger erupted uncontrollably, making him curse and roar like a wounded bull. He kicked the locked door violently, creating drama that passers by stood to watch, some with shocked faces, some giggling and egging Jim on. When he found MaCausland's door locked, he wrapped at the window calling him a double dealing hoor, before Teddy managed to haul him back to the car. He knew it wouldn't be long before the Guards came on the scene. Driving home, Jim hung his head morosely when Teddy thumped the steering wheel in frustration, incensed that he made a fool of himself and was ignoring Teddy's advice, only fueling the gossip mongers who were hard at work already.

Halligan relished his job the next morning, marching into the bar bright and early, his long sallow face like a man with a dose of jaundice.

"You stay out of Milford," he snapped, wagging his index finger. "Or there'll be a barring order issued against you."

"No man will tell me where I can or can't go in my own county," Jim resolved. "Not you Halligan or humpy Nevin Cox, blow-ins the pair of yous."

The Sergeant repeated his warning as he exited and Jim struggled to catch his breath, unaware of John Owen's ascent on the high stool until he spoke, looking at Jim with a quizzical expression on his haggard face.

"That sounded like a nice friendly wee visit," he smirked. "The friendly local sheriff doing his rounds I suppose."

"He can kiss my arse John, that's when he's not running up Nevin Cox's. What can I get you?"

He pulled two stouts and sat with John listening to the clock ticking and the youngsters playing on the street, a faint sound of static coming from the kitchen, when Ellen changed stations on the wireless.

Halligan was back the following morning, standing behind Cox at the back door, catching Jim off guard; nodding like a dashboard hound at every syllable Cox uttered. Jim's temper cracked, smashing the crate of empties to the ground, hissing at them to get the fuck out, they were trespassing.

John Owen was on the high stool again, shaking his head wearily, burdened by the weight of experience.

"You need to watch yourself on the buck next door, young Logue." There was no hint of disdain. "He's a Cox by name but a Fox by nature, don't forget that."

Jim's chest tightened, but he responded boldly to John's advice.

"Safe enough John, that string of misery won't get anywhere with me, he's not as smart as he thinks he is."

John seemed unconvinced, his glum mouth moving, saying Nevin was sly like a fox. Him and Ann smiling sweetly, hiding claws that only came out at night.

"Just watch yourself young Logue, that's all I'm going to say about that." There was sadness in his tired old eyes.

Jim moved down the counter and stood at the window watching Cathy skipping on the pavement, praying that John's advice was unwarranted.

Was he bloody seeing things, Jim wondered, when Halligan swooped again the following day, brash and lugubrious, accusing him of harassing his neighbors. He vowed that Jim would be bound over to the peace, only shutting up when he noticed Cathy and Malachy framed in the doorway. He turned towards them, but his watery smile did little to alter the anxious expressions on the youngsters' faces. They crept in past him, asking what was wrong, climbing onto the high stools, watching Halligan make his escape.

"Daddy, why were you outside last night, shouting up at Ann and Nevin's window?" Malachy's question made Jim's scalp contract, a sharp din rang in his ears.

He'd forgotten about that.

It felt like a good idea at the time, an opportunity to let Cox know what he thought of him and his mongrel brother, the great Fr. Manus, gentleman and scholar.

"You were saying bad things Daddy," Cathy's blue eyes were welling up.

"What kind of things Cathy pet? Was I singing?" Jim winked, a mischievous smile flickering at his mouth.

"You were cursing," Malachy offered.

"And shaking your fist in the air," Cathy added.

"Like one of the three stooges," Jim laughed. "Or Barney Cam when he stands on a rusty nail."

"O me soot! Me sucking soot!" Jim mimicked and they squirmed and giggled, sliding off the stools with their crisps and Cokes, asking to go to Mickey Floods to watch cartoons.

They needed their mother Jim realized, regretting his outburst the previous night. God's curse on the bloody Coxs', they were turning him into a raving lunatic.

Friday arrived and the entire house waited for Gracie.

All listening to hear her car on the Tome road, the gear change at the bridge and the revs that annoyed Jim, but not today; he wouldn't give two dams today.

Ellen was in the kitchen boiling eggs for a salad, knowing that Gracie would bring lettuce and new potatoes from the fields over west. The youngsters were whooping at the sight of the Anglia nosing up the last incline into the village, pulling in at the kitchen door. There were groceries to be carried in, along with Paula still half asleep in the front seat, hot and groggy. The chocolates from Aunty Hannah eclipsed the appreciation Gracie hoped the children would show for the fair isle jumpers her mother had knitted them. Jim reassured her they would love them when the cold edge of winter set in. He thought Gracie looked cheerful when Cathy hugged her around the waist and Malachy led her inside by the hand.

Jim yearned to fall at her feet crying and tell her he never wanted to leave her sight again.

Instead he carried her suitcase upstairs, pleased that Ellen had the bedrooms looking so well, sitting on the bed breathing in the smell of fresh linen, watching the floor length lace curtains swaying against the opened sash windows.

The school would reopen in a week, which meant that Gracie was busy with the last minute errands that always occupied her in the final days of August.

New textbooks arrived from Fallons in Dublin, with their colorful cartoon covers. That was the start of it. She would need to go to the Book Company in Letterkenny, for jotters and pencils. Into Toyland, for plasticine or Marla, as she called it. She would visit the Spinning Mill, for sewing needles and threads, including embroidery threads for the transferred doilies and runners the bigger girls worked on during autumn. Their first port of call though, would be the Bank, to deposit the month's takings, along with her Gaeltacht cheque. The cigar box under the bed hadn't quite burgeoned like July's, but profits were respectable, Gracie remarked, rendering Jim's learned off excuses redundant, lifting the worried look from his eyes. Things were back to normal.

They drove to Milford.

Jim at the wheel, promising to be her chauffeur for the week, pointing to the purple hills when she smiled and fixed his shirt collar, tutting that there was blood on it where he cut himself shaving.

She took control in the Bank and Jim waved his hand, telling Mr. Walsh that Gracie was the boss. She wasn't going to make the final payment on the mortgage, that could wait. She had her eye on a new car, a Morris 1100 that she'd seen a picture of in the Sunday Press. She put the money in their deposit account and headed across the street to Mc Mahon's. She'd write a cheque for him if the deal was to her liking, not for a moment expecting him to say that he didn't deal in Morris cars. Her face fell in disappointment, but Jim reminded her that it didn't matter a damn, didn't Roarty Motors in Letterkenny stock them and maybe it was time they dealt with someone else anyway.

She still sparkled as they walked up Milford street, past the Hotel, past Fields' and MaCausland, remembering what Teddy told him.

Hold your head up high.

Jim in his light grey suit, aware that Gracie drew glances in her pink shift and matching hair band. Yes indeed, they were a bit of class.

Gracie

All of October, now halfway into November, Gracie had been feeling strange. She wasn't dragging herself around like the last time she felt unwell. This was more of a paranoia, like a strange sensation that people were staring at her wherever she went, or avoiding her by crossing to the other side of the road on her way to school. When she walked into Mona's, people walked out without looking at her face and they were normally so nosey, standing in the shop long after their shopping was done.

Jim was frequently bad-tempered, unexpectedly so and without provocation. He denied it, saying she was imagining things. When she began to feel that even Ellen was different, quieter, no singing, she feared the black clouds were descending again. Maybe she needed to go and see Dr. Melly; that's what Jim would advise.

Oddly though, there were blissful moments and hours of blessed contentment. Jim would close the bar early on cold November evenings and cozy up on the sofa with Malachy and Cathy. They watched television while she sat opposite on the leatherette car seat, knitting, or writing up school notes in her navy blue ledger. Sometimes they listened to the radio, singing along with the big band sounds, laughing at Jim who hadn't a note in his head. He'd pretend to be offended, begging Cathy to hug him when Gracie scoffed, recommending he stuck to dancing. When pajama time arrived, Paula would climb in behind Gracie, sucking her bottle and listening to Jim reading stories from Arthur Mee, promising one last one before hot water bottles were filled and it was time for bed.

These were the moments when Gracie prayed silently, thanking God for her bounties and asking Mary, her blessed Mother, to protect them as a family and keep them safe from all harm.

Teddy still came down every Saturday with the usual crew and Geraldine would visit Gracie in the kitchen, sipping Babysham and smoking her fancy cigarettes. She made Gracie laugh, saying she couldn't live without a wee drink at the weekend, marveling at Gracie's fondness for orange juice. They never talked about private matters, sparing Gracie the humiliation of confiding that Dr. Melly warned her against alcohol, even though he knew she didn't drink. A tablespoon of Buckfast wine was permitted as a tonic, but only when she felt it was absolutely necessary. She kept a bottle behind the washing board in the scullery, for trying times when her energy sagged and she needed a boost. She did tell Geraldine about the protein drink Jim concocted for her after Paula's birth, made from Guinness and raw eggs and sugar, whipped into a frothy potion that would build her up, he said. They laughed and pulled repulsed faces at the thought of it.

Gracie

Gracie's favorite time to be in the bar was after mass on Sundays, since Jim heeded her advice and got Mandy the Post to play his melodeon, sitting at the big table, creating a jolly atmosphere until the last customers headed home for Sunday dinner. She juggled boiling pots on the range top and a roast in the oven, returning to the bar as Mickey Flood declared his arrival with his favorite mantra, 'There's a Big Flood in town today!' Jim pretended to tip his cap in Mickey's honor and high spirits swelled when Teddy sang Danny Boy. Gracie gave in and sang the Isle of Innisfree, knowing that Jim behind the counter, brisk and businesslike, was beaming with pride.

Master Ferry was in great spirits, having married over the summer and now expecting his first child; another miracle Gracie thought, as the last vestiges of tension disappeared from their classrooms. The big girls were back in Mona's choosing wool for their winter sweaters, though Gracie doubted they would have them for Christmas; they had spent too long on the embroidery this year. O'Mara visited in mid October, inspecting their work, commending the Master's initiative in setting up the libraries.

The new infants had settled in and there was little to complain about.

There was no one to fear or loathe, not now that Fr. Manus was gone. Life was calm and comfortable, without obvious discord or threat of mutiny, and yet; yet something felt wrong and Gracie couldn't put her finger on it.

Maybe she wasn't used to peace. Maybe it was too good to be true.

Why were the dark clouds gathering again when there was no need for them, when everyone was behaving and things were trucking along nicely.

Gracie was losing trust in herself.

The voices were back in her head, low this time, stealthier than before, making it difficult to hear what they said. Little vague murmurs that caught her off guard in the classroom when the Mc. Bride children pressed their faces against the window to spy on her, instead of playing hopscotch with the others. She watched Steven Dore holding court at the school gate, whispering to the older boys, who lent their heads surreptitiously, ending the disclosure abruptly when Malachy stood on the perimeter wanting to join in. When she asked later what Steven was talking about, Malachy didn't know; picking teams for five a side football maybe.

Tom and Sally were coming into the bar often, which was different too, especially on Sundays when they brought Mags and Maise after late mass and Malachy and Cathy took them upstairs to play. Sometimes they sat in the old Hillman, drinking Cokes and wolfing down bags of crisps, spoiling their appetites for dinner.

Tom's face was so serious, the way his gaze followed Jim up and down the counter, scowling like a man who wanted to protest, but was reluctant to take a stand. It was confusing, because Sally seemed like her old self, smiling and placid, listening to the melodeon and scraping the last of her Snowball with her finger.

Since September Gracie formed the habit of going home for lunch. She liked to sit with Paula and Ellen, listening to the news on the radio after she ate, walking through the bar saying hello to Neil Fada on his solitary perch at the counter. Jim's voice reassured her, in steady conversation that always stopped to ask the same question; any news today? It was an inquiry that Ellen had begun to echo. 'Any news today Mrs. Logue?', peering into Gracie's face, looking for something she might have lost there.

Jim was right. Her imagination was getting the better of her.

But why did Mary Bayers take her hand in both of hers when she stood in her kitchen last week, examining the mustard sweater she had finished, appalling Gracie, who withdrew from her sweaty grip, to hand her fresh hanks of wool for her next garment. Was she a silly woman after all, Gracie wondered, driving up Bridget Roarty's lane, determined to banish the creeping anxiety that would bring her down if she allowed it.

Bridget and herself conversed in Gaelic, fast and fluent, until her husband joined them and they switched to English. Was Bridget trying to camouflage concerned eyes behind her thick lenses, blinking repeatedly, expelling some unworthy thought from her mind. Her husband had never come in from the fields before, but here he was now, gaping like a toothless fool, fawning and expectant.

She felt light-headed driving home, telling herself to hold it together and concentrate on something nice, like buying a new dress for the ICA dinner dance or helping the children write their letters to Santa.

It was silly, but Gracie began to overcompensate for some nebulous thing she had done wrong. She smiled, wide beaming smiles, at Ellen, at Mona and Kitty Eddy, even at Ann Cox, who stared hard at her coming down from communion on Sunday morning, disgusted that Gracie looked so happy. It was usually the other way around, Gracie laughed to Jim in the car going home and he said she should pay no attention to the bitch, for the breeding was bad there. His knuckles were white around the steering wheel as he spoke and a feathery breeze touched Gracie's neck making her shiver, watching the fleeting fields, muddy and rusty in the winter sun.

Steven Dore was a well behaved boy, a willing biddable child. Gracie was shocked to see him being chastised sternly by Master Ferry one afternoon in late November when Gracie returned after lunch. At 3 o'clock she lingered in her classroom, wiping around stained ink wells and tidying her already tidy press, knowing the Master would wander in for a chat.

"I got a letter from O'Mara today," he said, walking up to the fireplace.

Gracie closed her press. "Well. What did he have to say?"

"He wanted to give a report on his October inspection and inform us that he was impressed with our work. He had a special word of praise for you Gracie and your meticulous notes; he mentioned the high standard of your Gaelic."

"Good," Gracie laughed. "That'll keep him happy for a long spell I hope." She changed the subject quickly. "I saw you giving out to Steven Dore earlier, what was he at?"

"He was at nothing. Nothing you need to worry about anyway."

Someone blew on her neck and she shivered. "Why would I be worried?"

"No reason. I caught him at lunchtime standing at the boy's toilet with an audience around him, filling their heads with nonsense."

"What was he saying?" The dying fire shifted in the grate.

"It was lies and nonsense." He was being evasive. "I warned him that I would leave welts on him if I heard him at that chat again."

"But what exactly was he saying?" She saw his gaze altering. "Was it something about me?" Her voice sounded shrill.

They stared at each other. Gracie searched for an answer in his close-set hazel eyes, staring back into her pools of blue, seeing the hurt that waited there, about to be unleashed.

"Tell me," she whispered.

"It was something he heard Andy at, a rumour carried home from Cox's, that he shared with his wife in the kitchen."

"About me?"

"About Jim." He sat on the desk nearest the fire, taking a deep worried breath.

Gracie sat at her table, aware that her legs felt weak.

"Nevin Cox is saying he has your place bought. The deal is sealed, only Jim is trying to go back on it. Steven says a lot of the youngsters have the same story from home, his daddy wasn't the only one who heard it.

The last ember fell in the grate. Hail Holy Queen, mother of mercy. Hail our lives, our sweetness and our hope. Sweet Jesus, come to my aid.

"Did you hear me Gracie, is this news to you?"

His voice sounded far away. At that moment she hated him. Him and Steven Dore and every man, woman and child who had listened to that rumour, or passed it on, across barbed wire fences or counter tops or kitchen tables, unable to disguise their venomous delight.

Please Jim tell me it's a lie.

That's what she'd open with, she decided, walking down into the village, hearing them all laughing and guffawing behind their closed doors, safe and secure, preparing evening tea with a new spring in their step.

She would have to trust Ellen, her only confidant now. She'd confront her as soon as she reached the kitchen, but not if Cathy or Malachy were there.

Paula was sitting in her cot drinking sweet tea from her bottle, wanting to be lifted when she saw her mammy, but there was no time for that. The other two were in Mickey Flood's, Ellen said, adding that she would go, now that Mrs. Logue was home. She was taken aback, ambushed by Gracie's question as she undid her apron. No, she had not heard that Nevin next door bought their premises. Then weakening under Gracie's gaze, she had heard a whisper of something, but she didn't believe a word of it. Of course she would stay an extra hour to do the bar. She'd send Jim up to the kitchen on the pretense that Gracie couldn't get the wireless to work.

"What the hell do I know about fixing a wireless?" His frustrated voice echoed up the passage. She didn't mean to speak so abruptly, but his face told her all she needed to know. Standing there in front of her denying, grandstanding, trying to squirm out of it, insisting he had made no deal with Cox.

How did I ever dance with you? Gracie thought. You have fallen so out of step with me.

She would march next door and demand to hear Nevin Cox's side of the story.

"You do that!" Jim shouted." Isn't that what Ann and him would love and the whole place watching you making eejits of us."

What should she do then?

She should keep her mouth shut and carry on as normal. Cox's nasty plan wouldn't work and he'd eventually run out of steam.

She floundered there in the kitchen, listening to him.

Her instinct deserted her. Words and phrases swirled around her head; it's nonsense, lies, nothing for you to worry about, all the parents have it, I made no deal.

Ellen would have to fix evening tea because Gracie felt unwell and needed to go to bed, maybe she was coming down with flu.

By Monday her legs had turned to steel and they balked at carrying her up to school to face Master Ferry's pursed mouth and worried eyes, the sea of eager faces following every move, every inflection of her body.

Steven Dore avoided her gaze when she walked through the Master's room, the gaze that pleaded with him not to tell

Malachy and Cathy what he had told the others. The others looked down at the floor, denying her the chance to silence them also.

While her pupils wrote, she stood behind them at the partition, scolding those whose eyes followed her, shouting, "Turn around Breda McBride, stop gawking and do your sums."

It was enough to turn them all back to their jotters.

While they rhymed off their tables, she stood at the window watching the lough, its windy swells petering into the bank, beside a pale blue rowing boat partially hidden in the bracken. Where was the Lady of the Lough now? Was she mourning the lost souls digested by the gluttonous lake? The innocent ones she failed to rescue? Maybe Gracie should pray to her, like she interceded the Blessed Virgin, or was that a pagan desire?

Unaware that silence had fallen, she'd turn to find the children watching her, waiting for instructions. The plasticine tins were hastily distributed and Gracie resumed her sentinel duty at the window, sure now that the Lady used darkness as her cloak, her black magic armour of deliverance. Time was suddenly dragging, and so was her resolve.

Friday finally arrived, bringing a slew of bachelor pensioners into the bar, hessian shopping bags at their feet, filled with tea and sugar and loaves of fusty bread, compliments of Mona. The Big Flood was in, along with John Owen and Cormac Brown, but Gracie stayed in the kitchen with the youngsters, unable to summon up the shy smiles and warm inquiries, when Mrs.Logue charmed them with her presence.

Jim left the bar from time to time to wonder how they were, winking at the children, his wriggling fingers threatening tickles, while he stole glances at Gracie. She pretended to write in her school ledger, resisting his charms, though she felt his need to show her he was sober.

Teddy came on Saturday evening without Geraldine. Gracie wished he would visit her in the kitchen, giving her a chance to ask him about the rumours. She knew it wouldn't happen, because he was Jim's friend, true and loyal, not hers. She heard strains of The Wild Colonial Boy floating above the garrulous chatter and she mounted the stairs, hoping Jim would close up before twelve. He was muttering to himself when he crept in behind her later. She pretended to be asleep, lying like a corpse, hearing Cox's name being cursed in oscillation with Fields and MaCausland. There was no smell of whiskey though that she could discern, no eiderdown flailing or pillow thumping either.

She rose early on Sunday morning to light the range, before Paula rattled her cot upstairs and Jim pounded the bedroom floor, wanting a cup of sweet tea. She wouldn't fight with Malachy and Cathy if they wanted to stay in their warm beds. She'd drive to Mass herself, knowing the oven would be ready for cooking on her return.

The bar was only half full after Mass, because Cox drew the bigger crowd on Sundays. That's how it always was in the village, although on this Sunday Andy Dore made a surprise appearance, with Sadie and Steven in tow. Gracie wondered why he was breaking with tradition, was there something behind it? She put her best foot forward, carrying Paula down to Jim, who sat her inside the counter, telling her to shake the Big Flood's hand and thank him for her wee brown hen. Gracie watched them, smiling, thinking that maybe her prayers after communion were heard. Andy Dore was watching too, gathering information to bring next door that evening and maybe Cox wouldn't find much comfort in the picture Andy would paint, Gracie hoped.

It was a vain hope.

That kept company with all her other hopes. Waiting in a shivering huddle to be annihilated, on Monday the 30th of November, the darkest day yet.

Jim hadn't opened the bar, Gracie noticed, walking home from school, Malachy and Cathy running in the kitchen door ahead of her. Ellen had homemade soup on the boil, serving it up with thickly buttered slices of pan loaf. The youngsters slurped noisily, hurrying to get out to play before darkness crept in, ignoring Gracie's warning that they would choke. She wondered where Jim was and when Ellen shrugged her shoulders she went down to the bar calling his name, knowing he was around somewhere because their car was on the street.

"I'm down here," his voice echoed.

The storeroom door stood ajar and she pushed it open, walking down the deep cement steps, shuddering in the cold cavernous den, trying to locate Jim with her eyes. He stood against the back wall holding a piece of paper in his right hand, watching Gracie's advance with the pained expression of a guilty prisoner facing the firing squad.

"Jesus Christ Gracie! Jesus Jesus wee Gracie!" He was weeping. "What in the name of God are we going to do!"

She had no reply.

Her heart stopped. She was certain of it. The blood curdled in her veins.

"This was put into my hand an hour ago by Guard Boyle, the retired buck from Buncrana," he held out the paper to Gracie.

"What is it?" she croaked, without reaching to take it.

"It's a summons, a fucking summons," he gulped. "O Gracie, my heart is broken."

He pushed the paper at her again. She took it and moved towards the light of the open door to read out loud.

'An Cuirt Chuarda, The Circuit Court, Ordinary Civil Bill, Form No. 2, Nevin Cox.........Plaintiff,and Jim Logue....... Defendant. You are hereby required within ten days after the service of this Civil Bill upon you to enter or cause to be entered with the County Registrar at his office at Lifford, County Donegal, an appearance to answer the claim of Nevin Cox,'

She paused, aware of Jim's distress, his furious weeping that rose to a crescendo, then fell away to sighs of despair. She attempted to resume reading, but he became hysterical, imploring her to read it silently to herself; he couldn't bear to hear it again. She complied, noticing Daniel MaCausland's signature at the bottom of the page, which confused her. He was their solicitor, but she didn't ask Jim to explain. She read it again and again with the same sentence standing out in high relief.

'AND TAKE NOTICE, THAT UNLESS YOU DO ENTER AN APPEARANCE YOU WILL BE HELD TO HAVE ADMITTED SAID CLAIM......'.

She waited until the weeping abated.

"You'll have to drive to Lifford tomorrow and explain to the County Registrar that this is all a mistake." There was terror in her voice. "You made no deal and you signed nothing; isn't that right Jim?"

"I'm not going to Lifford or anywhere near it."

He was a child, a recalcitrant child, spitting the words at her.

"But you'll have to Jim," her voice broke. "We could lose our home, we could be out on the street."

"Then we'll lose it! Let Cox take it, that's what's going to happen anyway, so what's the use in me going to Lifford!"

He hung his head, moaning in defeat.

Gracie was possessed with the urge to lunge at him and beat him around the head, screaming, BE A MAN! BE A MAN!

She watched the paper floating to the floor, suddenly aware of the stale smell of stout in her nostrils. She turned and walked heavily back up the cement steps, up into the fading November light.

Her hand was on the back door latch, opening onto the street, leading her through the deserted village, up past Mona's, her red winter coat buttoned against the cold. The coat Jim bought her in McGinny's of Letterkenny, after they got married, eight years ago. It was almost as good as the day she first wore it, except for the black astrakhan collar, slightly frayed. And she was heavier now, putting more strain on the black saucer buttons.

The school stood locked and silent in the gloomy dusk. She passed it, knowing Bunbin Hill towered above her and not one bird chirped to break the hush.

Gracie knew exactly where she was going.

She cut off through the damp fields leading to the lough, smiling at the memory of the blue boat, her breath rising and falling quickly in her chest.

The oars would be underneath the boat when she turned it over. She'd row out to the centre of the lake, where the Lady of the Lough would find her and answer her prayers. She could then go home to Jim and the youngsters, imbued with wisdom and love, knowing how they should proceed.

The cruel bracken would not surrender the boat, no matter how hard she looked. She stood, wretched and breathless, listening to the water lapping urgently at her feet; voices murmuring to her from the bare leafless shadows.

Go in. You have to go in, it's the only way she'll find you, the Lady of the Lough, your feet are already wet, wade in, don't look back, that's it, come along, peace is here waiting for you, keep coming, gently gently, row row row your boat, báidín fheilimí, d'imigh go toraigh, merrily merrily merrily merrily, life is but a dream. Mammy. Mammy. Mrs. Logue, Gracie, Gracie, Mrs. Logue! Mrs. Logue!

Jesus Christ Almighty!

Jim

~~~~

The wind was getting up. The noise of the back door flapping roused Jim from his slump in the storeroom. He lifted the summons off the cold cement floor where Gracie had dropped it and climbed the steep steps, weary and defeated. He pulled the back door closed, securing it against the wind, cursing the ancient bolt that bruised his fingers. There was no point in opening the bar on this doleful Monday evening. He'd have to sit looking at John Owen sucking on a miserable bottle of stout or listen to Cormac Brown hacking and spitting and regurgitating whatever putrid thing he had for dinner. Mind you, the thought of having to sit in the kitchen facing Gracie didn't fill him with ease either. The youngsters would be a distraction, so would the television. He doubted he could disguise the weight that sat on his chest, pushing up tears that stung his eyes. He wouldn't turn the light on in the bar either, attracting barflies who would expect Jim to entertain them late into the night, rescuing them from loneliness, and from themselves.

The youngsters were in from the street, he could hear them in the kitchen. Ellen's voice calling up the stairs to Mrs. Logue ; she was about to head home.

"Is she down here?" Ellen's bulk near the counter startled Jim. "It's time I went."

"Gracie's not with me," he tried to sound normal, hoping she couldn't see his eyes in the dim bar. Cathy and Malachy were there too, wondering where mammy was; they wanted french toast for tea like the Big Flood was having.

"Maybe she fell asleep on top of the bed, she does that sometimes." Jim suggested "Run upstairs Malachy and check."

She wasn't there.

The car was outside, so maybe she was over in Kitty Eddy's giving her wool, or in Mona's, buying slices of bacon for tea. Cathy ran across the street before Malachy could volunteer, but was back in jig time without Gracie. The shop was closing and neither Kitty nor Mona had seen her. They sat near the range, consoled by the heat of the kitchen and Jim's breath escaped staccato like, convincing Ellen she should stay a while longer. She'd try her hand at french toast she said, placing Paula on her daddy's knee.

The folded summons felt bulky in Jim's pocket as he hugged the child to him, swallowing back the lump in his throat that was threatening to choke him.

Where the hell was Gracie when he needed her and the bloody wind getting up, as well as the rain. If she had stayed at home all summer instead of running over to that fucking Gaeltacht, we wouldn't be in this mess now. If she was trying to annoy him she was doing a good job of it. Ellen was in and out of the scullery with dishes, when she shouted to Jim that someone was banging on the back door,would he go and see who it was. He rose, irritated that Paula was upset when he placed her back in her playpen, sure that Cormac

Brown was an unmannerly cur, out on such a night looking for drink. He would tell him to clear off up to Cox's because that's where he'd be drinking from now on, himself and all the other latchico's.

His anger dissolved when he heard Andy Dore's voice, low and urgent, telling Jim to open up quickly, he needed to see him. The bolt felt stiff at first, then slammed back mercifully to reveal Andy and Steven, standing in their black donkey jackets, pale and damp, pushing past Jim into the passageway leading to the bar.

"We have a serious situation on our hands Jim," Andy's face was ghostly in the dim passage. Steven watched Jim from under his eyes, fearful and expectant.

"We came on Mrs. Logue down at the lough Jim, it was a bad handling." Andy sounded crushed.

"O holy Jesus!" Jim howled. "Gracie's dead isn't she!"

Steven shook his head violently, grabbing Jim's arm as he sank to the floor, leading him to a seat inside the bar door, with Andy supporting him on the other side.

"It was the luck of God we came on her, a few more minutes and she was a goner," he stared at Jim making him understand. Jim's breath at last came rushing up his throat and he gasped in the belief that Gracie was alive, nodding at Andy as he spoke.

"We couldn't get her into the boat without it capsizing. I grabbed her by the shoulders and held on to her with all my might, praying that the weight of her coat wouldn't beat me. Steven rowed hard and we were nearly at the bank when the coat came off her, but the water was shallow and we managed to heave her to safety."

"What in the name of Jesus was she doing?" Jim shook his head in disbelief.

"She kept repeating something about the Lady of the Lough who was supposed to help people. She was confused, but she was able to walk with Steven and me until we got her into the trailer. I didn't want to drive the tractor over here to the village for fear of nosey parkers, so I brought her back to our house. Sally's looking after her. She might need to go to hospital, you'll see what you think yourself." Andy touched Jim's arm and Steven moved towards the door saying he would wait in the tractor.

"We'll go home Jim, come over when you're ready." Andy closed the back door quietly.

Now it was Jim's turn to trust Ellen, calling her down to the bar. She stood listening to him stoic and calm, ignoring his tear stained face, saving his pride, telling him she needed to put things in a bag for Gracie to take with him to Dores. She would stay the night and put the wanes to bed and he shouldn't worry about a thing, only bring Mrs. Logue home safe and sound.

He drove over the Tome road, imploring God's help between sobs and curses; cursing Nevin Cox for all the bastards under the sun and Ann and Manus and Fields and MaCausland, even Gracie for making a spectacle of herself and most of all himself and wishing to God he was six feet under.

When Sadie opened the door she led him to the fireplace where Gracie was dozing in a comfortable armchair, wrapped in a heavy woolen blanket, her hair still damp, wearing clothes that belonged to Sadie. He was sobbing, kneeling beside her, speaking coaxingly, asking her to open her eyes, he was there and everything was all right. She awoke startled and confused, overwhelmed to see Jim at her side. She sobbed with him, swearing she didn't mean to walk into the lough to harm herself. She only wanted to meet the Lady of the Lough and take advice from her. Steven had often talked about her helping people and she frightened Jim with the glazed look in her eyes. Sadie laughed lightly, saying the Lady of the Lough took a night off and Steven was filling in for her. They all laughed at this, even Gracie, whose cheeks flushed with color as she touched Jim's face, wiping a tear that sat silver and iridescent in the firelight.

"What we all need is a hot one," Andy winked, "Good and strong Sadie."

Sadie nodded, moving to lift the boiling kettle off the crook above the fire.

The rain pelted down on the corrugated roof and the wind howled in the chimney. They sipped their sweet toddys, sheltered and safe. Quiet conversation disguised the lingering distress that tragedy had bared her teeth, rash and ruthless, but they had driven her back, for now.

The mention of hospital alarmed Gracie and seemed to elicit a clarity in her, convincing Jim to take her home and send for Dr. Melly in the morning. Andy and Sadie agreed that a week in bed would leave her as good as new.

The rain eased as they helped Gracie into the car and Jim stood with Andy for a minute, aware of the momentum, unable to find the words he needed to express his gratitude, his relief. He wanted to ask him to be discreet, but that might insult this man who had saved his life and Gracie's and the youngsters. Andy read his mind.

"This won't go outside our four walls Jim, I'll make sure of that," he patted Jim's arm affectionately and turned towards the house. Remembering something, he asked, "What will I do with the wet clothes?"

"Do whatever the fuck you like with them Andy", Jim deferred, "I hope I never see them again."

"The coat might be lying at the mouth of the lough, me and Steven will have a look tomorrow."

"Please God it's buried deep in the water and if not you make sure to put it there."

He reached for Andy's hand then, giving it a manly shake, promising to have Sadie's clothes returned to her in a few days.

The children were asleep, unaware of the foiled tragedy that would not invade their dreams or wake them in the night. Ellen was sitting at the range. She sprang to her feet when Gracie appeared, clucking around, telling her there were two hot water bottles in her bed and an extra eiderdown, she needed to get the heat back into her. There was no scolding or judgement, just approval that Jim had brought her home, instead of taking her to hospital.

"I'll go down home now Jim," she announced, after settling Gracie in bed, "I'll be up early in the morning to get Malachy and Cathy ready for school."

As hard as he tried, Jim couldn't stop weeping. Gracie begged him to stop, rubbing his arms that encircled her in the bed, desperately needing to feel her beside him, to melt into her and never let her go. If only the night would last forever, wrapped warm and cozy, listening to the stubborn rain and angry wind, safe and protected in the blessed eternal darkness.

But time won't stop for any man, Jim knew, when reality woke him the following morning.

Cathy was refusing to go to school without her mammy. She stood on the landing crying and defiant, ignoring Ellen's command to come downstairs and eat her breakfast.

"Let her come in to me, it's alright Ellen," Gracie's voice beside Jim was surprisingly clear.

She sat up explaining to the child that she had the flu, which meant she needed to stay in bed for a few days to get all mended again. Jim lay listening to her voice soothing Cathy, promising that the big girls from the master's room would spoil her for the week, with songs and stories and drawing all day long. Eventually she relented and took Malachy's hand, trusting Gracie's words, knowing she would be the bravest girl in the class. Malachy handed Master Ferry the note informing him of his mother's illness, but no substitute was required; she'd be back in her classroom the following Monday.

"I'll drive down to Dr. Melly and ask him to call up to see you," Jim sat on the edge of the bed unable to look at Gracie.

"Wait and I'll go with you," she pushed the eiderdown away. "I'm well able to go to the dispensary. The whole place will be talking if they see his car at the house."

He turned to look at Gracie, her cheeks still flushed pink, her eyes bluer than he had ever seen them. She was shiny and new, he thought, lit up from inside with a mysterious wisdom gleaned from the mists of a redemptive lake and Jim wanted to listen to every word she said.

Teddy knew the law, she counseled. He was their trump card. He had seen summonses before and would know what their next move should be. They needed a new solicitor, now that MaCausland had gone rogue on them and was firmly in Cox's camp. She wasn't going to waste time convalescing, there were better things to do. She would not lie in bed weak and surrendered.

"We can't crumble now Jim," she said. "The only way we'll get through this is to fight it together."

"I suppose you're right, Gracie pet, but what if we lose. What then?" he couldn't help sounding doubtful.

"Christmas is around the corner. We need to think about the youngsters. We'll get through the coming weeks as normal as possible and do whatever Teddy recommends."

"Will I open the bar?" he asked. Part of him hoped she'd say no.

"It's our bar. Open it and run it like you always do, because the locals are waiting and watching, so don't play into their hands, or Cox's."

The mention of Cox made his fists clench, but he needed to keep a cool head and his powder dry, for the long battle that lay ahead.

"Another thing Jim, and don't get mad at me; stay off the whiskey. Just take the odd bottle of beer to pass yourself with the men and don't be telling them our business."

Her tone held no trace of blame or resentment, only an inference that they were in cahoots now, so he nodded, hoping her courage was contagious.

By Friday they had an appointment with Jonathan Fray & Co., the best firm of solicitors in Letterkenny, according to Teddy. They sat together in the waiting room, Gracie and himself, silent and awkward; Jim privately wishing she hadn't insisted on coming.

Mr. Fray cut a tall imposing figure. Jim liked him immediately, as he welcomed them into his office with robust handshakes. They drank in his lofty voice and serious eyes, while he inspected the summons with the cursory perusal of a decorated general who had won many battles.

They had until Wednesday to enter their Appearance and Defence, but the time frame was loose he said. They needed time, Jim and himself, to work out their game plan.

On Monday he would sit down with Jim and discuss strategy, but first he must hear the details of what exactly transpired between Nevin Cox and Jim, before he could extrapolate for the rebuttal. There was no necessity for Mrs. Logue to be present for this and although Gracie looked crestfallen Jim could have kissed him. He didn't want her sitting there when he'd stumble through his account of that doomed day in July, trying to relive the torturous haze of events which he'd dissected a million times and the facts never added up.

Two and two didn't make four.

It felt good in Fray's office on Monday afternoon, having an ally, someone who was living vicariously with him, walking every step of that July day in tandem, seeing clearly through the mist that had thwarted Jim for months, bringing in the light.

MaCausland was taking the case on behalf of the Plaintiff, Nevin Cox. He lodged his intent with the Registrar's Office, along with his Indorsement of Claim.

Did Jim want to hear what Nevin Cox was claiming? Probably not. He had to hear it anyway, before they could prepare their defence.

Besieged by the words Mr. Fray read out, Jim looked at the floor, holding himself tight inside, with every allegation coming at him in Cox's voice, mocking and evil.

Jim had agreed verbally on the second last day of July, to sell his premises and dwelling house to Nevin Cox and on the last day of July he agreed in writing to do so, for the sum of £1900. The sale was to be completed on the 30th day of October 1964. Jim snorted incredulity, twisting his face in exasperation, but Fray raised his right hand in dissuasion, indicating that it was inappropriate to protest, until he read out the entire claim. Mr. Logue would have to perform the said agreement and pay damages for not having done so to date. He would also pay Mr. Cox's costs. Now Jim could vent and provide Mr. Fray with the details that would constitute his defense.

"As God is my judge, I did not agree to sell my home or bar to Nevin Cox. Not in one million years." The ferocity of Jim's tone left the solicitor unaffected.

"Why the hell would I sell it for a measly profit of £100, when it's worth far more on the open market?"

"Indeed; then let that be the first point in our defense. We'll make an abject denial that such an agreement ever took place. Now, what about his claim that you signed a note or memorandum in the presence of Mr. Cox's agent, that is, Mr. Daniel MaCausland?"

"If I signed anything, and it's a big if, it would have happened in the bar that night and I know for certain that MaCausland wasn't there," Jim was warming up.

"You stated that John Fields, the Estate Agent, was the only man in the bar with you on the night in question, apart from Cox, who stood with you for five minutes without a drink and then left. Are you sticking with that ?" Fray's tone suggested that Jim should concur.

"One hundred percent. I might have had a few drinks in me, but I wasn't blind drunk," Jim sounded offended. "Agent my arse! Why he's using that title I don't know. What I do know is, John Fields was the only man in the bar with me that night."

Mr. Fray's amused smile curled at his lips and he nodded his belief that Jim knew his facts. They would refute the presence of MaCausland therefore, and the signing of any memorandum or document of any description.

"Now Jim, there is one other salient point to be included in our defense. You were drunk on the night in question and quite incapable of making any transaction with Cox, or anyone else for that matter."

"Do we have to put that in?" Jim was wary. "A man does have his pride, you know."

"It's vital that we use it, Jim. It's our best line of defense, we'd be fools not to. This case will be tried by a judge and we do know that most men, even judges, are partial to a drink. And most men would not appreciate being hoodwinked when they're inebriated, wouldn't you agree!"

Jim agreed reluctantly, hoping Gracie's eyes would never read that sentence or hear it being read out in court. He was already thinking up excuses to keep her at home on the day of the case.

By the end of the week their Defense was typed and signed by Johnathan Fray, but he had no intention of supplying it to the County Registrar or Nevin Cox just yet. There was no rush, he said, leaving them to stew was always his policy. The ten day rule was nebulous. MaCausland was cracking the whip and their vague reluctance and mild subordination would frustrate the hell out of him.

Jim drove home, a degree of optimism peppering his thoughts for the first time in weeks. He had space to think about the youngsters and their letters to Santa and ordering a goose for Christmas.

He couldn't look too far ahead though, just in case.

Still, Nevin Cox wasn't going to have it all his way. Jim had a new solicitor now and he would give MaCausland a run for his money, the fucking windbag. Fray wouldn't be long knocking the shit out of him. He had Teddy and Gracie standing firmly in his corner, giving him strength and purpose.

But what if Cox had proof that he signed something!

The memory of the ink-stained counter ambushed him, driving near the village lough.

He saw Gracie in her red coat, supplicating the Lady of the Lough, desperate and forlorn, before sinking beneath the clawing slimy reeds.

Did she know all was lost?

Just a matter of time before they stood on the village street, a pilgrim family, banished like Lot and his wife, with no reason to look back. His heart thumped against his ribs and he needed a drink, a good stiff one. Teddy would join him later for a few and he'd fill him in on proceedings with Mr. Fray.

He had to remember the good things. Gracie was alive and well. The Dores and Ellen were the only ones who knew what happened at the lough and they were allies now, he was certain. Everything would work out. He had to believe that. Keep the flag flying, as Teddy said. Remember Gracie's war cry: Don't crumble now!

He gripped the steering wheel tighter when the school came into view. No one, especially that slee'cy bastard Cox, was going to take their home from them. They would prevail.

Maybe Gracie's courage was contagious.

Nevin

It was a new year and Jim Logue was still acting the blackguard.

Nevin tried being reasonable, instructing MaCausland to give him a chance; sending solicitors letters, three to be precise, instead of hitting him with a summons immediately. His complete disregard for the gesture left them no option but to issue a warrant for the summons.

Sergeant Halligan was bursting to serve the boyo, but he couldn't get involved in a civil case. It was the only time he wished he was a civilian, he said, making Nevin laugh, while ensuring him his retired colleague from Buncrana would serve the bold Logue, no problem.

A fortnight passed before Johnathan Fray, Logue's solicitor, acknowledged it, sending in their Entry of Appearance on the 16th of December, as casual as you like. It dashed Nevin's hopes that Logue wouldn't reply to the summons and judgement would be granted to him without the hassle of a court case.

Surely when he heard their Endorsement of Claim, Jim Logue must have known he was cornered. Yer wan was as thick as the hosel of a hatchet though. She probably forced Fray to take the case, believing what she wanted, despite the truth staring her in the face.

The whole countryside knew the facts now. Ann and himself made sure of that.

Peter McBride couldn't have put it any better when he said, there was no need for two pubs in the village, it divided the community. Hughie agreed, adding that they did fine before Logue came along and they'd do better after he was gone. A unanimous murmur of agreement trickled around the counter, except for John Owen, who kept staring at his reflection behind the counter as if he expected to see someone different.

Andy Dore miscalculated badly, saying poor Logue had a young family and Christmas would be hard, knowing they were losing their home.

"He should have thought of that before he started bumming about the great premises he had and torturing Nevin to buy it." Ann rounded. "Sure he had Fr. Manus' head deafened about his great fortune and anyone else silly enough to listen to him."

"Funny I never heard him talking like that," John Owen said, "Did you Andy?"

When Andy shook his head Ann was incensed.

"I suppose you don't remember Mrs. Logue at your door either, Andy, soaked to the bone, out looking for knitters a few weeks before Christmas!" she challenged.

A blue vein on Andy's left temple throbbed and he growled that it was the first he heard of it.

"And Logue had to drive over to take her home. There's not much that goes amiss with me Andy," she winked at the McBrides.

"Were you in the lookout tower again?" John's question stung.

"As a matter of fact John, I was on my way to bed when I saw the car pulling up. I mean what kind of a headcase goes out on such a night, looking for skivvies to make more money for her, does she not know when she has enough!"

She stomped towards the kitchen, her arse high and proud and Nevin smiled, knowing John would wait a long time for his one for the road. Andy and himself were put firmly in their place. Since then they kept their gobs closed, especially Andy, whose visits were steadily declining. Did he know he was backing the wrong horse?

The Logue youngsters didn't need Andy's concern, Nevin noted on Christmas morning, when Malachy rode his shiny new bicycle up and down the village street, tinkling the silver bell on the handlebars. Cathy ran behind him, in a new red coat with fur cuffs and a matching fur hat, like a Russian princess. Ann would see them from the landing, but he'd remind her that their reign was almost over and they might as well live it up while they could. They were spoiled brats, looking down on the other youngsters, because their mother was a teacher.

Didn't the Cathy one tell wee Breda McBride that she owned the school and her mammy could slap Breda as much as she wanted to!

The Malachy fella was kicking his football dangerously close to their kitchen window of late. Once, he rattled the pane, frightening Ann that much, she ran out threatening to take the ball off him. He stood, defiant, sneering horribly at her, convincing Ann that yer wan was putting him up to it.

Nevin doubted that, but he changed his mind the following Sunday.

They were late going into chapel because Ann couldn't find her gloves and they walked quickly up the aisle to find the entire Logue clan sitting in their pew, refusing to budge; all of them focused on the altar as if wearing blinkers. Ann and himself had to retreat to the pew behind them flustered and perplexed. Poor Ann's shoulders twitched for the entire Mass, traumatised by the two older brats, who kept looking back at her, sticking out their tongues and squinting their eyes. She was in a daze going up to communion, but she still managed to smile at them as she passed the seat, even though yer wan refused to look up.

Logue himself didn't seem comfortable with her in charge of strategy, but he only had himself to blame.

The pretense at civility was gone.

Replaced by dirty looks and muttered insults under breaths. The volume rose in outrageous rants from Jim on the street, late at night, when his customers went home. There were sudden bangs of Malachy's football on their windows, along with the taunting prolonged ringing of his bicycle bell.

Danny Gallagher's take on it was accurate; where a wild duck lays her eggs, a wild duck comes out. Nevin was foolish to have been so kind to the Logue brats, but he was certain of one thing; they would never sit in his Zephyr again.

The Logues were playing a dirty game; continuing to inhabit Cox's pew every Sunday, no matter how early Nevin and Ann went up the aisle. They held their dignity though, genuflecting a few seats behind, bowing their heads to avoid the gleeful smirks aimed at them for most of the mass. It was unseemly behavior, but as Ann said; what would you expect from a cow but a kick.

On the last Saturday in January, Nevin couldn't believe his eyes, when Jim Logue drove a brand new car into the village, with yer wan sitting beside him smiling back to her two ears. She was wearing the new red coat she got for Christmas that matched Cathy's, with fur cuffs and collar, alighting from the motor, pretending she was Elizabeth Taylor. Gregory Peck got out in his belted crombie and the two of them stood examining the car, hoping the whole village was watching the performance. Nevin couldn't figure out what model it was from the landing window, but he could see it was dark blue with a deep silver grill in the front. It sloped at the back, with a huge rear window. Ann stood beside him, reading aloud the registration plate, like a great victory had been scored against them; CIH 714.

He ran downstairs and dialed the operator to put him through to MaCausland's of Milford. He phoned Manus too and both men were of a similar opinion.

It was bravado, plain and simple.

Mr. and Mrs. Logue should be saving every penny they could, because the cost of the court case would cripple them. Ann recovered her equilibrium when she heard that new cars can be impounded by the courts and new winter coats come in handy when you're standing on the street, wondering which road to take out of the village.

The new Morris 1100 was purchased in Roarty's Motors, according to Andy Dore, who still couldn't hold his water, on the odd occasion he did make an appearance.

"She's a lovely looking car, the latest model I believe," he said, settling himself on the high stool at his favourite end of the counter.

"She's a tidy motor," John Owen agreed. "Not a big heap of tin like the Ford machines."

Nevin didn't rise to the bait, but he couldn't control Ann.

"He must have more money than sense," she spat. "A born show off with nothing behind it." Peter and Hughie McBride were snorting their agreement, when John spoke again.

"Aye, it's hard to know what's behind a lot of things," he mused. "It takes a cute man to know that, or one who can see right through you."

He spoke to his own reflection in the mirror, ignoring Ann's livid countenance and the sarcasm of the McBride brothers, who reckoned John thought he was a kind of genius.

He certainly was more surly of late, Nevin thought, especially after drinking whiskey. His desire to be openly hostile was stymied by his last will and testament and he knew it. He relied on Ann's tolerance and the warm dinners she plonked before him most days, while he grumbled and spluttered at the counter, testing her kindness. The only thing John paid for was his drink, because Nevin wasn't about to set that precedent; doling out free drinks to every man who signed the dotted line. Old age settled heavily on John's shoulders, making his disgruntlement bearable.

Andy Dore was a different kettle of fish. His lips weren't as loose now, nor his patronage as frequent. Still, the term turncoat seemed harsh to Nevin, when Ann hurled it at him from the landing window, watching him heading into Logues. She missed the gossip he carried from next door, despising his new discretion. He refused to be drawn on the Logue state of play, no matter how charming or coquettish Ann was around him.

Barney Cam became the unlikely spy in the camp, regurgitating the odd tidbit that kept them in the know.

Tom Logue went clean off his head, when he discovered what Jim had done with his premises. Barney saw them fighting in the lower field and Sally running down the lane to separate them, with the aule mother limping after her, crying and scowling.

Mickey Flood got a contact in America for Mrs. Logue, who wanted her to send jumpers to New York for big money.

The Anglia Logue traded in, was bought by a fella up in Malin Head. He prattled away, making sense sometimes and sometimes making things up to ingratiate himself with Ann.

"It's hard to know if I should believe a word out of Barney Cam's mouth," she said, switching off the light before climbing into bed.

"Why, what's he saying now?"

"He said Mrs. Logue was seen tramping about the fields down at the lough, a few weeks before Christmas. It doesn't make sense," she doubted.

"That was the night you saw her getting out of the car, wearing Sadie Dore's coat and Logue's face was like thunder, do you remember?"

"No. That was the night she walked over to Dores looking for knitters. The worst night of the year and she decided to walk."

"Maybe she thought the walk would do her good," Nevin sniggered.

"Lord, you couldn't be up to her." Ann sniggered too. "But, do you know what I was thinking?" She didn't wait for an answer. "I was thinking she has her eye on a sight down near the lough. It's a lovely spot for a house. Joe and Mona own those fields. She'll be trying to buy one of them."

"Nice and near the school," Nevin suggested. "She'll build a log cabin like the Cartridges."

"Jesus!" Ann stiffened. "I'll talk to Mona tomorrow. That bitch is not getting one of those sites. She needs to clear out and take her brood with her so she does."

"Barney Cam is as thick as poundies," Nevin placated. "That was a yarn Neil Fada filled his head with, taking a hand at him. There will be all kinds of rumors circulating over the next few months and you'll have to take them in your stride."

She fell into a calm sleep, leaving Nevin wide awake, unsettled by Barney's talk, that signified nothing of course, but left him feeling uneasy all the same.

Andy Dore owned land near the lough too.

Maybe he'd already sold Logue a site. It would account for his new warryness and circumspection. His mouth that was once constantly flapping, was now as tight as a hen's arse. Only the greasing of a palm could explain such a transformation. He dreaded the idea of Logue and yer wan building a home in such a beautiful setting, eclipsing Ann's dream entirely. He wished Manus was there to throw light on the situation.

Logue's solicitors, Fray & Co., were making Nevin anxious too.

They sent in their Entry of Appearance on December the 16th, insultingly late and not another word was received since.

January moved on. February flew into March. And March brought snow and sleet and bitterly cold winds. Roads were impassable, putting Manus' plan to travel down from Enniskillen on hold.

Nevin stood in the empty pub incensed.

Fray still hadn't entered Logue's Defense with the Court Registrar and Nevin's fingers were itching to lift the receiver and ring Daniel's office again, only it would feel like badgering. He rang him that morning and his frustration was palpable.

"It's impossible for me to build a case until I see the contents of Fray's Defense document. I will ring you the instant I hear their Defense is entered." He slammed down the phone.

Snow lay deep on the street. Nevin stood behind the silent counter like a lovesick schoolgirl, willing the phone to ring. He listened to his heart beating, without a sinner to comfort or distract him.

Ann

Ann had rarely seen Nevin so nonplussed.

He usually took things in his stride, but this business with Logue had unhinged him slightly. It was March the 18th and Logue's solicitor still hadn't entered their Defense with the court. She watched Nevin stalking the pub, waiting for MaCausland to ring with good news.

The bad weather had hampered Manus' arrival, but like all things it passed and he landed on Monday, just after the phone call from Milford to say Logue's Defense had been delivered and Daniel could begin building their case.

Manus had been sanguine all along, reassuring Nevin that Logue's Defense would eventually be entered, even joking that lies took longer to concoct than truth. Fray probably hadn't a blade of hair left, trying to contrive a credible rejoinder for Logue.

Nevin and himself drove to Milford early Tuesday morning, to hear the details. Ann waited like a hen on a hot griddle for their return. When they arrived back Manus said Logue's rebuttal was simply a litany of lies, as expected.

Fray outlined six points in Jim Logue's Defense.

Whilst Ann understood some of them, she struggled with the finer details, cloaked in legal jargon. Obviously he denied agreeing to sell his premises and dwelling house to Nevin.

He denied signing any note or memorandum agreeing to sell. There was something about a statue of fraud, which Manus tried to explain to her without success.

"It's not a statue!" he said. It's a statute."

Ann told him to stop, he was giving her a headache.

Logue claimed also, that Daniel MaCausland was not Nevin's agent, nor was he present in Logue's bar on the night in question.

What did 'agent' mean, Ann wondered, but Manus was already reading point number five, which took her aback with the baldness of it.

At the time of making the alleged agreement, Jim Logue was drunk and incapable of making such a decision. Furthermore, Nevin and his agent knew he was drunk.

This point concerned Ann, but she made herself find the stupidity in it.

"Sure that'll go against him in court, won't it? He's going to disgrace himself saying he was drunk."

"It's a lie," Nevin answered. "He had a few drinks like the rest of us, but he knew exactly what he was doing."

"Precisely," Manus added. "It will be his word against many. John Fields will testify that Jim Logue was practically sober when he witnessed him singing the document of sale."

"Is John Fields the agent they keep talking about then?" Ann was far from satisfied.

"You could say that." Manus looked at Nevin as he spoke. "Daniel was the agent who drew up the Bill of Sale, however, it was Fields who witnessed Logue signing it."

Ann knew little about the law, except what had been demonstrated to her over the years, which was: unless a man signed the dotted line you had no claim to his house or farm or anything he possessed. She assumed a solicitor was always present when this occurred, but she didn't question Nevin or Manus about it.

They were confident that all the i's were dotted, all the t's crossed.

The truth was in the pudding, Manus said, in the signed memorandum they would produce in court on the day of the trial, proving Jim Logue a liar. The County Registrar would want all evidence handed in before the trial, but this was their big gun, staying dry until the courthouse beckoned.

John Fields was their prize witness, who would swear in court that Logue commissioned advertisements and brochures from him, proving his intention to sell.

He rang Nevin shortly after, and Ann stood on the stairs listening; shocked at the severity of Nevin's tone. He drove to Milford in the afternoon, saying he needed to see Fields, to put him straight on a few things.

Manus remained behind, keeping Ann company in the kitchen, both waiting to hear the pub door dinging, which it hadn't done since St Patrick's Day. Only the foolhardy like John Owen and Barney Cam had braved the blizzards, risking life and limb for the comfort of the high stool and human company. She wondered why Manus stayed behind. He must have read her mind, confiding that Nevin wished him to stay in the background, until the legal matters were resolved.

Gracie Logue hadn't missed a day off school since Christmas, which surprised Ann.

She thought this business would have her back in the big house, but disappointingly, not a bit of it. She did catch a bad cold the night she went rambling over to Dores in gale force winds and battering rain, confining her to bed for a week. Since then she hadn't flinched. A few of the big girls from the Master's room filled in for her, but none of the parents complained, not even the McBrides. Peter said they would only be wasting their time, when she had the full backing of Ferry and Monsignor McLaughlin.

Gracie Logue had the enemy firmly in her sight now and would fight to the death to defend her territory.

All attempts at civility were gone.

Instead, she was employing guerrilla tactics and using her children to upset Ann, setting her teeth on edge.

Malachy's football hit the kitchen window randomly and with such force, Ann jumped out of her skin. Sitting by the window was no longer an option, for fear of glass smashing into her face. It was impossible to prepare for the shock of it, impossible to catch him in the act. When she did manage to chastise him, he faced her down with brazen defiance, unhinging her so badly that Nevin forbade her to confront the brat again.

"Ignore him," he said. "If he breaks the window he'll pay dearly for it."

The Cathy one was showing her true colors too, dissolving Nevin's belief that she was a sweet wee thing. Sweet as a gooseberry, Ann harrumphed, when she stood on the footpath like a tinker's wane, hand on hip, pulling the most outrageous faces at Nevin and herself as they tried to get on with their day. She could sing too, the little bitch, breaking into a loud rendition of Secondhand Rose over in Mona's when Ann walked in, making her face burn with humiliation in front of Mona and Kitty Eddie. Secondhand Rose, sang to screeching pitch, over and over, because Ann once confided in Gracie Logue that her green pleated skirt was given to her by Nora, before she left the village.

It was downright sinful for Jim and Gracie Logue, using their children like weapons during the week, and running up the aisle on Sundays, like they were the bloody Holy Family.

The Sunday Nevin and herself had to stand like gombeens in the packed chapel, unable to get into their pew, was mortifying. Everyone watched to see how they would react, like two birds cast from their nest by a family of cuckoos. They retreated to the pew behind, with all the dignity they could muster, sure that the congregation were scandalized by what they saw.

Nothing Nevin said that Sunday could cool her burning rage. Only Manus found the right words.

"Cuckoos are migrating birds Ann," he chuckled, "and these particular cuckoos will soon be on their way, back to the dirt they crawled out of in the first place."

God! He had a way with him.

A way of centering her, so she could gather her wits about her once more. When he was with them everything fell into place. He soothed and predicted so sagely, heralding good news and fortune. He even taught Ann a new song, one to counteract Cathy's spiteful ditty.

Ann couldn't sing, but she did her best at the clothesline and on the street; walking past Logue's with Manus by her side, surveying the premises while they sang. It was a Jim Reeves song which Manus cleverly adapted to suit the occasion and they chimed together, 'You'll Have to Go.' They practically roared, making it impossible for yer wan not to hear the message, loud and clear.

'You can tell your friends there with you, YOU'LL HAVE TO GO!' Two can play this game Ann thought.

It wasn't a game though.

It was all out war, and the villagers were choosing their trenches wisely. All except the usual dum dums, like Cormac Brown and Johnny O'Donnell who made a habit of shooting themselves in the feet.

Mickey Flood was different. Ann wished he had patronized their pub, but there was no accounting for taste, and then again, water will find its own level.

John Owen was conflicted about the whole business.

Ann found his struggle amusing. It touched her how he longed to defect to Logue's trench, but rations were scarce there and the smell of defeat ominous. She observed his resentment of Nevin and herself with pleasure, delighted his baser needs were proving victorious. He showed no gratitude for the warm dinners and mugs of sweet tea. Still, he ate and drank with relish, ever aware that his last will and testament bound him to them for his remaining years on earth. Poor John, she almost felt sorry for him.

Andy Dore was a different matter; a turncoat, plain and simple, who no longer darkened their door.

"The bloody cheek of him!" Ann said, one morning at breakfast, when it dawned on her that he was now a firm fixture at the counter next door.

"Who the hell does he think he is?" "It's not long since he was piddling on my roses and tripping home with his galluses trailing behind him on the road."

"He's had his head turned," Manus mused, "which is unfortunate. He was a tremendous source of gossip from next door."

"Every detail he carried to us!" Ann mourned.

"He's a changed man of late," Nevin added.

"You sensed the change after that night in late November, didn't you Ann, when Gracie Logue called to Andy's home?"

"Indeed I did Manus. She wanted to recruit Sadie into the knitting circle and picked the worst night she could to go out in. Logue had to drive over to Dores and take her home. I watched them from the landing window and he did not look happy helping her into the house."

"But why would Andy be secretive about that? It's hardly a crime, being in the knitting circle." Manus was flummoxed.

"She was spotted down at the lough too," Nevin said. "Andy has fields down there and we think she's looking for a site off him."

"Ah! Making contingency plans," Manus' face brightened. "They'll be needing a new home soon, this is a good sign."

"She'll be building a beautiful log cabin on the nicest spot in the village, how is that a good sign? The bitch is full of badness so she is!" Ann almost cried.

"Now Ann, we don't know that for sure."

"But Nevin, you said that's what she was doing."

"It was only a thought." Nevin kept calm. "Joe and Mona have sites at the lough, but she didn't approach them. Joe told me so, we're probably on the wrong track."

"Then why did Andy stop coming in to us? I'll tell you why. Because he's after selling yer wan a site and he can't face us."

There was no appeasing her.

She despised Andy Dore and she loathed Gracie Logue, her nemesis, who was hell bent on spoiling her happiness. Wasn't it a terrible pity she didn't fall head first into the lough and sink without a trace.

Ann was mortified that her new sleuth was Barney Cam, stammering at her like an imbecile. She suffered him with enough gladness to hide her repulsion, watching his spittled lips moving when she questioned him about next door. He knew where they had purchased their fancy Christmas coats, but did he know who the hell they thought they were. No he didn't, only laughing at Ann like a silly gander, when she suggested the Royal Family. He knew the Morris 1100 was bought in Roarty's of Letterkenny, but did he know who Jim Logue was trying to impress. No, he didn't know that either. Only staring and slavering, as he watched Ann losing patience with him and getting redder and redder around the gills. He was unreliable, even when his story seemed plausible. John Owen's quips didn't help, only causing him to forget what he was going to say, especially the spicy details Ann hankered after.

She couldn't betray her contempt for Barney. Another general election was brewing and she needed him to carry the mountain of Blaney posters outside and plaster them on every inch of wall and gable around the village.

Manus showed no interest in local politics, preferring to sit at the range reading books about famous people, like Abraham Lincoln and some buck called Tolstoy. Nevin wasn't as focused on the election this time around, but he still drove the Fianna Fáil voters to school on Wednesday the 7th of April, confident Blaney would be re-elected.

Gracie Logue did the bar while Jim scoured the countryside for Fine Gael voters, carting them down to the village to vote for Paddy Harte. Tom was helping him, which left Barney flabbergasted and Ann dismayed. She rounded on the fool, who must have imagined the row between the brothers, apparently knocking hell out of each other the previous week, in a field below Barney's hovel. He swore it was true, there on the pub flagstones, reeking of dung, with John Owen bleating about blood being thicker than water.

Anyway, it didn't matter, Ann thought, pushing Barney out the door to make sure the Logue brats hadn't interfered with her posters.

Oddly, next door's crusade amounted to a few insipid pictures of Harte, blazoned across the school gate, where Cathy and Malachy stood guard, in case Barney would swoop. Ellen called them home for lunch though. When they returned, the Harte posters had vanished and the local men stood garrulous with amusement at Cathy's distress. Malachy told her to stop crying and called them a shower of fucking bastards. He took her hand, leading her back down to the village. His use of foul language didn't surprise Ann. Wasn't Danny Gallagher so right about the wild duck's nest. She expected retaliation, but there was none. They simply stuck Harte's face inside the bar window, where no one could disfigure it.

By the weekend, revelry was in full swing.

Fianna Fáil swept the board.

Barney Cam was promoted; setting bonfires along the route the cavalcade would travel. Down through the village and up past Mona's, stopping at the school where the locals would carry Blaney shoulder high, back to the pub..

Ann was exhilarated.

The 18th Dail of Ireland had a Donegal man in its cabinet. Was it not fitting after all?

The Local Government man now stood head and shoulders above Harte, Logue's man.

It boded well for the days ahead.

She told Nevin as much, watching him smile his belief that she was correct, knowing her movements up and down the counter would be sprightly that evening. She might even lilt tunelessly to Charles Bayers' fiddle.

Next door Logue celebrated Harte's election with his rabble of mavericks, including cousin Teddy, who drove down from Letterkenny with his posse in tow. It would be a late night, and Logue's denunciation was sure to reach their ears sometime in the small hours, until he burned himself out like he always did. Dragged back inside by yer wan, to simmer and lick his wounds.

It was nine years since the Logues arrived, to turn the village upside down.

Ann wasn't getting any younger. Neither was Nevin.

She watched Barney Cam lolloping to the lavatory, suddenly drained at the thought of the morning's cleanup. Nevin's back cracked a little louder now when he bent to stock the shelves, patiently waiting for his day in court. The thorn in his side was infected and would only be expunged by a phone call from MaCausland, confirming a court date. Tomorrow she would take the camphor balls out of Nevin's good suit and starch his dark blue shirt. A sign to heaven.

They were ready to bring this battle to a head.

Gracie 1965

Gracie turned the radio volume up when Butch Moore began to sing, but Jim barked at her to turn it off. How insensitive could she be? Why would he want to imagine walking the streets in the rain? Another letter arrived from Fray, which Gracie placed in the drawer with the rest of the legal correspondence, pushing it closed with effort. She read every legal document out loud to Jim, ignoring the despairing gasps he adopted lately, as if the words were killing him. There were no more secrets, no more hidden facts. This was the basis of the new covenant between them, fusing their determination to beat the enemy.

Gracie attended early Mass every morning, making novenas to St. Jude and St. Theresa of the Little Flower.

She was staying strong for Jim, but especially for the children.

The episode at the lough before Christmas left her shaken to the core.

She recalled the whispered conversations around the hearth, on long winter evenings when she was a child. The neighbors gathered in, vivid faces ruddy and plump by the light of the fire and the Tilley lamps.

Donal Mhór had died in the neighboring townland, a shooting accident that wasn't an accident. Their shocked tones wavered and swayed with the tragedy of his lost soul. Shaming his wife and children, denied the dignity of burying him inside the graveyard walls, where his own parents slept in peace. The ignominy of being buried in a 'cillín' on top of the hill, away from those who loved you. The stories of their lost souls terrified Hannah and Gracie. There were little babies up there too, in unmarked graves, under sod without their mammys to cry over them or bring them flowers. Babies Gracie and Hannah cried for some nights, imploring God to free them from Limbo and bring them to himself in Heaven.

Jim hadn't been angry with her, but she was mad at herself and the humiliation she could have foisted on her family, particularly the children. Her poor mother would have keened forever, for the sinful enormity of it.

It was out of her system now.

Maybe it had been a test. One she passed by the skin of her teeth, leaving her strong, like a mended break that thickened her courage and will.

Men could be weak, God knows she'd seen enough of their foolishness and Jim was no exception. She had no choice now but to listen to her mother's voice. 'Stand your ground.' And that's what she was doing.

Christmas tested Gracie severely.

Mocking her in Rainney's Store, when she chose toys for the children. Laughing at her from the mirror in McGinty's, blurring her reflection when Cathy said, "Mammy you look pretty in that coat." Her tiny fingers stroked the ermine cuffs, making Gracie swallow down the hurt in her chest that Jim must have noticed, because he stood behind her whistling his approval, saying Cathy should get one too. The sales girl went scurrying among the hangers, producing a tiny replica for the squealing child who held out her arms, allowing the lady to try it on her. Malachy tied the belt on his new trench coat, emulating Jim's walk across the shop floor, feeling very grown up amid their laughter at his antics. Paula was home with Ellen, but not forgotten as they searched the rails, finding a grey double-breasted coat for her, with gold military buttons that everyone approved of.

They made the best of it, stepping out to Mass Christmas morning with their heads held high. Ann Cox looked askance at Gracie on her way out of chapel, her goiter eyes hideous above her twisted mouth, making Gracie's skin crawl.

"Did you see the way she looked at me?" she asked Jim on the way home. "Lord but she's a hateful woman."

"She's like something that flew in on a broom," Jim laughed, lightening the mood, the car filling with mirth.

"Is Ann Cox a witch Daddy?" Malachy poked his head in from the back seat.

"She's a witch alright, watch yourselves on her." Jim made his voice low and scary.

"We know a song about a witch," Cathy offered. "Mammy taught us."

Spontaneously they began to sing along with Gracie, making Paula bounce on the back seat between her siblings, repeating the word witch over and over, adding to the fun.

"There was an auld witch who lived in a ditch, she picked up a penny and thought she was rich," they sang.

"And she was a hateful auld bitch," Jim added, singing off key, giving Paula a new word to repeat.

The fallout was inevitable.

Malachy became infected with spite, passing it on to Cathy, who excelled as his willing accomplice, both honing their skills of persecution against the Cox's.

They devised devilish little ways of torturing their new enemies, aware of Jim and Gracie's silent approval.

Tom grunted his disgust in the bar one evening, telling Jim he shouldn't involve the wanes in his mess. Mortified in front of Teddy and Mickey Flood, Jim snapped the whiskey glass from Tom's hand, flinging it into the sink. His brother stormed out, leaving the bar door swinging on its hinges, the cold air howling around the stools, until Mickey pulled it shut. He hadn't appeared in the bar since. Jim said he was a big loss and he could bloody well please himself.

It was true; the children were punishing Ann and Nevin in their own childish fashion, what of it? It was only what they deserved after all, Gracie reasoned, and Jim agreed with her.

"They forgot they weren't just dealing with me and you Gracie, when they got into this battle. We have a few extra foot soldiers they didn't bargain for."

He had a couple of whiskeys in him, but Gracie didn't mind. He'd been good lately, barely touching it at all.

"And they won't always be youngsters either," he warned. "Someday they'll be tall enough to look Cox straight in the eye and he better watch himself then."

"Her too," Gracie added.

Christmas was well and truly over.

The fear that it was the last one in their home haunted Gracie.

Jesus, where would they be this time next year?

The question would strike her out of the blue, draining every ounce of energy from her body. She prayed then; Sacred Heart of Jesus, I place all my trust in thee. She relied heavily on the tablets Dr. Melly prescribed, upping her dosage and ignoring the label that said take one twice a day. Sometimes she needed double that. On particularly dark days she reached under the scullery sink for the bottle of Buckfast, to help calm her racing thoughts and steady her shaking hands. She wished she could curse violently like Jim, or punch Ann Cox in the face, her and that charlatan priest, walking up and down past the house trying to provoke her.

He was the instigator.

Because Ann didn't know any Jim Reeves' songs, nor did she possess the imagination to change the words to suit their demand. 'You'll Have to Go.' Ellen turned the radio volume up, but Gracie said she wanted to hear what they were singing. Ann crowed the same words at the clothes line and when she crossed the street from Mona's in her threadbare pleated skirt. The skirt she begged off Nora, before she scuttled away back to Killygordon when Gracie got the school. Even Cormac Brown wouldn't wear it. She laughed, remembering the story Jim told her, sorry she missed the fun of seeing that spectacle. What else did she miss when she was over in the Gaeltacht; O Sacred Heart of Jesus I place all my trust in thee.

Gracie

Frank McGrory, the young tinker man, had been in the village yesterday. Malachy ran in to tell her, knowing she loved to watch him gyrating in the street, singing Blue Suede Shoes and Jailhouse Rock. She'd stand with the children, clapping and singing along, making sure to ask Frank in for a drink on the house. Didn't he deserve it, more than anyone? More than the spineless leeches who still brazened the bar despite the huge tab they declined to square. Frank was generous with his sweet voice and gentle ways. He brightened the day whenever he came around. So did his cousins, the hardy men who talked to Jim about horses and greyhounds and offered their skills in exchange for bottles of beer consumed in the bar with Jim. There was quiet dignity about them. The women were the same; peddling their small domestic items from handmade baskets swinging graciously from their weathered arms. They promised Gracie they'd pray for her and bless her with luck and health, like earthy Celtic witches, smelling of dark peaty smoke. Gracie always opened her door to them, ignoring the subservience they felt compelled to offer; sampling their tea towels and aprons before making her purchase. Yesterday she couldn't face listening to Frank, not when she fretted that soon enough she might be on the streets with him, asking to join in his bardic act by way of survival. They were merely a hare's breath apart. Such thoughts were getting the better of her!

Where would they be without Ellen?

Paula loved her. So did Cathy and Malachy. Little did they know that she shielded them from the campaign against Mammy and Daddy, threatening to dismantle their world.

They knew who the enemy was, but not really why.

Jim and herself told them the Cox's wanted to buy their bar and house, because it was a far superior building to their own. Daddy wouldn't let them have it, so they were angry and no longer their friends, or pretend friends, Gracie qualified. The children were not to speak or be pleasant to them ever again. They were nasty people, whose home and car was now out of bounds.

If the children felt like retaliating, let them. Gracie wanted Ann and Nevin to see the monster they had prodded and awakened. The brother priest was their heavy artillery, but big guns could miss their target. The sting of little slings and arrows was more effective in making the enemy feel besieged.

Master Ferry was besotted with his new baby girl, calling her Sinead, after de Valera's wife, a fact that went unnoticed by Jim, thank Blaises, because he liked the Master and Gracie didn't want him consigned to the burgeoning list of people Jim despised. Ferry's new daughter softened him, extending his empathy to feel Gracie's pain, though she hid it well, she thought. His smile was warm on chilly mornings, when she passed through his room.

He no longer begrudged her big fires, heaped with sods and hard black turf. Despite everything, Jim had worked the bog last summer, saving the turf even though his heart must have been aching. Andy Dore's tractor had carried every last clod into the shed, oblivious to the ill wind that was gathering speed and hurtling towards them.

Steven still avoided her gaze in school, yet she knew he was watchful, guarding her from afar.

He no longer held court at the school gate or the boy's toilet. Seeing Gracie break had cured his need to speculate and gossip. He felt heroic now, carrying himself with a manly quiet assurance.

With every day that passed Gracie tried to keep the flag flying.

The big girls finished their jumpers in time for Christmas. Certain families received the Puntai for their fluency in Gaelic. New songs were learned and new sums attempted and then she was busy teaching the English responses to the Mass.

Monsignor McLaughlin visited them in late January, telling the pupils about Vatican Two and the changes it portended. They listened dutifully, accustomed to his verbosity; words like vernacular floating over their heads. Mrs. Logue would enlighten them after he was gone, the swish of his soutane signaling a return to relaxed shoulders and blinking eyes. They embraced the responses that included them in the Mass for the first time in their young lives.

Gracie missed the Latin Mass, still insisting on bringing her Missal to chapel, despite what Jim thought.

The Monsignor faced them for most of the mass now, which unnerved Gracie, especially since she occupied Cox's pew with Jim and the children.

She hadn't planned the usurpation.

It just happened as she walked up the chapel aisle a few Sundays previously. She could feel Jim's feet dragging behind as hers kept moving, holding Paula's hand too tightly, making the child squirm, while her jaw set firmly in defiance. Malachy and Cathy followed her, forcing Jim to do the same. His face burned crimson but Gracie didn't care. It made perfect sense to her.

There was no such thing as owning a seat in God's house and Gracie was here to prove it.

Let Ann and Nevin Cox slither off to some other pew, stung and humiliated; wasn't it good enough for them.

Malachy and Cathy felt the victory of it, laughing at the deposed pair, whose confusion even Jim found amusing, having recovered his composure as they drove home in their new car.

"Did you see the steer on Ann when she saw us in her seat?" Jim laughed. "I thought she was having a fit on the spot."

"Her face was pure red daddy," Cathy squealed.

"And her head kept shaking," Malachy added.

"She was like a clocking hen pecking white wash off a wall," Jim said.

They laughed till the tears ran down their faces and Paula celebrated a new phrase, 'clocking hen', the repetition holding the mirth a while longer.

"Nevin is smarter than her," Gracie lowered her voice. *"He's fit to hide his feelings behind that long hound-dog face."*

"Because he's a sleekit bastard, that's why," Jim was suddenly angry, changing the atmosphere in the car.

The fun was over.

The purr of the Morris 1100 was no comfort, as silence descended and Gracie's thoughts returned to the looming court case. She knew Jim's were doing exactly the same.

Johnathan Fray had completed Jim's Defense, but took his time delivering it to the Court. Gracie was flummoxed, wondering why he was being so restrained. She nagged Jim about it, adding to his misery. He remonstrated, asking her what she knew about the law and shouldn't she let the expert do as he saw fit.

March was half over before Mr. Fray mobilized himself, entering their Defense two days after St.Patricks, not that it brought them much comfort. It amounted to Jim's word against Cox, only Cox had a coterie of allies to back up his claims.

Who would testify that Jim was blind drunk when he supposedly signed their home away?

Jim himself found the admission distasteful.

Where was Teddy on that critical July day? Or Mickey Flood?

Christ, even Cormac Brown would have done to place his grubby hand on the Bible and swear that Jim was hung out to dry. But no. Jim had to ride into battle half cocked on a mad horse, believing his foe was a friend. How often had she warned him about the Manus fella, with the unlikely clerical collar. Rasputin reincarnated; offering his evil advice to the two next door, who devoured it like ravenous wolves.

Jim said he had a man pegged within minutes of introduction, but his powers failed him miserably when they were most needed. Gracie couldn't fathom it. In the main, priests were anathema to Jim, yet he was spellbound by the only bad one he ever met.

She asked Mr. Fray if she could be a witness for Jim.

She would testify that never in all their years together did he raise the idea of selling their home and premises with her, never. She urged Mr. Fray to allow her, ignoring Jim's protests that he didn't want her taking the stand. Knowing him, he wouldn't want her in the courtroom or even in Letterkenny, when the time came.

He was fearful of seeming weak and emasculated. But Johnathan Fray didn't see it like that. Having Gracie in court would show a united front. Allow the judge to see the defendant's wife and mother of his children. It might do no harm to put her on the stand. If she broke down while up there, that would be no harm either.

Jim's sarcastic snort insinuated Gracie's inability to display emotion, particularly in public. He had only seen her crying twice. Once when the boycott shook her badly, and on that terrible night, when she sat broken and forlorn by Sadie Dore's hearth.

She hated crying. It made her feel angry and useless.

Lately though, tears were proving difficult to control.

She spoke sternly to herself in the classroom when her eyes stung, threatening to spill salty drops off her nose onto the tuning fork, down to the dusty wooden floor. Malachy was familiar with the signs of her impending gloom, pretending not to notice her welling eyes that made him moody and dour. Cathy would ask, "what's wrong mammy, are you crying?"

Ellen always came to the rescue, grumbling that mammy had been listening to sad songs again or cutting cruel onions. It helped Gracie to pull herself together, before the kitchen was filled with crying faces, including Jim's, that crumbled again and again, banishing Ellen to the bar until he managed to compose himself. The children cried with them. Paula made the loudest din, creating the distraction they badly needed, sobering them up, like rainbows after a heavy shower.

Those were exceptional moments.

Most of the time life went on, masquerading as normal.

Jim and herself spoke kindly to one another. The children watched cartoons or read stories from Arthur Mee, happy that Ellen was at the range making poached eggs for tea. Jim still ordered stock from Mulrines, opening the bar every morning at 11am, just as Johnny O'Donnell lurched into the village, joining Neil Fada at the high formica counter. Gracie drove to her knitters on dull Saturday afternoons, collecting garments that Ellen helped to press and parcel, ready for the railway lorry on Monday mornings.

Life went on, accompanied by a spectral cloud that hung menacingly low. At times impossible to ignore. Occasionally rising high and wispy and barely visible.

Hannah had taken to visiting them every Saturday morning from over west, sitting in the kitchen drinking tea and chatting in Gaelic with Gracie. She brought Gateaux Swiss Rolls and packets of Oatfield sweets wrapped in brown paper, placing them quietly on the sideboard where they sat torturing the children. Impatience overtook them as Gracie announced tea; slicing the cake and handing Malachy a packet of Emeralds to share with his sisters. He was to take a few down to his Daddy in the bar too.

Jim avoided the kitchen when Hannah was there, knowing what she must think of him. He was a different breed to her brothers, a fact he reveled in, in a proud sneering kind of way. Mícheal and Séan were quiet earthy men, who didn't smoke and rarely drank, only worked the land, enjoying the bounties it reaped. They felt blessed among family and good neighbors, God fearing men who recited the rosary every night of their lives.

"Oddballs!" Jim scoffed. "Sure you couldn't have a night's crack with them boys, God protect us."

Maybe he was right. But Gracie had yet to hear them speak badly of Jim, although they had cause to. Hannah saw Jim in various stages of intoxication over the years, but even now, knowing what he'd done, she displayed no hint of judgement, no look of, I told you so, on her face. Gracie explained to her the kind of people the Coxs' were, hoping she would see their guilt; setting the snare that Jim stumbled into.

Mary, her oldest sister, was sharp and outspoken. She wrote to her from Manchester, where she lived with her husband and six children, wondering what sort of mess Jim had landed them in. Her tone seemed cross and probing, convincing Gracie not to reply until the case was over and only then if the outcome was positive.

April brought another General Election, but she didn't have the stomach for it this time. It mattered little whether Paddy Harte got elected or not. It would make no difference to Gracie's life. That's what she said to Jim, when he ran up from the bar to watch the results being announced on Telefís Eireann, desperate for distraction. Tom and himself drove Harte supporters to the school to vote, for all the good that would do them.

"Will Paddy Harte make sure we don't lose our home Jim?" she asked, as he stared at the television.

"What the hell are you talking about Gracie?" he rounded.

"If he's that great a man, he'll have sway with the law," she was purposely provoking him.

"That's the thickness coming out now. You know damned well Paddy Harte can't interfere with the courts."

"I'll bet you Nevin Cox has Blaney working for him, making sure the jury is all Fianna Fáil boys," she fumed.

"But we know it won't be a jury," Jim tried to sound reasonable.

"Either way, the judge will be a Blaney man too. It'll be all sewn up before we put our noses in the courtroom door."

"In that case we won't bother our fucking heads going to court. According to you, there's no point." Jim's mouth was tight with rage.

Ellen came in from the scullery, bumping into him in the doorway. She raised her eyes at Gracie when he brushed past her into the bar.

"Someone's in a temper," she winked.

"Fianna Fáil swept the board again, Blaney's sure to get a big job this time." Gracie sat down near the range, exhausted.

A cold April light came through the kitchen window, making her feel nostalgic for a time long ago, she wasn't sure when. When Hannah and herself walked home from school maybe, aware that summer was coming, bringing baby calves and flowery spuds and new summer frocks.

She regretted annoying Jim and goading his temper, because he could shift the balance of guilt so easily. Why didn't she remember that, instead of sabotaging the new alliance they enjoyed lately, built on gentleness and affection. The new tenderness between mammy and daddy that gave the children security, like a warm Oxford blanket.

Did Ann and Nevin ever fight, she wondered, or were they constantly united in hatefulness and spite. The latter probably.

The children were in from the street announcing their hunger and Ellen was tying her scarf to go home. There were eggs to fry for evening tea and fresh bread she baked earlier. Good, Gracie thought. That might cheer Jim up, shorten the penance of sulking and silence. The children would make him laugh at the kitchen table, while she did the bar, and by bedtime the silent treatment would be over. She'd walk up to school in the morning, gathering the scraps of hope around her that lay for the moment, dying at her feet.

Jim 1965

If he could turn back the clock he would.

This time last year the world was perfect and he didn't even know it. His children were healthy and happy. Gracie was strong again and resilient; a bit too fixated on making money but what harm, didn't it beat squandering everything they had. Jesus! Wasn't he the unfortunate man to have rubbed shoulders with the Coxs, especially the Manus buck. He was evil. How did Jim not clock that. Was it because Gracie did, and his masculinity balked at her observation; so accustomed to dismissing her musings as the superstitious thinking of over west.

All along she'd been right about the two next door.

If her mother hadn't voiced similar misgivings, in her banshee shawl, he might have paid attention; especially when the plausible missionary made his entrance. But then you weren't supposed to speak ill of a priest, isn't that right, so what was a man to do? Stumble upon a nest of wasps and allow himself to be badly stung, that's what.

The fallout was terrible. The ugly repercussions of last July ransacked his brain, stealing completely the wavering faith he had in humanity.

The villagers nailed their colors firmly to the mast.

Jim retained his old guard, including Andy Dore, whose loyalty was now beyond doubt. John Owen's desertion was predictable, while not making his absence any easier to bear. His sharp mind and quick wit was too good for the donkeys next door, but he was a prisoner of his own making; a bit like Jim himself.

Everywhere he looked he saw enemies.

They streamed into Mass on Sunday mornings or up Milford street on Fair days, looking furtively under their eyes at the man who was the talk of the land. It was hard to decipher friend from foe. Jim assumed a curtness with all of them, signalling strength, though he did feel beleaguered.

He was safe out and about with Tom; that's when they weren't at each other's throats.

Tom could wilt with his eyes and cut with his tongue. Most people knew that and steered clear. Teddy's confidence was reassuring too and Mickey Flood's relentless charm, that didn't seem to notice twitching curtains or hostile backward glances.

The youngsters knew what was going on; kind of.

They were rogues, taking the opportunity to pay Ann back for her nastiness towards them.

Cathy's rendition of Second Hand Rose was a hoot. She sang it in the bar for John Owen, before he chose sides. She sat on the counter one Saturday evening singing it for Teddy and the boys. The wives came out of the snug to watch her, charmed by her sweet little mouth belting out the big number, delighted she was making them laugh. She lost all shyness when handbags opened revealing ten shilling notes. The men were generous too, pressing coins into her warm little hands, telling her she was the best girl in Ireland. Malachy hovered, siphoning the adulation that reached him too, with silver coins and manly pats, too heavy on his slight wee shoulders.

Gracie put the money in their Post Office books, bribing them with smaller amounts, deaf to their protestations. Jim knew she was right. He laughed as they wailed, appeasing them finally with a trip to La Scala.

Was it charity? Jim wondered. This kindness from their customers? Rainey day money they knew would be needed, when the bloody sky opened and the deluge washed them away.

He supposed that's why Gracie took on extra work, like the knitting circle and the Gaeltacht. She knew he was a loose cannon, liable to land them up on the dung heap.

Jesus! Why didn't she stay at home all summer, instead of leaving him to his own devices?

It was hardly worth the money, when they now stood to lose everything they owned. What was she thinking? He would never get an answer to that. But she could torture him with the same question. The one he tortured himself with a million times a day, driving his fist into walls, tearing clumps of hair from his scalp. Jesus Christ! No one knew the suffering he endured. Only Christ on the cross knew. Why did he go to Milford on that July day, led like a lamb to the slaughter. Tom had the answer.

"You're a fucking show off, always having to be the big fella!"

"Good man Tom, make sure you back me whatever you do."

"How could I back you, you bloody stooge? The Cox's saw you coming."

He got a punch in the jaw for that one, followed by a tackle to the ground that brought Sally and his poor mother squealing down the lane, angering him further with their pathetic wringing of hands, begging him to stop for God's sake. He drove home stultified, forgetting the youngsters, until Malachy asked him to slow down because Cathy was crying in the back seat.

Why was everyone crying? Jesus Christ Allfucking Mighty!

They needed to pull themselves together. If he'd had a bit more support they wouldn't be in this mess in the first place. God's curse on the lot of them; whining and blaming and driving him round the bend.

Gracie in the kitchen, singing along with Butch Moore, expecting him to smile; he should be happy about walking the streets in the rain. There was enough crying going on, without listening to it every bloody time you turned on the radio.

He felt better in December when Gracie told him their mortgage was negligible and they could definitely afford a new car. He doubted the wisdom of ordering a Morris 1100 though, after the rush of euphoria wore off, replaced by fretting and fear.

Still, Mr. Fray opined that life should go on as before, so he was taking his advice.

It gave him courage to look forward to the festive season and discourage Gracie's frugality, her inclination to scrimp.

No snakes and ladders this year or rag dolls or jigsaw puzzles.

Let Malachy have a new bicycle and Cathy her big dolly with long hair, like she asked for. Paula should get a teddy bear the size of herself, to sit with her in the playpen, soft and cuddly. Christmas called for new coats he reckoned, to warm bodies and souls; the perfect symbols of defiance in the face of adversity.

Did Ann and Nevin Cox think Jim should lie down and die, along with Gracie and the youngsters? Their faces in chapel Christmas morning intimated as much, livid with shock and offense. They looked stupid with it, making the children laugh, now that the devil inside them was wakened. Himself and Gracie laughed too and they tried to keep the merriment alive after Mass, driving home to unlock the back door for Andy Dore and the Big Flood, licking their lips and rubbing their hands in preparation.

Tom skulked in apologetically with Barney Cam behind him, warning Jim with his eyes not to be unkind. How could he be unkind, now that Cormac Brown and a handful more had presented themselves at his counter, raising their glasses stoutly and strong. The smell of roasting goose wafted down from the kitchen and Jim stood a drink for his comrades, coaxing them to sing louder, like a pledge that this time next year they would do the same again.

They didn't need to know that he already felt battle-weary, when two hours later he waved them out the same door they came in, hoping the few wee Johnny Walkers would carry him through the day.

Only Gracie could see his pain, as he could see hers, when they sat together watching Danny Kaye playing his cornet in 'The Five Pennies'. Cathy wept for the little girl whose legs didn't work like hers and he pulled her closer by way of comfort.

There in the warm kitchen, remorse clawed at his heart.

Sweet Jesus let this cup pass from me! Amn't I the luckiest and unluckiest of men!

Was Gracie's voice not a salve, announcing pudding and custard, distracting him for a little while at least.

This time next year. No No No Jim. Do not wander into that territory!

He must look forward, and rise above the gathering gloom threatening to weaken his resolve. Gracie needed him to be a man. She was fighting her own battles, which she seemed to be winning with Dr. Melly's help. Jim was grateful to him, although he never said as much.

He savored the prospect of collecting the new car. Himself and Gracie made a day of it. They had lunch in Gallagher's hotel and he urged her to drive the Morris 1100 home, letting the village see her behind the wheel of a brand new machine. She demurred, saying she'd prefer Jim to take the wheel, she was nervous of scratching it on its maiden voyage.

Barney Cam was Ann's new lackey. He jumped like a bandy goat into Cox's to splutter his guts when he spotted the car pulling in on the street. Jim blew the horn at the children, dancing on the footpath with Ellen, wide eyed with excitement.

It was a moment to remember. One to relish, standing there in the cold January sun.

Lent was around the corner, waiting in his grey depressing cloak, to cover the world in dust. Gracie wore the ashes like a suffering badge of honor, the poor sanctimonious wife.

Good moments were fleeting.

The bar stood silent all week, except for Mickey Flood, whose heathen visits were welcome. Cormac Brown tramped in when he should have stayed at home, only bothering Jim's head, having to listen to his nonsense. One could have a decent chat with the Big Flood and he didn't twitch like a spooked hare when the Monsignor stuck his pompous head around the door, as if he had jurisdiction.

"Yes Monsignor, how are we today?" Jim greeted, with forced conviviality.

"It's hardly worth your while staying open, is it Mr. Logue?" The tone was rhetorical but Jim answered regardless.

"O life goes on. Lent or no Lent. I suppose you'll be checking next door too?"

Mickey gave a little snort, never turning to acknowledge the cleric.

He made no reply to Jim's supposition, only glared through his dark spectacles for a long moment to confirm his authority.

"Make sure Mr. Logue that your establishment is closed on St. Patrick's Day, I presume you know the law." He turned; his shot had met its target.

"The bastard," Jim hissed. "What was he getting at? I know the law as well as any man."

He plunged a tumbler under the optic.

"He's a fossil Jim, an old relic from the past. Pay no attention to him," Mickey reasoned.

"Do you know what I'm going to do Mickey? I'm going to open up wide on Patrick's Day and the whole world can come in if they like." He swallowed down his whiskey.

"That's the spirit," Mickey laughed, raising his glass to indicate his desire for another.

Mandy the Post put his head in with another registered letter, but despite Jim's urging he refused to come to the bar Patrick's Day and play his melodeon.

"He's a spineless fool," Jim sighed.

"He's a good guy Jim, just a slave to the system, that's how it is in this great little country." Mickey was taking his leave.

"It'll make no slave outa me Mickey. I'll open up on Patrick's Day come hell or high water."

Gracie was aghast at the very idea of it. After all, Monsignor was the manager of the school. He would hold it against her, maybe give her the sack.

Jim stayed true to his threat though, opening after Mass, with a hearty fire lit and jugs of shamrocks festooned around the bar. Cox was closed tight and none of his tribe were tempted to defect, not even for the few hours that were in it. They were a miserable shower of shits. And just as Jim was thinking the whole business was a mistake, Teddy and his posse drove into town, transforming the drab atmosphere into a carnival of noise and color, raising spirits to the roof. The singing lured Gracie and the children down for the final hour, shy at first, watching Jim dancing outside the counter, hedging their bets. Then the easing of frowns into smiles, laughing with Teddy, who was wrapping the green flag round him, a hirsute growth of shamrocks trembling in his lapel.

Gracie shouldn't worry her lovely head, he told her, holding her around the waist. The Monsignor would have some job trying to replace a teacher like his wee wife, the auld bollocks.

Cathy was showing the Big Flood her dolly and Malachy pulled a stout for Andy Dore, giving him the correct change under Gracie's watchful eyes.

Another moment to cherish.

Would they be here for St. Patrick's Day next year? Sweet Jesus let this cup pass from me.

He cursed the pair next door, but he didn't dare wish them dead and buried, that would be bad luck. He detested the black hearted padrè. If he died roaring it would be a blessing!

Oh that he would wake up tomorrow morning and realize it was a bad dream, just fate sounding a warning note to keep him good and smart.

Lent crept interminably along.

Easterly gales blew through March, wrapping hoary frost around trees and fences, punishing every living thing. Jim haunted the bar, remonstrating with himself; a form of self-flagellation, interspersed with apologias spoken loudly in his defense. The stalwarts still braved the icy winds that dragged March along at a snail's pace, keeping Jim company and easing the drudgery of his recriminations.

And if March came in roaring, it sang serenely as it left, ending on the sweetest of notes.

The heat was sudden and unrivaled.

On the last Sunday of the month the bar was heaving with customers, lured by the thirsty sun. The men with their good shirts rolled to the elbows, the wives in summer frocks, flaunting the fear of casting clouts, astonished at their own bravery. Lent was suspended; putting everyone in high spirits. The children asked to wear their bathing suits and Gracie took them all by surprise saying lunch would be served outside. She drove them to the beach in the afternoon, with the picnic basket packed, the children already dressed for the occasion. Jim sat on the tartan rug watching them splash at the water's edge, wanting to be caught in the moment, as the children were. To really feel their wanton joy, instead of pretending to. Gracie beside him with her shoes off, knowing like him that if God answered them, they would never take these moments for granted again, ever.

March danced into April, still singing her sweet song, until the day of the General Election, when thunder rolled, bringing the heavens down in a deluge.

Tom arrived in the Hillman, expecting Jim to join him, taking Harte voters to the school to cast their votes, despite the tension between them. The outcome was a foregone conclusion anyway, which was oddly comforting to Jim. He felt no bitterness at Blaney's triumph and only mild jubilation at Harte's success.

Gracie goaded him about the outcome, needing to dump her anger somewhere. His counter attack was watery and lackluster. Was he running out of chutzpah, as Mickey Flood would say, or simply conserving energy for the battle ahead?

If March trundled, April galloped up to Psalm Sunday, throwing Easter at their feet impatiently, bringing Lent to a merciful end.

The deValera brigade were still swaggering up to Cox's, with taunting grins, as if Blaney was spawned from their loins. It jarred, but Jim had to be sensible now. There were too many nights when he lost control, using Johnny Walker to lambaste the two next door, pouring scorn on them long after bedtime. They stood watching him from the landing window, no doubt laughing at his plight. The whole village could hear him, Gracie said. It distressed the children too, this pathetic display of weakness in the face of the enemy.

"Keep the sunny side out my boy," the Big Flood sang. "Don't let your defenses down."

"You're right Mickey," Jim conceded. "The anger carries me away and I lose control."

"It's understandable son. You're playing right into their hands though."

He didn't know the finer details, Jim thought, because Mickey didn't ask questions, none of his customers did. They all knew the general outline of his situation, the quagmire he found himself in. The townland was swollen with gossip, oozing out like pus from a boil. Still Jim and Gracie kept their counsel. They wouldn't want Jim's truth anyway, preferring to concoct their own, various differing truths, whichever side of the divide you were on.

The new batch of Communicants were being prepared. Gracie wanted to please the Monsignor, who was possibly dismayed by her takeover of Cox's pew. Her temerity shocked Jim initially, but he quickly saw the justice of it, the crude symbolism of the gesture. The children embraced it, although Tom's words still rankled, because he was right, but you daren't say so to Gracie.

When they could breathe easy again they'd go on a family holiday, someplace nice. A hotel in Galway or Mayo, during the racing season and they'd stroll through the crowds with their feet barely touching the ground.

Waiting for a court date was excruciating.

The longing to have the case behind him, with the longing for it never to arrive, jostled for position. Gracie refused to install a phone and he couldn't use Mona's unless he wished the entire county to know his business. Teddy visited Fray's office for him, shaking his head as he entered the bar, relieving and disappointing Jim in one go.

But the date had to be set. So it was.

"You're wanted on the phone Daddy," Malachy's voice broke into his thoughts.

"Did Mona say who?"

Malachy shook his head. "Go on Daddy, hurry up."

He ignored Mona's beady eyes as he ran through to the kiosk, hearing Johnathan Fray on the line.

"We have a Notice of Trial Jim," he seemed upbeat. "May the 25th at 11am in Letterkenny courthouse, Judge Cooper presiding."

"Jesus!" his mind raced, "Is that good, I mean that it's not a jury?"

"It's standard procedure for Circuit Court Jim. Cooper generally sits on these cases."

The name meant nothing to Jim. Teddy would know about him, know how he operated.

"I'll accept the date on your behalf," Fray's voice again. "Come into me on Tuesday morning, we'll take it from there."

Nevin was in the Zephyr, Jim noted, as he crossed the street; driving up the Milford road to see MaCausland obviously, having heard the same news. Ann waved him off with a flourish, laughing at some pretend joke from inside the pub. She was a sickening bitch, he thought, but he smiled quickly when Cathy ran, skipping beside him to hold his hand.

"Who was on the phone daddy?" she asked.

"Nobody pet, just a man who sells sheep to Uncle Tom."

The boredom of the reply satisfied her. She ran off, calling Malachy's name, blissfully unburdened. Gracie listened to his news, her blue eyes unblinking, absurdly calm.

She was grateful First Holy Communion would be over before the trial, that seemed to console her greatly. Jim wanted to snort sarcastically and wonder if that was all she cared about, but his lips pursed in over his teeth, a reminder to keep his mouth shut. Ellen was in from the scullery and he couldn't cause a scene.

Teddy visited on Saturday morning early, knowing the news.

"So, you're getting a day out," he teased, sitting in the empty bar watching Jim stocking shelves.

"I feel as if I'm going to the gallows," Jim tried to sound amusing.

"You'll be safe enough in Cooper's hands. He's a Dubliner, but he can't help that," Teddy laughed. "He moved here years ago when he married a Letterkenny woman."

"I might have been better off with a jury."

"It's only in criminal cases that jury's are apportioned and you're not a criminal Jim, not yet anyway." Teddy laughed again. "You should see some of the boys that show up on jury's, auld fellas down from the hills and them as thick as pig shit. They wouldn't understand a quarter of what the judge was telling them. Christ you don't want boys of that caliber in charge of your fate, the Cormac Browns and Barney Cams of this world."

They both laughed then. The sight of Cormac in his hob nailed boots flashed before them and Jim couldn't help mimicking Barney.

"Baa Baaa, he's skilty your snonner, oh naw….. he's sninnicent your highness!"

"Get out of my court you snottery imbecile!" Teddy roared. "Jesus, can you image the performance?"

"What about Cooper though?" Jim was serious again. "He's not in with any politicians, is he?"

"From what I know of him, he's a straight arrow. A brilliant man with a brilliant legal mind and he doesn't drag cases out. He has a way of examining the evidence before him and making sound judgements based on it."

"That's me fucked then," Jim sighed, "If Cox can produce something with my signature on it."

"Now, now, you're heading down the wrong track," Teddy cautioned. "You don't know what Cox has or hasn't entered into evidence."

"John Fields will have given him whatever document he had with him that night."

"You don't know that either, and anyway that's what you have a solicitor for. Let Fray do the job you're paying him to do."

"Jesus wee Teddy, I was never so scared in all my life; it's a hopeless case I doubt."

"That's a great bloody attitude. Don't let Gracie hear you at that talk, or anyone else for that matter. Cox will get wind of it and think he's already the winner."

Jim had always bitten his nails, but now they were down to the quick. The Johnny Walker bottle yelled at him from the optic, joined by Mr. Bushmills and Mr. Jameson, a cacophony of temptation that hurt his teeth, making him long to take a hammer and smash the whole bloody bar to pieces.

It was a sad day, the day he bought it.

He should have purchased a farm with the money his mother gave him. A tidy wee farm, with lambs leaping in the fields and chickens clucking in the yard. He wouldn't be in this mess now. Why did Gracie encourage him to buy it, she wanted the bar as badly as him. Maybe more.

Dear Jesus let this cup pass from me!

The weeks wore on in a pained haze.

He watched Gracie walking to school, Cathy and Malachy running ahead, Gracie wearing her pinstriped jacket, the one she had from her maiden days. He didn't know where she got it. Maybe her sister Mary tailored it for her. The padded shoulders made her look strong, the gored darts pulled her in at the waist, walking there in the fresh morning sun.

Tractors complained on their way to the bog, some stopping at the invitation of the opened bar door. He listened to their weather predictions, optimistic forecasts for drying turf and saving hay. Inquiries if he was cutting bog himself this year. Why wouldn't he be? The cheek, asking such a question. Awkward coughs to drown the silence. Neil Fadá's long face looking longer, his morning solitude disturbed by thirsty bogmen.

Johnny O'Donnell appeared, loud and angry. Myxomatosis was destroying his snaring business. No one wanted infected meat. The plague was rampant. Jim had seen the dying rabbits in the fields around Tom's. He warned the youngsters not to touch them, knowing how tempting it was to pet the slow bloated bunny's who were normally fast and elusive. It took fourteen days for them to die. Fourteen days. That's how long Jim had before he faced the music. He wished Johnny would shut up about the rabbits. Why would a man who was snared in the trenches of World War One want to kill defenseless animals. He tried to focus on the present, but his mind churned.

No topic soothed, only hurt him more. Don't talk of the past, it's done and can't be changed. Don't go to the future, it's tainted, like the blue infected hills of slow painful death.

Mr. Fray advised him to take each day as it came and imagine the best possible outcome.

"Good judgement prevails; you must believe that. Nevin Cox will be exposed for the thief that he is. There's a preponderance of factors in your favor Jim," he said. "The 11am time is lucky. We won't have a tetchy judge on our hands, hungry for lunch and fatigued by lengthy morning judgements. He's a man in his early fifties, so he'll relate well to you Jim, as opposed to an old curmudgeon in his 70's."

Jim was warming to the analysis, but doubts intruded.

"What if I'm asked something trickery on the stand and I say the wrong thing?"

"It's unlikely that you'll take the stand. Put that fear out of your mind. I've engaged an excellent young barrister to represent you, he hasn't lost a case yet."

"When do I meet this young whippersnapper?"

"You'll meet him on the morning of the 25th. I passed on all the details to him so he can build his case."

"I thought I might meet him before then. Will Cox be meeting his barrister beforehand? I don't want to be the man going in like a gobshite, while Cox has his buko primed with all kinds of ammunition."

"Trust me Jim, Cox will have no advantage over you. He will be in the exact same position. Make sure you're there early Tuesday morning. I'll meet you inside the main door, myself and Mr. Joyce, your barrister, will be waiting. I don't need to tell you to look your best. Mrs. Logue will be with you?"

"She will," Jim said wearily.

"Tell her to dress demurely, no garish colors, we don't want the judge distracted."

He winked, rising from behind his desk, the noise of the chair rankling Jim's nerves, like the gates of hell opening before him.

"Go home and take every precaution to be physically and mentally fit for Tuesday Jim."

He drove home knowing what that meant. No whiskey between now and then. A hot bath Monday night, when Ellen's gone home and the youngsters are in bed. And a good night's sleep, if such a thing were possible. Would he open his bar on the 24th? He would, said Gracie. Worrying himself into a state of pessimism is what he'd do instead. Better to be listening to Mickey Flood's flamboyant optimism about seeing light when the heat is on, or Andy Dore's quiet reassurance that everything comes right in the end. That's what he needed to hear. Cormac Brown could offer his own brand of crude comfort, in phlegmy coughs and rhythmic hob-nail boots against the floor. Anything other than his own doomsday brooding.

His good suit was pressed and hanging on the side of the wardrobe. Gracie bought him a white shirt in McGinty's, with double cuffs and a pair of handsome gold plated cufflinks. He could pick out a tie himself, she said, one that made him feel lucky.

They gathered in on Monday evening, filling the bar incongruously.

John Owen shuffled to the counter, coughing away embarrassment for his long absence. Tom arrived, raising his eyes to heaven. Barney Cam waddled in behind him, splayed boots creating a dangerous arc as he approached the counter. Andy Dore and Steven sat at the big table, with Mickey Flood and Mandy the Post.

There was no melodeon playing.

Detached conversations floated, quiet and intermittent. Jim pulled bottles of stout, aware of the hush. Music was out of place at a wake and that's what this was, a send off, a final goodbye. A gathering in advance of death, to mark the demise of a seriously ill bar. Tom knew it too, staring at the whiskey glass turning and turning in his big weatherbeaten hands. No one broke ranks. No filthy jokes or indecent stories. Not a hacking spit or ripping fart. A stretch in the evenings postponed the dimming light, but dusk arrived, with a cool damp breeze creeping into the bar. Moths fluttered around the streetlight when Jim spoke to his tribe.

"That's it men, the last drink of the night. You all know what's happening tomorrow. Gracie and I appreciate your support and regardless of how things pan out, I'll see you all here again tomorrow evening. We'll grieve or celebrate together." He raised his glass of beer to the gloomy faces, smiling his sorrow.

The sun sank down behind Mona's, down into the lough, leaving torn shreds of fleshy pink at the sky's edge. Mickey Flood shook his hand, wishing him luck. Andy Dore waited outside with Steven, so they could do the same.

Jim watched them all taking their separate roads home, hearing the muted conversations drifting down from Cox's on the cool silent breeze. Were they up there still, plotting, nice and quietly invoking his demise! Best not to think about them, of all nights, not tonight.

He lay beside Gracie, but sleep wouldn't come. She knew the signs.

"Will we say a decade of the rosary?" she whispered "It might help us to nod off."

The slow litany of prayers ended and Jim turned to face her in the dark.

"I'm sorry wee Gracie, I'm so sorry."

"Ssh," She chided. "God will be with us. Now go to sleep."

He slept fitfully, waking at dawn to the blackbird's robust song, announcing his strength and defiance. The sound was replaced then by Ellen, letting herself in early, coming in the back door. Gracie stood at the bedroom window. He didn't know how long she was there, turning towards him telling him to rise, with courage and purpose in her eyes. The children would wake and wait for the sounds that lured them downstairs. The morning chill made Gracie shiver. She reached for her housecoat, saying she'd dress later.

Malachy and Cathy needed to know today was going to be different. She would think of something to tell them. A harmless lie to keep them from fretting. Ellen would give her a hand.

Jim shaved at the kitchen table, peering into the cracked mirror, grateful that at least his hands were steady, though his heart thumped in his chest. The children sat waiting for Ellen to butter their toast.

"Should I wear a picture-hat Ellen?" Gracie's question took everyone by surprise.

"I don't think so, Mrs. Logue. I have a feeling that hats are not allowed in court," Ellen trailed off, sorry she had mentioned court.

"You'll wear no bloody hat," Jim rounded.

The children watched her. Realization dawning on their faces.

"Are you not going to school today mammy?" Cathy asked.

Malachy put down his toast, waiting for an answer.

"Mammy and Daddy are going for a wee visit to Letterkenny," Ellen intervened. "One of the big girls is going to mind mammy's room. The two of them will be back before you know it."

"Can we go too?" Malachy asked, although he knew the answer.

"Not today." Jim spoke softly. "The car's acting up so we're leaving her in the garage, it's no place for youngsters. Go on to school and we'll be back as quick as we can."

"You're lying," Malachy's face darkened, his bottom lip quivering.

"Please tell us where you're going," Cathy begged. "We'll be good. You won't even know we're there."

"Please take us daddy, please please!" Malachy pleaded.

"Stop the fussing," Ellen scolded. "Get your school bags and away you go."

"We'll call into Rainey's if we have time and buy a wee toy each for you." Gracie promised, the appeasement failing miserably.

They stomped from the table without a backward glance, gathering their bags in the hall before walking up the street to school. Malachy slightly ahead of Cathy, both heads down and shoulders slumped; the weight of the world inside their satchels.

Tom and Sally arrived at 9. 15am, wearing their Sunday best, along with their funeral faces. There were no good mornings or nice weather, just nods of somber support.

Jim stood in his lightweight grey suit, the picture of success. Gracie in her pale blue, knee length shift, clasping her navy handbag, indication she was ready.

"We'll go," Jim announced. "We might as well travel in the same car."

Ellen stood on the path with Paula. Tom and Sally in the back. Gracie in the front seat touching her hair. Jim rolled down his window so Ellen could say good luck. The Zephyr had driven out of the village earlier, taking the lower road to Letterkenny.

"Take the high road past Lough Salt, it's quicker," Ellen advised.

Jim nodded, facing forward with grim determination.

The hills around Lough Salt rose before them and the sun played hide and seek, teasing the mirrored water with her rays. No one spoke. All lost in their own bleak reveries. Tom sighed heavily in the back seat from time to time. Jim's hand moved towards the radio switch but Tom said, "Leave it off, for God's sake." Gracie coughed lightly, breaking the tension. Still no one spoke.

They drove up the Port Road, anticipating the dreary building, rising above the other buildings, dull and austere.

"Park round the side," Tom directed, when the courthouse came into view.

The Zephyr was already there, parked at the front door, ahead and brazen; a signal of something it seemed, maybe advantage. They were on a steep incline, tempting Jim to drive into Cox's car, sending it scudding down the hill to destruction. Only the thought of denting his own bumper stopped him.

Keep it cool Jim, keep it cool.

He parked carefully near the deep pavement, pulling the handbrake tight.

The side door was open but they passed it, taking the main door instead, with its impressive stone columns on either side. Mr. Fray was in the front hall waiting, waving quickly in salute, impatiently, Jim thought.

It was only 10am.

They had time to spare, yet he hurried them down a long noisy corridor with a brusqueness that did little to calm Jim's racing heart.

Mr. Joyce, he presumed, waved from an open door on the left hand side, ushering them into a tiny room, crammed with filing cabinets and chairs arranged haphazardly by previous occupants. The young barrister looked extremely calm and extremely elegant in his black gown, worn over an expensive navy suit. Jim wished he could trade places with him, know what it felt like to be that self-assured, that confident. They sat, all four of them at his pleasant bequest, Tom and Sally feeling surplus to requirement.

"Good to meet you Mr. and Mrs. Logue," he shook hands with all four, pulling his chair nearer to Jim in a gesture of recognition. "ll be busy running between both rooms this morning." He smiled and Jim noticed his white collar sitting on top of a filing cabinet, temporarily discarded; his dark hair slicked with hair oil, his elegant fingers holding a gold pen, brown eyes that focused urgently when he spoke.

Tom and Sally rose, slightly embarrassed to be there, but he invited them to reconsider. Mr. Fray hovered in the background.

"No, no, stay," he said, "Johnathan will explain procedures to you."

He sat near the door and they raised their faces to Mr Fray, anxious to hear what exactly was taking place. Loud voices drifted in from the corridor. Words repeated. Find, fine; yes, yes; laughter, a woman's voice joyously uncontrolled. "We couldn't have asked for a better outcome!"

"Cox's party is upstairs," Jim's attention was on Jonathan now, watching as he spoke.

"I was talking to Daniel MacCausland before you arrived. He was waiting for his barrister and John Fields to arrive."

The mention of Field's name made Jim's scalp crawl, the knot tightened in his tummy. He knew he should respond, looking towards Gracie, her blue eyes lost on some foggy unreachable plain. Tom and Sally continued staring at the ground.

"Do we wait here until we're called into the courtroom?" He sounded like a child, like Malachy or his 14 year old self a lifetime ago.

"We were thinking Jim, Daniel and myself, that if there was a way of avoiding the courtroom we should take it." Mr. Fray sounded nervous.

Tom and Sally looked up. Gracie's gaze came into focus.

"What do you mean?" Jim was immediately irate. "Give up without a fight! Let Cox have the fucking lot. Is that it? Is that the neat wee plan you were hatching between you?"

"On the contrary Jim, you need to keep a cool head now, so we can negotiate a sound settlement."

"Settlement!" Jim's voice was dangerously loud. "The only settlement I want is to walk out of here today, still owning my house and bar."

"Please Jim," Gracie begged. "Will you at least listen to what he has to say?"

Tom shook his head in sympathy with her.

"If it were that simple, Jim, we could all go home now, but it's not. Mr. Joyce will go up there to find out what they're willing to accept. Let's have a modicum of patience and hear what they're thinking"

"Fuck what they're thinking" Jim said. "Your job is to listen to me, me and Gracie. We came here today for a court case and that's what's going to happen."

"It's always worth sounding out the opponent first, to see whether or not there's a reasonable compromise we can reach, without going into court," Mr. Fray explained.

"What if they're not reasonable?" Jim asked. "What then?"

"Then we'll take our chances in the courtroom, in front of Judge Cooper."

"And may the best man win," Tom ventured.

"Precisely," Fray agreed, watching Mr. Joyce leave the room to go upstairs.

Gracie's gaze was trained on Jim, hoping he would see her silent imploration, but Jim continued glaring at Tom whose wisdom he scorned.

Mr. Fray began to pace near the tall sashed window, Jim's attention drawn to the barrister's stiff white collar sitting on the filing cabinet, temporarily discarded.

Gracie flinched when the door opened briskly, revealing Mr. Joyce, still calm and elegant. He huddled with the solicitor muttering, both nodding before turning to Jim.

"Well Mr. Logue, they have aimed the first shot across our bough," he smiled, "but we're not going to dignify it of course."

Jim had no idea what he meant and he knew he wasn't the only one, judging by the expression on Gracie's face, not to mention Tom and Sally's.

"They're claiming that you instigated the sale of your home and premises," Johnathan spoke, "that you signed the deal and now they want it honored."

Tom's exasperated moan brought blushes, interrupting the solicitor who continued quickly.

"Of course that's not what we're going to do, so let's start again. What would you be happy with Jim, yourself and Mrs.Logue that is?"

Jim looked at Gracie, certain her mind was set like his own.

"We need a bargaining chip Mr. Logue," Mr. Joyce said. "Something to offer Mr. Cox that doesn't involve losing your home." His smile was beginning to get on Jim's nerves.

"Give him a bit of a bog," Gracie spoke abruptly. "He's mad for turf."

Jim's collar suddenly felt tight, but Mr. Joyce dignified her proposal.

"Is there anything else we could add to this bit of bog?" he asked

"I have a few good store rooms," Jim was thinking now too, "He was always jealous of that. Should we offer him one of them, along with the bog or are we making arseholes of ourselves!"

"Try that Mr. Joyce," the solicitor encouraged, "suggest also that each party will pay their own costs; it might sweeten the pot."

It was a hopeless shot Jim knew, one Cox would never accept. A glimpse of Gracie's beseeching eyes only added to his fury and frustration.

Mr. Joyce returned presently, not at all perturbed by the rejection, simply regrouping to sharpen their efforts.

Cox's barrister, Mr. Kerr, was at their door with a new proposal.

Mr. Cox would accept the entire bog along with the bar and storerooms, allowing Mr. and Mrs. Logue to retain ownership of their dwelling house. Mr. Logue would have to pay all expenses.

Jim was out of his chair, incensed.

"The dirty bastard! The lousy dirty bastard, he can go and ..."

Gracie was on her feet, forcing him to sit back down. "Please Jim! In the name of God will you try to keep control of yourself!"

"You can take it that my client rejects your offer," Mr. Joyce confirmed. "Give us a moment please to consider a counter proposal."

Tom rose, saying he needed a breath of fresh air, and Sally, who wouldn't stay in the room without Tom, left too.

Jim lit a Sweet Afton, drawing the smoke into his lungs like a prayer, exhaling angrily, barely able to contain his temper.

Mr. Joyce and Mr. Fray pulled their chairs nearer to Jim and Gracie, with renewed purpose. Forbearance was needed, they said. Some compromise that would resolve the case to everyone's liking.

The rehashing of events began and Jim moaned at the prospect of grappling with the past nine months again, the nightmare that haunted his every living moment, asleep or awake. Gracie touched his arm gently, reminding him of their pact; together they would survive. His nod allowed the re-hashing to resume.

He had been offered £1,900 for his home and business; it wasn't a bad sum. What if Cox increased the offer to say, £2,500, would the Logue's agree to that?

Jim mused, impressed by such a sum, knowing Cox would never pay it. Gracie sat with her arms folded like a tightened spring, unwilling to concede yet, despite the generous offer.

"You can try that if you like," Jim almost sniggered, "but I know Cox won't go for it."

No one asked Gracie what she thought, Jim's opinion seemed paramount. She said nothing, for now, but Jim knew she would not be silent in the heel of the hunt. He didn't know what frightened him more, the final judgement or Gracie's random moods that could change from minute to minute.

Mr. Joyce rose to leave, but a knock at the door stopped him in his tracks.

Teddy put his head in, wondering how they all were and could he talk to Jim for a moment. He nodded deferentially at Mr. Fray and Mr. Joyce, waiting for Jim to go with him.

"How's it going?" he asked in the corridor. "Are you making any progress?"

"None," Jim was blunt. "This is going into court Teddy, as sure as I'm standing here. Cox won't be happy until he owns every slate I possess, it's as simple as that. Gracie seems to be considering a deal, at the moment anyhow, but I feel we should take it all the way."

"Say nothing; but a wee bird told me Cox doesn't want to go into court. John Fields seems to be acting up, not complying, I doubt."

"What does that mean, is it good news for me?"

"Maybe the evidence isn't as strong as they thought. Going into court might suit you better than Cox. Whatever document Fields has, he's reluctant to bring it into court. I think that's what's going on up there. Say nothing though, you'll only get me into trouble. Go back in and see what happens."

Tom and Sally were sitting on a bench in the corridor and they waved at Jim, implying their intention of staying where they were. Jim returned to the tiny room, wondering how to use what Teddy had told him. Maybe Fields had a conscience after all, but Cox and MaCausland would bully him into compliance. Should he call their bluff?

Sacred Heart of Jesus I place all my trust in thee.

"I have my mind made up," he said, after lighting another cigarette. "I want my day in court. We both do, don't we Gracie."

She nodded slowly, searching his face for a clue to this sudden epiphany. All eyes on her now, suddenly remembering her presence.

"Are you sure Jim?" Mr. Fray sounded concerned. "A signed Bill of Sale would be a damning piece of evidence against you."

"Are you sure?" Jim asked for effect, "that such evidence exists. If I did sign anything, and I'm pretty sure I didn't," he glanced sternly at Gracie, "I was drunk, remember. You said that was our wild card, didn't you?"

"Mr. Joyce, do we know whether Daniel MaCausland's witnesses submitted all their evidence or are they still withholding some?" Mr. Fray looked at the young barrister, both men unsure of their footing.

"Mr. Fields was summoned to produce all documents pertaining to the case, however I'm unsure if he complied or withheld them until today. If he produces them in court that will suffice."

"I'll ask you both, one last time; do you want to take this into court and let the judge decide the final outcome?"

Jim looked at Gracie, his eyebrows raised, waiting. She held his gaze too long, testing everyone's patience, finally nodding, as Jim began to sigh.

"Then we'll take our chances and do as Mr. and Mrs. Logue has directed. Go up Mr. Joyce and let them know our decision."

Minutes later he returned, accompanied by Mr. Kerr, who wished to remind Jim again; there was no question that Mr. Logue had signed a memorandum to sell his home and premises to Mr. Cox. In fact, John Fields was above with the document in his pocket, ready to produce it in court.

"So you say, Mr. Kerr," Johnathan's voice was clipped. "However, my client has made it perfectly clear that he will have his day in court." He glared at Cox's barrister, nodding curtly his acknowledgement before withdrawing from the room.

Johnathan's eyes were now trained on Mr. Joyce, both men wondering if Jim was making the right decision.

"What do you think of the state of play?"

Jim's question took them by surprise. He stood lighting a cigarette, throwing the spent matchstick on the windowsill.

Gracie remained seated, watching Jim carefully as if he might become hysterical, but he simply looked at both men, waiting for an answer.

"If you're asking whether they're bluffing, I don't believe they are Mr. Logue," Mr. Joyce answered. "Mr. Kerr is adamant that the signed memorandum is in their possession, which is a damning piece of evidence against us, I would say."

"We'll hold our nerve for the moment," Johnathan Fray said, "see what they come back to us with."

Jim dragged deeply on his cigarette and Gracie joined her hands in her lap, praying silently to the Sacred Heart or St. Jude or maybe the Lady of the Lough.

Mr. Joyce looked quickly at his watch, just as the door opened revealing Mr. Kerr again, a little red faced, not quite as calm, wearing his black gown this time. There was no legal head-huddling. Cox's barrister delivered his message to the entire room.

"Mr. Cox feels that Jim Logue can save face, by selling his licence to him for the sum of £500, without admitting liability; allowing Mr. Logue's family to retain their home and dwelling place for life. It's a fair proposition. I'll leave you to consider."

The air in the room changed.

Gracie was on her feet now, no longer willing to remain silent and forgotten.

"The licence is worth far more than that," she spat, "if he's serious about the offer, tell him we'll deal at £1,000!"

Jim's face darkened, but he didn't show signs of dissent. He held his tongue until Mr. Kerr exited the room.

"Are you for real woman!" he roared, "I thought we agreed to go into court. You're making us look fucking stupid now. Cox is upstairs having a right laugh at us."

His irritation spilled over, verging on madness, but Gracie held her nerve, returning Jim's incredulous stare, knowingly calm.

"Mrs.Logue may be making the wisest decision Jim," Johnathan Fray offered. "If they produce the signed Bill of Sale in court, the Judge is unlikely to rule in your favour, despite the circumstances on the night in question." He widened his eyes at Jim in a gesture of collusion.

Before anyone could speak, Mr. Kerr had returned saying £600 was his client's final offer, accept it or take your chances in the courtroom. He would wait outside in the corridor, but time was of the essence.

They had 10 minutes before their case was called. All three men looked at Gracie.

"Tell him it's £1,000 or nothing." she said, "otherwise we go into court."

Mr. Joyce ran, the clatter of his shoes up the corridor, as Jim and Johnathan sat watching Gracie pace near the window, refusing to look at Jim's angry face.

The clatter of two sets of shoes down the corridor, bringing Mr. Joyce and Mr. Kerr back into the room. Breathless, Mr. Kerr delivered their final, final offer.

"Mr. Cox, being a man of good character and Christian charity, is reluctant to see Mr. Logue and his family forced to leave their home. Therefore, he will buy the Licence to Trade from Mr. Logue for the sum of £800, allowing the family to retain ownership of their home and remain there forever, without the right to run a public house of course. And no harm done."

It was two minutes to eleven. The door closed behind Mr. Kerr and Jim sighed bitterly. His back was to the wall.

"Call Tom in," he said.

Mr. Fray left, returning quickly with Tom.

They were all on their feet, huddled together in the tiny room, grappling with the choice that faced them.

Jim looked at Tom, his older brother. What did he think of Cox's proposal?

"Do you want to sell the licence, Jim?" Tom asked

"Of course I don't, Tom. You know that, the world and its mother knows that! But I'm not the only one involved in this decision."

He watched Gracie's eyes, more resolved than his own, needing her response.

She wondered aloud. "Could Jim buy another license sometime down the road, and run the bar again?"

It was doubtful, fairly improbable, Mr. Fray reckoned.

Jim would be bound by the Intoxicating Liquor Act, which would prevent him from obtaining a new Licence to Trade for a variety of reasons, not to mention the likelihood that Cox would seek a barring order against such an endeavor. Jim could always buy another public house in a village or town away from his current location, that was certainly an option and he would have the means to do so.

The clock was ticking.

They had five minutes left when Tom boiled it down concisely. Jim could take a gamble and let the judge decide. Or he could agree to the offer on the table, without the risk of losing everything.

John Fields was on the high stool laughing. There were ink stains on the counter. Nevin Cox shook his hand. Images, like bolts of lightning, flashed in Jim's mind. He slumped against the wall and Gracie gasped.

"We'll take it," he whispered. "We'll take the deal."

Mr. Joyce vanished. They watched the door close, standing near Jim, listening to his troubled breaths, escaping in long painful sighs.

No one looked at Gracie.

She sat with her hands back in her lap, praying thanks this time, to whatever saint had come to her aid.

"You did the right thing," Tom broke the silence.

"Well done Jim," Johnathan Fray moved towards him. "It was your decision to make and I believe you made the right one." He patted Jim's shoulder affectionately, ignoring the trembling mouth betraying his client, damming the tears that were threatening his manhood.

Sally was still outside in the corridor and Tom left to rejoin her. Mr. Fray left also. He would meet Cox's legal team in the judge's chambers, to hammer out the terms of the settlement. It could take a while. Jim should stroll across to Gallagher's Hotel for a drink.

Gracie stood, reminding them of her presence.

"I beg your pardon Mrs. Logue," Johnathan Fray apologized, "of course I meant Jim and yourself should retire to the Hotel and I'll find you anon, when Jim's signature is needed on the final draught of the settlement."

They sat in the empty lounge, gratefully alone. Jim's hand trembled when he raised the glass of whiskey to his lips. Just one good stiff one he promised, knowing Gracie wouldn't object.

No man ever needed a drink so much.

She sipped tea, switching her focus to stare blankly at the shadows behind Jim's head. He no longer seemed angry, more relieved that it was over. Thank God there was no one to greet them with false smiles and wide inquiring eyes.

How are you both, how are things?

Jim would say, 'Oh grand, I just made a balls of my life and that of my children. Yeh, I lost my business, threw it away actually.'

Gracie would say; 'We're great! We just sold our business. Got a hefty price for it too. It was difficult trying to run a bar while teaching and rearing young children. Jim is still farming. And yeah, we had our money made on it, hee, hee.'

At twelve o clock the barman approached them with a message from Mr. Johnathan Fray. They were to return to the courthouse. They sat in the same small room breathing easier, resignation quietly dawning. Tom and Sally were nowhere to be seen.

Mr. Fray arrived with the typed pages in his hand. Seven stipulations read aloud to Mr. and Mrs. Logue, the words bouncing around the filing cabinets, swirling around their heads; catch me if you can. Their foreheads frowned, trying to catch the salient points amid the legal jargon, the ones that really mattered.

The £800 would be placed in a joint account for both solicitors, to be paid to the Defendant upon confirmation of the Licence transfer to the Plaintiff.

Each party would pay their own costs.

The Defendant must undertake not to carry out the business of Publican or Licenced Vintner in his premises, AS FROM TODAY.

The Defendant will continue ownership of his dwelling house and empty premises and neither party needs admit liability.

Cox's signature was already on the final page, Jim noted, along with John Field's and Daniel MaCausland's. Jim signed slowly, in his best hand. Mr. Fray added his signature, dated the 25th of May, 1965.

It was done and dusted.

Tom and Sally were in the corridor, as they left the tiny space for the last time, walking to the main door, along with Johnathan Fray. A lone man stood clapping his hands in the foyer, the sound reverberated along the high ornate ceiling. He smiled at the party descending the stairs. Sergeant Halligan, dressed in his civies, beaming. He walked towards Cox's party, his hand outstretched in triumph. "Well done my man! Not a bad day's work, hah!" Words echoing down the hall.

Jim was pulled up short, stung to his core. And then, without compunction, Nevin Cox turned to where Jim stood and he smiled, striding towards him, his arm outstretched to shake Jim's hand.

"No hard feelings," he said.

Jim's clenched fists sprang from his side as Tom lunged, barring his aim.

"You treacherous bastard," Tom spat. "No man here will ever shake your hand. You got what you wanted. May it never bring you a day's luck till the day you die!"

"The nerve of the man!" Sally exclaimed, watching Cox slink back to his triumphant party waiting for him by the door.

They returned to Gallagher's Hotel to consider their own victory, however hollow.

Driving back to the village was going to be tough.

The final goodbye had yet to be said. Jim knew it would happen that evening, with his faithful crew around him. Fuck the court ruling. Nobody would stop him, not tonight. They would watch the ship going down together.

Malachy and Cathy

Mammy and Daddy weren't fooling anyone. We knew for ages that something was wrong. They were keeping secrets. Not nice secrets like where our birthday presents were hidden. Secrets that made them whisper in the scullery and raise their voices downstairs when they thought we were asleep. At night Daddy would punch the wooden partition in their bedroom making us cry because Mammy was crying.

Poor Mammy.

We always worried about her because we loved her so much.

And poor Daddy.

We loved him so much too and we knew he wasn't a bad man.

He had a temper sometimes, when we couldn't ask him anything without making him mad. But he was silly too and knew how to make us laugh. Especially after he got cross with us for no good reason. He'd look at our wee sad faces and we knew what was coming next. The fishing rods appeared from under the stairs and off we'd troop to the village lough. Three adventurers. Away to catch pink trout for tea. If he felt really bad we'd drive up to La Scala. Sitting in the big peoples' seats beside Daddy. Eating chocolate and waiting for the trailers to end so the main picture could start.

We lapped up those moments. Because we never knew when the fighting would take off again. Shouting cruel things at each other. Making each other feel sad and lonely. It was piggy in the middle, with us as piggy. Trying to catch the spiteful words they threw before they reached their target. Sometimes we caught them; but often we didn't.

We hated Ann and Nevin Cox.

So did Mammy and Daddy. That wasn't always the way.

For a while we liked Nevin because he could be kinda nice. Giving us sweets and taking us for runs in his big bouncy Zephyr. He wasn't funny like Daddy though.

We never liked her. Even though she thought she was funny. And we never laughed at one thing she said, or did. There was something cruel inside her. Like she could tell you how nice you looked and be pinching you at the same time, until it stung, mercilessly.

Daddy used to like Fr. Manus, but that was before November.

Before himself and Ann started walking up and down past our house , looking at the upstairs windows singing, 'You'll Have to Go!' They made Mammy cry and drop stitches in her knitting. Ellen got cross then, telling us to smarten ourselves up, that Mammy's eyes were watery because she'd been cutting onions. Her eyes were watery nearly all the time though. In school; in the car; at Mass on Sundays when she had no onions in her pockets or handbag. We knew because we checked.

Our hearts were always pounding, waiting for something bad to happen.

Like Mammy losing her job in the school; which felt like our school, like we really owned it. We stayed behind with her when she tidied her press and put fresh ink in the inkwells. We'd pretend to slap the big boys and girls with the swishy rod that lay on the Master's desk. He wasn't slapping as much lately all the same. Not since he got a baby. Ellen said, "At least he knows what it's for!" Daddy laughed and said, "The other buck thought it was for stirring his tea!"

This was one of the secrets big people spoke about in a low sideways talk. We longed to be in on it. When we asked Ellen why Master Ferry liked stirring his tea she couldn't answer cos her false teeth fell out with the laughing.

We tried not to think about the other secrets. Bad things happening as Christmas came around.

The pounding was joined by flutterings in our bellies. The Big Flood called it 'butterflies in your tummies'. He gave us a wee brown hen each and we ran down to sit on the Tome bridge and compare dates to see whose penny was the oldest.

We knelt at the crib, lighting candles for the Baby Jesus, thanking him for our new coats and Raleigh bike. Mammy cooked a big goose and after dinner we sat watching a sad film that made us all cry. Only Paula didn't cry. She rolled across the floor with her huge pink teddy; but instead of making us laugh we cried even harder, without knowing why.

In the New Year we heard Mr. Fray's name for the first time. Long brown envelopes kept coming to the house. Daddy had to sign his name in Mandy the Post's notebook before Mandy handed them to him with a crooked smile on his face. Mona was always shouting across the street that Daddy was wanted on the phone, making him curse and kick things out of his way. Mammy bossed Daddy in a sharp tone she never used to use and her mouth set in a hard straight line.

Daddy didn't laugh much any more and he was rarely funny. He sighed deeply and said, "Jesus" a lot, making us remember our pounding hearts and fluttering butterflies that didn't go away even when Christmas was over and there was nothing to be excited about.

When we were on our own in the kitchen Daddy would ask us how we'd like to be wee tinker wanes living on the side of the road. Wouldn't Mammy look good going round houses selling statues and dish cloths. Maybe we could sing like Frank McGroarty and people would throw money at us in the street. The pounding got faster then and Mammy would tell him to shut his mouth before hunting us up to bed.

We didn't like who we were; at all.

When we walked to school or played on the street there was always some auld man stepping out in front of us or behind us, wondering were we Jim Logue's wanes. Fixing us with one eyed stares.

The auld women in Mona's asked the same question, sticking their chins out like they had a third eye to see us better with. They were ugly auld crones in their torn stockings and smelly knickers. If John Owen was in the shop he would say, "Them's young Logue's alright, the best wee wanes in the parish!" The crones would clack their pink gums in rage, saying, "I'm sure they are!"

Daddy hated everyone who didn't drink in our bar.

Mona was a nosey auld bitch. Mandy the Post was a stupid auld fucker. The McBrides and McClaffertys were a shower of bastards. And deValera, he was the biggest stupidest bastard of them all. We looked for evidence that this was true and in the end we agreed with Daddy. Andy Dore was a right fella. Along with Johnny O'Donnell and Neil Fada. The Big Flood and Teddy had the best hearts and Mr. Fray was a gentleman.

Mostly though; they were a shower of fuckers and bastards and hoors.

We remembered that.

Walking to school without Mammy on that May morning, trying not to cry. We repeated 'hoor', over and over, louder and louder, trying to sound like Cormac; 'HOOOR!' It didn't make us laugh. But it kept us from crying.

That day. The day they went to Letterkenny. Felt like a thousand days.

When the car finally revved into the village Ellen couldn't keep us from running out the door.

Mammy was behind the wheel. Daddy beside her looked like a man we hardly recognised. Uncle Tom and Aunty Sally were in the back and they glowered up at Cox's as they got out of the car. Tom helped Daddy up the stairs to bed and headed home, saying himself and Sally would be back later.

Mammy and Ellen stood in the passageway down to the bar whispering more secrets. We wished we could be like Neil Fada's dog. Neil said his dog could hear ten miles away and he knew what Neil was going to say before he even said it.

At 8 o'clock Daddy came downstairs. His good suit looked a bit rumpled but we recognised him again. We were happy about that.

It was still bright outside and Mammy had the bar door opened wide letting the last of the sun's rays fall in on the cement floor.

The McBride and McClafferty men passed up. On their way to Cox's. Their heads down muttering. All scrubbed clean with Carbolic soap. Their necks the same colour as the soap.

Ellen was at the kitchen window with us. Watching. Waiting for something to happen. Her breath near our ears sounded loud through her nose. It caught suddenly when she saw who was coming.

Johnny O'Donnell, lurching past Mona's. Neil Fada and Cormac Brown beside him. All in their Sunday suits. Ellen said, "Good man Neil. Good man. You're all welcome tonight."

Cars drove into the village beeping their horns. Parking everywhere, like a cavalcade after an election. Teddy and his crew and all the wives and someone shouting, "Go on Logue ya boy ya!"

Mandy the Post arrived with his melodeon. Who appeared only Charles Bayers with his fiddle and Mary in tow preening like a parrot.

Mammy told Ellen to take us down to the bar, lifting Paula from her cot at the same time.

"It's the last night we'll ever be open," she said, coughing hard to dislodge something stuck in her throat.

Daddy was at full tilt behind the counter, serving everyone at the same time. Teddy got behind the counter with him and Daddy shouted, "Get in here Tom and give us a hand!".

The drink was flowing, and Daddy never once opened the drawer and Mammy didn't care one bit. Men and women kept putting money in our hands; mainly notes, hardly any coins at all.

Next we knew , Daddy was dancing a hornpipe outside the counter; his shoes rapping the cement, keeping time for Mandy and Charles, making a lovely sound. Teddy wrapped the green flag round him one last time and Ellen warbled the Hills of Donegal. Daddy dying for her to finish so he could say the one about Sam McGee.

We never knew you could be happy and sad at the same time. Laughing and crying; caught between victory and defeat. Daddy raised his glass to the bar and Ellen held our hands too tight, hurting us. And we were grateful.

We walked to school on Wednesday morning behind Mammy.

The bar door was locked tight. It was still locked when we walked home at lunch time. Mulrines lorry was pulling away. Every last bottle from behind the counter, every last crate from the store, gone.

For weeks Daddy sat at the range with his head down, saying, "Jesus! Jesus!" We counted how many times he said it. It was twenty three times, a day.

Mammy watched him sighing and shaking his head with a look in her eyes we hadn't seen before. The pounding in our chests started up again, telling us she couldn't stick him for much longer. No more than he could stick himself.

The last Saturday in June. Daddy put a boxy brown suitcase in the boot of the car, banging it shut. We sat in the back seat with Paula, watching Mammy closing the kitchen door, wearing her pale blue frock.

Daddy started the engine. We tickled Paula. Trying not to look at Daddy's face. The face that told us he was going away and might never be back. Adam. Sneaking his last glance at Paradise.

He pulled down the visor, shielding his eyes from the sun. Mammy didn't bother with the visor, only frowned out the windscreen, angrily. All the way to Letterkenny.

We drove into the bus depot. The engine kept running. We wouldn't be getting out.

Daddy turned around to face us. As soon as he spoke the elastic bands in our throats snapped.

"Now you two be good when I'm away."

"No Daddy! Stop Daddy!"

"Listen to me now, be good for Mammy."

"No Daddy! Please Daddy!"

"Do what she asks you and don't be bold."

"No Daddy! We're not listening. Don't go! Please! Please wee Daddy! Don't go!"

He stood on the tarmac. The sun beaming down on his white shirt. His suit jacket lying on the square boxy case. Mammy put her arms around his neck and kissed his cheek and we slapped at the rear window screaming his name. He turned towards the long red bus without looking back.

Mammy got behind the steering wheel and drove away. Her side face told us nothing. Just driving away there. Changing gear as smoothly as she could.

For a while our sobbing stopped. Until we came to the village lough. The car slowed and Mammy's breath rose dangerously. Breaking in a howl of broken gulps, bringing the car to a jolting halt. We joined her. Our backs arched, howling at the sky. No way to control it now. The agony that burned through us, scalding our hearts.

Mammy wiped her eyes roughly, trying to see the road. The engine caught again. Her hands back on the wet steering wheel.

We wept past the lough. Past the school. Past Kitty Eddy's and Mona's. The sun high above our house, glinting on the big silver letters saying, Logue's Bar. All control gone. Still weeping as we pulled in at the locked bar door.

END

About the Author

I was born and raised in a small village in Donegal. After attending college in Dublin, I taught English and Religion in a suburban secondary school there, for 30 years.

Taking early retirement in 2012 gave me the freedom to concentrate on my writing.

The Big Smoke Writing Factory helped me find my voice, convincing me that "Gracie" was the story I really needed to tell. It's historical fiction, literary style, set against the background of post civil war politics and the austere climate of de Valera's Ireland.

The story is based on my parents' early years together and the ill fate that befell them then. I guess I wanted to set the record straight, I hope I have done it justice.

My debut novel was, 'College Girls' a coming of age story, also mined from my own experience of flat life in the capital, when I attended college and it's a story filled with humour and drama and resilience!

These days I spend most of my time back in the hills of Donegal, with the odd visit to the capital. I continue to write and am presently working on a new novel.

Please Review

If you enjoyed this book, I would really appreciate if you could spread the word or leave a review on Amazon or Goodreads. Your opinion counts and it does influence buyer decision on whether to purchase the book or not. Thank you!

Other Books by the Author

College Girls

College Girls is a coming-of-age story, full of fun, energy and emotion. Cathy, a recent boarding school graduate, moves to Dublin for college and finds a flat with two other boarding school survivors, happy to be away from oppressive nuns and an unhappy home. Despite the dismal conditions of the flat, all three are determined to make the best of it.

As the Troubles in Northern Ireland intensify, the girls must learn to navigate their new lives in a city seemingly oblivious to the struggles across the border.

Dublin offers them bohemian revelry, in a city slowly moving out of the hippy era. The girls experience heartache and betrayal, all the while staying connected through music and youthful exuberance. They learn about life and more about themselves while navigating the city's uncertainties.

Captivated by Rosie, the girl from the flat above, they make naive and impulsive decisions, leading to hurt and betrayal. Despite this, College Girls is full of humour and poignance, shot through with music from the 70s, as it celebrates friendships between young women and the pitfalls of growing up in an ever-changing world.